THE MISEDUCATION OF EVIE EPWORTH

July, 1962. The fastest milk bottle-delivery girl in East Yorkshire, 16-year-old Evie Epworth is tall as a tree and hot as the desert sand. She dreams of an independent life lived under the bright lights of London (or Lee__). The two posters of Adam Faith on her bedro__ wall ("brooding Adam" and "sophisticated __am") offer wise counsel about a future beyond __al Yorkshire. Her role models are Charlotte Bront__ Shirley MacLaine and the Queen. But, before she __an decide on a career, she must first deal wit__ her future step-mother, the manipulative an__ money-grabbing Christine.

If Evie can r__ __e her bereaved father from Christine's pin__ __d over-perfumed clutches, and save the farmh__ __ from being sold off then maybe she can move __ __th her own life and finally work out exactly wh__ __s she is meant to be

SPECIAL MESSAGE TO READERS

THE MISEDUCATION OF EVIE EPWORTH

MATSON TAYLOR

LARGE
PRINT

First published in Great Britain 2020
by
Scribner
an imprint of Simon & Schuster UK Ltd

First Isis Edition
published 2021
by arrangement with
Simon & Schuster Ltd

The moral right of the author has been asserted

A catalogue record for this book is available
from the British Library.

ISBN 978–1–78541–937–9

Published by
Ulverscroft Limited
Anstey, Leicestershire

Set by Words & Graphics Ltd.
Anstey, Leicestershire
Printed and bound in Great Britain by
TJ Books Ltd., Padstow, Cornwall

This book is printed on acid-free paper

For mum
(for looking out for me)

and dad
(for putting up with me)

CHAPTER
ONE

Wednesday 13 June 1962

I am the wind. I skeet across tarmac and whoosh over dale. Birds skate along my amorphous limbs and the sun bakes down on my back. I am a sirocco, hot as the desert sand. I fly. I loop. I race.

I'm also Evie, as old as the hills (16½), as tall as a tree (5ft 11), and as wise as time (perhaps). A dog-loving, celery-hating, never annoying, always enjoying, at times corduroying, (brackets-deploying), daughter of Arthur, and the fastest girl with a milk bottle in East Yorkshire.

My milk-delivery speed is not usually worthy of comment. Under normal circumstances, I'm to be found doing my rounds either on foot, with a few bottles in an old basket, or on my bike, in which case I carefully balance the basket up front, leaving the bike front-heavy and ripe for an accident if I brake suddenly (as I often do).

Today, though, I'm flying.

I've borrowed Arthur's other child: his MG roadster. If he knew I'd taken the car, he would not be happy. Luckily he's currently in his trusty old Land Rover on a shopping trip to Leeds with Christine, our housekeeper,

1

stocking up on a new shaving brush (him) and "just a few little bits and bobs" (her). Despite being only eight years older than me, Christine (hoarder, moaner, heifer) always makes it very clear that she is an Adult and I am not, although in Christine's world being an Adult seems to consist of little more than listening to Mantovani LPs, drinking Babycham and wearing cleavage-bolstering dresses.

I have been warned about driving Arthur's pride and joy before. It is one of many things classified as Off Limits. Other things that are Off Limits include the telephone, the drinks cabinet, the bull (yes, this is the country), the attic, assorted ornaments and vases, and — by far the largest category — Christine's Things, a group of objects that seems to be growing in number with the speed of a virus.

I've broken the Off Limits car rule today because this morning is the occasion of my first ever hangover. Somehow my brain knows to tell me that being on a bike would not be good (but why doesn't it say anything about driving a car?).

Yesterday, at 4.02p.m., I finished my last O level exam. Chemistry. By 5.30p.m. I was slumped in the corner of my best friend Margaret's father's barn slugging a perm-inducing mix of spirits from an old dandelion and burdock bottle. The day before, Margaret (girl guide, practical, destined for teaching) had suggested we get "something fizzy" so that we could celebrate the end of our exams. She'd supply the food and I was tasked with getting two bottles of Babycham from Christine's stash at the back of the

2

pantry. As if trying to remember about titration numbers and endothermic compounds hadn't been mentally exerting enough.

The pantry is a dark cave of plenty. Its shelves are lined with tins, packets, bottles and jars, all standing like soldiers on a parade ground, best face forward and ready for action. The back of the pantry slopes down and it's there, tucked away, that Christine keeps her Babycham. Usually there are dozens of bottles of the stuff, herd upon prancing herd, but last night there were only two. Two bottles. Two very conspicuous bottles. So I made do with the drinks cabinet (Off Limits — see above), decanting half an inch of everything into the most innocent-looking bottle I could find.

Initially my drinks-cabinet cocktail wasn't a success (Margaret said it was like drinking vapour rub), but after a while we both decided it didn't taste so bad after all. It was definitely helped down by Margaret's food: two bags of crisps, a Melton Mowbray pork pie, some sherbet dips and a box of Terry's Neapolitans. I can remember lots of dancing (with each other and with assorted hay bales) and lots of falling (falling off things, falling over things, falling under things), but the rest of the evening is a bit of a blur.

Fourteen hours later, I woke up in bed (how did I get there?) wearing my Adam Faith nightie back to front and with my hair clumped together in tufty knots well beyond the means of any brush known to man (or woman). I lay still for a few minutes, letting life — and the room — settle, before realising that I was late for my milk run, a small and select clientele made up mainly of family friends (the milk run is my principal job around the farm along with some occasional hay spreading and cow scrubbing). Downstairs a note on the kitchen table (*Gone to Leeds. Back 6ish. Dad.*) reminded me that there was nobody around to enforce the Off Limits rule and so here I am, in Arthur's MG, flying from village to village, the very model of a very modern milkmaid.

To look the part, I have wrapped an old woolly scarf around my hair and become Grace Kelly in *High Society,* or at least the part in *High Society* where Grace Kelly is driving Frank Sinatra round lots of empty country lanes, the part where they hate each other before they realise that they actually love each other. But instead of Frank in the passenger seat serenading me with "You're Sensational", I'm stuck with eight milk bottles in a basket, rattling and chinking (a micro-symphony of impending doom).

My life up until this point has been nothing special: a patchwork of school, Guides, cows, lost mothers, the Brontes, lacrosse, and Adam Faith. But now adulthood has arrived. Exciting things will happen. Life's great adventure will unfold.

I will become A Woman.

What *kind* of Woman I will become is still very much up for discussion. Arthur is set on farmer's wife. Christine, unhelpfully, has suggested either hairdresser or bus conductress. Margaret thinks I should become a teacher (of what? Cocktailology?). And me? What kind

4

of Woman do I want to become? I honestly have no idea.

Different future Evies whoosh constantly through my mind. Librarian. Florist. Vet. It's exhausting. Sometimes my head feels like a sputnik, rocketing around the world at great speed but without ever actually getting anywhere. Maybe I should become a cosmonaut? Do cosmonauts need a good pass at O level Chemistry? I read in Christine's *Woman's Realm* magazine that becoming a Woman is basically all about efficient typing skills and good deportment (of which I have neither), but I suspect it's probably a bit more complicated than that.

The road ahead is clear (literally if not metaphorically) and I push my foot down on the accelerator, encouraging the engine to heights of high-pitched crooning that even Frank would struggle to reach.

Hedgerows and trees race past me as I fly. It's a beautiful sunny morning and the bright blue sky looks like it's been borrowed from a Spanish summer and stuck on top of our lush green Yorkshire fields. The early morning heat brushes my bare arms and I can taste its warmth in my mouth. Soaring and plunging, I am unstoppable. A force of nature. A wild wind-faerie. Will being a Woman always feel like this?

The hedgerows race.

The engine croons.

And the milk bottles chink.

I am Evie, a speeding joyous blur of scarf and smile.

Gulping in the view ahead, I see someone in a field. A man. And some cows. I shield my eyes with my hand, trying to get a better view.

It's dear old Mr Hughes, a farmer from the next village.

I wave.

Mr Hughes doesn't wave back.

I blink, trying to make out what's going on.

Is he dancing?

I blink again.

Is he swinging? Swaying?

Corralling? Herding?

From somewhere, the words to "Jerusalem" jab-jab-jab themselves into my brain.

And then, just like that, mid-skeet and *whoosh*, I have a moment of clarity: Mr Hughes, flat-capped and trousers down, is singing the hymn at the top of his voice while thrusting rhythmically into the back of a cow.

Suddenly everything slows down.

My head inches round, transfixed by the strange coupling. My jaw drops and I feel a thread of spittle hanging from my mouth. Fat beads of perspiration appear on my forehead and my eyes feel as big as pan lids. My hands follow my head, edging the steering wheel round to the right.

The engine *crooooooooooooooooooons*.

The milk bottles *chiiiiiiiiiiiiiiiiiiiiiiiiiiiiiiink*.

And Mr Hughes serenades the world with his arrows of desire.

6

The MG clatters as it exits the smooth tarmac of the road and mounts the rough dirt of the bridle path. My head feels both hollow *and* very heavy. How is that even possible? What's happening? Is it all some kind of divine punishment for breaking the Off Limits rule twice in twenty-four hours? I see a tree stump, gnarled and brutish, immediately ahead and then . . .

I'm out of the car and flying through the air. Milk bottles whoosh past me like little white missiles. I am the wind, flying over hedgerow, a startled gust. All of a sudden I feel very hot. The ground disappears and I melt into the sky.

I am Evie, sixteen and a half, as wise as a tree, as tall as time, the fastest milk bottle in East Yorkshire, hurtling towards Womanhood.

This is all really strange.

CHAPTER
TWO

Wednesday 11 July 1962

I am woken by a loud thump of cured ham.

"What do you mean I'll have to go on the bloody bus?"

That's Christine, assembling a cold tea and clearly not happy about having to rely on the vagaries of the East Yorkshire Bus Company to get her to bingo.

I must have nodded off. It's four weeks since the crash and the colourful assortment of pain-relief tablets I need to take every day makes me drowsy, or "dopey" as Christine puts it. I have been out of hospital for two days and am missing the attention of all the middle-aged nurses desperate to mother me. In hospital, I was the star patient: young and glamorous (you don't get many MG-driving sixteen-year-olds in East Yorkshire), with a whiff of excitement and scandal. The Hull Royal Infirmary's answer to James Dean, but a marginally better driver.

"We can't leave Evie on her own, Christine. She's an invalid."

That's Arthur, my surprisingly — given the state of his MG — doting father. He's locked in a battle of wills with Christine over his services as a taxi driver. For the past six months he's taken Christine, her mother (Vera) and Mrs Swithenbank (Vera's friend) to bingo on a Wednesday night, but tonight he wants to carry on listening to the cricket on the radio and is using me as an excuse to get out of it.

"Invalid!" The cured ham takes another thump. I hope I'm not going to be expected to eat any of it. "You heard the doctor. There's nothing wrong with her bar a few cuts and scrapes. She could fall out of bed and land straight in a warm bath, that one."

She's right. The consultant at the hospital said I was very lucky. I told him I was a Sagittarian, the lucky sign, and began to explain to him about the lucky charm on my necklace (my mother's wedding ring), but he stopped me and said he just meant that it's a good job I'm so young. A young body is a rubber body, apparently, and this rubber body bounced its way safely through a field of muddy grass after coming flying out of Arthur's MG. I don't remember any of this, though, as I had passed out, which, according to the consultant, is why I "fell so well" — an odd way of putting it seeing as I was trussed up in a hospital bed, at the time, with a thick scratchy neck brace and more bandages than an Egyptian mummy.

But it hasn't all been good luck. When I got back from hospital, a big Christine-shaped dollop of bad luck was waiting for me at the farmhouse. Apparently she's now our live-in housekeeper.

Much more convenient for everyone, said Arthur.

Much easier to keep an eye on everyone, said Christine.

There's no escape from her. She's everywhere. Like a bad-tempered pink fog.

Since Christine started working as our housekeeper ten long months ago, after a fateful meeting with Arthur in the Red Lion (village pub and unofficial labour exchange), our once lovely kitchen has gradually turned into her trophy room. Her chief prize is the gleaming new electric cooker, prim and pert and very pleased with its own modernity. It replaced our nice old Aga, a huge beast which threw out as much heat as a steam train. Christine didn't like the Aga because:

1. "It smells" (really more the fault of Christine's cooking than the Aga).
2. "It's got a mind of its own" (it takes a special kind of person to be outwitted by a kitchen appliance).

The Aga's days were numbered after one memorable incident involving Christine, the Aga, three coiled Cumberland sausages and a particularly gripping episode of *Take Your Pick!*. No food, as such, was produced, just a burnt cruddy mess and more smoke than a London pea-souper.

The kitchen now also houses, among other things, a pink glass vase full of dusty plastic flowers, a small china figurine of a dinner-suited Mantovani, a knitted pink doily plonked in the middle of our lovely old table, and a plague of pastel-coloured Tupperware bowls. The bowls are all over the kitchen. Little pots of plastic springing up like mushrooms. They've replaced a huge emerald-green tureen which we used to keep more or less everything in, from buttons and keys to coins, pencils and spark plugs. The tureen was an heirloom from my mother's grandmother and had survived two world wars but didn't survive Christine's love of British Home Stores' kitchenware department. Even the large black-and-white photo of my mother, Arthur and me (taken in winter 1946, when I was four months old, an ample mass of wool and lace with a tiny beaming face) has been sent off to Arthur's study — replaced on the kitchen wall by a photo of Christine and Arthur in front of Buckingham Palace and another one of Christine meeting Perry Como outside the Manchester Free Trade Hall.

But, despite Christine's handiwork, traces of the kitchen's previous custodian still linger if you know where to look. Objects and spaces offer up secret bits of information like a discreet hallmark tucked away on a silver candlestick. Christine's shiny new cooker, for example, sits in the same space as the Aga, but it's much smaller, exposing an Aga-shaped block of brightly coloured wallpaper that sings out against the old, faded patterns around it. A noisy silence. Then there are the hooks in the pantry ceiling, meant for game and bird but left untouched for years, reminders of a time when the kitchen was run by someone who must have been considerably more skilled in the culinary arts than the present occupant.

And, unused and unknown, hidden deep inside the second cutlery drawer, is an art deco nutcracker inscribed with the initials DM. Diana Melville. My

11

mother. A beautiful affirmation. An idea I can't quite remember.

Thump.

It's the poor cured ham again, a proxy casualty of our very own cold (tea) war.

Arthur is hovering, clearly uncertain of the best way to engage in battle. He looks scared (or do I mean scarred?).

Thump.

Christine is a formidable opponent. Her hair is up in rollers, a modern-day Medusa, and the stench of Amami setting lotion wafts across the room like clouds of mustard gas.

"Arthur," she says, staring at him with the intensity of a serial killer.

Thump.

"I'm sure Evie will be fine on her own for half an hour. They did let her out from hospital, remember?"

Thump.

Thump.

Arthur coughs.

"I just think we should wait a few more days until she's left on her own, that's all. Probably best to keep an eye on her." He's smiling as he speaks but it's the kind of nervous-hopeful smile that I use when I'm explaining to Maureen, our village hairdresser, what style I want (something hip) but know that she isn't actually listening and will do exactly what she wants to do anyway (something with a vicious fringe).

12

Christine closes her eyes and breathes in deeply. Will she explode?

"Just (*thump*).

A (*thump*).

Few (*thump*).

Little (*thump*).

Scratches (*thump*).

And anyway," she goes on, pointing at me with the carving knife. "She's got her book to keep her company, haven't you?" The way she says "book" makes it sound like she's holding the word with laundry tongs. "What are you reading?"

It's *Laxdcela Saga,* an old Icelandic saga about the Norse myths. Why am I reading the most obscure book in my entire collection just when Christine asks to see what I'm reading? Why couldn't I have been reading *Wuthering Heights* again? I can see her eying the book with great suspicion. Christine's reading doesn't really extend much beyond *Woman's Weekly* and the Littlewoods catalogue.

Arthur bought me the book on a family day out to York Castle Museum. The trip was his idea, a way for Christine and me to spend some time together, although why either of us would want to do that I have no idea. I was tasked with choosing the destination. Initially I suggested Whitby (where better to take a bad-tempered blood-sucker?) but Christine rejected it because the sea air plays havoc with her fringe. So we went to the museum. We spent an hour wandering around the castle and its recreations of ancient city streets before Christine got bored and suggested a trip to Browns department store, where she quickly sprang back to life and managed to persuade Arthur to buy her some new leather boots and a set of "Ye Olde York" coasters. Afterwards, sitting in Bettys and having a toasted teacake, Christine said that she couldn't understand why people were so interested in The Olden Days as it all looked a bit grim and dirty. Christine's version of The Olden Days is fairly broad, starting with the First World War and then working backwards, taking in the Victorians, the Tudors, the Normans, the Vikings and the Romans in one huge blurred unwashed historical pageant.

"Laxatives Saga! What kind of name for a book is that? *Laxatives* Saga." She's shaking her head in disbelief (I know the feeling). "Have you seen what she's reading, Arthur?"

I think about correcting her but, from past experience, know that this probably isn't a good idea. (I once pointed out her use of split-infinitives in Selby *Woolworth's* and, after an initial confusion with split ends, it led to quite a nasty scene next to the *pick "n" mix*). Laxatives Saga it is then. The heroic tale of Unnr the Deep Minded, Hakon the Good and Olaf the Peacock as they set off in search of bowel Valhalla. A classic. I wonder what *our* Norse names would be . . . Arthur the Phlegmatic. Arthur the Put Upon. Arthur the Lost Soul. And his Brünhilde? Christine the Acquisitive. Christine the Sausage Burner. Christine, Naggiest Nagger of the North.

And what about me? Who would I be?

14

"What's that, love?" Arthur is miles away. At The Oval, to be precise, where someone has just bowled a flipper off a sticky dog and hit a Chinaman, or something like that.

"I said have you seen what Evie's reading? You're not even listening, are you?" Christine picks up a jar of pickled onions and unscrews it as if she were breaking the neck of a small animal. "I don't know why I bother. I have to do everything in this house."

(This isn't strictly true as Vera, Christine's mother, seems to be round here every day doing all the chores for her.)

Thump.

Slam.

Crash.

The ham looks like it's been through the St Valentine's Day Massacre. In fact, the whole kitchen has the feel of a crime scene. Even the potted plants look stressed. Christine picks up the bread knife and butchers a cottage loaf.

Trying to ignore the drama and concentrate on the radio, Arthur is now doing his best to hide behind a copy of the *Yorkshire Post*. He is a great believer in the *if you can't see it, it doesn't exist* school of thought and is adept at using the large newspaper to block out anything he finds troublesome or stressful: a bad day on the farm; a poor cricket over; Christine in a funny mood. Life. Death.

"Sorry, love. Barrington's just hit a six."

A noise like an angry gas leak spurts from Christine's side of the kitchen.

15

I decide it's best to leave them to it for a bit so I head to the downstairs loo. Not for any biological reason (I have the bladder control of a Shire horse) but because it's a place of sanctuary and escape. Compact and safe. With a lock. For such a small room, there's a surprising number of accoutrements. There's a big pile of old *Wisden* magazines in the corner (Arthur), a pink knitted loo-roll cover in the shape of a doll (Christine), and, perched on the windowsill, an Oxford dictionary (me).

I love flicking through the dictionary. It takes me off to another world, a world where a melange of esoteric people do pulchritudinous things meritoriously. Or at least a world with fewer doilies and hairnets. I sit down on the loo and open the dictionary at a random page.

Histrionic (adjective — theatrical performance, display of emotion for effect.)

Hmm, sounds like Christine.

Another page.

Jejune (adjective — lacking interest/significance, dull.)

Christine again.

You can see why I do this, can't you?

When I come back into the kitchen, the conversation has finished and, unfortunately, an air of victory hangs over Christine. She's sitting on Arthur's knee and when they see me, they both look a bit sheepish. Arthur quickly taps Christine on the bum and she gets up and walks back to the table, looking over at me in a very cat-who's-got-the-cream-ish way.

16

"Your dad's decided to run us to bingo after all," she says, smiling smugly (adverb — *in a way that shows excessive satisfaction in oneself*).

"Oh," I say, looking over at Arthur. He's retreated behind his *Yorkshire Post* and is doing a very good job of pretending he isn't here. "But I thought he wanted to stay and listen to the cricket?" I ask, knowing it'll really irritate her.

Christine stops assembling the cold tea and puts her hands on her hips.

"Well," she says, cracking the word like a whip. "He's decided it's much *safer* to take us in the car. There are a lot of *nutters* around, you see, and it'd be *dangerous* for us to be out on our own."

Dangerous? For who? The combination of Christine, Vera and Mrs Swithenbank would be more than a match for most small armies, never mind one lone nutter.

"You can't be too careful these days, isn't that right, Arthur?" Christine goes on, smiling at him and wiping her hands on a Bolton Abbey tea towel.

Arthur looks up over his *Yorkshire Post*. "Of course. More than happy to run you there." He ducks back behind the paper and a disembodied voice adds, "No trouble at all."

"Such a gentleman, your dad," says Christine, more loudly than is strictly necessary. "They don't make 'em like him any more." She smiles over at Arthur and then turns her attention back to the plates of ham, lettuce, pickle and tomato in front of her. I decide to do the sensible thing and get as far away as possible, heading off to my bedroom. As I leave the kitchen, Christine is doing something to a radish that she has seen Fanny Craddock, one of her heroines, do on TV. It involves a potato peeler and lots of patience. Christine has the potato peeler but not the patience. Sure enough, within a few seconds, the radish pings out of her hand and scuttles across the table. She takes another and exactly the same thing happens. It's radish carnage. Christine, eyeing the radishes like a maniac, is muttering something under her breath. Walking up the stairs, I hear a muffled scream followed by the pained, manic cackle of a woman pushed to the edge by a punnet of small root vegetables.

Up in my bedroom, a Christine-free zone and general haven of loveliness, I lie on top of the soft, flowery eiderdown and begin to tally up the events of the past few weeks.

Dramatic car crashes: 1
Broken bones: 0
Hospital visits from Arthur: 18
Hospital visits from Christine: 2
Hospital visits from Margaret: 11 (I think she might have been bored)
Letters written to Adam Faith: 3
Replies from Adam Faith: 0
Disturbingly vivid dreams involving Mr Hughes and a cow: 5 (hopefully just a side effect of the tablets)
Ideas about what I could do in the future: 28

Decisions made about what I should do with the rest of my life: 0

The Future is strange. Before my O levels, it seemed far away, something that only other people worried about (scientists, politicians, old people). It was a hazy, unreal half-thought that involved weddings, jobs, babies and tailored suits, not necessarily in that order. But all of a sudden, it's here. I always used to think of The Future as a happy, crowded, noisy place with lots going on, but now it feels big and empty, a huge silent space, like an enormous aircraft hangar with a tiny me rattling around it. What am I going to do in The Future? I still have no idea.

As an insurance policy, under Margaret's guidance, I have put my name down for sixth form. I have no great burning desire to study A level English, History and French, but then again have no great burning desire to do anything else either. I am happy to be a little cloud and get blown more or less where the wind takes me. And at least sixth form means that I won't get buffeted into any wholly inappropriate life by Christine (our very own gale). Christine has decided to take the idea of my return to education as some kind of personal insult. She is campaigning hard for my life in an ivory tower to end before it even begins. Torn clippings from the job section of local newspapers have mysteriously started to appear around the house (*Shop assistant needed. No experience required*). Every time I see one, I'm reminded of the small scraps of newspaper that Arthur sticks on his face when he cuts himself shaving.

19

Christine thinks these clippings are subtle messages that will send me cartwheeling into the world of work, part of a subliminal arsenal to be deployed in her cunning psychological war. In reality, they are as subtle as the Blackpool illuminations. Naturally, I ignore them.

Sixth form starts at the beginning of September. Today is 11 July. That leaves two months to find a Future. Easy. I can do that. Can't I? Surely it can't be that hard.

As I'm lying on my bed pondering Life and the unappealing prospect of Christine's cold tea, I look up at the two big posters of Adam Faith on my wall. In one of them (a freebie from *Melody Maker*), Adam is staring at the camera, brooding and looking rugged and masculine. He's wearing a mustard-coloured blouson (which matches his lovely blond hair) and his smile lights up the room like a million candles (well, perhaps not quite a million). In the other poster, bought on a day trip to Scarborough, he is the living embodiment of sophistication. He's wearing a well-ironed white shirt, navy cardy and bow tie. A bow tie! He is pop aristocracy and I love him. No matter how bad things ever get, I'll always have Adam.

Evie and Adam. Adam and Evie.

Together forever in our very own garden of Eden (otherwise known as Yorkshire).

I quite often speak to Adam on my walls. He can be a great help and, to be honest, he's one of the better conversationalists in the village. Which Adam I speak to depends on my mood. Today I definitely need Sophisticated Adam.

I sigh (trying to catch his attention).

"What would you do?" I ask him. "It's so confusing. There are all these different Futures. Which one's best for me?"

I open the drawer of my bedside table, get out a list of jobs given to us by the careers service at school, and then read them to him.

"Shop assistant, veterinary assistant, library assistant, dental assistant . . ."

(How come the only Futures open to women are always as someone's assistant?)

"Perhaps I could be your assistant?" I ask Sophisticated Adam.

He doesn't say anything. Perhaps I should have asked Brooding Adam instead.

I carry on working my way through the list (bookkeeper's assistant, showroom assistant, clerical assistant), but before Sophisticated Adam can offer me any useful advice there's a knock on the door.

"Tea's ready in five minutes," Arthur says, poking his head into the room.

"Thanks, Dad." We both look at each other and smile. "So you're going to miss the cricket, then?"

"Miss the cricket?" He arches his eyebrows in mock shock. "Certainly not. I'll have the transistor radio with me. You don't think I'm going to let bingo get in the way of *Test Match Special,* do you?"

I start picking at my corduroy skirt and let out a massive sigh, like a huge deflating beach ball.

"Hey, what is it, love?" says Arthur, coming in and sitting on the edge of the bed. When he sits down, I notice the light streaming in from the window glistening in the Brylcreem in his hair like flecks of stardust.

"It's Christine," I say.

For a moment there's almost silence, the only sound coming from the distant clatter of tea assemblage downstairs in the kitchen.

I look at Arthur.

Arthur looks at me.

(We are experts of restrained communication, Arthur and me.)

And then he sighs — just a little one, not a beach-ball one.

"Christine?" he says. "Come on, love. We've spoken about Christine, haven't we?"

Yes, we have spoken about her. Several times. The last time was on the way back from hospital when Arthur told me she'd moved in. Her moving in is good news, apparently, because:

1. She's a big help around the house (this is not true — her mum does all the housework).
2. I need a female role model (again not true — I've got loads already: Charlotte Brontë, the Queen, Shirley MacLaine).

Arthur also keeps going on about how the farmhouse is plenty big enough for one more. This is true. But it's also big enough for a herd of cows and Arthur hasn't asked any to move in.

I stop picking at my skirt and look straight at him.

"I don't like how she bosses you around," I say.

"Bosses me around? Don't be daft! No one's bossing anyone around." He pats my knee. "Look, it's no trouble at all running Christine and the others to bingo. Better to be safe than sorry, isn't it?"

He gives my leg a little squeeze and then looks out the window wistfully (*adverb — with a feeling of regretful longing*).

"Sometimes it's better not to force things," he goes on, turning back to me and smiling. "Just let things be. You know, let people be."

He stands up and brushes his hands through his stardusty hair.

"Now then, try and be nice to Christine. She's doing her best — and even Christine can't burn a cold tea," he adds, winking and walking out the door.

Alone again in my room, I lie back down on the bed and think about Arthur. When I was little, we'd go hunting for frogspawn and tadpoles in the stream, catching them in a mini-net and then keeping them in jam jars on the kitchen windowsill. We'd go off to the pictures in York and Leeds (he took me to see *Lady and the Tramp* six times) and he'd buy me chocolate ice cream in the intermission. We had days out all over Yorkshire. To Headingly cricket ground, where he'd buy me a comic and I'd read about "Belle of the Ballet" and "Nurse Susan Marsh" while he'd watch the Test match, or out on the Moors, where we'd fly my big red kite and climb over the rocks and eat crisp sandwiches and lemonade and butterscotch fudge. And he'd take me out on the farm, of course. He'd sit me on his knee on the tractor, driving around for hours, dodging cows and singing nursery rhymes. Later on it would be his Land Rover, where I'd sit and move the steering wheel while he controlled the pedals (perhaps, in hindsight, not the best way to learn how to drive).

I pick up my favourite photo of Arthur. It was taken before the war, when he was really young, not that much older than me now. The photo's black and white but you can tell he's wearing a pair of baggy white shorts and a coloured T-shirt with a white collar. His football kit. He's running, leaning into the future, and behind him you can see hundreds of flat-capped men standing on a terrace watching him, row after row of little white faces all staring at him and the ball at his feet. There would have been thousands there, close to twenty thousand, Arthur thinks. That's forty thousand eyes all looking at Arthur.

A Yorkshire gladiator. Dynamic and unafraid.

But what happened? That's what I don't understand. How did someone who plays in front of twenty thousand men every Saturday, week in, week out, become the man who hides behind his *Yorkshire Post* and goes along with pretty much anything Christine says?

Interlude

2 May 1936

It was the final day of the season.

The final minute of the final day.

Arthur Epworth, the new signing that year, was running up the pitch with the ball. The Yorkshire flyer, that's what they called him. The fastest man in the league.

He was just outside the 18-yard box now. He chose his spot then blasted the ball past the keeper into the back of the net.

The crowd exploded, the roar barrelling round the ground. A heaving mass of noise and waving caps.

The ref blew his whistle. Full time.

"Well done, lad," said Mr Barrett, the team manager, putting his arm round Arthur's shoulders as he reached the side line. "Great game."

"Thanks, Mr Barrett," said Arthur, wiping the sweat from his forehead with his shirt. "We didn't do too bad, did we?"

"You did very well, son. We'll be joining those buggers up in League Two next season. Anyway, get yourself inside now," Mr Barrett went on. "You'd better get tidied up. We've got a posh do later at the Mansion House, remember."

At the end of every season, the mayor put on a civic reception for the club. This year, with promotion secured, it would be an especially grand affair.

Arthur grimaced. A posh do at the Mansion House was not his idea of a good Saturday night. He wasn't one for fuss.

"Do I have to go?" he asked.

"'Course you have to go, son. It'll be bloody good. A real celebration. Now come on, get yourself in there," he said, gesturing towards the players tunnel and the changing room just inside.

"And anyway," shouted Mr Barrett, as Arthur walked off, "you might just enjoy it. You never know who you might meet, lad!"

CHAPTER
THREE

Wednesday 11 July 1962

Tea was uneventful, a relatively quiet affair involving quite a bit of surreptitious gristle-removal thanks to Christine's poor ham-buying skills, plus some polite conversation about:

1. Mrs Bridewell's dog (pregnant again)
2. Harold MacMillan (looking old)
3. The new village postmaster (a bachelor)

Afterwards, the three of us settle into our usual pre-bingo routine. For Christine, this involves retreating up to "her" bedroom for half an hour's "titivating", for Arthur it means falling asleep listening to the cricket, and for me it means waving Evie's Wand of Brilliance over the kitchen and tidying up the tea things.

I have a routine, built up from years of experience. First I clear away all the glasses and cups and saucers (you can't eat anything in Yorkshire without an accompanying cup of tea). Then I get the plates, stacking them up as I go around the table, the big plates at the bottom and the smaller ones on top, carefully scraping any leftovers onto the top plate to create a pyramid of crockery and unwanted food. This is easy with something like a cold tea — what can go wrong? — but far more challenging when Christine has actually cooked something, which greatly increases the likelihood of leftovers and potentially risks leaving a pile of food so large that balancing it all on a small plate requires the engineering skills of Isambard Kingdom Brunel.

Suddenly there is a cheer on the radio and a voice from The Oval says something about someone being bowled for nine. Arthur twitches and drops the *Yorkshire Post* onto the floor. The grandfather clock in the hall strikes six deep, pendulous chimes and I hear Christine slam the bathroom door upstairs (she has the lightness of touch of a heavyweight wrestler). Outside, the cows are starting their evening mooing and then . . .

Ra-ta-ta-ta-ta-ta-ta-ta-tat.

The back door is beaten with the ferocity of the guns of *The Guns of Navarone.*

(Our house is full of noises, sounds and sweet airs that give a fright but hurt not.)

"Yoo hoo. Only us," says Vera, Christine's mum, coming in and immediately parking her handbag on the kitchen table. Mrs Swithenbank, her friend, is just behind, obviously struggling, her ample frame wrapped — despite the balmy weather — in several layers of black clothing.

(The two of them together look like a seaside variety act: Mrs Swithenbank, a tall, wide-berthed battlecruiser whose limbs have a heft that defy gravity; and Vera, small and angular, as thin as a thistle and just as spiky.)

"Oooh, Evie, love, could you get me some water? I'm parched," says Mrs Swithenbank, balancing on a small kitchen chair that seems inadequate to the task. "It's this weather. I'm not built for it. It's like the bloomin' tropics." She wipes her forehead with a little hanky. "Look at me," she says, dabbing at her cheeks. "I've had enough of this heat. I'm sweating like a fat lass in a chippy."

Mrs Swithenbank has a way with words. She could be a poet.

"Vera, Doris, lovely to see you," says Arthur. "Have a seat, Vera."

"I'll stand thanks, Arthur," says Vera. "Better for my varicose veins."

We hear a lot about Vera's varicose veins. They are a bottomless font of conversation for her, coming in just behind the weather, the good old days, foreigners and, well out in front, "our Christine". ("Our Christine", another only child, could well be singlehandedly to blame for the terrible reputation of the rest of us.)

Vera's varicose veins, we are repeatedly told, give her a lot of gyp. She is a martyr to them. She doesn't know what she's done to deserve them but we're all pretty sure the war and the Germans have something to do with it because, according to Vera, the war and the Germans seem to be to blame for almost everything.

Where will the conversation go from here?

"Nice out," says Arthur, falling back on a classic.

"Aye, nice out," replies Vera. "They say tomorrow'll be even hotter."

This is not good news for Mrs Swithenbank and her hanky. "Even hotter?" she exclaims. "Oooh, I'm sweltering already. If I'd wanted to live in a hot country, I'd have married Mussolini." (This would have changed the course of world history considerably. There's no way Mrs Swithenbank would have let Mussolini get mixed up with Hitler. She says you can never trust a vegetarian.)

While all this has been going on, I've been getting Mrs Swithenbank a glass of cold water.

"Here you are, Mrs Swithenbank," I say, putting it down on the table in front of her.

"I do wish you'd call me Doris, love," she replies.

I will never be able to do this. Mrs Swithenbank has the stately presence, not to mention volume, of a Spanish galleon — possibly even a whole armada. She is no Doris. She will forever be Mrs Swithenbank to me. Calling her Doris would be like calling the Queen "Liz".

Every time I see Vera and Mrs Swithenbank together, I'm struck by how very different women are. The two of them are like chalk and cheese — a scrawny little piece of chalk and a tremendously oversized round of stilton. How many different versions of Woman can there be?

(And, even more importantly, which version will I be?)

Arthur, clearly uncomfortable with the number of women in the room, is trying to make polite chit-chat with Vera and Mrs Swithenbank, but he's struggling. He's very much a man's man. The female sex remains pretty much a mystery to him. The constant stream of village gossip provided by the two women might as well be in Swahili for all the sense it must be making to Arthur. He valiantly attempts to keep up, feigning interest in Mrs Swithenbank's neighbour's pools win (£38 4s 2d) and the "goings on" at number 28, but I can tell that he's actually just straining to hear the cricket. When it's his turn to contribute to the conversation he is gossip-free and flounders quite badly but recovers by telling a number of outright lies about the quality of Christine's cooking.

As soon as he's spent a polite-enough amount of time with Vera and Mrs Swithenbank, Arthur makes his excuses and disappears off to his study, leaving me with the Yorkshire Inquisition.

"So then, Evie, love, tell me . . . are you courting yet?" asks Mrs Swithenbank, getting straight down to business.

Courting is very important for a girl around here. We're not allowed to court (that would make you a hussy) but we are expected either to be courted (like in the olden days) or be courting (v. modern, like Princess Margaret). The only women who do not have to worry about being courted are:

1. Married women
2. Old women
3. Ugly women

To be honest, the last thing I want is to be courted by a boy from the village. Most of the boys around here are a waste of time, not to mention brutish and feckless (*adjective — lacking initiative or strength of character*). I will wait for Adam Faith or, if I can't have him, at least someone who comes from more sophisticated climes, like Leeds. Anyway, I'm not sure where Mrs Swithenbank expects me to have conjured up a boyfriend from since I last saw her as I've been in hospital for the past four weeks (which I remind her).

"Aye, love, I know that, but what about all those nice doctors in the hospital? There must have been some young 'uns? You could do a lot worse than getting yourself a doctor, you know."

"Like Dr Dawson in *Emergency — Ward 10*," pipes up Vera. "He's very nice. Lovely eyes. Mind you, Evie, I'm sorry, love, but I don't think you've got much chance of getting a doctor. They usually go for the petite, bubbly type."

Charming. (I am as tall as a tree, remember.)

"Don't be so daft, Vera. They'd be lucky to have her!" says Mrs Swithenbank.

Vera, never one for tact, presses on. "I just meant, Doris, that Evie's a bit tall. Men don't like that. They like to feel in charge. She needs to wear something a bit more, well, *shortening*."

Shortening? What clothes are shortening? Maybe she's seen a pair of magic Alice-in-Wonderland pedal pushers — *wear me and shrink*.

"And she should smile more. She'll be up against all those nurses. It's like a bear pit in some hospitals.

32

They're all after a doctor, you know. It's the only reason they go into nursing."

"What about Florence Nightingale?" I ask.

Vera gives me a Funny Look, then carries on.

"Yes, I can see you as a nurse. Much better than all this daft talk about going back to school. What's the point of more bloody exams? I mean, what have exams ever done to help anyone?"

"But, Vera," says Mrs Swithenbank, "Evie's a clever young lass. Happen she's going to be one of these modern women needing qualifications."

"Modern women! I'm a modern woman," says Vera, adjusting her hairnet, "and I get by quite happily with absolutely no qualifications. It's high time Evie stopped beggaring around at school and got a job. Our Christine was working before she even left school and look how well she's done for herself."

Oh.

What does Vera mean *Christine's done well for herself?* Does she mean by invading our home and bewitching Arthur? Surely Christine will just be a temporary aberration in our otherwise calm and pastel-free lives?

With perfect timing, Christine walks into the room.

A sickly fug of lavender accompanies her. Is it possible to suffocate on Yardley? Mrs Swithenbank gets her hanky back out of her handbag and begins wafting it in front of her nose.

"We were just asking Evie if she's started thinking about a job yet, love," says Vera.

Christine, narrowing her eyes, takes a step forward and surveys the battlefield.

"Of course she wants a job. Who doesn't?"

(Well, Christine for a start.)

"She'd have her own money and be able to get her own place. It can't be nice being cramped up in that tiny little room all day and night," she says, half-heartedly waving her hand around in the vague direction of my bedroom upstairs.

"Who says I'm cramped up?" I ask. I've got the run of the whole house, not to mention nearly a hundred acres of fields, three barns and a stream full of Great Crested newts. I certainly don't feel cramped up.

Annoyed, yes. But not cramped.

Christine pulls a face.

"Oh, I just thought you might be a bit squashed up there," she replies, walking across the kitchen. "Well, we're all living on top of each other, aren't we? Three sardines in a battered old tin. All these pokey little rooms. I thought you'd like to . . . *Owwww*. That bloody bear."

Christine starts hopping around on one foot, red faced and sweary. She's stubbed her toe (again) on a large ceramic bear that stands next to the bin.

"For God's sake. How many times have I said to get rid of it?"

Lots.

The bear is awful but ever since I found out Christine hates it, I've become very attached to it. It's meant to be a dancing bear, standing on its hind legs (as tall as a chair). I don't know what dance it's meant to be doing but it isn't the Twist or the Shimmy; it doesn't even look like it could manage the Hokey Cokey to be honest. My mother inherited it from her father and, apparently, she hated it too (that's why he's in the corner next to the bin).

"I'm going to throw this bloody thing out once and for all," Christine says.

She tries to pick it up but fails to budge it.

"Leave it," I say. "I really like it."

"Really like it?" says Christine, screwing up her face like a cabbage.

"Yeah, it's lovely," I lie.

"What are you talking about? It's horrible."

Christine's right. It is horrible. But not as horrible as Christine.

"He's really handsome. Look at his distinguished face."

(To be honest, the bear looks a bit simple and he's got funny eyes.)

"What? Are you crackers?"

"And he's very useful."

"Useful?" says Christine, crossing her arms. "How?"

I have a quick look round the kitchen, taking in the various rural-scened plates on the walls, the rusty tin of Vim next to the sink and the unused brass cooking utensils dangling in the alcove.

"Cap holder," I say, spotting one of Arthur's flat caps on the back of a chair. I take the cap and pop it on the bear, making him look a bit like Lenin. "There, you see. Very useful."

"Don't talk daft," she says. "I want it out of here. Now."

"And I want it in here," I reply. "Now."

We stare at each other, locked in mortal combat like two noble warriors. Well, one noble warrior and one horrible old lavender-breathing dragon.

Christine looks round the room for help but Vera and Mrs Swithenbank are sat at the other end of the table deep in conversation about the price of faggots. She tuts, gives me a Look, and then stomps out the room, knocking the cap off the bear as she walks past.

I pick the cap up, put it back on the bear and smile, happy in our little victory.

By the time Christine comes back in, Vera and Mrs Swithenbank are in the final stages of their pre-Bingo routine. You can feel the air of anticipation. Vera, busy fiddling with her hairnet and glancing at her watch, is clearly the most excited. For Vera, Wednesday evening bingo offers all the glamour of the Monte Carlo Casino for the price of two halves of stout and a bag of pork scratchings. Mrs Swithenbank, managing to keep her excitement much more under control, is hoisting up the prodigious (but sagging) gusset of her thick tights ("just getting everything ready for t'car journey").

I, meanwhile, have started washing up and am trying to fish out some nasty-looking chunks of ham gristle from the washing up bowl.

"Oh, Cinderella," says Christine, coming over to the sink. "Don't worry, one day you shall go to the ball!" She laughs, clearly very pleased with her joke. "But not tonight. You'd love bingo, though. Number three, cup of tea," she shouts, going all theatrical. "Sweet sixteen, never been kissed. Forty four, droopy drawers. See, it's made for you." She crosses her arms, smirking. "It's all part of growing up and becoming a woman, you know."

Not to me it isn't. I can't think of anything worse than sitting in a room for two hours and competitively listening to numbers. Is this what lies ahead of me? There must be more to being a Woman than Wednesday night bingo.

And, anyway, if I'm Cinderella, who does that make Christine?

Arthur pops his head round the kitchen door and tells us "ladies" that he's going to get the Land Rover started.

Vera looks extremely relieved. She has checked her watch an unnatural number of times in the past few minutes and has been looking even more manic than usual. I think bingo might be addictive, like cigarettes and jelly babies. (If bingo were ever wiped off the face of the earth, I'm sure Vera would miss it far more than she misses her husband, Derek, who was also wiped off the face of the earth when his ship hit a German mine in the middle of the Atlantic in 1940.)

Christine looks up from her compact. "Ay, come here," she says to Arthur, gesturing with her head and doing her best sultry smile (thinking she looks like *Jane Russell* but actually looking about as sultry as *Bertrand* or *Jack*). "Your tie's not straight. Let me sort it out for you."

She puts her hands up to Arthur's tie and wiggles it around a bit. Arthur tenses up then glances down at Christine and visibly relaxes. She sorts out his tie, puts her hand up to his cheek and strokes it gently. "There, that's better," she says, simpering up at him. "Much smarter. You look like Cary Grant now." And she brushes some imaginary crumbs off his shoulders.

"Thanks, love," says Arthur, squeezing her hand.

"You're welcome. I'm glad I have my uses. And it's nice to see you looking so handsome. I must be the luckiest girl in Yorkshire." She winks at Arthur. "And thanks again for taking us tonight. You're my knight in shining armour." And she taps him on the bum. (I feel physically sick.)

"Now, go and get the car started," she goes on, taking her compact back out and checking her lipstick. "We'll be with you in a sec."

"Are we all ready, then?" says Mrs Swithenbank, giving her tights one last tug. "Time for off. It's my lucky night tonight. I can feel it in my waters."

"Think you're going to get the big one tonight then, Doris?" says Christine. "Twenty quid'd come in very handy. What would you do with it?"

"Oh, I'd be straight into Hull for a better telly. One of those new big ones. And I'd get a nice new cabinet for it too. And a wireless for the bedroom."

"Your house'll be like a Rediffusion showroom, Doris," says Vera. "It can't be good for you, all those tubes and knobs and invisible rays. *I'd* have the house

38

done up. New everything. Fancy new settee and armchair. And some nice china knick-knacks."

"Ooooh yes," says Christine, clearly invigorated by the prospect of new china knick-knacks. "We could go up to York and get some proper posh ones."

"What about you, Evie, love?" asks Mrs Swithenbank. "What would you get with twenty pounds?"

What would I get? Would twenty pounds be enough to fly somewhere in a plane? Somewhere hot and exotic. Spain, perhaps, or Italy. I could walk barefoot on a warm beach and feel the sand in my toes and wear a big straw hat and stripy top. Or maybe go to London and stop in a really nice hotel and eat oysters and go to parties with Nancy Sinatra and Sofia Loren. Would twenty pounds be enough for that? I'm too embarrassed to say either of these things though and so just end up saying I'd get a tartan skirt and some books, and then save the rest.

"Lovely," says Christine, flatly.

"And what about you then, Christine, love?" asks Vera in an uncharacteristically sparkly voice. "What would you get?"

"Well . . . what would I get? I think I'd get a few little things for my bottom drawer. A nice tablecloth, perhaps, and some fancy serviettes. Maybe some underwear too, something a bit slinky. And a new dress. A lovely one with lots of ruches and bows." She waves her hands extravagantly around her waist and thighs. "Something beautiful and big and . . ."

Baaaaaaaaaaaaaaaaaaaaaaaaaaaaaaaaaaaaaaaaaaaaaaaah.

She is cut off by the sound of the Land Rover's horn, signalling the chauffeur's impatience to get going. The three of them grab their handbags and bustle out of the kitchen whooping and laughing. Mrs Swithenbank comes over to me on her way out and gives my wet hands a little squeeze.

"Enjoy your book," shouts Christine as she leaves. "Laxatives bloody Saga!"

And the door closes.

Phew. A bit of peace and quiet at last.

CHAPTER
FOUR

Thursday 12 July 1962

It's the morning after bingo night. Mrs Swithenbank's dreams of bingo glory came to nothing (the £20 jackpot went to a well-upholstered lady from Goole), but Vera won a new chip pan and apparently spent all night clinging on to it as if it were the Koh-i-Noor diamond.

I spent all night thinking about Christine. She's always buying new Things. Or, rather, getting Arthur to buy her new Things. The problem is, the more Things Christine buys, the harder it's going to be to get rid of her. Her clothes, the Tupperware and china knick-knacks, her Mantovani LPs, the horrible electric cooker — they're all mini anchors, weighing her down and making her immovable. Like a septic tank.

"Mini anchors?" says Mrs Scott-Pym, our wonderful old neighbour. I've popped round to cheer myself up (as I often do). She's currently busy folding buttercream in a huge caramel-coloured mixing bowl and, even though I've now officially Grown Up, I'm hoping she'll still let me give the bowl and wooden spoon a good finger-clean.

Mrs Scott-Pym is a balm to life. She has the magical ability to make time stand still (in a good way) and cheer me up if I'm feeling stretched or out of sorts. I have no idea how she manages to be so comforting but I think it might be a combination of:

1. Her clothes. She *always* dresses in calming colours, generally maroon, navy, bottle green or sky blue, and her cashmere twinsets precisely match the shade of her pleated tweed skirts. And she *always* wears a double-looped chain of pearls (I like consistency).

2. Her generosity. She's a constant source of books, jam, Browns' gift tokens, assorted baked goods, and magazines (or "periodicals" as she calls them). She has the brilliant knack of giving me the right book at the right time (Katherine Mansfield, Fanny Burney, Jacques Prévert), although when she gets it wrong it can be *very* wrong (John Cleland, for example, and his stiff staring truncheons).

3. Her house. Perfectly proportioned like one a child would draw. It's a wonderful pattern of books and parquet and old, expensive-looking furniture. If the Queen Mother were ever to move to Yorkshire, this is exactly the sort of house she'd live in. It has a calm, ordered timelessness that Christine would instantly ruin with the addition of man-made fabrics and cheap knick-knacks.

4. Her cooking. Bliss. This other Eden. Adam Faith in culinary form.

"Yes, mini anchors. All Christine's Things", I explain, "are like little mini anchors. And she keeps getting more and more of them. I'm worried that she'll never leave."

Mrs Scott-Pym keeps folding the buttercream. The mixture makes a lovely squelchy sound as she folds it. "I see. Very rum business. I'm surprised, I must say. I thought your father had more sense." After a few more seconds, she stops folding the buttercream and looks up at me. Her eyes have the sharp intelligence of a gold-crest and her body, small and lithe, makes her seem even more birdlike. "I'm sure he'll buck up soon and realise what he's got himself into. Now, could you pass me a tea towel, please?"

I could listen to Mrs Scott-Pym speak all day. Her vowels, like Mrs Scott-Pym herself, are as trim as a hockey stick and as grand as Harrods. Everyone else in the village says *towel* with two great swinging syllables but she needs just the one.

She folds the tea towel three times before cupping it in her palm and using it to open one of the range doors. A hot waft of sweet air rushes out.

"I'm afraid men have a habit of doing silly things, dear, and your father's no different," she says, taking assorted cakes out of the oven and placing them on wire cooling trays across the kitchen table. "It's difficult for a man to turn down the charms of a young lady, even when those charms are somewhat questionable."

Somewhat questionable? To me her charms are *entirely* questionable, based mainly on low-cut tops and her bowling-ball chest.

How can men be so stupid? Seeing as they're in charge of just about everything, you'd think they'd have the brains to be able to see beyond a pair of large boobs. How can such overwhelming power have been achieved with such distraction?

A great howl interrupts my thoughts. Is it the collective howl of womanhood expressing rage at hundreds of years of oppression and general drudgery?

No, it's the great howl of Sadie, Mrs Scott-Pym's dog, expressing her desire to be allowed in from the garden so that she can become more intimately acquainted with the delicious baking smells wafting out from the kitchen window. She is working herself into a howling frenzy, watching Mrs Scott-Pym through the French windows that lead out onto the garden terrace. Long streams of spittle dangle down from her jaw and attach themselves to the glass when she howls. The bottom half of the French windows look like they've been splattered with the deranged web of a psychotic spider. (I'm constantly amazed at Sadie's capacity to produce drool. Whenever I hear about a drought somewhere, I think of her amazing water-producing ability and wonder if we could send her there.)

Mrs Scott-Pym opens the French windows and a great clattering of paws signals Sadie's entrance. She heads straight for the table, a silver line of spittle tracing her path, and sits in anticipation, her eyes darting from the baking to Mrs Scott-Pym and back again. "Who's my best girl, then?" says Mrs Scott-Pym, breaking off a chunk of cake and handing it to Sadie, who takes it and in return covers Mrs Scott-Pym's hands in drool and crumbs. Mrs Scott-Pym picks up a tea towel and uses it to wipe off the drool (I dread to think what Vera would make of that).

Sadie is an English Setter and her long drooping muzzle reminds me of Mr Macmillan, the prime minister. If it weren't for all the dribble, she would look a very noble hound — as noble, in fact, as Mrs Scott-Pym. There is nothing she likes more than having her pink bits rubbed (Sadie, that is, not Mrs Scott-Pym) and she is often found on her back with her legs stretched upwards, tail excitedly wagging in anticipation of a good belly rub.

"I thought this *aventure* with Christine would all blow over soon," says Mrs Scott-Pym as she fills a pan with water. She puts the pan on the range and then balances a large glass bowl in it. Sadie looks up but decides that pans of water are not as interesting as chunks of cake. "Could you pass me the chocolate, please, dear? It's in the middle cupboard," she says, pointing to a cupboard I'm standing next to. As I fumble around in the cupboard looking for the chocolate, Mrs Scott-Pym folds up her tea towel and sighs. "Of course, things would have been very different if your mother were still here."

And there it is. The huge, enormous, unfair *if* that hangs over everything I do. If my mother were still alive, things would be very different.

I would know about fragrances and handbags and permanent waves. I would know which colours suited me. I would know how to make vanilla custard and macaroni cheese and how to have sophisticated parties for artistic friends. I would know that watching old men having sex with a cow in a field is not conducive to good driving. I would know how to get Adam Faith to marry me. I would know which Future would be best for me. And I would know how to get rid of Christine and all her horrible Things.

I would know everything.

If.

I pass the chocolate to Mrs Scott-Pym. She breaks it into small pieces and drops each piece into the glass bowl. As the water in the pan boils beneath it, the bowl tinkers gently against the sides of the pan.

Mrs Scott-Pym stares into the glass bowl. What can she see? Apart from pieces of chocolate, that is.

I think now would be a good time to talk to Mrs Scott-Pym about the disappearing objects in our house, and so I tell her about the Aga, the photos, the tureen, an armchair, a painting of a lady in big hat, and an elephant's leg umbrella stand. All gone. Vanished. Victims of Christine's push for lebensraum (*noun — additional territory considered necessary, especially by Nazi Germany, for economic expansion*).

"Hmm. I see," says Mrs Scott-Pym, using a wooden spoon to move the pieces of chocolate around in the glass bowl. I can hear the water simmering away but the chocolate still looks rock solid. "That's very worrying, dear." She stops stirring. "It's not right, at all," she goes on, flashing her goldfinch eyes around the room and shaking her head slightly. "Look, would you mind taking over for a moment whilst I go upstairs for something?"

And I take control of the wooden spoon and tinkering bowl while Mrs Scott-Pym leaves the room.

The chocolate pieces stare up at me. I give them a Good Prod. There are slight smears of chocolate on the glass but most of the chunks remain stubbornly intact. I give them Another Prod. Does prodding aid the melting process? Does it encourage heat dispersal? Is a wooden spoon an effective aid to thermodynamics? I wish I'd paid more attention to physics at school (or is it chemistry?).

I try Yet Another Prod followed by a Good Stir.

Nothing.

It's beginning to annoy me now. Why is it taking so long? I'm not sure baking is for me and I make a mental note to cross it off my list of potential jobs. I'd love to have the chocolate melted for Mrs Scott-Pym by the time she comes back downstairs so I decide to use my initiative and add some boiling water. That should speed things up.

The moment the water touches the chocolate, success strikes. The chocolate melts. Ha! I am a culinary genius. Perhaps I should be a baker after all.

But instead of turning into a smooth luxuriant gloop, the chocolate hardens and before long it's going claggy. I rush the chocolate off the heat but it now resembles something you'd find hanging off the rear end of a sheep. A few seconds later, and it's turned into a bowl full of rabbit droppings.

"Thank you, dear," says Mrs Scott-Pym, coming back into the kitchen. "It's always nice to have some help."

I stand in front of the bowl and smile, hoping she won't notice the pebbly mess.

She walks towards me with something in her hand. It's a small tatty book, with a few bits of folded paper sticking out. "I've been keeping this safe for a long time," she says, holding the book out with both hands as if it were a precious relic. "I wanted to wait until the right moment to give it to you. And now, I think, is very much the right moment."

I take the book and look down at it. It's black with a burgundy spine. Its cover is hard but slightly dimpled like the peel of an orange. There's a small white panel on the front, bordered with a simple pattern of tiny red ropes. On the panel someone has written "Recipes" in a now-faded blue ink.

"It's your mother's recipe book, Evie," says Mrs Scott-Pym. "She lent it to me in the war and it just got put on a shelf and stayed there."

My mother's recipe book. I hold it tightly, a suggestion of another life, squeezing it, rubbing it, trying to imagine my mother's art-deco-nutcracker hands flicking through its pages.

"I took it upstairs and put it in a drawer when we lost her," Mrs Scott-Pym goes on. She reaches up and adjusts her silver hair-slide. "I couldn't bear to see it in the kitchen every day." She stares at the book; she is in the room but at the same time seems a million miles away. "She was a good cook, your mother. Very good. She did a course in Paris, you know."

What? A cookery course? In Paris? Why hasn't anyone told me before that she did a cookery course in Paris? It all seems absurdly glamorous, given the farm and the cows and Arthur.

I smell the book. It reminds me of autumn. I smell it again, longer, deeper, breathing in its dusty absence. Inside, the edges of the paper are turning brown and some of the newspaper cuttings have yellowed. There's writing everywhere — my mother's writing — looping and leaning, a beautiful riot of blue ink. Some of the recipes I recognise, like *Lemon Syllabub* and *Caesar Salad* and *Veal and Ham Pie,* but many others come from a different world, like *Asparagus Ice* and *Vermicelli Souffle* and *Bouillabaisse.*

"Mind you don't let Christine get anywhere near it, dear," says Mrs Scott-Pym, gesturing at the book.

I'm only half listening, though, as I'm still carefully turning every page and incanting recipe names to myself: *Cod Normande, Gainsborough Tart, Gaufres au Caffe, Potage Saint-Germaine, Collier's Pie, Lobster a la Creole, Devilled Chestnuts.*

O brave new world that has such meals in it.

Mrs Scott-Pym is looking at me, smiling. I'm going to have to say something but I have no idea what. "It's wonderful, Mrs Scott-Pym," I try. "Really wonderful. Thank you." I go over and give her a kiss on the cheek, carefully avoiding Sadie (and her dribble). The recipe book has instantly become the most precious object in my possession, trumping two signed fan-club photos of Adam Faith and even my mother's wedding ring. Unlike the ring, the recipe book feels alive, every line of it a moment lived. "I love it," I say. "Such a beautiful thing. It's amazing. Thank you."

"No need to keep thanking me, dear. It's yours. I was just keeping it safe until the right moment. I think what with all this awful Christine business, now's the time to return the book to its rightful owner, don't you?" and she gives my hand a grandmotherly squeeze.

What kind of woman was my mother?

Arthur almost never speaks about her. Whenever I try to ask him anything, he falls silent and disappears into his deep sad eyes. Other people seem to avoid talking about her. They just look uncomfortable and unsure.

She died when I was six months old, just a chubby little gurgling baby. I know what she looked like, of course, from photos and from a lovely painting of her that Arthur has in his office, done when she was sixteen (like me) and looking very glamorous (not like me). But I don't know what she was like as a person. In fact I don't really know that much about her at all. Just basic snippets that get repeated back to me over and over again (attractive, kind, tall), making her more like a character in a badly written book than a real person. It's not like Margaret, who seems to know everything about her mother: her waist size, her annoying habits, her favourite song. And she knows her mother's voice too, as present as air, all around her every day. Singing, shouting, soothing. I wish I could remember my mother's voice. Sometimes I try to imagine it but all I end up with is a young Mrs Scott-Pym or Celia Johnson in *Brief Encounter*.

My mother is a mystery to me, a beautiful jigsaw with lots of pieces missing. Was she funny? Radiant? Clever? Or was she moody? Bossy? Clumsy? (I have definitely inherited the clumsy gene from someone.) Now, with the news of the cookery course in Paris, I've found out she could speak French. What else could she do that I don't know about? Ski? Play the banjo? Fly a plane?

"Oh, your mother really was wonderful," says Mrs Scott-Pym, looking at the recipe book and smiling. "A real gem. Very good company. Beautiful too. Just like you."

She sits down at the kitchen table, resting her chin in her hand.

The room pulses in the summer heat. It feels like an important moment has arrived.

"I don't really know much about her, Mrs Scott-Pym," I say. "Not as a real person anyway."

Mrs Scott-Pym is silent for a few seconds, then she smiles and words tumble out of her mouth like a giddy, happy dictionary: witty, friendly, tender, bright, refined, thoughtful, graceful, chic (not a word usually associated with our particular corner of Yorkshire). It's all incredibly wonderful to hear but at the same time a bit terrifying. I don't think I'll ever be able to live up to my mother, no matter how hard I try.

I look down at the recipe book in my hands.

"What type of Woman do you think I'll be, Mrs Scott-Pym?" I ask.

She stares at me with her sharp, birdy eyes. "You'll be your own woman, Evie. That's what Diana would have wanted."

A rush of light suddenly bounces around the room. I love it when people say my mother's name. It's like she's living again, even if only for a second. I let the golden flare of her name burst over me.

"Young ladies today can do anything they want and it's about time too," she continues. "It was very different when your mother and I were young. We weren't really expected to do anything other than look pretty and play tennis." She bends down and strokes Sadie (who's busy attending to her pink bits). "No. You should do whatever you want to do. Be whatever type of woman you want to be."

I'm not sure that really helps.

"Do you have any idea what you'd like to do yet, dear?" says Mrs Scott-Pym, breaking off a corner from the warm madeira cake and giving it to Sadie. "Have you thought of a career?"

A Career? Oh. That sounds even more terrifying than a job. How can I possibly be expected to decide on a Career? I can't vote yet. Or drink (officially). Or drive (officially) for that matter. Actually I don't think there's much I can do officially at the moment other than work and smoke.

I tell Mrs Scott-Pym that I have no idea what I'd like to do and that I seem to change my mind every few minutes. "It's exhausting," I carry on. "It makes my

head spin. I think I've settled on something and then —
bang — a new idea comes along. At the moment, I
quite fancy being an air hostess. Or maybe a vet."

Sadie glances up at me and whimpers.

"I see," says Mrs Scott-Pym, sounding unsure. "And
what does your father say?"

Arthur doesn't say much. The range of careers that
he thinks suitable for women is limited, to say the least.

"He thinks I should become a farmer's wife," I tell
Mrs Scott-Pym.

"Really?" She somehow manages to weigh the two
words with half a dozen different meanings, each one
tucked inside another like a Russian doll. "And what do
you think about that?"

"Not much," I tell her. I explain how people are
always telling me what they think I should do. How my
best friend Margaret's convinced I should become a
teacher. How the careers lady at school suggested the
typing pool at York City Council or receptionist at one
of the big law firms up on Micklegate. How Christine's
mum, Vera, thinks I should become a nurse or a
secretary ("Secretary?" repeats Mrs Scott-Pym, losing a
syllable). And how Christine herself, whose career
planning seems to have consisted of little more than
tight dresses and come-hither smiles, thinks I should
become a hairdresser or bus conductress.

Mrs Scott-Pym wipes her hands on a tea towel.
"Hmm. Well, you're a very different girl to Christine. I
wouldn't worry too much about what she thinks you
should do, dear." She twists the tea towel and uses it to
flick away a fat summer fly that has begun to explore

the baking. "Or anyone else for that matter. Be your own woman, Evie. It's the only way to be happy. I'll help you." She folds the tea towel and hangs it neatly on the oven door handle. "And your father will help you."

Arthur?

I'm not sure Arthur will be much help. Even before Christine he was always really busy (milking, calving, herding), but since she barged her way into our lives he's been more distracted than ever. He's like a swan, apparently gliding serenely across the water but actually paddling away frantically beneath the surface in a constant battle to keep Christine happy. His initial attempts to do this, mainly a bunch of flowers, the odd pub dinner and industrial amounts of Old Spice aftershave, have given way to ever more baroque pursuits: horse-racing at Doncaster; afternoon tea in Harrogate; fish and chips in Scarborough. Thanks to Christine, trips to the retail wonderlands of York and Leeds (not his natural habitat) have become a frequent part of Arthur's life. He's always either just bought something for her (handbag, Mantovani LP, family-size box of Milk Tray) or is on the verge of buying something for her. Trying to keep Christine happy has turned into another full-time job for Arthur. I don't think he has much time left to help me "be my own woman".

I try to explain all this to Mrs Scott-Pym but it isn't easy. I can feel her growing disapproval as I go on. Poor Arthur. I feel like I'm dobbing in a friend at school. "And now it looks as if she'll stay forever," I say.

"Hmm, what a bally mess," replies Mrs Scott-Pym, shaking her head.

"I know. It's horrible. Actually, Mrs Scott-Pym," I go on, "I've got something to confess."

"Confess?" She smiles. "Whatever have you been doing?"

"Well. It's to do with Christine."

I pause and take a deep breath.

Here goes.

"It was bad enough before when she was around the house all day working," I say, "but now she's moved in with us it's awful. Really awful. She's everywhere, day and night, nagging. With her horrible music and ugly whatnots."

Mrs Scott-Pym grimaces.

"I really don't like her," I go on, glad to finally get the words out.

"I see," says Mrs Scott-Pym, sitting down. "But, Evie, dear, whatever's happened to your father? Surely he can see what she's like?"

"Well, it's difficult," I explain. "She's quite tricksy. One minute she's super lovey-dovey and being nice and fluttering her eyes and pretending to be interested in tractors and rubbing his shoulders and laughing at his bad jokes and telling him how handsome he is. And the next she's horrible. Like a big pink witch. A big, grumpy, bossy pink witch. I think she's cast a spell on him," I add, waving my hands around in dramatic spell-casting way, hoping to look scary and magical but probably appearing about as spine-chilling as Mrs Tiggy-Winkle.

"What's that, dear?" says Mrs Scott-Pym, I think momentarily bumfuzzled (*adjective — confused and distracted*) by my sudden burst of am-dram witchcraft.

"I said Christine's tricksy, Mrs Scott-Pym. She can be really horrible to him but then he just forgets all about it the moment she's nice to him. It's like she's using some kind of magic." I try another quick blast of magic finger-waving. "Black magic probably, given the amount of chocolate she gets through."

Mrs Scott-Pym fails to acknowledge my brilliant joke. "Mmmm," she says, looking over at the bookcase. "Christine sounds a real scarlet woman to me."

I have no idea what Mrs Scott-Pym is going on about. Christine is definitely more pink than scarlet.

"Yes, a scarlet woman," she repeats, standing up and wrapping a malt loaf in some greaseproof paper. "Definitely. Now, let's get you a few things, dear, and then you can get going. I'm sure you've got plenty to be getting on with." And she thrusts the malt loaf and a still-warm bloomer into my hands and ushers me towards the door.

I have the distinct feeling I'm being got rid of.

As I walk back down Mrs Scott-Pym's gravelly drive, the smell of baking bread hangs like honeyed mist around me. I'm desperate, of course, to have a proper look at my mother's recipe book. It's singing — throbbing, fizzing — noisily in my hand and it takes every ounce of patience I have not to sit down in Mrs Scott-Pym's front garden and start flicking though the pages immediately.

Instead I head for the stream that winds through our fields. There's a particularly nice spot on a bend, complete with weeping willow and a stepping stone. On a sunny day, I often come and sit here because:

1. It's usually nice and quiet.
2. I can rest my feet in the water, letting the cool liquid lap against my ankles and pretend I'm paddling on a beach somewhere charming and urbane, like Saint-Tropez or Filey.

As I nestle down into the grassy bank and dip my feet in the stream, I open my mother's recipe book. I immediately feel like I've landed in a foreign country. *Poule au Pot. Sauerkraut. Duck à l'Orange. Pitcaithly Bannock. Esqueixada. Baked Gurnet. Iles Flottante.* I have no idea what virtually any of it means (did my mother never have chips, egg and beans?), but it's not just the recipe names that leave me flummoxed; the actual recipes themselves do too. Most of them are written in English but it's not exactly an English I recognise — it's a bit like the Chaucer we did at school where you can have a good guess at some words but definitely need a dictionary (or Margaret) for big chunks of the rest of it. For example, there are a few nice easy verbs (chop, melt, pour), but lots of others (coddle, bard, ream) that you really need to be Mrs Beaton to make any sense of. And then there's all the French, flamboyantly scattered around everywhere. Some of it I recognise (*pomme, pêche, petit pois*), but a lot of it is beyond me (I would have no idea what to do with a *bouillon* or *veloute* let alone how to *buleter* flour or *mortifer* a rabbit).

And then I see a recipe that catches my eye. *Tomate tout-en-un.* Well, it's not exactly the recipe that catches my eye but what my mother has written next to it in big capital letters: S.E.S. And underneath "Super Easy Supper!" (another small piece of my mother's jigsaw drops into place: a love of acronyms and exclamation marks).

That's more like it. I'm all for anything that's *super easy.* I scan through the recipe and am very pleased to see that it's not entirely gobbledegook. Basically, it looks like you fry an onion and some garlic in olive oil (I'm not sure about this — everyone knows that you fry with lard and put olive oil in your ears). Then you empty a tin of tomatoes into the pan plus some spinach leaves and simmer for ten minutes. When it's almost done drop two eggs into it all and let them poach. Then sprinkle on some cheese ("any will do") and stick it under a grill until the cheese is brown. Serve with "a *baguette*" (a type of pointy French bread that featured quite heavily in our textbooks at school — the French always seem to be buying them or eating them or losing them).

My stomach lets out a rumble, so I tear off a piece of Mrs Scott-Pym's still-warm malt loaf and tuck in. At the bottom of the page, my mother, in her beautiful looping writing, has written "from Daphne, 1936, Deauville" and drawn a little doodle of a woman wearing a very stylish hat. I have no idea who Daphne was but I'm sure I'd like her.

58

I put the book down and tear off another piece of malt loaf. Lying on the grassy bank with my feet in the stream and my head in Deauville (wherever that is), I feel I may have just glimpsed a new world. A new Future.

CHAPTER
FIVE

Friday 13 July 1962

"Can you put your foot down, Arthur, love? I'm almost dropping anchor back here."

That's Mrs Swithenbank. Her imminent bowel movement has been the main topic of conversation for the past five minutes. She started having problems as we drove through Scalby and we've had a running commentary ever since.

I am crammed in the back of Arthur's Land Rover between Mrs Swithenbank and Vera. I don't know what's worse: the sharp protrusions of Vera's skeletal body or the jelly-like folds of Mrs Swithenbank and her spreading flesh. Arthur and Christine sit regally up front, immune to our discomfort and a safe distance from the threat of Mrs Swithenbank's tummy troubles.

"Ooooh, come on. Get a move on," says Mrs Swithenbank.

Christine spins round. She doesn't look happy. Mrs Swithenbank's bowels are spoiling her plans. We are on our way to the Royal Hotel in Beverley for dinner, or luncheon as the hotel insists on calling it. Apparently we're having a slap-up meal to celebrate some good news. Christine, wanting to share the good news with as many people as could be crammed in the Land Rover, invited Mrs Swithenbank along, but she's clearly regretting it now.

"Leave Arthur alone, Doris," she snaps. "He's doing a great job. Could you just try and have a little more . . ." Christine pauses, obviously searching for the right word . . . "decorum, please?"

"Decorum!" says Mrs Swithenbank. "You try having decorum when you've got the Bombay bloody trots."

Vera leans forward and, stretching out straight across me like a bony accident waiting to happen, grabs Mrs Swithenbank's hand. "Try to keep your mind off it, Doris," she says. "Think of something else. Look at the view," and she points out of the window.

The view is hardly distracting. We are bang smack in the middle of farming country and the view consists of field after very flat field of cauliflowers.

"Keep my mind off it!" exclaims Mrs Swithenbank. "Vera, King Kong couldn't keep my mind off it at the moment," she goes on, holding her belly with one hand and the car door with the other. A menacing gurgle reverberates around the back of the car. "Oh, it's no good. We're going to have to pull over."

"Almost there, Doris," says Arthur, glancing nervously in the driver's mirror. In the reflection, I can see a sheen of sweat on his forehead. It's a very sunny day, the type of day that would normally be classed as glorious. It doesn't feel particularly glorious at the moment, though. The Land Rover is boiling, more cooker than car. Christine has banned the opening of any windows because she doesn't want to have her hair blown around and arrive at the Royal Hotel looking as if she's been "dragged through a hedge backwards". Arthur wipes his forehead with the back of his hand. "Just another couple of minutes to go. Hold on."

"Just think how nice the toilets will be at the hotel," says Christine, more to Vera than Mrs Swithenbank. "I bet they're proper posh."

"Oh yes, I bet they're lovely," replies Vera. "I wonder if they have their own towels, you know, with a nice motif on. Do you think I could get one in my bag?"

"Never mind the bleeding towels," shouts Mrs Swithenbank. "Can we just stop beggaring around and get to the hotel. *Ooooh*."

"Let's sing something to keep your mind off it, Doris," says Vera (rather optimistically to my mind).

"Do I look like I'm in the Sally bloody Army, Vera?" says Mrs Swithenbank, now clutching her belly with both hands.

"Come on. It'll distract you. What about, 'It's a Long Way to Tipperary'?"

Mrs Swithenbank gives Vera a Look that Christine would be proud of. "What about Arthur putting his foot down and getting us to the bloody hotel?"

"Arthur's doing his best, Doris," snaps Christine, fixing her eyes on the road and decidedly not looking back. "For goodness sake. It's not all about you, you know."

This is rich coming from Christine.

"Just another minute and we'll be there, Doris," shouts Arthur in a forced happy voice.

Vera, though, is not going to be beaten by Mrs Swithenbank's dicky tum. If Vera has decided that a sing-along will help, then a sing-along we shall have.

"*Rule Britannia, Britannia rules the waves*," starts Vera, waving her arms in front of her as if conducting the Halle Orchestra.

"*Britons never never never shall be slaves*," the rest of the car joins in. Perhaps it's all a bad hallucination brought on by the multi-coloured pills the doctor gave me.

Unfortunately, it very soon becomes clear that:

1. It isn't a hallucination.
2. Nobody knows any of the verses of "Rule Britannia", only the chorus.

We are stuck, then, repeating the same words over and over again.

"*Rule Britannia, Britannia rules the waves,*
Britons never never never shall be slaves.
Rule Britannia, Britannia rules the waves,
Britons never never never shall be slaves."
(This must be what hell feels like).

Everyone, except Mrs Swithenbank, is looking quite jolly and Vera even starts clapping. I decide on the path of least resistance and join in. I hope Adam Faith never finds out about this.

"*Rule Britannia, Britannia rules the waves,*
Britons never never never shall be slaves."
Mrs Swithenbank is half singing, half moaning. I can feel her flesh shaking as she fights to keep control.

Sitting next to her is like being forced to sit next to a geyser and hoping it doesn't erupt.

"*Rule Britannia, Britannia rules the waves,*
Britons never never never shall be slaves."

We turn a corner and see a sign for the Royal Hotel. It feels like a religious vision.

"*Rule Britannia, Britannia rules the waves,*
Britons never never never shall be slaves."

Arthur (still using his forced happy voice) tells Mrs Swithenbank that we'll be at the hotel in two ticks. This might be one tick too many. A deep rumbling bass, like someone playing the very low notes on a contrabassoon, emerges from Mrs Swithenbank and so begins the most extended bout of wind that I have ever heard. We all start singing more loudly, looking out the windows and pretending we can't hear. Mrs Swithenbank's wind stretches continuously across two and half choruses of *Rule Britannia*. It is very impressive.

The car finally turns into the driveway of the Royal Hotel, sending the gravel scattering as Arthur speeds to get to the parking area. Mrs Swithenbank has gone very pale.

Arthur starts to pull up in front of the hotel's main entrance but before the car has come to a complete stop, Mrs Swithenbank shoots out the door, her huge frame going this way and that like a load of barrels falling off a moving lorry. It is the fastest I have ever seen her move. "See you inside," she shouts, looking straight ahead as she charges up the stairs and into the hotel.

Finally, we have silence. I feel like I need an ear transplant.

"Well," says Christine. "Some people." She shakes her head and tuts.

"Poor Doris," says Vera. "She's always had a very sensitive tum."

Arthur looks through the driving mirror, smiles, and asks me if I'm all right. I nod. I have survived Mrs Swithenbank's Delhi belly relatively unscathed. He winks at me and then turns to Christine and Vera.

"Well, ladies. Welcome to the Royal Hotel. Are you ready to dine in style?"

Vera giggles coquettishly (the stuff of nightmares) but Christine already has the car door open. "Come on, let's get in," she says. "I don't want to miss anything." And she swings her legs out of the car and onto the gravel. "I'm starving."

The Royal Hotel Beverley feels a considerable number of steps up from the Selby Berni Inn, Arthur's usual venue of choice when he wants to push the boat out a bit. From the driveway, an imposing portico (complete with stone lions) guides you up to a large double door, each side of which is tastefully dressed with imposing brass embellishments (*noun — something intended to add beauty or interest*). The doors open up onto an enormous marble-floored entrance lobby. There is not a fake Tudor beam or maroon paisley carpet in site. It all feels more Castle Howard than Berni Inn. Flanking the entrance doors are two of the most extravagant arrangements of flowers I have ever seen, taller than me

65

and wider than Mrs Swithenbank. Down one side of the room stands a swanky reception desk (more flowers) manned by an extremely well-tailored lady with grey hair, and down the other is a huge fireplace and a very impressive assemblage of chairs. In the centre of the lobby, a staircase rises up and then twists round to the left *and* the right (just in case you don't know which way to go). The lobby even smells expensive. Does Arthur really know what he's doing bringing us here?

We are doing our best to live up to the surroundings. We had very clear orders from Christine to get dressed up for the occasion. Arthur is in a navy blue suit and looks surprisingly handsome. I'm used to seeing him in a shirt and tie (usually with a pullover, like every other farmer in Yorkshire), but it is strange seeing him out of his brown chords and brogues. I didn't realise he scrubbed up so well. Christine, Vera and Mrs Swithenbank, meanwhile, with their array of matching accessories, look like they've just stepped out of a clothes catalogue. Shoes, hats and gloves are all colour-coded to the exact shade, as if they'd been dipped in a big vat of the same dye. Such eye for detail is obviously another important part of being a Woman. (Will the list never end?)

And me? I am a vision in green tulle and red polka dots. I'm wearing a sticky-out dress that Arthur got me last year. This is only the second time I've worn the dress. The first time was at Margaret's New Year's Eve party and I felt like a Hollywood star. Now, though, seven long months later, I have a feeling that the dress makes me look like a Christmas tree.

"Can I help you, sir?" says the extremely well-tailored lady with grey hair on reception. She has the welcoming demeanour of Mrs Danvers.

"Yes, we've got a table booked for lunch. It's Mr Epworth," says Arthur. "We're a little early, I'm sorry."

"That's quite all right, sir," she replies, sounding like she's speaking to the butcher's boy. "The table is ready for you. Would you like to come through to the dining room, Mr Epworth, *mes-dames*?" Christine almost purrs with pleasure at being referred to in French but I can see that it has put Vera on her guard.

"Well," says Arthur, glancing round, "we're just waiting for someone actually. I'm sure she won't be long."

"Oh, would that be that the lady who came in just before you, sir?" Her tone suggests that Mrs Swithenbank made quite an entrance.

"Yes," says Arthur, looking rather sheepish, "that's right."

There's an awkward silence.

She looks down at her desk and then back up at Arthur.

We all smile nicely at each other.

Mid smiles, Mrs Swithenbank comes walking back into the room, moving considerably more slowly than the last time I saw her. "Ay, Vera," she shouts over the polished marble, "you should see the lavs. They're lovely."

The extremely well-tailored lady with grey hair holds out her hand in the direction of what must be the dining room. "Shall we proceed to the table now, sir?" she asks Arthur, and we all traipse off in her wake, already slightly deflated.

If anything, the dining room is even more impressive than the hotel entrance. Tables are spread out at a discreet distance from each other, like highly starched little islands on a parquet sea, and each table has a king-sized flower arrangement holding court in the middle. A wall of French windows leads out onto a pebbled terrace and beyond that lies a lawn any cricket team would be proud of. We walk past a large photograph of the Queen (thankfully this doesn't lead to more "Rule Britannia") and then past a long table loaded with assorted silver banquet dishes and tureens. The smell is incredible, a mix of flowers, meat, lemons and money.

We are taken to a round table next to the French windows. So far we have maintained a dignified silence, but as soon as the staff have us seated and furnished with menus, Vera starts.

"Well, I don't know who Mrs Fancy Pants on reception thinks she is. Did you see that look she gave us?"

"Snooty old cow," says Mrs Swithenbank.

"Doris!" says Christine. "It's just how people are in places like this. It's called being refined." She smooths the napkin on her knee. "It's a very upper-class establishment, remember."

Upper-class establishment? Why is Christine speaking like a holiday tour guide?

"Well, I didn't like her attitude," says Vera. "You'd think she'd never been to a privy the way she looked Doris up and down."

"Aye, I shot through that reception shouting for the lav — she had a face like thunder. Just stood there. No help at all," says Mrs Swithenbank, rolling her eyes. "Thank God for a little foreign chappie who pointed me in the right direction. I thought I was going to follow through."

Christine tuts and gives Mrs Swithenbank a Look.

"Well, we're all here now," says Arthur at his jauntiest. "We can just relax and enjoy ourselves, can't we?" He smiles at Christine. "It's lovely having you all together."

He picks up his menu. "Now what would you like? Don't hold back, this is a celebration after all." He glances around the table. "Have all three courses if you want."

A celebration? All three courses? What's happened to the financially cautious Yorkshireman that was my father? I notice Christine looking smugly at Vera and feel a sudden urge to whack her with the flower arrangement. I pick up my menu instead.

Rather than the shiny plastic-coated menus of the Berni Inn, the Royal Hotel's menus are *handwritten* on *real* paper, very thick paper, too, not like the stuff we have at school. And most of the menu appears to be in *French*. This will not go down well with some on the table.

I scan the menu, doing my usual trick of going straight to the puddings, and enjoy a moment's precious silence.

69

It's a very short moment.

"What's all this?" says Vera. "I think they've given me the wrong menu. It's all foreign. I can't understand a word."

"It's French, Vera," says Arthur. "A lot of the food here is French."

"French?" says Vera. "What are they doing with French food? We're in Beverley."

Christine looks up from her menu. I can spot traces of a frown gathering on her face (I know the signs well). "It's a fancy restaurant, Mum. I told you," she says. "Arthur's brought us somewhere really nice." She turns and does and her best Jayne Mansfield smile at Arthur then turns back to Vera. "The French just makes it even fancier. It's that kind of establishment."

I can't believe she just said "establishment" again. She will be clutching her imaginary pearls next.

Mrs Swithenbank, meanwhile, has bypassed the French and gone straight for the prices. "'Ow much?" she exclaims, loudly. "Three and a tanner for a starter! Ay, Arthur, you're going to need a mortgage to pay for all this. Have you banged your head?"

"It's a special occasion, Doris," says Christine, curtly. "We wanted to push the boat out."

I can't imagine Christine doing much boat-pushing. She's definitely the type who'd get someone else to push the boat. In fact she'd probably sit in the boat as it was being pushed.

Arthur is beginning to look as though he is pushing a very heavy boat indeed. I don't know whether it's the stress of being surrounded by women or the stress of

70

seeing the astronomical prices. Either way, he's looking decidedly uncomfortable. I give him a reassuring smile and return to the menu.

The menu is like a summarised version of my mother's recipe book. I imagine her in Paris testing out the various exotic-sounding delights in between sipping wine and chatting with her sophisticated friends. *Mousse de saumon avec pain grillé, soufflé au frontage, canard à l'orange*. I'm sure there'd be a hint of an accordion playing outside on the street. And probably a glimpse of the Eiffel Tower through the window.

"'Ere, Arthur. What on earth's *Bo-we-yuf Bour-gwig-non*?" asks Mrs Swithenbank.

(The city of light dissolves and I'm back in Beverley.)

"*Boeuf Bourguignon*, Doris. It's delicious," replies Arthur. "Diana used to make it." (My mother's name! For a second, the room is shot through with colour.) "It's quite rich. I'm not sure it's a good idea if you've got a funny tum. Probably best to stick to something light."

"Yes, you have to be careful with foreign food," says Vera. "It's all oil and garlic. We don't want any problems on the way home, Doris."

"No, we bloody don't!" says Mrs Swithenbank, grabbing her stomach with both hands. She turns to Arthur. "So what exactly is *Bo-we-yuf Bour-gwig-non*, then, Arthur?"

Arthur leans back in his chair. I think he's enjoying his moment in the linguistic limelight. "Well, the best way to explain it is sort of like a beef stew."

71

"Beef stew?" says Mrs Swithenbank. "Well why don't they just put that?"

"It's French, Doris," says Christine, putting her menu down on the table and crossing her arms. "It's a French beef stew. We're in a French restaurant. We're not in a Lyons' cafeteria now, you know."

Mrs Swithenbank ignores Christine. "And what about *coke-ow-vin*?" she asks Arthur.

"*Coq au vin*," replies Arthur. "Chicken stew."

I'm beginning to feel that the English language sucks the romance out of food. No wonder you pay so much extra for food with a French name.

"Chicken stew?" says Mrs Swithenbank. "Ee, it all sounds right tasty to me. Happen that foreign food isn't so bad after all, Vera."

Vera doesn't look convinced. If pie and chips were on the menu, I know what Vera would be having.

"So cock is chicken, then, Arthur?" asks Mrs Swithenbank.

"That's right, Doris," says Arthur, "well done. We'll have you dining with de Gaulle before you know it," and he does a jokey wink. I love it when he's like this.

"Well, it's not so hard after all, is it, this French business?" says Mrs Swithenbank, looking very pleased with herself. "A lot of it's just an English word with a funny accent. A bit like Brummy, really."

Arthur spends the next five minutes going through every item on the menu and explaining it all to us. I had no idea about his extensive knowledge of fine dining and I can't help feeling some filial pride. Vera and Mrs Swithenbank are also obviously impressed with Arthur's ability to make sense of the menu and they listen to him as if he were deciphering the Dead Sea Scrolls. Christine just sits there smiling proprietorially.

An elderly waiter with a moustache comes to take our order. He is wearing a bow tie and looks very smart, apart from what seems to be a large white tablecloth wrapped around his waist like a skirt (this must be another French thing, like kilts and the Scots).

"Are you ready to order now, *mesdames, monsieur?*" says the waiter, looking around the table. His French accent has the note of authenticity that a Yorkshire farmer will never attain. There's a general nodding of heads and then the waiter turns to Mrs Swithenbank, pen poised above pad, and says, "*Madame?*" Both Christine and Vera look miffed about not being asked first but Mrs Swithenbank beams a huge smile and dives in.

"Oh, right. I'll have the asparagus to start, please," she says, using what must be her best telephone voice, "and then I'll have the *Coq au Vin.*" She pronounces *Coq au Vin* very carefully and makes it sound like a dish that, if not quite from France, does at least have a passing acquaintance with the continent. I'm impressed.

"*Bien, madame. Merci,*" says the waiter with a little bow of his head. "And you, *madame?*" He turns to Vera.

"Well, I'd like to start with the asparagus too, please," says Vera, seeing Mrs Swithenbank's telephone voice and raising it with the Yorkshire version of a BBC continuity announcer. "And then I'd like a Kiev cock."

73

The waiter looks up from his pad. "*Madame?*"

"A Kiev cock, please," confirms Vera.

The waiter looks flummoxed.

"Chicken Kiev," intervenes Arthur, smiling at the waiter.

"Ah, chicken Kiev," repeats the waiter, visibly relieved. "*Bien, madame.*" Vera gets a little bow. "Thank you."

"I thought cock was meant to be chicken," snaps Vera to no one in particular.

"It is, Vera," replies Arthur. "But only some of the time."

"Oh, I can't keep up with this bloody language," says Vera, clearly vexed. "It's no wonder the Germans walked all over France in the war."

The waiter's pen hovers over his pad for a second or so longer than is strictly necessary and then he looks up, smiles, and proceeds to make his way round the rest of us.

"Well," says Arthur when the waiter leaves the table, "it's really lovely to have you all here today."

"Yes," says Christine, looking at Vera and Mrs Swithenbank. "Arthur and me have been wanting to do this for a while but we had to wait for Evie to get out of hospital and feel a bit better."

I get the feeling that my being in hospital has been a cause of great personal annoyance to Christine.

"You've certainly brought us somewhere grand, Arthur," says Mrs Swithenbank.

Arthur beams.

74

"Must be costing a pretty penny," she goes on.

"Well, you can't take it with you, Doris, can you?" replies Arthur while Christine gives Mrs Swithenbank yet another Look.

"The Royal Hotel Beverley is a very special establishment," Christine says, sounding like an advert in the local paper, "and we wanted to bring you all here to share some good news." She glances over at Arthur, who is somehow managing to combine smiling with looking quite uncomfortable. She reaches over and holds his hand. "Are you going to say a few words, Arthur?"

"Yes," says Arthur. "Yes, of course." He coughs (I think mainly just to free his hands from Christine's iron grip). "Well," he continues, looking like he's in need of a big French hole to swallow him up. "Like I said, we're very happy to be here with you today. It's smashing. Really smashing."

Christine and Vera look at each other and do a smile so smug it should be in the Guinness Book of Records.

"You might be wondering why we've brought you all the way out here. Well, it's because there's some news we'd like to share with you." He looks over at me and I can see little beads of sweat starting to gather on his forehead. "Some really good news."

Christine, now doing her best mafia-boss smile, reaches out and holds his hand again.

"We've been thinking about this for a while now," continues Arthur, "and we both feel that it's the right thing to do." He blinks. "Absolutely the right thing to do." I can see the skin on Christine's knuckles whiten as she tightens her grip on Arthur's hand. "Christine's been with us for a while now and I hope Evie will agree that it's been a very happy time."

Everyone turns to look at me. I can see that I'm expected to make some acknowledgement of our very happy time so I marshal my mouth into a smile but it isn't easy (I think I may have lost control of my facial muscles). As a diversionary tactic, I nod frantically and raise an empty glass to Christine. This seems to have done the trick as everyone swivels back round to look at Arthur.

"Anyway, I'm not one for speeches," says Arthur,

". . . but I'm very happy to say," (my mouth feels dry)

". . . that Christine and I," (my hands feel clammy)

"are getting engaged."

What???????

Suddenly I am high in the air looking down. I see myself sitting at the table, shocked and shaking and trying not to cry. I look confused. Broken. Sitting opposite me, Christine is being hugged by Vera, giant cocky gloats crackling across their faces. Next to Vera, Mrs Swithenbank smiles nervously over at Arthur but Arthur doesn't notice because he's staring at me, straight at me, his eyes full of hope and fear.

Poor Arthur.

Christine is a bossy, gold-digging trollop who will rule over him with the clemency of a renaissance pope.

I'm going to have to save him.

It's going to be a busy summer.

Interlude

2 May 1936

"What a Bobby Dazzler!" Arthur Epworth thought as he looked at himself in the mirror. He was wearing his York City FC blazer and couldn't decide whether he looked like a matinee idol or a shop dummy.

"You look very dapper, lad," said Mr Barrett, coming up and standing next to him. "We might just make a gentleman out of you yet."

"Not much chance of that," replied Arthur, quickly turning away from the mirror and facing the club manager. "I feel a bit of a chump in all this to be honest."

"As long as you don't start playing like one, lad."

They both smiled.

"Now, come on. Let's be having you. We've got the team bus waiting outside. We can't keep the great and the good of York waiting all night at the Mansion House just for a young rascal like you."

CHAPTER
SIX

Saturday 14 July 1962

The world's strange, isn't it? Take wind. (Not the Mrs Swithenbank kind of wind. The other kind.) Where does it come from? Is there a giant fan somewhere making new wind every day or does the same wind just keep going round and round and round forever? And stiletto heels. Are they really a Moral Danger? That's what a man said on the telly last week. Would they be less of a Moral Danger if men wore them? Helen Shapiro wears stilettos and she doesn't really strike me as being very immoral. Or dangerous. And cows. You put grass in one end and you get milk out the other end (well, not exactly the other end). How does that work? And how come the white milk comes from a brown cow that eats green grass?

I often get lost in philosophical musings. My brain skips around like a young rabbit: bouncy, full of energy, but without ever actually getting anywhere.

Today my musings revolve mainly around the events of yesterday.

The engagement.

Christine celebrated the announcement with all the grace and subtly of a Roman triumphal arch. It was engagement *this* and wedding *that* every course. Relentless and unstoppable. Like toenail fungus.

And so here are I am, walking up Mrs Scott-Pym's drive at nine in the morning. I know a cup of tea and a slice of something nice will be waiting for me. And a friendly ear. Well, two friendly ears actually. Four if you count Sadie.

The drive is gravelled and each footstep triggers a satisfying crunch. When I breathe in, it's not the aromatic balm of her cooking I smell but the perfumed assault of countless flowers coming from the garden's densely packed borders. The smell of summer.

And then suddenly I hear a lady scream.

And a man shout.

And then lots of people screaming and shouting.

I'm momentarily alarmed but then I hear what sounds like a hundred violins doing something very dramatic and I know it'll just be opera. Mrs Scott-Pym loves it. She often has it on in the morning and says it gets her going and ready to start the day. I'm not so sure. Opera's just a lot of orchestra and shouting to me. If I were a character in an opera, I'd be very worried as I think your chances of being thrown off a tower or stabbed to death in a bullring are pretty high. I'm going to stick with Adam Faith.

As I get nearer the house, the shouting, screaming and orchestra get louder and louder. Mrs Scott-Pym's gramophone is the size of a cow. I am madly jealous. I have a pastel-blue portable Dansette turntable in my room and it just can't compete. Opera singers seem pretty loud anyway and the huge gramophone cabinet just makes them even louder. I would love to give some of my records a spin on Mrs Scott-Pym's gramophone. It would be good to use it to play some proper singers, people who can hold a tune without yelling or dying.

I let myself into the house and find Mrs Scott-Pym sat in her sitting room (why aren't all rooms named after what we do in them? I'd love a daydreaming room and Christine could have her very own nagging room). Mrs Scott-Pym's sitting room has the same kind of refined elegance as Mrs Scott-Pym. Stately. Lithe. Comfortably grand. A big fireplace topped with a slightly clouding mirror takes up most of one wall and in front of it a sofa and two very upright armchairs surround a small table covered in magazines. Mrs Scott-Pym is sitting on the sofa, a copy of the *Radio Times* on her lap and drinking what looks like a glass of sherry. Sadie is at the other end of the sofa, clearly unimpressed by all the noise.

Mrs Scott-Pym looks up, smiles, and mouths something. I think she said *hullo, dear* but it's hard to tell because the music is so loud.

I shout hello and ask her how she is. Three times. Mrs Scott-Pym, gesticulating gracefully, mouths something else then gets up and turns off the music, mid-scream. The room is suddenly quiet, except for the muffled *thump-thump-thump* of Sadie's tail wagging on the sofa. "There," she says. "That's better. Now, how are you? How was the meal yesterday?"

As we both sit down, I tell her about the hotel, and the food, and the extremely well-tailored lady with grey hair. I tell her about Mrs Swithenbank's tummy troubles and Vera's Kiev Cock. I tell her how handsome Arthur looked and how I looked like a Christmas tree. And I tell her about the engagement announcement and about Christine behaving as if she were the Supreme Commander of the Allied Forces.

"Little madam," says Mrs Scott-Pym, her quick bright eyes narrowing slightly. "I knew something was wrong, dear. I can read you like a book."

(I'd love to be read like a book. I'd be something experimental and French, tricksy and clever, something that never uses the letter M or full stops. Or maybe something northern and gritty, something set in a bicycle factory with lots of moral ambiguity and A-line skirts. And what about everyone else? What sort of book would they be? Arthur would be the *Wisden Almanack*, of course, or maybe a history book or a biography. Mrs Scott-Pym strikes me as a World's Classic, probably with a leather cover. Margaret would definitely be an encyclopaedia — full set — and Mrs Swithenbank would be something hefty but no-nonsense, like a dictionary. Vera already is a living, breathing book of bingo cards. And Christine? What would she be? Gothic horror.)

Mrs Scott-Pym sighs. "I must say I'm disappointed in your father, though. Very disappointed." She gets up, making another disapproving noise (half groan, half tut), and walks towards the kitchen. "I'll get you some tea, dear. Keep an eye on Sadie for me, will you?"

I take Mrs Scott-Pym's place on the sofa. Sadie is oblivious to her new sofa companion as she has just buried her head deep in her belly and is manically snorting around her nethers. I try to pull her head away but she's having none of it. She has the single-mindedness, not to mention technique, of a pig snuffling for truffles (*noun — a rare underground delicacy often found with the aid of trained swine*). It's probably best just to let her get on with it so I sit back, relax, and flick through the *Radio Times*, hoping to find something on Adam Faith.

After a few minutes, Mrs Scott-Pym comes back into the room carrying a tray. I start to stand up so that she can resume her previous spot on the sofa but she tells me to stay where I am and instead comes and sits next to me, shunting Sadie along a bit.

"Now, dear," she says, putting the tray down on the small table in front of us. "I'm going to talk to you about something important but I want you to promise not to tell anyone."

Oh no. She's not going to talk about Sex, is she? I couldn't bear that. Margaret's mother had a long talk to her about Sex a few weeks ago and Margaret still can't look her in the eye. (Apparently the talk started with a detailed explanation of Margaret's "woman-hood" [in the manner of an engineering report], then moved on to an elaborate metaphor involving the correct technique to stuff and plump cushions, before finally ending with lots of talk of buds of passion and life-giving fluids.)

"Yes, of course," I say, trying to sound nonchalant.

"Good," says Mrs Scott-Pym as she pours some tea from the pot, catching a few stray leaves in a tea-strainer that she's perched on the rim of a china cup. "Well, it's a rather awkward subject," she goes on, adding milk to the tea and placing the cup and saucer down in front of me. "And I'm not really sure where to start."

Right, it's definitely Sex, then.

"Well, I suppose I should start back in 1936, when Mr Scott-Pym and I were trying for a baby."

(I wish I could do Arthur's trick and hide behind a *Yorkshire Post*.)

"I was forty-two. Far too old to have a child really. We'd wanted children for a long time but, for whatever reason, it just didn't happen." She hands me a plate with a large slice of madeira cake on. "We'd more-or-less given up. It hit Edward even harder than me, I think."

Edward was Mrs Scott-Pym's husband. He died before the war so I never met him but I know what he looked like because there are some photos of him on the sideboard. His lovely old car is still parked up in Mrs Scott-Pym's garage, unused, packed away like a museum piece.

"Well," continues Mrs Scott-Pym, "one day I received a small package in the post; it was a couple of books and a letter from my old nanny's legal executor. Poor Nanny Thompson had died and she'd left me the two books. She was seventy-six, I think. A good age. She was always in such good health." She looks lost in thought for a moment, transported back to another age until I slurp my tea and bring her back to 1962. "Anyway, one of the books was a collection of Hans

Christian Andersen's fairy tales that we used to read together in the nursery; it had beautiful illustrations. Quite decadent. All very Aubrey Beardsley."

I nod, even though I have no idea what she's talking about.

"And this is the other book." She picks up a small leather-bound book from the tray. "A book of Yorkshire magic. You reminded me of it the other day when you were telling me about Christine and your father. You said something about her casting a spell on him. Black magic, wasn't it?"

Yorkshire magic? Black magic? I suspect this is possibly more like sherry magic.

"Anyway, Nanny Thompson was always talking about faeries and spells and the magic of olde Yorkshire. Every story seemed to involve some kind of hocus-pocus. When we went on walks, she'd point out elf trees and enchanted streams and go on for hours about the spirits of the air. It was all terribly exciting when I was young, of course, but as I grew older I used to think that she was perhaps a bit gaga. Poor old dear." Mrs Scott-Pym looks down at the book and turns it over in her hands. "Naturally, by the time I was sent the books I thought the whole thing was absolute rot so I just put them on a shelf and got on with my day." She puts the book of Yorkshire magic down on the table and tucks a stray wisp of white fringe back under the silver clip in her hair. "That evening, Edward came back from work looking terribly fretful. I knew something was wrong as soon as he walked in. I was sitting here, you

85

know, on this very sofa," she taps the sofa, "reading and having a sherry."

I try not to look at the half-empty glass of sherry currently on the table in front of Mrs Scott-Pym and instead ask her what was wrong with Mr Scott-Pym.

"Well, Edward was a journalist, a staff writer for the *Yorkshire Post*. That day the Spanish generals had launched their coup and it looked pretty certain that there was going to be civil war. The editor wanted someone over there, boots on the ground as it were, so he asked Edward to go to Madrid. He was one of the few chaps at the paper with no family so it just seemed the right thing to do. He was worried about leaving me alone, dear man. That's why he looked so anxious. I expect he was worried about walking into a war too, of course, but he never spoke about that."

I had no idea about any of this. A journalist! A war correspondent! Spain! Mrs Scott-Pym was already the most interesting person in our village by far and now she's got the added glamour of journalism and the Spanish Civil War.

I've got a million questions in my head, not least how does any of this connect to the magic book, but I think it's best to start with the basics. "What happened to Mr Scott-Pym?" I ask. "Did he go Spain?

"Yes, he went. He had no choice really. When an editor says jump, you jump. At least that's how it was in those days." She stops to have another mouthful of sherry. The house is so quiet that I can hear her swallow and then lick her lips. "Anyway, when the shock had worn off, he asked me about my day so I told him about the package from Nanny Thompson and showed him the books. We had a jolly good laugh about the magic book — Edward was a rationalist to the core — and then that was that. Within a week, he was off."

"So he went, then? Over to Spain. To the civil war. That's incredible."

"Yes, well, I suppose it is. We did a lot of incredible things in those days."

Mrs Scott-Pym looks out across the room and sighs. I look too and see hundreds of tiny particles of light (or, as Christine would call it, dust) floating in the solid beams of sun which stream in though the large sash windows, each speck bobbling along on its own random drifting journey. Glimmering little boats searching for a port.

I wonder why Mrs Scott-Pym hasn't told me before about her husband and the Spanish Civil War or his job as a journalist. I know some things about him, of course: where he went to university (Durham); his first dog (chocolate lab); his favourite colour (navy blue, like me). But not much. Just a few incidental facts (more scattered jigsaw pieces). But then, I suppose, how well do we ever really know anyone? How well do I know Margaret or Mrs Swithenbank or Christine? How well do I know Mrs Scott-Pym? As a real human being, I mean, not just as a lovely old lady who lives next door and gives me books and cake.

"Evie, dear, would you like some more tea?" Mrs Scott-Pym has stopped looking out the window and is staring straight at me. I've got a horrible feeling I've been daydreaming.

"Ooh yes, thanks, Mrs Scott-Pym. That'd be lovely."
I pass her my cup and lean back on the sofa, trying to look as though I've been paying attention. "Did Mr Scott-Pym write many stories about the war? Was he in Spain long?"

"Well, he was meant to stay there for however long it lasted," says Mrs Scott-Pym, pouring more tea into my cup. "Everyone said it would all be over in a few months but it got very nasty and dragged on for more than three years. Terrible thing."

"Three years! You didn't see each other for three years?" I am seeing the *Yorkshire Post* in a new light.

"Three years?" repeats Mrs Scott-Pym, sounding puzzled. "What, Edward? No, it was much less than that, dear. He was only out there a few months." Sadie is lying with her head in Mrs Scott-Pym's lap, a skein of dribble stretching from mouth to skirt. "He came back early," she goes on. "He had to, you see. I was expecting."

My mouth drops wide open (I hope I'm not dribbling like Sadie).

"You look shocked, dear," says Mrs Scott-Pym, smiling and stroking Sadie's head. I could swear her eyes are twinkling.

I *am* shocked. And confused. My head's full of questions again, pinging around like giddy marbles. "What happened?" I ask Mrs Scott-Pym. "Was everything all right? Were you okay? Did you lose the baby?"

I didn't mean to ask that last one. It just came out.

"Lose the baby? No, dear. Not the baby. I lost my husband. Poor Edward," she says, wiping Sadie's dribble from her skirt. "I sent him a telegram, of course, as soon as I had confirmation from the doctor. He was overjoyed. He got straight on to his editor and was given leave to come back. They sent another chap out there. Edward set off home immediately, carefully making his way through Spain, then over the Pyrenees and across France to London but then, just outside Kings Cross, hanging around for a train to bring him back to York, he was knocked down by some drunken fool in a coal lorry." She stops talking and exhales deeply. Poor Mrs Scott-Pym (and poor Mr Scott-Pym, too). "It's ironic really. We'd all been worried about him going over to Spain and the war but in the end he was killed in a wretched road accident here at home."

I don't know what to say, so I just say sorry. Several times. In several different ways.

Mrs Scott-Pym reaches over and holds my hand.

"Oh, it was a long time ago, dear," she says. "Life goes on. It always does. And of course, I have Caroline now."

"Caroline?"

"Yes, Caroline. My daughter. *Our* daughter."

A daughter! Just how many secrets can one person have? Especially a nice old person who wears tweed and listens to opera.

"I didn't know you had a daughter, Mrs Scott-Pym," I say.

"Well, one never really talks about one's children very much, dear. It's not the done thing, is it? Anyway, she lives up in London and has her own life there."

London.

A scent of something glamorous and sophisticated wafts into the room.

"Come with me. I want to show you something," says Mrs Scott-Pym, taking my hand. She leads me through the sitting-room door, into the hallway, and then up the stairs. This is all very exciting because I've never been upstairs in Mrs Scott-Pym's house. Downstairs is like a second home to me but somehow upstairs has always felt more intimate, private, something to be glanced at only from a distance. As we're walking, Mrs Scott-Pym tells me about her daughter.

Apparently she lives somewhere called Holland Park and works in Chelsea "doing something in fashion" (which Mrs Scott-Pym says in a way that makes it clear she disapproves). She moved to London straight after boarding school and did a secretarial course but "never got very far with it" (more disapproval). And she's twenty-six.

She sounds amazing.

By now we're in Mrs Scott-Pym's bedroom. I feel like an Elizabethan ambassador, led through various public chambers and into the Queen's inner sanctum. Mrs Scott-Pym sits on the edge of her bed and beckons me to sit next to her.

"Here. This is Caroline," she says, passing me a large photograph that she's taken from her bedside table. The woman in the photograph is staring right at the camera and laughing. She's beautiful. She's wearing pedal pushers and a stripy T-shirt and she's swept a huge pair of round black sunglasses back onto her hair, like an Alice band. She's standing in the middle of a small street somewhere, surrounded by shops and mopeds and life.

"She's lovely, Mrs Scott-Pym," I say, stating the obvious. "Really beautiful."

"Yes, dear, she gets her looks from Edward. He was such a handsome man." Mrs Scott-Pym laughs. "The most handsome man in Yorkshire, my mother always called him."

I can see that there are more photos of Caroline on Mrs Scott-Pym's dressing table. Baby Caroline. Caroline in school uniform. Glamorous Caroline looking very grown up in a ball gown.

"Well, the reason I'm telling you about Caroline now is this book," she says, waving the book of Yorkshire magic. "Edward's news that night when he came back from the office saying he had to go to Spain really hit me. I knew that I was on the cusp of being too old to have children but the thought of him going off to a war seemed to make it all so definite. We would have to resign ourselves to the fact that it would be just the two of us forever and I'm not sure I was quite ready for that. When he was upstairs changing, I sat on the sofa trying to make sense of it all. The book was still there from when I'd been showing it to Edward earlier and so I started flicking through it. Of course, I thought the whole book the most frightful nonsense but I just needed something to take my mind off the day's news." Mrs Scott-Pym laughs to herself. "Well, it certainly did that; it's all such mumbo-jumbo. At the top of every page there are these dreadfully fey titles: *songs to do this* or *songs to do that*. Look, I'll show you," and she opens the book randomly at several pages. "Yes, here's a good one. *Songs to Turn a Bad Man Good*. I think we should send that one to Mr Macmillan, don't you? And look, here's another one. *Songs to Drain a Cuckold's Rage*. Really! One for Sir Clifford Chatterley I think, dear," she chuckles. "Well, I ask you, what poppycock. The book was so absurd that at least it stopped me thinking about Spain and the bally war. But then something caught my eye. I'll never forget it. *Songs to Make a Childless Couple Sing*. I knew that it was all hogwash, of course, but I couldn't help but read on."

Mrs Scott-Pym pauses and starts flicking through the book again.

"Ah, here it is! Look," and she passes me the book, open at a page that has *Songs to Make a Childless Couple Sing* written across the top in ye-olde-worlde writing.

I look down at the book and read the first line. *Take 6 leaves of barrenwort and 2 cloves of nutmeg*. It sounds like a pretty bad song.

"Are you meant to sing this, Mrs Scott-Pym?"

"Sing it? No, of course not, dear. They're not really songs. Whoever published the book just called them that to make them sound more mysterious. They're more like recipes and lists of things to do."

"Oh, I see," I say, as though it all suddenly makes sense (which it doesn't). "What happened next? Did you follow the recipe?"

"Well, yes, I did actually. Despite thinking it was all a waste of time. What did I have to lose? Getting all the 'ingredients' together was something of a trial, though. I seem to remember running round after oysters, sows' whiskers and all kinds of nonsense. And then I put it all together and made a . . . well, a potion I suppose. I took the horrible thing every morning for the next few days, read out a few silly rhymes and that was that. Edward went off to Spain. Of course, I didn't say anything to him about it. He'd have thought I'd gone completely mad."

Quite.

Mrs Scott-Pym looks at the book and puts it down on her bedside table.

"A few weeks later, I started to feel off colour," she continues, "and then it just got worse and worse so I went to visit my doctor. When he told me I was with child, I couldn't believe it. The rest of the story you know. I sent a telegram to Edward telling him about the baby and he came straight back to be with me. And then suddenly he was gone."

Just like that.

It's all so unfair. Just as everything looked like it was going so well, it all went horribly wrong. (Now I can see why Mrs Scott-Pym likes opera so much.)

"No, dear, come on, don't cry," says Mrs Scott-Pym, looking up at my watery eyes. "No need to be maudlin. I'm only telling you all this because I have an idea. Something that will help you." She holds my hand again and rubs my fingers with her thumb. "You see, I was very old when I had Caroline, far too old to have a baby really. It was only when I followed what was in the silly old book of Yorkshire magic that Caroline came along."

"Oh. So the magic in the book makes babies then?" I ask (this is very different from what Margaret's mum said).

"Well, no. Not quite, dear." Mrs Scott-Pym gives me a doubtful look. "But the book must have helped. It must have done something, you see. Some magic or whatever it is you want to call it. There's something there. Something that works. You reminded me of it when you were telling me about Christine using magic to snare your poor father."

"But I was only joking, Mrs Scott-Pym," I say. "Christine's the least magical person I can think of. There's not a whiff of mystery about her. There's more wizardry in our old Hoover than there is in Christine. I don't *really* think Christine used any magic to charm Dad," I add. "I think her charms are more . . . humdrum than that. More . . . obvious."

"Yes, dear. But you got me thinking about the book again — it hadn't come into my mind for years. I just thought it might perhaps help."

She taps my thigh with the book.

"I had no idea where the bally thing was and had to turn the house upside down looking for it. Eventually I found it tucked away on a shelf in the study, next to some of Edward's ornithology books. I had a good look through it and found this." She hands me the open book. "I think it might just be what you need."

94

I take the book and look down. At the top of the page in the terrible ye-olde-worlde writing is the title for that particular page's magic spell.

Songs to Unshroud a Scarlet Woman.

I take a big breath. "But Mrs Scott-Pym . . ."

"Now I know what you're thinking, dear. That I'm a barmy old lady."

That's exactly what I'm thinking.

"But I'm also a barmy old lady with a twenty-six-year-old daughter who by rights just shouldn't be here. Now, Christine is clearly a young lady on the make. A scarlet woman if ever there was one. And your father is clearly incapable of looking after himself, so we need to help him. And this," she stabs at the page with her index finger, "is how we're going to do it."

Interlude

2 May 1936

Arthur had never seen anything like it. At least not in real life.

York Mansion House was alive with light: candelabras, candlesticks, mirrors. And diamonds too. Every woman seemed to be wearing them. The whole place sparkled.

They were up in the ballroom, a grand first-floor room with a wall of floor-to-ceiling windows. It was the end-of-season gala, an annual affair in which city celebrated club. The team was lined up at one end, smiling politely through speech after speech while the invited dignitaries looked on. The Lord Mayor was saying something about York's finest and then there was some applause and then a joke and then Mr Barrett, the manager, was shaking the mayor's hand. More jokes. More clapping. When would it all end? Then, from nowhere, Arthur heard his own name and felt a slap on his back from a teammate. He blushed, looked down at the floor and then out across the scrum of clapping hands and smiling faces.

And that's when he saw her, standing near the door, talking to friends and laughing. She was the tallest woman in the room, dressed in an elegant navy-blue gown that made her look like a film star. When the applause stopped and the speeches resumed, she glanced over her shoulder and caught him staring at her. She half-smiled, arched an eyebrow, and then turned back to her friends.

He spent the rest of the night trying to watch her without making it too obvious. Once or twice, he even managed to manoeuvre himself close enough to see her eyes, dark and shining, he thought, like newly polished leather.

And then, just like that, there she was. Standing next to him, smiling. As bold as brass.

"Well, aren't you going to ask me to dance, then?"

"Sorry?"

"I said aren't you going to ask me to dance. It seems only right given that you've been staring at me all evening."

She held out her hand.

"I'm Diana."

CHAPTER
SEVEN

Saturday 14 July 1962
It's been a very strange day and it's still only half past ten in the morning.

Mrs Scott-Pym is convinced that a magic spell will help rescue Arthur from Christine's scarlet-woman clutches. The spell involves getting Christine to eat two hedgehog quills, the bark of an ash tree, a "fairy sack" of hydrangea petals, and one of her own buttons. Simple, then. *Songs to Unshroud a Scarlet Woman* also involves some more mundane ingredients (eggs, butter, orange rind), meaning that if you get a bit distracted, as I often do, it could easily be mistaken for a recipe from *Woman's Realm*.

I've been tasked by Mrs Scott-Pym with acquiring one of Christine's buttons while she takes care of everything else. I have no idea where she'll find hedgehog quills or how she'll measure a fairy sack of flower petals, but it's beside the point really as the whole thing is clearly bonkers. I have decided to humour Mrs Scott-Pym, though, because:

1. She's so nice
2. She makes such lovely cakes

So I'm back at home pretending to look for a button. What I'm actually doing is sitting in the kitchen reading *Tender is the Night* (hardly a glowing advert for adulthood) and working my way through a bag of ready-salted crisps. I'll give it a couple of hours and then go back and say I couldn't find a button anywhere in Christine's wardrobe (Christine, queen of man-made fibres, is very much the type of person who looks like she's at home in zips and Velcro fastenings). Hopefully by then Mrs Scott-Pym will be occupied by lunch and I'll be able to divert her away from magic and back onto a slightly less strange subject, which, let's face it, could be more or less anything.

Just as I'm finally getting to another good bit in the book (we're back in the Ritz bar), I hear some clickety-clack footsteps on the courtyard slabs outside. It's Christine. I'd recognise her bossy gallop anywhere. So much for having a couple of hours relaxing in the company of Riviera sophisticates.

"Got your head in a book again?" she says, coming in and closing the door behind her. "You should be careful. You spend so much time with your head bent over a book, it'll drop off one of these days." She walks over to the kitchen table and deposits her handbag on it. I briefly think about explaining the biology of a neck and spine to her but decide against it.

"I'm just finishing off a chapter and then I'm going out," I say, words universally understood to mean *leave me alone*.

"Well, I'm glad I caught you," she replies, pulling up a chair and sitting across the table from me. "I thought it'd be good for the two of us to have a little chat."

A Little Chat. Three words that, on the surface, appear harmless but in Christine's hands have the potential to wreak havoc and destruction on a grand scale. I put my Adam Faith bookmark in *Tender is the Night*, place the book on the table next to my crisps and prepare for battle.

Here goes then. A Little Chat.

"It's about the wedding," she starts, leaning back in her chair, her arms crossed and her eyes narrowed.

(Oh. The Wedding.)

"Or actually," she goes on, "it's about *after* the wedding." She makes a good stab at a smile but can't quite pull it off.

"What about after the wedding?" I ask, trying not to be distracted by her pink coral-feather earrings.

"Well, when your dad and me are man and wife, I'll be your new mum."

"What?"

"After the wedding. I'll be your new mum."

"Actually, you'll be my step-mum," I correct her.

(I think it's only right that we get this nice and clear from the start.)

"Like the one in Cinderella," I add, just for good measure.

The room is silent for a second.

"Mum. Step-mum. It's all the same really, isn't it?" Her smile turns even more vinegary than usual. She grabs one of my crisps and bites hard. "Your dad's *so* pleased I'm here to help you, you know. He thinks you need someone to give you some womanly advice and guidance. Someone you can talk to about women's things." She smiles. "Someone you can *listen* to."

I sniff and take a crisp.

"Anyway," Christine goes on. "I wanted to have a little chat with you about this idea of yours of going back to school. I mean, what's the point? They're not going to be able to teach you how to read any better, are they?" As she speaks, she picks up *Tender is the Night* and glances at its cover.

"I don't know why you're bothering with books like this," she says, her lips curdling around the words. "Why you don't read proper ones like *Woman and Beauty* or *Housewife?*"

"They're not books," I point out.

"Not books? 'Course they are. They're there to be read, aren't they?" She shakes her head and rolls her eyes. "People don't just look at the pictures, you know. Speaking of which, you'd have thought they'd have put a better picture on the front of this," she says, looking at *Tender is the Night*. "It looks dead boring. Although, to be fair," she goes on, "they say you shouldn't judge a book by its cover."

(She's wrong, of course. You should always judge a book by its cover. Anyone who's ever actually read a book knows this.)

She sniffs and then casually tosses *Tender is the Night* back on the table. "Now, look, I'll tell you what you want. You want to stop cramming your head with silly ideas and start thinking about getting a nice little

101

trade. Something that'll keep you busy. Something that'll bring in a nice wage. Something that'll get you some independence. Well, at least until you get married."

"But I've already got a job," I say. "I'm earning."

"Job! What job?"

"The milk round. I deliver milk and Dad pays me. It's called capitalism," I add, knowing that she won't like me using an "*ism*".

Christine leans forward and screws up her face.

"I thought you did that for free?"

"No, I get seven shillings a week for it," I tell her. "How else do you think I can afford a weekly *Melody Maker* plus a new LP and a pair of pop socks every month?"

"Ow much!" says Christine, sounding remarkably like Mrs Swithenbank. "Seven shillings? We'll see about that. And taking money from your dad is not earning. You need to forget all this rubbish about going back to school and get a proper job instead."

A proper job. Or a Career, as Mrs Scott-Pym would say. That's not actually a bad idea. I imagine myself as an Independent Woman. Like Mrs Scott-Pym's daughter, Caroline. I could go to glamorous parties and film premieres and meet friends for cocktails in sophisticated bars. Yes, I think I'd like having a Career. It'd be great. I could be a doctor. A journalist. A lawyer.

"I've got you a job shampooing at Maureen's salon," says Christine, helping herself to another crisp. "She'll take you on trial for a couple of weeks and if you're any good, she'll let you stay. For now it's just Thursdays, Fridays, and half-days on Saturdays."

What?!

"You get four shillings plus tips. Not bad for less than three days' work. And don't go messing it up," she says, stabbing the table with her finger. "I've had to go through no end of appointments to get you the bloody job. It's cost me a small fortune."

She sits back, sighs, and starts looking at her scarlet fingernails.

"But I don't want to be a hairdresser," I tell her. I know my limitations. Sagittarians might be lucky but you wouldn't want to let one loose on your hair. We are clumsy and absent-minded. Not a good combination when perm lotion or a pair of scorching hot tongs are involved.

"I've spent hours in that salon trying to get you a job. Hair, hands, feet. I've had them all done," she says, not looking happy. "It hasn't been easy, you know. You're not the only girl in the village who wants a job there. And what thanks do I get? None at all. None." She looks round the room, looking for sympathy from the kitchen cupboards and empty chairs.

I wonder if anyone has ever used an F. Scott Fitzgerald novel as a murder weapon. (*Tender is the Night* has a good heft to it; it'd definitely do more damage than *The Great Gatsby*.)

"Look, young lady," she says, jabbing a scarlet finger at me. "You need to start growing up."

"That's exactly what I have been doing," I tell her.

"You've had it far too easy," she goes on, talking to me but at the same time managing to completely ignore me. "Do you know how many jobs I've had? I've scrubbed floors, pulled pints, picked fruit, washed windows, polished brass, packed eggs, laundered god-knows-what, fed babies, plucked chickens, served idiots, wiped arses. I've done it all. Just to scrape together enough money to live on and keep me in nice clothes."

(Just for the record, she's currently wearing a ham-pink sleeveless crimplene blouse.)

"You don't know you're born, young lady. You need to start standing on your own two feet. Stop sponging off your dad. It's ridiculous." She sits back and folds her arms, bunching them under her boobs so that her cleavage forms two large railway arches. "You need a job. You need to stop all this school nonsense. And you need to get used to not having the bloody farm around."

What?!

Christine stops mid-nag and stares straight at me.

"What do you mean, *get used to not having the bloody farm around?*" I ask, watching Christine shuffle uncomfortably in her chair.

"Look," she says, straightening out some imaginary folds in her skirt. "We can't go on living in this rickety old place. It's 1962 for god's sake. We have to move with the times, you know. It's like a pokey old museum here. All dark and dingy. Look at this tatty old kitchen."

"What's wrong with the kitchen?" I ask, looking around. "The only thing that's wrong with it is your

104

horrible new cooker." (Christine's incinerator of choice.)

"Listen, my new cooker's the only bloody thing that's not an antique," she replies, getting up and stroking it like the women do on the quiz shows on Granada Television. "I'm trying to drag this place into the Twentieth Century but it isn't easy. *What's wrong with the kitchen*, she says. What's bloody right with it, you mean. Look at it. We need everything new, proper fitted units and a nice Formica top, not this crabby old wooden thing. Just think of the germs."

(To be honest, with Christine's cooking, germs are the least of my worries.)

"And then there's the bathroom," she goes on. "We need something up-to-date. A nice pink suite with big cabinets and maybe even a corner bath. And we need a bar. And fitted carpets. The whole place is like a stable . . ." I'm only half listening, though, as I'm still trying to process what Christine has just said about getting used to not having the bloody farm around.

"But I don't understand," I say, interrupting her, mid-renovation. "How has all this got anything to do with the farm?"

"Don't you see?" she says. "It all needs pulling down and starting again. There's no point beggaring around doing a bit here and a bit there. We need to start from scratch. Tear the whole place down and build something new. Something nice and modern."

"What? Tear the farmhouse down? You can't do that."

"Of course we can. Look, do you think I'm going to live in this dump when I'm married?" She glances round the kitchen and pulls a face as though she's visiting the local sewage works. "And I'm not having you telling me what I can and can't do. Anyway, you'll be off soon. You can't stick around here forever you know. I don't want you under my feet after the wedding."

"But . . ."

"And don't answer back," snaps Christine. "You've always got a clever comment."

(Is that meant to be a bad thing? I think the world would be a far better place if people were only allowed to speak if they made a clever comment. Christine would be mute for a start. In fact I suspect everywhere would be a good deal quieter.)

"You can stick your rotten fitted carpet right up your corner bath," I shout. I know it's not a clever comment but it's exactly how I feel. My face is getting red and I think I might be about to cry.

Christine stares at me, pursing her lips and tapping her fingers on the side of her leg. Through her eyes I can see all the cogs in her tiny brain turning round and round. "Look, don't cry," she says, switching to the voice she uses with Arthur when she wants something. "It'll be proper fancy. You'll see. With all modcons. Double glazing. Central heating. It'll be lovely when it's all done." (She's beginning to sound a bit like an estate agent.) "We'll be the envy of the village. I'm even thinking of having a water feature outside."

She comes and puts her hand on my shoulder, probably trying to be reassuring but it's actually quite unsettling.

Surely Arthur can't know anything about this? And anyway, I don't see how a new house means I should get used to not having the farm around. We've got nearly 100 acres of land, a stream, and countless barns. Even Christine can't need a house that big.

"Look," she says, still using her nice voice. "Your dad wanted to tell you this but you might as well know now. Knocking this place down, building a new house and then kitting it out will cost a small fortune. So the whole lot's going." She flicks her hand cheerfully. "It's being sold to a developer. He's going to turn it all into a brand new housing estate. It'll be lovely."

She says lovely like it's spelt with a capital L. Maybe two.

"We're having the best plot of course and the developer's going to build us a special house. The biggest on the estate. Different from all the others. With a nice-size garden. And a curvy driveway."

A housing estate? On the farm?

But what about the newts?

And the cows?

And me?

"But you can't do that," I say. "You can't sell the farm."

"Of course we can," she snaps, taking her hand off my shoulder and going back to her usual bossy voice. "We'll get a brand new house out of it. And plenty of money." She stands up and walks towards the kitchen door. "Enough for holidays to Spain. Or even America. We'll be part of the jet-set."

"More like the shampoo-and-set," I say.

Christine ignores me.

"Me and your dad'll be like . . . like Frank Sinatra and Elizabeth Taylor."

Rubbish. Christine is as much like Elizabeth Taylor as I'm like Richard Burton.

"Anyway, I'm off," she says, opening the door and letting in a waft of summer air. "I can't stay around here talking to you all day. Some of us have things to do. Now, you think on about that job with Maureen in the salon," she goes on, attempting a smile. "You need to sort yourself out and stop loping around. A job'll do you good. School! What do you want with more school? I ask you."

And she walks out and slams the door behind her.

This is awful. The farm. The farmhouse. Arthur. I can't believe it's all going so wrong. At least now Christine's gone there's some peace and quiet. Except for the *tick-tock* of the Grandfather clock that is. And a cow mooing outside. Poor old thing. It's not going to be happy on the new estate.

I have no idea what I should do. Suddenly *Tender is the Night* and the French Riviera don't seem so appealing. We can't sell the farm. It's just wrong. My mouth feels dry and claggy, so I get up and pour myself a glass of dandelion and burdock from the fridge. As I drink, I find myself staring at the bright patch of wallpaper uncovered when we got rid of the nice old (big) range oven and installed Christine's (mercifully small) cooker. The wallpaper is made up of large colourful flowers, warm and inviting. I start tracing the shape of the flowers with my fingers, following the curves of every petal and stem. And then, mid-trace, I feel the sudden urge to sit on the floor and lean against all the brilliant colours, tucking my knees under my chin like I used to do when I was little.

I don't think I'm ready to be an Adult.

It's all far too complicated and messy. Not to mention unfair. And cruel. In fact being an adult is so far proving pretty unpropitious (*adjective — disappointing, not very promising*). It's not at all what I thought it would be like.

They don't tell you about this part of being an adult in *Bunty* or on the telly, about having your life torn asunder and being thrown into a world of enforced coiffured labour, wicked stepmothers and grisly water features. I'm actually beginning to feel that it would be much simpler to stop being an Adult and go back to being a little girl.

Arthur's little girl.

And I close my eyes and push my back up against the bright flowery wallpaper, hoping it sucks me in and takes me far away.

After a while, when I've finished my drink and daydreamed my way to Paris and back, I go upstairs. I really need some good advice. Luckily, I have two of the finest minds in the village waiting for me.

Sophisticated Adam and Brooding Adam.

I lie on my bed and stare at them, a double knickerbocker glory of Adam loveliness.

Usually I only talk to one Adam at a time (they are the jealous type), but today is an emergency: I need them both.

"You're going to have to stop Christine," says Brooding Adam, smouldering.

"You're going to have to do something before it's too late," says Sophisticated Adam, flashing his super-white shiny teeth.

I sit up, taking in their words and trying to think of a plan.

"This calls for drastic action," says Brooding Adam.

"This calls for belief in the power of old ladies and Yorkshire magic," says Sophisticated Adam.

They look at each other, then look back at me, and together they say:

"This calls for buttons."

Interlude

7 November 1939

"Come on, Lieutenant Epworth," said Diana, gesturing towards the door with her head. "If you don't get me over the threshold soon, the war'll be over and done with."

"Erm," said Arthur, balancing his new wife in his arms. "Slight problem there, I'm afraid. The keys are in my pocket. And I seem to have my hands pretty full at the moment."

Diana laughed. "Let me help you," she said, pushing her hand into Arthur's pocket. "Voila! Nos clés," she said, pulling out the keys and giving them a good jangle.

"Oh, I love it when you speak French," said Arthur.

"And I love it when you speak English," said Diana, swapping her expensive vowels for the blunt, flattened Yorkshire ones of her husband. "Now, *allez*, let's get this door open." And she reached out with the key towards the door. Arthur bent his knees, lowering his precious cargo so that she could put the key into the lock. Diana snapped the key round to the right and the door swung open.

"Here we go, then," shouted Arthur, holding Diana tightly. "One, two, three!" and he strode over the threshold, hugging his wife close to him, his fingers pressing deep into the folds of her elegant tweed suit.

The wedding had been a quick one, in the registry office, with crowds of other couples waiting outside, like a market on market day. A mad, matrimonial rush caused by the war. Her father hadn't come, of course. She'd done everything she could to get him there but he was implacably against the wedding. He'd tried to stop the relationship right from the start, invoking the spirit of Diana's dead mother and, in the end, cutting her off from the estate. He bought them the farm, though, a small settlement he called it, something at least to confer some kind of respectability on his son-in-law.

"It's a little dark in here, isn't it?" said Arthur, looking around the room. He was sitting on a chair with Diana side-saddle on his lap, her arms draped over his shoulders. The chair was the only piece of furniture in the entire house. It looked very old and very rickety but neither of them cared. Today, now, together in their first home, even the rickety old chair was perfect.

"Dark? Really? Do you think so?" said Diana. "I think it's snug. Cosy. I'll be able to make it lovely, darling, don't worry."

Arthur smiled. Diana had wonderful taste. It was one of the many things he loved about her. She had an eye for things. A knack of making something look just right. It was the same with colours too, he thought, looking at what she was wearing. Taste. She understood it. It was another language she was fluent in, like French.

"Look, that spot over there is just right for a range oven," said Diana, pointing to an alcove running along one wall. "And behind it, we'll have some lovely wallpaper to brighten up the room. Something happy."

"Perfect," said Arthur. "I'll leave it all to you."

"Yes, somehow I knew you were going to say that."

"Some of us'll be busy fighting Hitler, you know."

"And some us will be busy doing everything else!" replied Diana, kissing her new husband on the forehead.

"Anyway," said Arthur. "I've got a bone to pick with you."

"Really?" said Diana, curling the word around Arthur like a mink stole.

"Yes, really. You've been here a whole twenty minutes with your wonderful new husband and you haven't even offered to make him a cup of tea."

"Oh, I think you'll find, Mr Epworth, that the lorries haven't arrived yet with your sugar."

She always teased him about the number of sugars he took in his tea. The first time he'd been to call on Diana, she, Arthur and her father had been in the sitting room making polite conversation when Mrs Henton, the housekeeper, came in and asked if they would like some tea. Tea was ordered and a few minutes later she returned carrying a tray with a teapot, some crockery, and assorted cakes. When Mrs Henton asked Arthur if he took sugar, he replied, "Seven, please." There was a moment's awkward silence and

113

then Diana looked up at her and said, "Mrs Henton, I think we may need a bigger sugar bowl." Arthur's sugar intake had been a running joke ever since.

Diana pushed her hand through Arthur's hair. "You know there's nothing I'd love to do more than make you some tea," she said. "But we're waiting for the removal men, remember? Until they come, we're stuck I'm afraid. No tea. Only me." And she flicked his fringe and then wrapped her arms around him.

The front door fell victim to a burst of loud knocks.

"They're here!" shouted Diana. "Come on," and she ran through into the hallway, Arthur in quick pursuit.

When Diana opened the door she was surprised to see that, rather than a flat-capped removal man waiting outside, there was a small, middle-aged lady in a rather smart maroon tweed suit.

"Oh, hullo," said the lady. "I live over there." She pointed in the direction of the chocolate-box Georgian house next door. "I'm your neighbour, Rosamund Scott-Pym. How do you do?"

Diana took the lady's hand and shook it heartily. "How do you do? I'm Diana Epworth and this is my husband, Arthur."

"It's so good to have someone living in the farm house again," said Rosamund. "It must have been empty for well over a year now."

"Yes, it's a bit of a wreck inside," said Diana, thinking of the empty rooms and bleak decor. "But it's such a lovely spot. We both fell in love with the place straight away. I'd love to invite you in but I'm afraid we're waiting for our removal men to arrive. We haven't a thing!"

"Oh no, I quite understand. I don't want to bother you. I just wanted to say hullo and give you this." Rosamund held out a wicker basket full of little pots and bulging paper bags. "It's just a few things to help you out in the first day or so. I know what it's like moving in to a new home and now, what with the war, everything's so much more difficult than before."

"Oh, that's far too kind of you," said Diana. "Our things will be here soon. We couldn't possibly."

"No, really. It's nothing at all," said Rosamund. "Just a little something to welcome you to the village."

"Well, if you're sure," said Diana. "It's very kind of you, Mrs Scott-Pym. You must come round once we're not quite so upside down."

"That would be lovely," said Rosamund. "And, please, do call me Rosamund."

"Thank you, Rosamund," said Diana. "And you must call me Diana."

"Do you know, I have a feeling we're going to be very happy here," Diana said to Arthur as she watched her neighbour walk back down the drive. "I think it's going to be home for a long time."

"I hope so, love," said Arthur, pulling Diana close.

Diana let herself fall into the familiar warmth of Arthur's arms. "I want us to grow old here," she went on. "Have parties here, play tennis here, have our grandchildren here, just be very happy here, living out our dotage under the warm summer sun."

CHAPTER
EIGHT

Saturday 14 July 1962

I am drowning in pink. Asphyxiated. Strangulated. Suffocated. Pink. Pink. Pink. Everything around me is pink. Pink bedspread, pink curtains, pink wallpaper, pink cushions. It's like being stuck in the middle of a huge pink jelly.

I'm up in Christine's bedroom in search of a button. I must be mad. How can a button stop Christine and her pneumatic boobs and grasping scarlet hands?

Her wardrobe is huge. Solid slabs of dark wood stand on fat wooden-doughnut feet, giving it the chunkiness of another age (Neolithic). On the doors, there's some carved panelling that reminds me of the wardrobe in *The Lion, the Witch and the Wardrobe*, except that in Christine's wardrobe instead of easing past fur coats and discovering the secret world of Narnia, I'm far more likely to squeeze through a wall of acrylic blouses and find myself in the Razzmatazz bingo hall in Scunthorpe.

Christine would be furious if she knew I was about to have a good rummage through her clothes. Her bedroom is strictly Off Limits. I am living very dangerously, like Marlon Brando.

Here goes, then.

The doors creak open to reveal an orgy of pastel. Christine's taste is the colour palette of a box of fondant fancies. The wardrobe is stuffed full of clothes, all scrunched up against each other, fighting for air. Almost every hanger is different. Wire ones. Wooden ones. Plastic ones. Heavily upholstered ones with lacy frills and bows. All jutting out here and there at odd angles. It makes my head hurt.

I wonder what my mother's wardrobe was like. If it was anything like her recipe book, it would have been very swish. I imagine a sleek line of clothes, all colour co-ordinated and elegantly spaced. She'd have beautifully shaped wooden hangers, all exactly the same, and the whole thing would smell as fresh as a spring day or as sophisticated as a Monte Carlo nightclub.

Christine's wardrobe smells of mothballs and medicated toilet rolls. The mothballs are balanced on top of some of the clothes and at the bottom of the wardrobe, shoved under everything, there's a big pack of Izal, Christine's loo roll of choice. It all smells a bit like walking into a chemist. No wonder Christine douses herself in so much lavender water.

I grab a hanger at random. Out comes a yellow dress. Egg-custard yellow. Around the middle is a big bow, making the dress look like an enormous yellow present waiting to be unwrapped (not a pleasant thought). The material is shiny, hard and coarse: half polyester, half scouring pad.

This is quite good fun. I pull out another hanger. On it is a skirt the shape of a half moon and almost the size

117

of one too. Its colour can best be described as fungal green. Now that it's free from the scrum of clothes surrounding it in the wardrobe, the skirt springs out like a horizontal jack-in-the-box.

I can't resist it.

I'm going to have to try it on.

Finding the right hole to put my legs through in the mass of petticoat and ballooning skirt is not easy but eventually I get everything lined up and ease the skirt over my pedal pushers. It seems to weigh a ton and I imagine there's probably more material in this one skirt than in my entire wardrobe. I am very aware of my increased circumference and feel very bottom-heavy but manage to waddle cautiously over to the pink-framed mirror.

Staring at me in the mirror is a different Evie, one who looks like the fairy we put on top of the Christmas tree (minus the wings). It's funny how different clothes can make us become different people. Am I going to be the type of Woman who wears sticky-out skirts? I wish choosing a Future could be a bit more like trying on clothes from a wardrobe. You could pop on a Future and give it a whirl. See how it fits. Jig it around a bit. Then try on another. Instead, choosing a Future all seems so final and definite. Once the choice is made, you're stuck with what you're wearing for the rest of your life, even if you look a right clown in it.

I ease my way out of the skirt, which involves a great deal of wriggling and contortion, and pull out another hanger. This time I hit the jackpot. It's a pastel pink see-through baby-doll nightie, one of Christine's favourite outfits. (She often wears it in the evening to watch telly, her legs sprawling across the sofa like rolls of fleshy pastry.) The nightie has little pink satin bows ranged over its flimsy surface and the bottom is trimmed with pink fur. It somehow manages to be both hilarious and horrifying at the same time. It looks quite petite for Christine (chest-wise); it must be like trying to get a couple of blancmanges in an envelope when she puts it on.

I pull it on over my top, preparing to be wowed by my new-found allure (*noun — the quality of being attractive and enticing*).

Unfortunately one of the little pink satin bows gets caught on the zip at the back of my top and I'm left stuck, half in, half out, flailing around with one arm free but the other one locked in a pink claw hold, bent back on itself awkwardly inside the nightie. The top of my head is sticking out of the neck hole but the rest of my head remains wedged inside, making the room look even pinker. I'm trapped, stuck inside a pink diaphanous hell. I try to struggle out of it but this just seems to make things worse. I'm terrified of tearing the paper-thin material but equally terrified of being stranded in the nightie until Christine gets back from York.

"*Ding-dong.*"

Oh God. The doorbell. I manoeuvre carefully over to the window, my arms locked in place like a headless chiffon statue. Through the window, in a pink blur, I see Margaret waiting outside the front door.

"*Ding-dong. Ding-dong.*"

She rings the doorbell again and then looks at her wristwatch (she has the brittle patience of all very organised people). She'd have me out of the baby doll in a jiffy (if not even quicker). I shout to her to come in but she obviously can't hear a thing. I try to open the window but it's not easy with only one free arm and restricted vision. I can see her looking around impatiently. I've got the window handle in my hand now but am struggling to lift it off the rusted latch. Margaret sighs, looks at her watch again then turns and begins to walk down the front path.

This is awful. I have one final desperate push at the handle and it flies off the latch, almost propelling me out of the now-open window.

"Margaret," I cry. "Come back!"

She looks up. "Evie? Is that you? What are you doing?" she shouts, sounding baffled (not something that happens very often). "What have you got over your head?"

"Never mind that," I shout back. "I'm stuck. Can you come and help me?"

"Hold on." And I hear the reassuring sound of the front door opening and closing and then the deep thud of Margaret's sensible shoes on the stairs.

"What's going on?" she asks, coming into the room. "What are you doing? Why are you wearing that pink thing like that? What's happened to your head? And your arm?"

It's always like this with Margaret. She is a leaking barrel of questions.

120

"I was looking through Christine's wardrobe for a button and I just ended up trying a few things on. I'm stuck."

"Looking for a button?" says Margaret. "What were you looking for a button in Christine's wardrobe for?" Being with Margaret is like being stuck in a never-ending episode of *What's My Line?* I can't tell her the real reason I'm looking for a button — Margaret is hewn from pure logic and if I told her that the button was for a magic spell, she'd think I was mad (not unreasonably).

"Never mind that now. Could you just help me out of this, please? I'm getting pins and needles in my arm and all this pink is making my head hurt."

"What were you doing putting a nightie on over your top?" she asks, helping me out of my chiffon cage.

"I just wanted to try it on. See what it was like." She might ask a lot of annoying questions but Margaret's a dab hand with a zip and a satin bow. In a couple of ticks, I'm released. I decide to share my news with her. Maybe her supersonic brain can come up with a better solution than a magic button.

"Christine's got me a job shampooing at Maureen's salon," I tell her. "She thinks I should get a trade."

"You can't do that. You'd be a rubbish hairdresser. You're far too clumsy."

Harsh but true (she knows me well).

"Who'd be mad enough to let you loose with a pair of scissors? They'd end up looking like Yul Brynner," she adds (unnecessarily I think).

"It's been a strange few days," I say.

We sit on the bed and I tell her about everything that's happened. The engagement. The wedding. The farmhouse. The farm.

"What?" says Margaret when I've finished. "But Christine can't do that. You can't let her get away with it. Horrible old cow. You have to stop her." And there, in that brilliant shining moment, is why Margaret is my best friend.

"I need to do two things," I say, sounding far more in control than I feel. "One. Find some way of getting Christine out of our lives. She's only interested in Arthur and the farm because she thinks they'll keep her in handbags and foreign holidays." Margaret nods enthusiastically. "And two, find someone much nicer for him."

(Which could literally be anybody.)

"Oh, I forgot. And three, find a Career and become an Independent Woman."

Margaret stares at me as if I'd just started speaking backwards.

"Independent woman? A career? What about your A levels? What about university? Do you mean you're going to work in Maureen's salon instead? As a shampooist? Or is it a shampooer?" she adds, ever the pedant.

"No, I'm not going to work at Maureen's salon," I say. "But I am having second thoughts about going to sixth form, yes." Margaret looks baffled. "I could get a job and wear a pencil skirt and buy a car and go to glamorous receptions. I could be a Modern Woman," I

122

continue, trying to sound sophisticated, "like Natalie Wood or Jacqueline Kennedy."

"But I don't understand," says Margaret. "What will you do?"

I have no idea, of course, so I say the first thing that comes into my head.

"I could move to London and do a secretarial course and then do something in fashion."

"What?" says Margaret, almost falling off the bed. "Move to London? A secretarial course? Do something in fashion? What are you talking about? Don't be daft. Anyway, real people don't work in fashion."

"Caroline does," I say, enjoying saying the name.

"Caroline?" says Margaret. "Who's Caroline?"

Am I allowed to mention Caroline? I don't think Mrs Scott-Pym said anything about it being a secret, even though it is. Well, *was*. Too late now. Margaret the interrogator is in full flight.

"Caroline who? Do I know her? What does she do? Where does she live?"

"She's Mrs Scott-Pym's daughter," I answer. "She lives in London and works in fashion."

"But Mrs Scott-Pym doesn't have a daughter."

"Yes, she does."

"No, she doesn't."

"Yes, she *does*."

"No, she *doesn't*."

I sense this could go on a long time. Margaret is not very good at being wrong.

"Caroline is Mrs Scott-Pym's daughter. She was at boarding school and then went straight to London to

123

do a secretarial course but now she works in fashion. I've no idea what she actually does and I'm not sure whether Mrs Scott-Pym knows either."

"Oh, I see," says Margaret.

(Evie 1: Margaret 0.)

"How funny." She wrinkles her forehead. "What a turn up for the book!"

(This has always struck me as a strange phrase. Where did it come from? It makes no sense at all. Other "book" sayings are much more straightforward. *To do something by the book* is clear, ditto *to be in someone's good books*. *To be double booked* is heaven [two books!], bettered only by being *tripled booked* [a good trilogy, like *The Oresteia* or Pippi Longstocking]. *Balancing the books* always brings to mind me on a bike. And *every trick in the book* makes a lot more sense now that Mrs Scott-Pym has told me about her book of Yorkshire magic.)

"It's the first I've heard about Caroline too," I say. "Mrs Scott-Pym told me about her this morning. I don't know why she's never spoken about her before. It's all very strange."

Good strange, I mean. Not bad strange. She definitely doesn't sound bad strange. More of a wonderful, beautiful strange, enigmatic and mysterious, full of life and colour like the big stained-glass windows in York Minster when the light comes streaming in.

"Caroline Scott-Pym," I say, more to myself than to Margaret. "It's the type of name that you'd find at glamorous parties, ones with actors and politicians."

124

"And foreign diplomats and aristocrats," says Margaret, joining in.

"I bet she'd be wearing a fabulous dress with a really elegant hat," I say, twisting up Christine's pink baby-doll nightie and plonking it on my head. "And she'd be drinking champagne."

"Or maybe smoking with a fancy cigarette holder," says Margaret, holding an invisible cigarette in her hand. "And making clever conversation with a handsome man."

"Yes! Or dancing with him," I say, grabbing Margaret's hands and pulling her off the bed for a dance.

"He'd be a French general," shouts Margaret as we fling each other around the room. "All dark and swarthy."

"Or maybe a racing driver," I shout back.

"Or an artist."

"Or a singer."

"Or a pilot."

"Or a film star."

"Or a Lord."

"Or a farmer," I shout, and we both collapse on the bed laughing.

"Hey," says Margaret. "Perhaps Caroline knows Cliff Richard. It sounds just like the kind of party he'd be at." Cliff Richard is Margaret's big crush. She has every record, a Cliff Richard wall clock, and even a Cliff Richard eggcup. I think if Cliff Richard asked Margaret to marry him and not be a teacher, she would have an

125

existential crisis. I don't know what she sees in him. He is no Adam Faith.

"Of course he'd be there," I say. "And Helen Shapiro. And Petula Clark. And Billy Fury. It'd be like *Juke Box Jury* or the *Six-Five Special*. They'd all be there."

"God, wouldn't it be wonderful," says Margaret, yanking Christine's nightie off my head.

"Come on," I say. "Let's go and listen to some music in my room — we can stick the volume on full while everyone's out." And we put Christine's clothes back in the wardrobe, dancing around and singing "The Young Ones".

As we leave the room, I slide my hand into my pocket. There, tucked safely away in my pedal pushers, is a large round pink button that I pulled off the back of Christine's baby-doll nightie.

Success.

I squeeze the button hard and have a sudden urge to pull it out and kiss it.

CHAPTER
NINE

Saturday 14 July 1962

It's like a scene from one of those Dutch still-life paintings you see at the City Art Gallery in York.

A strip of bark lies upturned on a table next to two fat blousy hydrangea flowers. Beside them, an egg, a crumpled bag of flour, and an opened bottle of Cointreau. To the right stands a silver salt cellar and a small cut-glass bowl filled with grated orange rind. Two hedgehog quills rest cryptically on a white china saucer and, sitting on a sheet of greaseproof paper, is a glossy block of golden butter. At the side of the table is a noble hound, her eyes locked on the golden butter. Out of her mouth, a glistening rod of shiny drool reaches down almost to the floor like an ancient stalactite. She is the embodiment of Dog. Magnificent. Proud. Hungry.

And then a smell like rotting broccoli starts to drift around the room.

"Oh, Sadie. For heaven's sake," says Mrs Scott-Pym, wafting her hand in front of her nose. "Not again."

Sadie, somehow immune to the smell, keeps staring at the butter while Mrs Scott-Pym opens a kitchen window.

"There, that's better," says Mrs Scott-Pym, wafting the air with her tea towel before turning her attention back to me. "Now, how did you get on, dear? Did you manage to get a button?"

"Ta-da!" I say, pulling the button out from my pocket. It's been safely tucked away in there all afternoon, jigging along with me through countless bops and Adam Faith and Cliff Richard sing-alongs. If Margaret knew she'd spent a few hours dancing around with a soon-to-be-magical button, there'd have been a tornado of questions. Much easier to keep it a secret.

"Well done, dear," says Mrs Scott-Pym. She takes the button and has a good look at it. "Hmm, it's very big. And very pink. Wherever did you find it?"

I'm not sure Mrs Scott-Pym is ready for the world of chiffon baby-doll nighties. She must sleep in something but it's very difficult to picture her in anything other than a skirt and twinset. Maybe Caroline sends her silk pyjamas from London. Or, far more likely, she has a nice comfy winceyette from Browns in York.

"I got it from one of Christine's nighties," I tell her. "It was dangling on a loose thread so I expect she'll just think it's dropped off."

"Well done, dear," she says, passing the button back to me. "Although to tell you the truth, I was expecting something smaller. Something, perhaps, a little more delicate and dainty."

(Delicate and dainty? Mrs Scott-Pym clearly doesn't know Christine or her wardrobe very well.)

"Still, we can easily break it up," she goes on. "Nice and small, Evie, dear. We don't want her choking!"

128

No. That would be terrible, wouldn't it.

Mrs Scott-Pym busies herself at one end of the table with flour and butter and her huge cream mixing bowl and I'm sent down the other end with a dark-green pestle and mortar.

I place the button at the bottom of the mortar's slippery-smooth basin. It makes a satisfying little tinkle as it settles in place. I steady the mortar with my left hand and raise the pestle up in my right hand. I am Evie, Queen of the Kitchen. Destroyer of Buttons.

Here goes.

As soon as the pestle crashes into the button, it shoots up the side of the mortar and whizzes out across the kitchen, hurtling through the air until it hits the window (*ping!*), then bounces back on itself and flies straight at Sadie, hitting her on the back of the head.

Sadie yelps, spins round and chases the button across the floor.

"Don't let Sadie get the button, dear!" shouts Mrs Scott-Pym. "She'll never let the bally thing go."

The button rolls under the table, closely followed by Sadie. I dart round the other end of the table so that I can grab the button before Sadie gets to it but I'm too late. Sadie stops it with her paw and wolfs it up into her mouth.

"Sadie!" shouts Mrs Scott-Pym as Sadie positions herself strategically under the kitchen table and begins chewing on Christine's button. "Come here. Give that button to me." Sadie doesn't move. She's far too pleased with her new toy and sits there sampling its pink delights.

"Sorry, Mrs Scott-Pym," I say, crestfallen.

"No, it's quite all right, dear. Nothing to worry about. She won't be able to eat the thing — it's so big. I just don't like the thought of putting it in Christine's cake after it's been in Sadie's mouth. It's not very hygienic."

No.

It isn't, is it.

What A Shame.

"We'll need to give it a good wash," says Mrs Scott-Pym.

Yes.

Of course.

A Good Wash.

"I'll do that," I say, trying not to sound too keen. "It's my fault Sadie got hold of the button."

Mrs Scott-Pym is trying to coax Sadie out from under the table and I get the impression that she's not really listening to me.

"For heaven's sake, Sadie," she says. "Come here." She grabs Sadie's bum and drags her out across the floor. "Now, are you going to give me that button, then?" she asks, tugging open Sadie's mouth and yanking the thing from her drooling muzzle (Mrs Scott-Pym would make a terrifying dentist).

"Here you are, dear," she says, passing me the button. "Would you mind giving it a good wash, please?"

"Absolutely," I say. "Don't worry. I'll make sure it's nice and clean before it gets in Christine's cake."

I walk over to the sink, turn on the tap and swoosh an empty hand around under the running water, keeping the drooly, slaver-covered button well out of the way in my other hand. I give the button a quick wipe on my pedal pushers and then hand it back to Mrs Scott-Pym.

"Here you are. Squeaky clean."

"Thank you, dear. You're such a help."

(I am an evil only child.)

"But it still needs to be broken up," she goes on, handing me back the button. "It would be a bit of a giveaway if we put it in the cake like this, wouldn't it?"

Oh yes. I'd forgotten. Why is it that my brain skips along at high speed but never seems to get anything done? I wish I were one of those people who had focus. Like Margaret. Or President Kennedy.

"You might as well do these at the same time, dear," says Mrs Scott-Pym as she passes me the saucer with the two hedgehog quills on. They look like tiny shrunken spears or a pair of very glamorous modern earrings (there's not much call for either in our village).

I look down into the mortar. A big pink button and two hedgehog quills. It's hardly haute cuisine. What would my mother make of it? I imagine her mortar would be full of tasty things like fresh herbs and exotic oils. Or at least something edible. Something recognisable as actual food.

"Are you all right, Evie, dear?"

Mrs Scott-Pym is looking up from her mixing bowl, staring straight at me.

"Sorry, Mrs Scott-Pym. I was daydreaming again."

"Don't worry, dear, that's fine. Daydreaming's good for the soul I always think."

Really? My soul must be as strong as a lion, then. And I thrust the pestle into the mortar, feeling like I could roar.

After a few minutes grinding, prodding, roaring and daydreaming, the mortar's contents are reduced to a little pile of grey-brown-pink grains.

"Here you go," I say, passing it to Mrs Scott-Pym.

"Well done, Evie. Your mother would be proud of you."

A shower of glittery stars rockets round the room.

"Now, could you pass me that bowl, please?" she continues, pointing to another cream mixing bowl standing on the kitchen worktop. "We need to divide this mixture up so that only Christine gets the magic ingredients in her cake. We don't want your father eating Christine's button, do we?"

No, we certainly do not.

I pass Mrs Scott-Pym the bowl and watch as she takes a dollop of the mixture and decants it into the new bowl.

"Are you ready?" she says, picking up the mortar. "Make a wish." And she upends the contents of the mortar into the bowl, coating the cake mixture with a dirty-pink snow. I cheat and make two wishes:

1. To get rid of Christine from Arthur's life (obviously).
2. To go on a driving holiday with Adam Faith

(preferably somewhere with mountains and a stream and lots of nice places to be serenaded).

Mrs Scott-Pym is now pummelling away at the cake mixture with the vigour of a combine harvester. Within seconds, the button-quill dust has disappeared into the mixture. She is an alchemist, capable of turning base metal (a nasty pink button) into gold (a magic-button cake).

"Now then," says Mrs Scott-Pym, putting down the bowl and dabbing at her forehead with a tea towel, "nearly all done." She spoons the *magic* mixture into one bun tray and then spoons the *non-magic* mixture into another bun tray. "There we go. All over bar the shouting," she goes on, sliding the two trays into the big oven in her range. "Time for a sherry I think."

The whole *Songs to Unshroud a Scarlet Woman* thing has been much easier than I thought. Cooking is usually hard enough and baking even harder so I was expecting magical baking to involve labyrinthine complexity (not to mention the odd spell or two), but Mrs Scott-Pym's magical buns seem to revolve mainly around very generous amounts of butter, sugar and Cointreau. There are the non-magical ingredients (normal):

   3 ounces plain flour
   I ounce spelt flour (the Biblical flour, according to
      Mrs Scott-Pym)
   4 ounces butter (salted)
   4 ounces caster sugar

2 eggs

2 tablespoons Cointreau (plus several for the cook)

2 teaspoons baking powder

a good dollop of marmalade

some orange zest

a sprinkling of salt

And then there are the magical ingredients (not normal):

a button (pink, although any colour will do)

2 hedgehog quills

a sprinkling of ash tree bark (to be collected at dawn apparently, which would not go down well with some witches I know)

1 "fairy sack" hydrangea petals

The flours, salt and baking powder are all put in a big bowl and mixed up. Then, in a separate bowl (baking seems to involve a lot of washing up), the butter and sugar are whipped and whisked and whizzed to an inch of their life. When it's all looking light and fluffy (which takes forever), add the eggs (one at a time), then the marmalade and orange zest and finally some of the Cointreau (folding and beating all the time). Then (if you're not totally exhausted at this point) add the dry bowl (flour etc.) to the gloopy bowl (butter etc.) and stir again. DO NOT EAT ANY OF THE CAKE MIXTURE (the hardest thing so far). Now comes the magical part. Grind up the button, the quills and the bark and cut the two petals into tiny pieces and then throw them all into the bowl. Give it a final good mix and — ta-da! — you have some magical bun mixture, ready and waiting to *unshroud a scarlet woman* (after it's all been baked and drenched in more Cointreau, of course).

"And here's what I suspect you've been waiting for," says Mrs Scott-Pym, handing me the non-magic cream bowl. The bowl is lined with cake mixture, fold after lovely unctuous fold of it. "You really do remind me of your mother, you know," she goes on, as I get to work with my finger, scooping up all the yummy remnants. "She had a sweet tooth too."

"Really?" Another piece of my mother's jigsaw drops into place. Chic, French-speaking, kind, cow-loving, bright, and now sweet-toothed. She sounds wonderful.

"Does Caroline have a sweet tooth?" I ask. Mrs Scott-Pym definitely has one. Her house is cake heaven. If Mrs Scott-Pym has a sweet tooth does that mean Caroline has one too? Is that how it works with mothers and daughters?

"Caroline? Oh, well, yes. At least I think so. I used to get Bettys to send her a tuck box every term when she was at school. And she seems to be no better now." Mrs Scott-Pym folds her tea towel and sits down on a kitchen chair. "From what I gather, she spends most of her time in London at Italian coffee shops and bakeries."

Caroline must be great. A good heap of Audrey Hepburn mixed with a splash of Jane Fonda and a sprinkling of George from *The Famous Five* thrown in too.

"Is Caroline like you, Mrs Scott-Pym?" I ask, sitting down next to her.

"Like me? No. Not really. She looks far more like Edward, I'd say. It's the red hair. And the brown eyes. Oh, and she's tall like Edward too."

"Tall? How tall is she?" I ask. (As tall as a tree? As tall as me?)

"Oh, she must be almost six foot," Mrs Scott-Pym replies. "I used to think she was never going to stop growing."

A red-haired Amazon warrior who eats cake.

"I bet she's lovely, Mrs Scott-Pym," I say. "What kind of person is she? Does she take after you?"

"No, dear. She certainly does not take after me. Actually, I really have no idea who she does take after. She's very much her own woman," she adds, looking down at the tea towel in her hand.

Very much her own woman. That sounds great. I wish I could be very much my own woman.

"What do you mean, Mrs Scott-Pym?" I ask. (I know I sound like Margaret now but I can't stop myself.) "How is she her own woman? She must take after you in something."

Mrs Scott-Pym's bright eyes dim a little. "No. We're very different." She shakes her head and sighs a deep sigh (which seems to be a pretty important part of being an adult). "Very different indeed."

"She must be super glamorous," I say. "Do you think I could be like Caroline, Mrs Scott-Pym?"

She takes another step towards the door and then stops and turns her head, looking back at me over her shoulder. "No, dear. I don't think you want to be like Caroline." She is staring straight at me but it feels like she's talking to someone else, and there's a sadness in her voice that I haven't heard before. She takes a wisp of grey hair and tucks it behind her ear. "No," she sighs again and covers her eyes with her outstretched fingers. When she moves her hand, I notice her eyes are pink and wet. She rubs her hands with the tea towel and then starts walking again. "Now, how about we all sit outside whilst the cakes are in the oven?" she goes on, back to her usual non-sad voice. "They'll be another quarter of an hour or so yet and it's such a lovely evening, it'd be a shame to waste it."

This is true. Even though it's now well gone six, the summer sun is still bright in the beautiful rectangle of sky caught in the kitchen window. I love summer. I love feeling its warmth on my skin and seeing the clear blue sky stretch out over the fields. I love hearing the birds sing and the constant background buzz of bees and heat. I love that the air feels so alive — a balmy, joyous fizzy drink to be gulped down.

And ice cream is everywhere. I love that too.

What could possibly go wrong in summer?

Interlude

16 July 1952

Rosamund Scott-Pym looked out through the French windows onto the terrace outside. The two girls were relaxing on deckchairs, chatting and laughing and listening to some terrible American music on the wireless.

It was the start of the summer holidays and Rosamund's daughter, Caroline, had a school friend staying for a couple of days. Flora. A nice girl whose father owned an engineering works in York. Rosamund hoped that Flora might be a steadying influence on Caroline (if, indeed, Caroline could be steadied). For the past two terms Rosamund had been getting letters from school about Caroline and her unruly behaviour. "Undisciplined", one had said, "fractious and disruptive". "Improper". "Rebellious". She'd tried talking to her but it was no good. Caroline was impossible. A feisty, intractable sixteen-year-old whom Rosamund was unable to control.

A yelp from the floor called Rosamund's attention back to the kitchen.

"Gladstone! Sorry, my best boy, have I been neglecting you?"

She bent down and stroked his neck, catching his soft curls in her fingers.

"What will we do with her, eh?" she asked, looking into Gladstone's gentle eyes and tickling him under his chin. "What a mess. Fourteen teas and coffee, that's what Edward would have said about her, isn't it?" She paused, lost in the past, the only trace of 1952 being the girls' voices and their tinny music coming from outside.

"I've just come to get some lemonade, Mummy," said Caroline, walking into the kitchen.

Rosamund looked up.

Caroline was wearing her swimsuit. In the kitchen. How absurd. It wouldn't have been allowed in Rosamund's day, of course, not at home. Whatever would people think?

"Of course, dear," she said, deciding it was easier not to say anything about the swimsuit. "There's some ice cream too if you like."

"That'd be lovely, Mummy. Thank you." She was standing next to the refrigerator pouring out two glasses of lemonade. "Mummy?" she went on, in a tone that immediately made Rosamund aware she was after something. "You know we were talking about me staying in York and doing that secretarial course?"

"Yes, dear," replied Rosamund. It was Caroline's latest idea. She was desperate to leave school and get on with real life (whatever that is, thought Rosamund), and now, the summer after her O levels, she seemed to be trying out an endless array of possibilities.

"Well, Flora says I can board at hers. Their house is enormous, eight bedrooms apparently, up on The Mount. She'll be there for the next two years whilst she does her A levels. It'd be perfect."

Rosamund looked at her daughter. How had she grown up so quickly?

"And what do Flora's parents say about this? Are you sure they're quite ready for a tearaway like you?"

Caroline stuck out her tongue.

"I'm sure you'll warn them all about me," she said, taking the two glasses and making her way back outside. "Oh, and by the way, I thought Flora and I could clean Daddy's car later on, if you like? It'll make a nice change from sitting out in the sun."

And with that she strode off out of the kitchen, heading back to the terrace and the joyous summer sun.

CHAPTER
TEN

Saturday 14 July 1962

"Oooh, it's lovely. Really lovely. Aye, you don't get many of them to the pound, do you?"

That's Mrs Swithenbank, admiring Christine's new engagement ring.

I've just got back from Mrs Scott-Pym's. It's eight in the evening and Christine is sitting at our kitchen table showing off the ring to Mrs Swithenbank. Vera and Arthur are also gathered around the table. Vera looks ridiculously excited. Arthur less so.

"It's a *princess* diamond," says Christine. "Like Petula Clark's."

"Mr Brice, the nice young man from the jeweller's, recommended it," says Vera. "He was *so* helpful. *So* nice," she goes on, making Mr Brice sound like he had just donated a spare kidney rather than sold Arthur an engagement ring. "Such a lovely manner. And he had lovely nails too."

"Well, what do you expect, Mum?" says Christine. "It's York's *finest jeweller's*. She leans over towards Arthur, smiling triumphantly, and adds, "*The Jewel in Yorkshire's Crown*."

She is speaking like an advert again. I expect it's all the time she spends reading the local papers and watching Granada Television (Mrs Scott-Pym says that commercial television shrinks the brain).

"Oooh it was lovely," coos Vera. "You should have seen it, Doris. There were diamonds everywhere. And rings. And fancy watches. It was like something from the telly."

"They took us off to our own little room, Doris," says Christine, still extending her hand to show the ring with maximum effect. "It was proper posh."

"We had mahogany chairs, Doris," says Vera. "Ma-hog-any. I thought I was in Castle Howard."

"Very nice," says Mrs Swithenbank.

"They brought out all these rings and put them on little black velvet cushions," continues Vera. "Everything was so elegant. Mr Brice was very particular. He had such a nice delicate manner."

"Aye, it's a different world, York, isn't it?" says Mrs Swithenbank.

"And Mr Brice got me a black velvet cushion too, Doris. To rest my hand on," says Christine. "Like this." She reaches over for the tea cosy, folds it up and rests her hand on it.

"Well," says Mrs Swithenbank. "I can see it might be tiring holding your hand up all the time."

"Oh, it was wonderful," says Vera. "I felt like royalty."

"I know," says Christine. "I bet Princess Margaret gets treated like that all the time."

"Aye, I bet she does, love," says Mrs Swithenbank. "Well, I think the ring looks smashing."

142

"Aww, thanks, Doris," says Christine, her fingers still extended. "I'm glad you like it. Are you putting the kettle on, then, Mum?" she adds, flicking her head round to Vera. "I think we're all ready for a brew."

Vera gets up from the table, takes off her jacket and pulls on a flowery wrap-around apron. She now looks identical to millions of other Yorkshire women, like Chairman Mao's floral army (but possibly even more dangerous). Up until now, Vera has been in her "York best", an outfit saved for special occasions: a boxy jacket, pleated skirt and blocky shoes. She is the walking embodiment of 1949. Christine is also in her "York best", an understated combination of tight pencil skirt (pink), tight bolero jacket (pink) and terrifyingly pointy shoes (pink). She looks like a well-inflated flamingo.

"Evie, love, stop skulking over there and come and sit down next to me," says Mrs Swithenbank, patting the empty chair next to her.

"I wasn't skulking," I say. Just observing. And staying out of Trouble.

"Here, Evie, come and have a look at my ring," says Christine, wiggling her fingers like a crawling caterpillar.

I lean forward and stare at the ring. The only other engagement rings I have ever seen are Elizabeth Taylor's and Zsa Zsa Gabor's. It's not a good comparison.

"It's lovely," I lie. "Really lovely."

"Yes, it's gorgeous, isn't it?" says Christine. "Mr Brice says that when you lift it up to the light, you can see 128 colours in it." She does some more caterpillar wiggling. "How many can you see?" she asks, shoving the ring under my nose.

I stare at the ring.

"Loads," I lie (again). "I can see loads of colours. All sparkling. It looks lovely." I am playing a tactical war and the shimmering multicoloured diamond ring is a battle that I'm happy to let Christine win. It will soon be my turn to let loose the power of the magic-button cake (what am I saying?).

"Watch yourself," says Vera, pushing past me and putting the large brown teapot on the table. A little splurt of weak tea comes out of the spout and falls onto the lacy table mat. "We'll just let it brew for a few minutes. Have you finished with the tea cosy, love?"

"Mmmm," replies Christine, still busy looking at her ring.

Vera reaches over and grabs the cosy, pulling it over the glossy brown teapot. "Oooh," she sighs, sitting down. "That's nice. There's nothing like putting your feet up at the end of a busy day, is there?"

"You relax, Vera, love," says Mrs Swithenbank. "It's hard work getting around York. All those bloody cobbles play havoc with my corns."

"Oh I know. I'm shattered," says Vera, leaning over and rubbing her shins.

"A bit of cake would be nice, Mum," says Christine, finally taking her eyes off the ring. "We're meant to be celebrating my new piece of elegant engagement jewellery remember."

(I wonder which advert that was from.)

144

"Christine, love," says Mrs Swithenbank. "Your mother's just sat down. Let her have five minutes while the tea brews."

"Doris, we can't celebrate my new ring with just a cup of tea," says Christine. "Mum doesn't mind getting the cake, do you, Mum? She likes to keep herself busy. It keeps her trim," she adds, looking Mrs Swithenbank up and down.

"I've got some cakes," I say.

"What?" says Christine.

"Cakes. I've got some cakes." I hold up Mrs Scott-Pym's bag. Inside is a tin box filled with twelve fairy cakes; one of them is my secret weapon, the V2 rocket of buns.

"What are you doing with some cakes?" asks Christine.

"Mrs Scott-Pym made them. To celebrate the good news. I helped her. We've been baking all afternoon," I explain, taking out the tin box and putting it on the table.

"Well, that's right nice of her," says Mrs Swithenbank, smiling and rubbing her hands.

Christine and Vera stare suspiciously at the tin box.

"That's very nice of Rosamund," says Arthur, who seems to have perked up at the mention of cakes.

"Let's have a look, then," says Christine, grabbing the tin box and taking the lid off.

Inside are ten fairy cakes, each finished off with a large swirl of buttercream and a dollop of marmalade. There are two other buns. One is blue and the other is pink. Arthur and Christine. In cake form. Mrs Scott-Pym is a genius.

"Ooooh, aren't they lovely," says Mrs Swithenbank. "What a nice thought."

"Well," says Christine, "you'd have thought that she'd have bought a cake rather than making her own. She's got more money than she knows what to do with. She could have got something right nice from Bettys. Something big."

"That's right, love," says Vera. "She thinks she's so much better than the rest of us. So *La Di Da*, with her sash windows and lined curtains."

"Eee, have you two heard yourselves," says Mrs Swithenbank, looking at Christine and Vera. "I think it's right neighbourly. Evie, love, can you get us some plates?"

I get Mrs Swithenbank some side plates and she passes round the buns while Vera pours the tea.

"I've never had a blue cake before," says Arthur, picking up his bun and having a good look at it. "You don't see much blue food, do you?"

"There's a good reason for that, mister," says Christine, smiling coyly at Arthur and tapping the end of his nose with her finger. (*Yuck.*) "Oh, honestly, I don't know what she was thinking. I mean, who eats blue food? It looks horrible." She looks down at her pink bun. I do too. It is sitting in front of her like a ticking bomb. Tick. Tock. She looks over at Arthur. "Do you want to swap?" she asks, doing something strange with her eyes.

Swap? No! How can someone so obsessed with pink want to swap a pink bun for a blue one?

I look at the pink bun.

And then the blue bun.

And then the pink bun again.

"Oi, what are you looking at?" says Christine. "Don't get any ideas about having these; they're for us. You get the rammy old fairy cakes and we get the special cakes, don't we, Arthur? His and hers."

"Or hers and his," says Arthur, swapping the plates round so that the ticking pink bomb is in front of him.

I love him dearly but sometimes it's not easy having Arthur for a dad.

"Oi, you. You're as bad as your daughter. You don't think I was serious about swapping, do you?" she says, her hand now rubbing Arthur's leg. "Pink's *my* colour."

(Yes, we've noticed.)

"So the pink cake's mine," she continues, switching the plates and fluttering her eyelashes and trying, I think, to look seductive. "I'm a beautiful pink English rose, remember."

(More like a bossy pink English pig.)

"Now then, are we all ready to toast the happy couple?" says Mrs Swithenbank.

"Woo hoo!" shouts Vera. "My little girl is getting married."

"And she's got a lovely ring to show for it," sings Christine, waving her hand in the air and showing off the ring again.

"Well, here's to Arthur and Christine," says Mrs Swithenbank, raising her cup of tea. And we all raise our cups of tea and say, "To Arthur and Christine."

Right. Eat the cake, then. Tick. Tock.

Christine picks up her plate with one hand and holds the pink cake with the other, moving it slowly up to her mouth.

Just as she's about to bite into the cake she looks at me and then puts the cake back down on the table, untouched.

"Oh, I forgot," she says. "Shush. There's something I want to say."

Everyone goes quiet, even Vera.

"We're not just having one celebration today," says Christine. "We're having two."

Vera and Mrs Swithenbank exchange glances.

Arthur suddenly looks very anxious.

"It's a double celebration because as well as celebrating my ring and the engagement we're also celebrating Evie's new job." What?!?

Everyone cheers (except me).

"Oh, congratulations, Evie, love," says Mrs Swithenbank, patting me on the thighs. "That's smashing news. What's your job, then?"

"She's got a job at Maureen's salon," says Christine, helpfully answering for me. "Shampooing and helping out. Maureen's going to train her up." Christine sits across the table smiling at me. I have a strong urge to stuff my butterfly bun in her face but I don't. I focus on the pink cake. (Tick. Tock.)

"Well, yes," I say. "Maybe."

The cake. I just need Christine to eat the cake.

"I thought I'd give it a go," I add, desperate to stop the talking and get everyone eating. "You know, just to

148

try it out. See what happens." And I bite into my fairy cake, hoping to lead by example.

"Evie, that's great, love," says Arthur. "It's wonderful news. Why didn't you say anything? I'm really pleased for you." He is smiling more than I have seen him smile in a long time. "You'll be set up for life. People will always want their hair doing, won't they?"

"Oh, aye," says Mrs Swithenbank. "You'll be all right now, Evie, love. Someone like you, with a bit of brains and all those books, well, you'll be running your own salon before you know it. Come here." And she gives me a big hug, pressing my face into her monumental chest. "In fact never mind one salon, love, you'll have a whole chain of them. I can see it now. Evie's Top Crops."

"Evie Mends Ends," shouts Arthur.

"Evie's Lavish Locks," shouts Vera.

"Evie Cuts Loose," says Christine, looking down at her ring again.

"Well done, love," says Arthur, lifting up his blue cake as if he were toasting me with a glass of champagne. He gives the cake one more quizzical look and then bites into it.

Tick.

Mrs Swithenbank, meanwhile, is attacking her butterfly bun with gusto, sending buttercream up the sides of her mouth and Vera is nibbling away at her cake with little ratty licks.

Tock.

Christine lifts her pink cake up. Yes! She opens her mouth. Yes! And —

"Oh, silly me. I almost forgot. It's actually a triple celebration."

"Triple celebration, love?" asks Vera.

Arthur looks anxious again.

Mrs Swithenbank looks befuddled, although it's hard to tell whether this is because of Christine's triple-celebration announcement or because there's a blob of buttercream on the end of her nose.

"Yes, triple celebration," says Christine. "Good things come in threes. That's what they say, isn't it?"

(No, when you're an only child, good things come in ones.)

"Come on then, love, let's be having it," says Mrs Swithenbank, still with the buttercream on her nose. "What are we celebrating?"

"Well," says Christine. "It's to do with the farm."

Arthur now looks even more anxious.

"We've sold it," Christine blurts out. "To a developer." And she waves her arms up in the air, obviously waiting to be showered in bank notes.

"Ooooh, love, that's fantastic," shouts Vera, putting her cake down on the table and throwing her arms round Christine.

"Hold on," says Arthur. "You know we agreed not to say anything, love." Shiny droplets of sweat have started to appear on his forehead.

"Sold the farm to a developer?" asks Mrs Swithenbank. "What do you mean?"

"Well, nothing's finalised yet, Doris. We're still talking about it," says Arthur, looking simultaneously extremely uncomfortable and (for Arthur) pretty angry.

150

"I need to talk to Evie about it," he goes on, turning to me. "I was going to tell you about it over the next couple of days, love. They're offering a lot of money. It'd set us up. You could get your own car. Get your own hair salon even. You'd be sorted for life."

Christine is leaning across the table, listening to every word (she has the hearing of a field of radar antennae).

"Oh, it's fantastic news. It's like winning the pools," shouts Vera. "Well done, Arthur."

"Well, Vera, like I said, nothing's been decided yet," says Arthur, giving Christine one of her own Looks.

"What do you think about it, Evie, love?" Mrs Swithenbank asks, turning to me.

Everyone stops talking and looks at me.

What do I think about it?

I look down at the cake in front of Christine. I think of Mrs Scott-Pym's little book of Yorkshire magic. I think of *Songs to Unshroud a Scarlet Woman*. I think of Mrs Scott-Pym getting pregnant. And I think of Caroline, as tall as a tree, living in London and doing something in fashion.

Now is not the right time to talk about selling the farm. I need to focus.

"It sounds great!" I lie (yet again — I am turning into a mythomaniac: *noun — someone with a compulsive propensity to dissemble*). "Come on, let's celebrate!" And I throw myself back into my fairy cake.

Arthur beams an ecstatic smile, leans over and kisses me ("brilliant, love"). Then he pushes his hand through my hair, gives me a hug, and has another bite of his cake. Christine, meanwhile, has had a big slurp of tea and is picking up her cake. She looks as smug as a pug in a rug. As she lifts the cake up, she glances over at me, narrowing her eyes. (Tick.) She leans forwards slightly and opens her mouth. (Tock.) She moves the cake up to her lips, holding it there for a second before lifting it up to her nose and giving it a big sniff.

"Mmmm, smells quite nice," she says. "Orangey."

Just.

Eat.

The.

Bloody.

Cake.

She moves the cake away from her nose and — finally, wonderfully, horribly — puts it into her mouth.

Bingo. I experience a rush of excitement. This is what being at an Adam Faith concert must feel like.

I stare at Christine, watching for something magical to happen, but the only sign of any magic is her ability to make the cake very quickly disappear.

"Mmmm. This isn't bad," she says, licking her lips in between mouthfuls. "Nice and orangey."

Is that it? No lightning bolt or thunder crash?

Yorkshire magic is certainly very untheatrical, not like magic on the telly.

"*Argh!*" shouts Christine, making everyone jump.

"What is it, Christine, love?" asks Vera. "What's happened?"

(Hurrah. It's the magic!)

"It's the bloody cake," says Christine, spitting a dollop of mangled sponge out of her mouth and onto the plate. "There's something rock hard in it."

(Oh. Not the magic then.)

Christine puts the plate with the spat-out cake down on the table. We all stare at the moist grubby mound of sponge, orange zest and pink icing.

"Are you all right, love? says Arthur, looking unsure.

"It's probably just a nut," says Mrs Swithenbank. "Won't do you any harm."

"It wasn't a bloody nut, Doris," says Christine, starting to investigate the spat-out cake. "I know a nut when I taste one." She has a good prod around with her finger. "Look!" she says, holding up a small pink thing. "I told you there was something."

I'm beginning to get a bad feeling about this.

"What is it, love?" says Vera. "Give it here. Let me have a look." Vera takes it and holds it up to the light. "It feels smooth. And I think I can feel a ridge." She puts it close to her eye and then holds it out at arm's distance. "Do you know what . . . I think it's part of a button."

"What?" says Christine. "Part of a button? How the bloody hell did that get there?" She snatches the pink object and has a good look at it. "I think you're right,

153

Mum. It's part of a bloody button. What on earth does she think she's playing at, putting a button in my cake?"

"A button?" says Arthur. "Are you sure?"

"Of course I'm bloody sure," snaps Christine.

"Well, these things happen, love," says Mrs Swithenbank. "It's all part of having something homemade."

"Homemade? Doris. The old cow put part of a button in my cake."

"Come on, love," says Arthur, smiling his best saintly smile.

"It's just an accident."

"Accident? A button? In a cake?"

"Aye, no need for a face like thunder, love," says Mrs Swithenbank. "It must have just dropped in. Let's see," and she reaches over for the button.

"Get off," says Christine, pulling the button away. "I want to have a good look at it." She stands up and walks over to the kitchen sink. "I'll give it a quick rinse."

Right. I need some Yorkshire magic now.

Please.

Christine turns on the tap and shoves her hands and the button under the running water. She looks to be giving it a good rub.

"Oh, bugger," she shouts.

"What is it?" asks Vera.

"I dropped the bloody thing," Christine replies. "It almost went down the plughole." She turns her head round to look at Arthur, leaving her hand and the button under the running water. "Arthur. How many times have I asked you to get this plughole covered? Mum dropped a teaspoon down there yesterday." She tuts and rolls her eyes.

"Sorry, love. I'll —"

"*Aaaaaargh!!!*"

Christine lets out another scream, this time one that could break solid rock.

"My ring!" she yells. "It's just gone down the bloody plughole." She's screaming like a whole troupe of opera singers (but using some very un-operatic language). Vera and Arthur run around trying to calm Christine down while Mrs Swithenbank sits at the table finishing her cake, muttering something about U-bends. At least one cup and saucer lies smashed on the kitchen floor and I wouldn't be surprised if more crockery ended up there very soon.

Obviously I do what any self-respecting only child would do and sneak out the door. As I walk upstairs, I hear Christine shouting, "It's all the fault of that bloody woman and her bloody cake," and I have a nasty twinge of guilt.

Up in my room, I go and lie on top of the bed. Sophisticated Adam and Brooding Adam look down on me from the wall but neither of them offers much help to be honest. It's horrible. I never thought there'd be a problem that one of the two Adams couldn't ease. I don't even feel like putting on my Dansette. It's all too much for me, so I close my eyes for a moment, hoping for some peace and quiet. Floating in the dark void, I see my mother's recipe book and her elegant looping writing and then I realise that what I want more than anything else in the world right now is to be lost in the flow of her beautiful blue words.

Rolling, rolling, rolling.

Eh?

La La La La La La

I can hear a strange non-musical music. Am I dreaming?

Dum Dum Dum Dum Dum Dum

Actually, it sounds more like a nightmare.

Rawhiiiiiiiiiiide.

This is not a good way to wake up. It's Christine and Vera singing, a combination of all the worst sounds in the world rolled into one.

I have a muzzy head, partly caused, no doubt, by falling asleep fully dressed on top of my bed but also partly caused, I'm sure, by the horrible wailing coming from downstairs. I look at my watch. It's ten o'clock. What on earth are Christine and Vera doing making all this noise at ten o'clock at night?

Perhaps the singing is part of the spell? It is called *Songs to Unshroud a Scarlet Woman* after all. Maybe it's some kind of hideous compelling magical infliction, like in that film *The Red Shoes*, but instead of dynamic thrusting ballet we get Christine's flat notes and tone-deaf wailing.

I need to investigate.

When I walk into the kitchen, the singing is replaced by shrieks of laughter. Four bottles of Babycham and a half-eaten pork pie are sitting on the kitchen table.

"Oh, Evie," says Christine, looking up from her glass. Vera is wiping the kitchen table and giggling away to herself. "Did we wake you up?"

"No, I just came down for a drink," I reply, scrutinising her for any signs of magical intervention. She looks exactly the same. It's very disappointing.

"Your dad's at the pub," Christine goes on, gesturing with her glass towards the door. She's sitting on one of the kitchen chairs with her legs stretched out and her feet up on another chair. She looks like a jump in a junior gymkhana.

"Are you feeling okay?" I ask, hoping at least for some magical aches and pains.

"Okay? Oh, yes. Everything's fine now. We got the ring back. Look," she says, holding out her ring hand and wiggling her fingers again. "Isn't it lovely?"

"Mmmm. Lovely. So you're not feeling any different at all, then?"

"Different? No. What do you mean?"

"She means now that you've got the ring, love," says Vera, looking up from her wiping and being helpful for once. "Now that you're engaged."

"Yes, that's exactly what I meant. Now that you're engaged. Do you feel any different?" I ask. "Older perhaps?"

Christine gives me a Nasty Look.

"Older *and* wiser," she replies. "Wise enough to know that there was something funny about that cake today. I haven't forgotten about the button, you know."

Oh God. The button.

157

"I don't know how it happened," I say. "Mrs Scott-Pym had been doing some sewing in the kitchen before we started baking. A broken button must have found its way into the cake mixture somehow."

"Mmmm," says Christine, not looking at all convinced. "Well, to show Mrs Scott-Pym that there are no hard feelings and that we're all very grateful for her cakes, Mum and me have been doing some baking too, haven't we, Mum?"

"We certainly have, love," says Vera, looking over from wiping the sink and giving us a glowing smile (it must be the Babycham).

"Yes, we wanted to thank her for such a kind, neighbourly gesture and so we thought she deserves a nice bit of cake too. Sitting around all day in that big house of hers on her own. It can't be easy for her, can it?"

Christine has a slurp of her drink while Vera nods enthusiastically.

"And do you know what," Christine continues, "we've really enjoyed making the cake, haven't we, Mum?"

Cue more nodding from Vera.

"Mother and daughter together. In the kitchen. Baking. It's been lovely. It reminded me of when I was little and we used to make butterfly buns together. Mum'd always let me make the wings and then lick out the bowl, wouldn't you, Mum?"

"Oh yes, love," sniffs Vera, now busy wiping the table. "You used to love it."

"And it got me thinking about you, Evie. You know, we're not so different after all, you and me."

What? Christine and me are as different as night and day. Cake and ale. The BBC and ITV.

"We're both young women trying to do our best, two only children setting out on life's big adventure," she says, reaching over and squeezing my hand. It's not a pleasant feeling (partly because her ring digs into my bone), but it is, admittedly, a nice gesture.

She pulls a sad face and flutters her eyes a bit.

"Two daughters who've lost a parent."

Oh. I've never thought of Christine as a bowl-licking, parent-losing, only child before. I'm beginning to feel a bit bad about her almost losing her ring down the kitchen sink . . .

"Now, I know you're such good friends with Mrs Scott-Pym," she goes on. "So I thought it'd be nice if you took the cake round to her tomorrow. Mum and me just want to finish it off. Make it look fancy. Something grand like she deserves."

This is a new Christine. Still pink (and scarlet) but with a strange veneer of something alien. Something unnatural. Something hitherto unknown to her.

She's being nice.

Of course, I've seen her being nice before — smiling (occasionally), laughing at Arthur's bad jokes, not kicking Mr Carr's goat when it chewed her hem — but they're all things that required no effort. I've never seen her actually *do* anything or put herself out in any way to be nice (unless she's after a new LP or a pair of boots or something).

"Yes, of course," I say to Christine. Maybe part of being an Adult is knowing when to change your mind about someone. Learn to accept them. Embrace Forgiveness (*noun — a conscious decision to release feelings of vengeance towards someone who has harmed you*). "It's really nice of you," I go on. "I'm sure Mrs Scott-Pym will love the cake."

"Awe, thanks, love," Christine replies, giving my hand another little squeeze and then sitting back and crossing her legs. "I'm sure she'll love it, too."

CHAPTER
ELEVEN

Sunday 15 July 1962

It's quarter past nine the next morning and the bright blue sky is hanging above our village like a wonderful huge sheet pegged out along an infinite washing line. There's not a cloud in sight. It's already warm and you can tell it's going to get much hotter.

I'm outside Mrs Scott-Pym's back door. My arm is killing me because I'm carrying Christine's and Vera's cake for Mrs Scott-Pym and it weighs a ton.

I give the door a quick knock and then step inside. There's a lovely bready smell in the air and a faint whiff of oranges but no sign of life. I put the cake down on the kitchen table (accompanied by a solid thud) and then pop my head round the sitting-room door and shout "hello". There's no reply. Not even a howl from Sadie. I hover in the doorway, unsure what to do next. I was looking forward to seeing Mrs Scott-Pym and telling her about Christine and the button, hoping that she'd somehow be able to find some traces of magic.

As I stand holding the sitting-room door open, I notice that there's a new photo on Mrs Scott-Pym's sideboard. It's the photo that Mrs Scott-Pym showed me yesterday, the one that was on her bedside table.

161

Caroline. She looks amazing. She has her head cocked back and it looks like she's laughing. She's standing in the middle of a narrow street; lines of washing stretch from one side to the other and all the shops seem to be called things like *lavanderia* or *pasticceria*. It's definitely not Yorkshire. The street is full of life and lots of people are milling around but it's Caroline who draws your attention. She's staring straight at the camera. Daring you to look back.

I try calling Mrs Scott-Pym one more time. Nothing. She must be out. I expect she's taken Sadie for a good walk somewhere (as she often does). I could sit and wait for them to get back but sometimes they're gone for hours so probably best to leave the cake on the kitchen table and go and see Margaret instead.

It's actually late afternoon before I get back to Mrs Scott-Pym's.

I've spent most of the day with Margaret. We took a picnic and went for a long bike ride out through the lanes and over the fields and ended up going all the way up to the river. We are both good on bikes. My long giraffe legs make light work of pedalling and Margaret has thighs as thick as tree trunks, stuffed full of muscle, and capable of producing more power than most steam engines.

When I walk in, I find Mrs Scott-Pym on her knees scrubbing the floor. She looks very pale and a bit grey around the eyes.

"Are you all right, Mrs Scott-Pym?" I ask. "What's happened?"

She puts down her scrubbing brush and wipes her brow with the edge of the flowery apron (*primus inter pares* of flowery aprons) that she wears over her cashmere and tweeds when cleaning.

"Oh, it's Sadie," she says. "She's not well, poor old thing. She's embarrassed herself on the kitchen floor. Several times."

"Oh no," I say, bending down so that Mrs Scott-Pym doesn't have to keep looking up. "Poor Sadie. Where is she?"

"She's in her basket," she replies, gesturing towards the sitting room. "She must be exhausted. The poor old dear looks rotten."

Mrs Scott-Pym looks rotten too. Her skin is damp and her eyes look red and watery. "Here, let me do that for you," I say, taking the brush. "Are you sure you feel all right, Mrs Scott-Pym?"

"Well, not really, dear," she says. "I've had a nasty stomach cramp all afternoon."

"Oh no," I say, again (I really must work on my vocabulary). "Look, why don't I make us some tea? I brought a cake round earlier; we could have a slice."

The remaining colour drains from Mrs Scott-Pym's face.

"Thank you, dear, but I'm not really feeling up to any food. I had some of your cake this morning and then again after lunch. I'm afraid I don't really think it's agreeing with me." She holds her stomach and takes a sharp intake of breath. "Whatever did you put in it? It's very . . . rich."

Oh. The cake.

"Christine and Vera made it," I say. "They did it to say thank you for the cakes you sent round yesterday."

"Oh, I thought it was strange, you making a cake," says Mrs Scott-Pym. "I must say I was quite surprised when I walked in and saw it. Anyway, it was very nice of Christine and Vera to go to all the bother. Very nice indeed."

Very. Nice. Indeed. Three words not usually associated with Christine and her crab-apple mum.

"Did you give any of the cake to Sadie, Mrs Scott-Pym?" I ask.

"Well, yes, you know what Sadie's like with cake. She's such a greedy old thing. She's had two big pieces. Wolfed them down."

I see.

"Thank you, dear," says Mrs Scott-Pym as I help her onto the sofa. "You're such a help. I don't know what I'd do without you, you know."

"And I don't know what I'd do without you, Mrs Scott-Pym," I reply. It's true. I really don't know what I'd do without her. Not only is she lovely and sweet and generous and kind but she's also the only sane person around for miles.

"Here," I say, putting a blanket over her legs and belly. "Are you sure you don't want me to get you anything? Some water, maybe?"

"No, dear, thank you. I'm fine." (She doesn't look at all fine.) "Now, tell me, how did you get on last night with the cake? Did Christine eat it?"

"Oh yes. Eventually. It took her a while to get it down because she kept making announcements."

"Announcements?" says Mrs Scott-Pym, making the word sound very common. "Whatever do you mean?"

I tell her about Christine announcing to everyone about the job she's got me and the plan to sell the farm. As Mrs Scott-Pym listens, her face gets redder and redder.

"Ridiculous girl," she says. "Wait till I'm feeling better. I'm going to go and talk to your father. It's obvious what's happening. That young woman is taking advantage of his big heart." She takes my hand and gives it a little squeeze.

As we sit holding hands, I look over at the sideboard.

"Mrs Scott-Pym?" I say.

"Yes, dear?"

"Why did you move the photo of Caroline downstairs?"

Everything holds its breath for a moment. The air. The room. Mrs Scott-Pym.

"Well, dear, I just thought that maybe it had been shut up in my bedroom for too long. I think perhaps it looks much better down here on the sideboard, don't you?"

"Oh yes, I think it's perfect down here. It's a lovely photograph."

"I'm glad you like it, dear. I like it too. Very much, in fact. I think I may have been very silly hiding it away upstairs."

"Caroline definitely belongs downstairs," I say. "She's so glamorous and beautiful. If she were my daughter, I'd have photos of her everywhere."

Mrs Scott-Pym doesn't say anything; she just nods and smiles a little smile.

"Mrs Scott-Pym?" I ask, readying myself for another Caroline question.

"Yes, dear?"

"Did Caroline always want to do something in fashion?"

"Caroline? Well, no, not really, dear," she says, looking very pale again. "She just drifted into it, I think. I'm not really sure. It's all a bit of a blur, to be honest. She was never one to plan things."

Just drifted into it. Never one to plan things. I like her even more now. I want to be like Caroline, drifting and not planning. I think about my A levels. Doing them doesn't feel very drifty. And I think of Margaret, planning everything with the precision of the D-Day landings. And then I think about Caroline, living in London and doing something in fashion.

"Owwww," says Mrs Scott-Pym, suddenly clutching her stomach and bending forward.

"Are you okay, Mrs Scott-Pym? You really don't look at all well. Should we phone the doctor?"

"No, it's only a bit of stomach pain, dear. I'll be all right in a moment."

Her forehead is covered with sweat and her face is almost translucent. She is bent right over, her body just about touching her legs, a compass that doesn't quite close.

166

"Can I get you anything?" I ask.

A loud gurgling noise comes from under the blanket.

"I think I might just go upstairs for a moment, dear," she replies, obviously in pain. "Excuse me." And she shuffles off the sofa and across the room to the hallway and beyond.

I hear her going up the stairs and then the loud slam of the bathroom door being thrown quickly closed. After a few seconds, I hear the unmistakeable sound of someone being sick. Poor Mrs Scott-Pym.

I look over at Sadie, slouched in her basket. She really doesn't look very well either. Her eyes are bloodshot and she's covered in drool. Her tail, usually erect and bobbing, is curled around her, lifeless and sad.

Upstairs Mrs Scott-Pym is being sick again. The horrible wrenching noise comes and goes and in between I can hear her taking big deep breaths. I wonder whether I should go and help her but then I'm sure she just wants to get on with it on her own. Better out than in, as they say.

I pick up Mrs Scott-Pym's *Country Life* and start flicking through, looking mainly for photos of dogs. Just as I find a particularly handsome terrier, I hear a loud bang and then a horrible scream coming from upstairs.

I rush into the hallway and look up. Mrs Scott-Pym is at the top of the stairs. She looks like she's slipped. She's got one foot hovering backwards over the top stair, the other one precariously balanced two steps down; her arms are flailing around desperately grasping at nothing.

Her entire centre of gravity looks wrong.

She suddenly doubles over, grabbing her stomach. And then everything happens in slow motion. As she bends, she hits her head on the banister. Crack. She loses her footing and topples forward, crashing her shoulders down onto the stairs. She screams. Her legs flick up behind her, arching over her shoulders before slamming down on the stairs and crumpling underneath her. And then, like a deadweight sack of coal, her flaccid body crashes down each step.

Bang.

    Bang.

        Bang.

            Bang.

                Bang.

                    Bang.

                        Bang.

                            Bang.

                                Bang.

When she lands on the final step, she just lays there, staring at the floor, limp and still.

Interlude

12 May 1945

The crunching of the gravel under her feet reminded Diana of the driveway of her childhood home, bringing back memories of bicycles and nannies and grand cars and Rex, her basset hound. She smiled. Another life, one far removed from Arthur, the farmhouse, and the war.

She bent down to inspect some almost-opened peonies, their thick, heavy petals bunched together tightly, like a mass of brightly coloured artichokes on sticks. When she stood up, she was aware of a slight twinge in her back and an ache in her knees. A good soak in the bath. That's what she needed. Best not to overdo things. She'd been with the cows all morning, milking and then checking the calves, something she found oddly relaxing.

She carried on walking down the gravel drive, a small black book in her hand. She walked up to the house and then took the path round to the back. The days when they'd used each other's front door had long gone.

"Rosamund!" exclaimed Diana as she turned a corner and saw Rosamund Scott-Pym on all fours on the grass. Rosamund's backside was facing straight up at Diana so that all Diana could see of her friend were her rear-end, legs and feet. All very veterinarian, thought Diana.

Rosamund cocked her head round. "Diana! What a dreadful welcome. I'm so sorry." The two women laughed. There were twenty years between them and yet, over the war, they'd become good friends. "Here," she said, manoeuvring round on all fours, "I want you to meet Gladstone."

An English Setter puppy lolloped into view.

"Oh, he's adorable," said Diana, running over to the puppy. "But you can't call such a lovely little thing Gladstone!"

"Why ever not?" said Rosamund. "He looks like a Gladstone to me."

"Gladstone?" said Diana, bending down and stroking the puppy. "Well, it's so Victorian, Rosamund. I just think of declamatory old men with long heards."

"And that's exactly what he'll be one day, dear," said Rosamund. "An old man with a heard."

The puppy busied himself licking Diana's wedding ring.

"Well, he's certainly adorable, whatever you call him," said Diana, curling her hands around the puppy's head. "I thought you said you were going to get a girl this time?"

"Well, yes, I wanted a girl but then this little one insisted I pick him. You should have seen him showing off. He was like Gary Cooper. I couldn't resist." Rosamund leant down and blew on the puppy's belly.

170

"I'll get a girl next time. For my dotage. She and I can become the two mad old dears of the village."

Diana laughed, finding the thought of them all growing old together in the village very comforting. "Well, every village needs its share of mad old dears, doesn't it?" she said. "Oh, by the way, I brought you this," she went on, passing Rosamund the little black book. "It's the recipe book I told you about."

"Oh, thank you, dear," said Rosamund, taking the book. "I must say, I love the sound of all those grand French recipes. It'll be like reading a beautiful work of fiction. I'm sick to the back teeth of hearing about Woolten pies and the national loaf." She began flicking through the book. "Onions! Oysters! Mmm, how lovely. Although, if I'm honest, I'd settle for just being able to get my hands on some decent flour again."

Diana craned her head back and stared up into the vivid, blue sky. "Oh, it feels good, doesn't it?" she said. "After all these years, we must be near the end of the war now, surely?

"Let's hope so." Rosamund was playing with the new puppy, letting him chew her finger. "I think we've all had enough, haven't we? What those poor boys must have been through. Speaking of which, how's Arthur today, dear?"

"Oh, hearing up," said Diana. "The crutches are driving him mad, I think."

It had been almost six months now since Arthur had been injured near Reims and sent back to a military hospital in Leeds. His legs had been trussed up for a couple of months and at one point the surgeons had worried that there'd be permanent damage. But they let him come home at Christmas and he'd made good progress ever since. His left leg was still badly splintered and he had to go everywhere on crutches, but it all seemed a small price to pay really compared to what others were going through.

"He worries about what will happen to him now, after the war," said Diana, plucking a daisy from the grass. "With his legs, he says he won't be able to go back to playing football."

"You've got the farm, dear. That's work enough, surely?"

"Yes, that's what I tell him. But I'm not sure it's enough, Rosamund. I'm not sure his heart's in it."

Rosamund stopped playing with Gladstone and looked directly at Diana.

"His heart, Diana, is wherever yours is. Anyone can see that."

Diana smiled at her friend and then peered up into the swimming-pool sky, the summer sun lapping around them.

"How's Caroline by the way? she asked after a few moments. "When is she next home?"

Caroline had spent the last year boarding at a school in York. It was her first year away; she was eight. It was Rosamund's old school, a grand Edwardian affair that turned well-bred little girls into women of the Empire. Caroline had taken to the school immediately, as a cat takes to a new home, making it her own.

"Early July," said Rosamund. "She's loving school. I knew she would. She's such an independent little thing.

I just hope they manage to drip-feed some sense into her somehow."

"Well," said Diana, breaking into a huge smile. "By next summer, we might just have a little playmate for her."

"Darling!" exclaimed Rosamund. "A baby!"

Diana beamed, her eyes bright and alive. "You're the first person I've told, Rosamund."

"A little war baby. How wonderful! Well, we have to celebrate," she said, embracing Diana. "Keep Gladstone company, would you? I'll just be a moment." And she stood up and then cantered off into the house.

Diana looked down at the little puppy on her lap. Soon it would be a little baby sat there. A bundle of wool and lace. A little boy or a little girl. Either would be wonderful, of course. When Arthur and she had spoken about it, they'd both said they had no preference. But secretly, deep down, Diana wanted a little girl, an ally, an accomplice. A beautiful mischievous partner in crime.

"Here we are dear," shouted Rosamund, coming out of the house carrying a large tray. "A celebration fit for the King."

"Rosamund!" exclaimed Diana. "Whatever have you got there?"

"Champagne, dear."

"Champagne! Where did you get that?"

"I've had it since before the war. I've been saving it for the right time and I think this is very much the right time, don't you?

"Oh, you're an angel," said Diana, still stroking Gladstone. "Champagne reminds me of before the war, all those parties and balls. I haven't had a glass for years, you know."

"Well, I can think of no other way to celebrate such good news," said Rosamund, untwisting the little golden cage that held the cork in place.

There was a loud pop, triggering a round of high-pitched barks from Gladstone, and then a gush of champagne came bubbling out. "Congratulations, dear," said Rosamund, catching the champagne expertly in a tall, fluted glass. She passed the fizzing glass to Diana and poured another for herself. "Here's to baby Epworth," she said, sitting down on the floor and raising her glass.

"Baby Epworth," said Diana, chinking Rosamund's glass.

The two women took a sip. And then another. The sips turned into gulps.

"God, that's good isn't it?" said Diana.

"Nectar, dear," replied Rosamund.

"You really are such a good friend," said Diana, reaching out and taking her hand. "I don't know what I'd do without you, you know."

"And I don't know what I'd do without you," said Rosamund, putting her free hand on Diana's. "Now, come on, drink up. It's medicinal, you know. Good for baby."

Diana licked her lips. "Mmmm, baby loves it."

"Naughty baby!" said Rosamund, wagging her finger.

174

Diana laughed and put a hand on her belly. "Oh, I'm sure it'll be the naughtiest little beast in the entire county."

"I like naughty," said Rosamund. "It shows character. Have you had any thoughts yet on what you'd like to call your naughty little beast?"

"Well," said Diana, hesitating slightly. "Arthur wants Reginald if it's a boy."

"Reginald?" said Rosamund.

The two women exchanged a blank look.

"It was Arthur's father's name," explained Diana.

"I see," said Rosamund, arching her eyebrows. "And what if it's a girl?"

Diana paused, suddenly aware of the sound of a wood pigeon cooing.

"Evie," she said, unfurling the word as if she were shaking out a freshly laundered sheet. "After my mother, Evelyn."

She leant back, tasting the name in her mouth and feeling the sun warm her face.

"Well, let's just hope it's a girl, then, dear!" said Rosamund, holding up her glass. "To Evie. The naughtiest little girl in Yorkshire."

CHAPTER
TWELVE

Thursday 19 July 1962

"Eeeeeeeeeebbbieeeeeeeee."

What does Margaret want? Can't she see I'm busy?

"Eeeeeeeeeebbbieeeeeeeee."

I feel a tug on the back of my top.

"The bat maraid zuboutta tart."

What?

I can hardly hear a word she's saying because my face and ears are submerged in a barrel of water. Dozens of apples are bobbing around my head. I'm thrashing around like a run of salmon but I just can't get an apple to stay in my mouth.

Margaret and I are at our village fete. Every year I try the "apple bobbing" stall and every year I fail to get an apple. This year will be different. This year I am a sophisticated young woman, like Maria in *West Side Story*. I will not be beaten by a piece of fruit.

I surface, gulp down some air and then set off again after the apples. My mouth is stretched wide open and I have a feeling I must look like one of those sea monsters you see on old maps. Chasing the apples round the barrel is like trying to herd cats. Just as I think I've got one cornered, it bobs up past my nose and floats off calmly to one side. I pull up again, snorting in some air while I scan the surface of the water for my next target. I spot an apple that looks a bit smaller than the others and swoop in, dragging the apple underwater with the killer moves of a Serengeti crocodile. I chase it downwards, submerging my head fully and splashing what feels like half a barrel of water down my back. Suddenly — bingo! — the apple bobs into place, docking into my mouth like an egg in an eggcup. I bite into its crisp, bitter flesh and heave it out of the water, triumphant. Water is dripping down my top and my hair is wringing wet but I don't care because I beat the apple. That's the only thing that matters.

"You're soaked," says Margaret, not looking at all impressed.

The boy on the stall, Geoffrey Brown, a bulldog-looking fourteen-year-old with spots, hands me a towel. "Here, wipe yer'self down," he says, staring at the apple in my mouth. As I start drying myself off, he points at the apple, still in my mouth, and says, "Not bad. For a girl."

I look down at Geoffrey (he barely comes up to my shoulders). I am trying to give off the air of a sophisticated older woman, aloof and unobtainable, but it's not easy when you have an apple stuck in your mouth.

"How about a kiss?" he says, puckering up his lips so that he looks even more bulldoggy.

"Kiss this, Geoffrey Brown," shouts Margaret, clipping him round the ear. "Come on," she says, grabbing my hand and yanking me away so hard that the apple drops out of my mouth onto the floor. "The hat parade's about to start. I was trying to tell you when you were messing around in that barrel," she adds, still not acknowledging my bobbing skills.

"Hold on a sec," I say, nipping back to return the towel to Geoffrey. As I thank him, holding out the damp towel, he looks up and smiles. Quick as a flash, I dunk the towel in the barrel, drenching it thoroughly, and then cover his head with it, giving it and him a kiss, somewhere, I hope, in the vicinity of his forehead.

There. I feel better now.

Not bad for a girl, indeed. It's 1962 for heaven's sake.

Margaret has been watching me.

"What did you do that for?" she asks. "Why did you kiss him?"

"I don't know," I answer. "I just felt like it. Everything doesn't have to be planned, does it?"

"What?" says Margaret.

"Nothing. Where's the hat parade, then?" I ask, trying to divert her from more questions. The hat parade, during which the women of the village march round the show ring in home-made hats and bonnets, is one of the traditions of our annual fete. It fulfils two purposes:

1. It's a chance for the women to show off their millinery skills and generally untapped creative flair.

178

2. It gives all the men a break from parading round the ring with cows and sheep so that they can have a quiet half-hour in the beer tent.

"It's over here," says Margaret, pulling me through the crowd. "We'll miss it if we don't get a move on." (For someone so obsessed with facts, quadratic equations and the periodic table, Margaret, every year, is surprisingly keen to see the hat parade.) She leads the way, dodging past people and assorted animals. As we bob along, we pass stall after stall of fete activities. The flower-arranging competition. The lucky dip. Guess the weight of the sheep (for men). Guess the weight of the doll (for women). The raffle. The bric-a-brac stall. The stocks (complete with wet-sponge projectiles). And, largest by far, the Women's Institute stall, a super-organised affair made up of leaflets, cakes and absolute authority.

As we pass all the cakes, I think of poor Mrs Scott-Pym. She would usually have been one of the stars of the cake stall (and a very strong contender for the fruitcake competition) but neither she nor her cakes are present this year. This is because she's been in hospital ever since she fell down the stairs. Poor Mrs Scott-Pym is black and blue all over and has a something called a herniated disc (which sounds like something you'd find in a car engine), but essentially she's okay. She's in a small private hospital in York and has her own room, complete with carpet and a wireless. According to Vera, it'll be costing an arm and a leg —

perhaps not the best way to phrase it, given the circumstances. I went to see her yesterday, taking an assortment of books, chocolates, flowers and magazines with me. The doctors say she's probably going to have to stay in hospital for a while, so I've been charged with looking after Sadie. Christine won't let dogs in the farmhouse so Sadie's still living round at Mrs Scott-Pym's but I've been spending as much time there as possible, partly to keep her company and partly to keep out of the way of Christine and all the talk of weddings, housing estates and pink bathroom suites.

Just along from the W.I. stall is the show ground, a small piece of grass surrounded by assorted deckchairs, benches and upturned buckets. The hat parade has already started and the procession is in full swing. The days of displaying stylish little hats are long gone (if indeed they ever existed in our village) and for the past couple of years the hats have all looked like they've been borrowed from a particularly flamboyant pantomime dame.

Vera is a hat parade veteran. She takes the competition very seriously. She came second last year, wearing something that involved a stuffed budgerigar, and has her sights firmly set on the top spot today. We've had no clues about the theme of this year's hat other than being told it's something modern.

And then I see her. She looks Modern. Terrifyingly Modern. She looks like she's just walked out of an episode of *Quatermass*. Vera is wearing a black leotard and thick black tights, all covered with glittery little stars, and on her head is balanced an enormous shiny globe, covered in tin foil, screws, buttons and bits of mirror. Three knitting needles, wrapped in foil, stick out of the top of the globe, looking like a DIY television aerial. Across her chest, she's wearing a sash with TELSTAR written on it, which is just as well as otherwise people might think she'd come as a Belisha beacon. Rather than looking embarrassed, as most people would, she is walking round the parade ring with all the swagger of Napoleon surveying his troops.

"Is that Christine's mum?" says Margaret, her voice curling upwards in shock. "What's she wearing? Did you help her make it?"

"No, of course I didn't!" I say, quickly disowning all knowledge of the tin-foil Telstar. Vera's satellite hat is definitely more world's worst than world's first and I feel slightly peeved that Margaret could think I'd had anything to do with it. "She looks ridiculous."

To be fair to Vera, though, she's not the only person who looks ridiculous. Among the many hats featured in today's parade are a basket of fruit, a mini loo (complete with chain), a huge knitted teapot, a suggestive-looking missile, a tartan-clad Dundee cake, a Spitfire, and a cloud (basically, industrial quantities of cellophane and some extra-strength hairspray).

Vera's main competition, I think, comes from Mrs Gaythorne from Willow Farm. Her hat is a replica of the Statue of Liberty, but instead of a torch it's holding up a white Yorkshire rose (obviously playing the patriotic card). To complement the hat, she's wrapped a big Stars and Stripes flag around herself and the whole outfit is finished off with a pair of cowboy boots.

181

As I gawp, I pull out a pair of sunglasses from my pocket and rest them on top of my head, sliding them back slightly on my still-wet hair.

"What are you doing?" asks Margaret. "Why are you wearing your sunglasses like that? Why don't you put them on properly?"

"I like them like this," I tell her, using my hands to comb down my wet hair. "It's hip." I stretch my arms up into the sky, taking in the heat, and smile, thinking of the photo of Caroline wearing her sunglasses pushed back on her head, the one where she's surrounded by life and laughing under a summer sun.

"Hip?" echoes Margaret. "They're meant to protect your eyes not your hair. I can't see the point of it. You should get a nice Alice band."

"Sssssh," I say, sounding bossier than I meant. "Look. They're going to announce who's won."

Mr Stephens, a big, bald cardboard box of a man who runs the village Post Office, picks up a megaphone and steps into the middle of the ring. He's accompanied by our vicar, Reverend Wroot.

(There are two important things to know about Reverend Wroot:

1. He has the ruddiest face for miles [quite a feat when nearly all your neighbours are farmers]. This has led to him being known as Reverend BeetWroot.
2. He is what Mrs Scott-Pym calls *low church*, which apparently means he's allowed to wear

rainbow-trimmed vestments and the occasional set of wooden beads.)

As Mr Stephens starts speaking, someone (at last) turns down the *South Pacific* soundtrack LP that's been playing all morning on an old wind-up gramophone. Mr Stephens makes a couple of announcements and then Reverend Wroot takes the megaphone, telling everyone that the quality of hats this year is the best it's ever been and so this year is a particularly hard year to judge (he says the same thing every year).

I look over at Vera. She is standing very erect, possibly even on tip-toes. Her thin, twig-like body is dwarfed by the huge round Telstar sitting on her head. She looks like an oversized lollipop.

Reverend Wroot is now busy comparing the women in the hat parade to the hanging gardens of Babylon (I think). He goes on a bit and there's a fair bit of eye-rolling from onlookers. The women in the parade have fixed smiles and are trying to look as relaxed as possible. It doesn't fool me though. I'm glad I'm not the one who has to decide whose hat is best. Reverend Wroot is a brave man. The wrath of the devil is as nothing compared to a group of discontented Yorkshire women.

The results are announced in reverse order (like in Miss World). By now quite a crowd has gathered round, mainly women but also a few stray men, probably waiting for the cows and sheep to come back into the show ring again. I wave at Vera and flash her an

183

encouraging wink but her gaze and rictus smile are locked on Reverend Wroot so she doesn't notice me. You can feel the tension in the air. This is what it must feel like at the Oscars.

"So, without any further ado," says Reverend Wroot, after rattling on for what seems like hours (the Almighty, bric-a-brac, Cary Grant), "I'm very happy to announce that third place in this year's hat parade goes to Mrs Thorneycroft and her splendid WC."

Everyone claps and Mrs Thorneycroft (petite, clairvoyant, gammy knee) shuffles over to the winner's podium, a rickety homemade affair modelled on the one they have at the Olympics. She steps up into third-place position and beams, twirling the loo chain around like a flapper girl twirling her beads doing the Charleston.

"Well done, Mrs Thorneycroft," says Reverend Wroot, smiling beatifically. "And, after much deliberation, I'm very pleased to announce that second place goes to Mrs Gaythorne for her wonderful evocation of the spirit of Yorkshire-American friendship." Cue more clapping as Mrs Gaythorne (bad perm, flower arranger, suspected nudist) takes her place in runner-up position on the podium. She is trying to look happy but you can tell that she's more than a bit miffed. Vera on the other hand looks ecstatic and is clapping so hard I worry she may soon need the attention of one of the two St John's Ambulance volunteers hovering by the beer tent.

"And now," says Reverend Wroot, clearly enjoying the attention, "we come to the overall winner of our wonderful hat parade."

Vera is looking manic. Her smile stretches upwards so much that her cheekbones look like ping pong balls.

"We have a much-deserved winner," the reverend goes on. "A hat that encompasses both the skill and craft of the old world and the beauty and science of the new world."

I think Vera will need oxygen soon if he doesn't get a move on.

"It gives me enormous pleasure, then, ladies and gentlemen, to announce that the winner of the 1962 hat parade is . . ."

Reverend Wroot pauses dramatically.

Time stands still.

The village holds its breath.

". . . Vera Bradshaw."

Vera throws her hands up in the air and screams. Everyone applauds politely while Vera makes her way over to the podium. From the other side of the ring, I can see Christine pushing her way through the crowd.

"Wooooo! Well done, Mum," shouts Christine, elbowing her way past a couple of young girls. "You did it. Wooohoooo!"

Vera, still waving and screaming, steps up to the winner's place on the podium. Reverend Wroot shakes her hand and gives her the traditional prize: a large tray of meat from Jackson's butchers. Christine is now over by Vera's side, waving to the crowd and eyeing the tray of meat.

"God. What's she wearing?" asks Margaret.

"She's Telstar, the satellite," I tell her, happy to be one up on Margaret's encyclopaedic knowledge for a change.

"No, I know that," says Margaret. "I meant Christine. What's she wearing?"

Today is the day that Christine and Arthur will officially announce their engagement. Christine told us that she wanted to wear something special for the occasion and I think she's managed it. She's wearing a pink leopard-skin sticky-out skirt and a spangly pink boob tube with a big pink bow in her hair, an outfit that takes its inspiration not so much from the pages of *Vogue* as from a saucy seaside postcard.

The applause has now stopped and someone has cranked up the *South Pacific* soundtrack again. The winners leave the podium to the strains of "There is Nothin' Like a Dame", with Vera still waving with one hand and balancing her considerable tray of meat on the other. Everyone else is milling around chatting, having a good look at all the hats.

"What do you fancy doing now?" I ask Margaret.

She shrugs.

"The flower-arranging competition?"

We look at each other for a second and then both screw up our faces.

"What about here?" I ask. "What's on next?"

The millions of brain cells in Margaret's head whizz around at high speed.

"Er, cows, I think. It's probably the Ayrshires."

"Great, that's us," I say, picturing Arthur strutting his stuff with one of our better-looking cows. "Let's stay."

186

Margaret nods and pulls up an upturned bucket. I grab one too and we both sit under the dreamy sun, nattering about cows and life and Cliff Richard and hula hoops.

After a few minutes, Margaret points over to the far side of the show ring. I look up and see a procession of cows, each one led by a man. Arthur is second in the parade. As he walks into the show ring, a rush of pride comes over me. He's wearing his smart cords, best tweed jacket, a maroon waistcoat, and shirt and tie. In a nod to the modern world, he's decided to go capless, and his Brylcreemed hair gives him the appearance of a rural Elvis. He could do far better than Christine.

"Oh, look at your dad," says Margaret. "He looks really dishy!"

"Shut up," I say, part embarrassed and part exploding with pride. "You're meant to be looking at the cows."

"I was just saying, that's all," says Margaret, nudging me with her elbow. "The cow's not bad either."

The cows keep coming, each one led into the show ring by a man. Fat men. Thin men. Tall men. Small men. Old men. Young men. Handsome men (well, Arthur). All men. Why aren't any women allowed to lead in the cows? It can't be that hard. We just get lumbered with the Pantomime Dame hats and miss out on all the farming fun. I think I would make a good cow-leader. Miss McMinn, our lacrosse mistress, says I have an excellent gait.

The cows (and men) are nearly all in the ring now and I'm just telling Margaret about an article in Mrs

Scott-Pym's *Listener* magazine ("As You Like It: Shakespearean Imagery in the Lyrics of Adam Faith") when suddenly I see something that causes me to stop mid-sentence and stare.

It's old Mr Hughes.

With a cow.

Smiling and licking his lips (Mr Hughes, not the cow).

As he walks into the ring, images of Mr Hughes in a field with a cow flicker across my brain like the champagne-fuelled dreamy bit in *Dumbo* (complete with disturbing "Jerusalem" soundtrack).

"What's wrong?" asks Margaret, peering into my face.

I can't speak. Mr Hughes is busy stroking the cow and whispering something in her ear (sweet nothings?).

Margaret pulls at my arm.

"Are you okay?"

"Errr . . ." Suddenly my brain feels very sluggish. I think I'm in shock.

"Hello?" She knocks gently on my head with her fist, as if she were knocking on a door. "Is anybody there?"

My eyes are fixed on Mr Hughes and the cow. Is it the same cow? The one that I saw him with when I had my accident in Arthur's MG? Mr Hughes looks around, sees me, raises his cap and smiles. I'm sure he winked.

"Loo," I say, getting up quickly. "It's just come on. I'm desperate."

"What, just like that?" asks Margaret, looking baffled by my sudden lack of bladder control.

"Yes. I'll be back soon. Hold the fort," I say before dashing off as quickly as possible. I can hear Margaret grumbling behind me but I don't care. All I can think about is the memory of old Mr Hughes in a field, flat-capped and trousers down, thrusting rhythmically into the back of a cow.

I decide I need a drink. A good strong tea. And possibly some cake. So I make my way to the refreshment stall.

As I get closer to the stall, I see the gargantuan figure of Mrs Swithenbank looming over an equally gargantuan tin teapot. The teapot looks like it's been around since the war (First not Second) and is a bit battered but still in fine fettle, all of which could equally be said of Mrs Swithenbank. She is standing watch over the refreshment stall with all the authority of a Grenadier Guard or the Queen Mother.

She beams a warm, welcoming smile in my direction.

"Evie, love," she says, uncrossing her arms and tapping the tin teapot. "Have you come for a brew?"

"Oooh, please, Mrs Swithenbank. I've been over at the hat parade. Vera won."

"Did she now," she replies, pouring my tea into a robust-looking cup. "Well, she always puts on a good show. And, by, she certainly puts in the effort. She's been buggering around with that hat for months."

She passes me the cup, resting it on a saucer as thick as a roof slate.

"Between you and me, I can't see the point of it, love. I've got better things to do than sticking buttons and old loo rolls or whatever on my head."

She glances round at the next-door stall.

"Hey, have you had a go on the tombola yet? There are some lovely prizes this year."

I look over at the tombola stall. It's full of exactly the same stuff you can buy in the village shop. Mint Imperials. A bottle of Compton's gravy browning. Some Lily of the Valley talcum powder. A tin of marrowfat peas. Three bars of Lux soap sello-taped together.

"I've got my eye on the washing powder," says Mrs Swithenbank. "It's family size. It'd keep me going all year."

"Lovely," I say, trying to muster as much enthusiasm as possible over a giant box of Oxydol.

"And what about the cake stall, love?" she carries on. "I know what you're like with your sweet tooth. Although it won't be the same this year without poor Rosamund. The things that woman can do with an egg and some flour." Mrs Swithenbank sucks on her lips. "How's she doing by the way?"

I give her a full update of Mrs Scott-Pym's health, dwelling on the herniated disc and a particularly nasty bruise that looks like Ireland.

"Oh, poor Rosamund. I was in such a state when they told me. I didn't know whether it was Pancake Tuesday or Sheffield Wednesday. You're a good one going to see her," she says, resting her hand on top of the huge teapot. "I bet she loves having you around."

"I love having *her* around," I say. "I miss not having her next door. It seems strange without her."

190

"She'll be home soon enough, love," says Mrs Swithenbank. "Don't worry."

Just then, our always chirpy village butcher, Mr Jackson, sidles up to the refreshment table with his wife (cat lover, thick set, serial abuser of the church flower rota). "All right, Doris, love?" he says, winking at Mrs Swithenbank. "Two teas, please. Three sugars in each. Don't be holding back, now."

Mrs Swithenbank turns to greet Mr Jackson and his wife. Soon they're all deep in conversation (weather, Scotch eggs, hovercrafts) and so I decide it's time for cake and wander off.

The cake stalls look amazing (unlike the tombola). There's the "buy a cake" stall, populated by a variety of mouth-watering cakes and buns, and the "cake competition" stall, basically lots of similar-looking fruit cakes topped with great swirls of almonds and glace cherries. I know Christine has entered the fruitcake competition this year but I don't know why. Her basic cooking is bad enough so I can't see how she can hope to master the advanced technical skills needed to bake a fruitcake.

"Would you like a cake, dear?" says an old lady with a blue rinse. She must be part of the W.I. They have a monopoly on cakes at the fete. They're like the Sicilian Mafia. The W.I. run all cake stalls here and woe betide anyone who comes near the fete with a cake if they're not on W.I. business.

"Yes, please," I say, eyeing a Battenberg cake (the Adam Faith of cakes). I ask for a slice and, while the old lady is cutting me a piece, I glance round at the *non-cake* W.I. stall next-door. It's significantly less interesting than the *cake* W.I. stalls. There are a few books for sale, some bossy leaflets (Keep Britain Tidy, Eat Your Greens), but mainly the stall is loaded with lots of "how to" booklets. How to Make Jam. How to Clean Lace Curtains. How to Protect Your Family from Atomic Attack. The W.I. seem to think they know everything, or at least know how to do everything. They are like an institutional version of Christine.

"There you are, dear," says the old lady, handing me a slice of Battenberg cake. "That'll be thruppence, please."

I give her the money and head back to the show ring.

Back at the show ring, there's a lot of excitement. The fruitcake competition winners are being announced. I can see that second and third place are already up on the podium: an unknown lady with big hair is standing in third place and Mrs Barton, primary school teacher and W.I. bigwig, is standing in second place. Reverend Wroot is making another long speech so I nudge my way through the crowd and join Margaret. Luckily she's managed to save an upturned bucket for me.

"Where have you been?" whispers Margaret, looking cross. "I thought you were just nipping to the loo."

"I got waylaid," I tell her. "I was ambushed by a Battenberg cake."

She gives me an unimpressed look.

Somebody shushes us and I hear Reverend Wroot say: "So I'm very pleased to announce that the winner of the 1962 fruitcake competition is . . ."

Cue overly dramatic pause.

". . . Christine Bradshaw."

What?

Christine?

Everybody is clapping and some people are even cheering. Christine makes her way over to Reverend Wroot and the podium, smiling and waving to the crowd. Vera, giddy with excitement, is bouncing up and down, the huge Telstar rocking precariously on her head. Christine steps up onto the top of the podium, still waving, and shakes Reverend Wroot's hand. Then she takes the prize, a bouquet of white roses and a large bottle of Cherry B wine, and curtseys to the crowd, as if she'd just been awarded an OBE or the Nobel Peace Prize.

"I thought you said Christine can't cook," says Margaret.

"She can't," I reply, shaking my head. "I don't understand. She could even manage to burn a tin of soup. There's no way could she manage a fruitcake."

Christine has now put the wine down and grabbed the megaphone from Reverend Wroot. She's still holding the bouquet in her other hand, swinging it down by her knees like a big wooden club.

Oh God. She's going to make a speech.

"Thank you, everyone," she starts, her voice booming through the megaphone. "Thank you. I just want to say a few words. I'm so glad that all the judges enjoyed my cake. I'm sure all the cakes were delicious but some just happen to be more delicious than others."

What?

"I want to thank all the lovely ladies of the W.I. for organising everything today. I think, given their age, they've all done a wonderful job."

Polite applause from the crowd (with the exception of one or two W.I. ladies).

"I also want to thank my wonderful mum, Vera, who taught me everything I know about cooking and baking."

More polite applause. Everyone turns to look at Vera, who is busy waving and bowing, putting Telstar through some very demanding manoeuvres.

"Today's a special day for me. A very special day. And not just because I've won this wonderful competition."

She waves the bouquet in the air.

"Today's a special day," she continues, the huge pink bow in her hair flapping against her eye in the breeze, "because as well as winning this, I've got a very special announcement to . . ."

She pauses, clearly searching for the right word.

". . . announce. Is Arthur there? Can someone get Arthur Epworth? Arthur!"

Christine shouts for Arthur, setting off a clamour of *Arthur* shouts that spread through the crowd. After a few seconds' waiting, Christine looks bored (and annoyed — I know the signs).

"Well, we were going to tell you together but I've started now, haven't I? I might as well go on."

She coughs, clearing her throat for dramatic effect.

"A few days ago Arthur and me went to Bawden's, York's finest jeweller . . ."

Suddenly there's a noise around the show ring. A hushed murmur. People have turned away from Christine and are looking at someone very tall who's walking through the crowd. Christine, looking distracted and straining to see who it is, carries on.

"The reason . . . we went to Bawden's . . . was, er, to . . ."

The crowd opens to let the person through. It's like the parting of the Red Sea, but with a lot more tweed.

Christine lifts the megaphone away from her mouth, using it to shield her eyes from the sun so that she can see who it is.

"Arthur?" she shouts. "Is that you?"

Is it Arthur? I hope it's not Arthur. Please don't let it be Arthur.

"Who's that?" asks Margaret, squinting at the person walking out from the parted crowd.

I stare at the magnificent figure now standing bang smack in the middle of the show ring.

Everyone is staring.

"It's Caroline," I say, my eyes as big as dinner plates. "Caroline Scott-Pym."

A flame-haired bullet of exotica fresh from London and the future.

CHAPTER
THIRTEEN

Friday 20 July 1962

> Battenburg cake slices eaten yesterday at the
> village fete: 3
>
> Dances with Margaret to the *South Pacific*
> soundtrack: 5
>
> Tombola prizes won: 1 (a family-size pack of Atora
> shredded suet)
>
> Best in show for our cows: 0
>
> Best in show for Christine and Vera: 2 (incredible)
>
> Amazing new neighbours magically arrived to
> make the world a better place: 1

I'm in the kitchen, getting breakfast but also getting
very excited. Today's going to be brilliant. I'm off to
Leeds. With Caroline Scott-Pym. In a Mini. I can't
believe it. I'm feeling slightly hysterical and think I
might explode. It's like birthday, Christmas and a new
Adam Faith LP all rolled into one.

We arranged the trip at the village fete yesterday.
Caroline walked straight up to me, through the crowd,
right across the parade ring, and said, in a deep

luxuriant purr, "Hullo, Mummy's told me all about you. I think we're going to be very good friends."

She's amazing.

Apparently she needs to go to Leeds to get some food (food! from Leeds!) and has asked me to go along with her to keep her company. I'd be pretty excited about a trip to Leeds at the best of times but a trip to Leeds with someone who wears huge black sunglasses and lives in London and does something in fashion has taken my excitement to a whole new level.

So I'm sat having a very quick brew and a couple of slices of toast, desperate for it to get to 9.30 so that I can go next door.

As I'm draining my mug, mid slurp, the creature from the pink lagoon walks into the kitchen. It's Christine. Carrying a hairdryer. Her head is full of rollers and she's wearing her pink baby-doll nightie complete with, inexplicably, a pink feather boa. One end of the feather boa is looped round her neck and the other hangs down her back, making her look like a frilly pink Godzilla.

"Oh," she says. "You're still here, then. I thought you were meant to be going out?"

"I am," I reply, hoping (as usual) that she doesn't sit down. "I was just about to leave. I'm going to Leeds with Caroline."

Christine walks over to the cooker and plugs the hairdryer into a wall socket. Why is she doing her hair in the kitchen? Why can't she just stick to her room? She's spreading all over the house, squirting for territory.

"Caroline? Ah, yes. Caroline Scott-bloody-Pym. Arriving like she owns the place, with her bloody London ways. Spoiling my announcement like that. I had the crowd eating out of my hand and then she turns up and everyone's talking about her and not about me."

(This is true. Caroline's arrival sucked up all attention in the parade ring, forcing Christine to postpone her engagement announcement and slink off the podium unnoticed. It was like watching the Moon trying to outshine the Sun.)

"She's a stuck-up cow, you can tell," she goes on. "Just like her mum. I don't like her."

And she shakes her head, as if that's the last word to be said on the subject.

"I think she's lovely," I say.

"Well, you would, wouldn't you," she replies, stroking the feather boa. "I suppose you odd-bods need to stick together. And what on earth was she wearing? A funny little striped school dress and bright blue stockings. She looked like a clown."

"A clown? What are you talking about? She looked stylish and hip."

"Stylish and hip? Yes, if you think Andy Pandy looks stylish and hip. Anyway, enough of Miss Fancy Pants," says Christine, giving her feather boa a dismissive flick. "Let's talk about something far more important. How does it feel to come from a family of winners, then? Best hat *and* best fruitcake. We got the double. Just like Tottingham Hotspurs." She waves her hands in the air as if she's lifting an imaginary trophy. "Maybe you might be a winner too someday, Evie. Or then again maybe not," she adds, looking down at her nails. "Everyone said how good Mum looked. She was the best by miles. She looked incredible, like something from a film."

I'm not sure which film Christine means. *The Mummy? The Bride of Frankenstein? It Came From Outer Space?*

"And did you see Edna Gaythorne's face when they announced she'd only come second. Oh, it was a picture. The jealous old cow looked furious. I loved it."

Christine is in full rant now, going on about how much better than everyone else's Vera's hat was. I have to admit Vera's hat was quite good by the (admittedly strange) standards of our village fete, but the way Christine's talking about it makes it sound like Vera's Telstar hat is up there with the great artistic achievements of the Italian Renaissance.

"And then, of course, I won too. Best cake in the village. Better than all those silly old biddies. Oh, it's good to be a winner. Another Bradshaw victory. Like mother, like daughter."

She laughs but then suddenly pulls an exaggeratedly sad face, like one of those annoying French mime people.

"Oh, Evie, I'm *so* sorry. You wouldn't know about that, would you? Mother and daughter, I mean. Me and my big mouth."

I fight the urge to crack her with the teapot.

"Don't worry." I smile. A proper smile (sort of). "It's fine. Well done. I can definitely see why you won best *fruitcake*."

Christine smiles. A proper smile (sort of).

We look at each other, smile to smile.

Battle lines drawn.

"Hmm. Yes, best *baker*," Christine corrects. "You should give it a go sometime. It'd be good for you to try *baking* a cake rather than just stuffing your face with them."

She puckers her lips.

"The cake must have been difficult to make," I say. "A lot of skill involved I bet. Very technical."

Christine's lips are still puckered. She looks like a pink rubber duck.

"It was dead easy, actually." She crosses her legs. "It turns out I'm a natural. Well, you've either got it or you haven't. That's what they say, isn't it?"

"Funny how I didn't see you baking it though," I say.

Silence blows into the room. The grandfather clock in the hall ticks then tocks then ticks then tocks.

"Well, you wouldn't, would you," she replies. "I baked it round at Mum's. I didn't want to use this old place, with its dirt and germs. No, of course not. Everyone knows you can't bake a prize-winning fruitcake on tatty wooden worktops like these. You need proper Formica surfaces."

She stares at me with the welcoming presence of anthrax.

"Ah, okay," I say, trying not to sound too much like Dixon of Dock Green. "You made the cake for Mrs Scott-Pym round here though, didn't you?"

"Yes, of course I did," she snaps. "That didn't need to be prize-winning. Any old cake's good enough for the batty old crow next door."

I feel my nails digging into the palms of my hands.

"You know the cake made Mrs Scott-Pym really ill, don't you?" I say. "And that's why she fell down the stairs. She was being sick. Sadie too, and she had some of your cake."

"What's she doing giving my cake to a bloody dog?" Christine's voice shoots so high they can probably hear it in space. "Me and mum sweated hours over making that. Cheeky cow. She deserves to come a cropper."

"No," I say. "Mrs Scott-Pym deserves a nice quiet life with a sherry, a good book, and Sadie. She doesn't deserve to go flying down the stairs and end up in hospital with a herniated disc and lots of nasty bruises. What, exactly," I ask, clanging every syllable with the strength of a big hammer, "did you put in the cake to make them both so sick?"

We stare at each other across the table. (This is what trench warfare must feel like.)

"Nothing. She's just a silly old woman who's fallen down some stairs. Nothing to do with me. Just like the missing button on this nightie is nothing to do with you," she adds, holding out the nightie.

Oh god, the button. Trust Christine to remember.

"It was a big pink button," she goes on. "Just like the bits of button in that cake Mrs Scott-Pym made for me. Funny, that, isn't it? So many coincidences. But, then, that's life, I suppose. At least we all know where we are now."

She sits back and crosses her arms.

"Anyway, pass me my hairdryer, will you."

I grab the hairdryer and point it at Christine as if it were a Martian laser gun. Perhaps I could just evaporate her?

"You'd better get used to handling one of those," says Christine smirking. "You're starting at Maureen's salon tomorrow."

"What?"

"Make sure you're there for nine o'clock sharp. Maureen says Mrs Thwaite's booked in for a curly perm; she'll need shampooing."

Christine is unstoppable, like smelly feet or the Black Death.

"I can't start tomorrow," I say, dumping the hairdryer on the table.

"Rubbish. You can and you are. It's all sorted. Your dad's over the moon about it. You wouldn't want to disappoint him even more than you already have, would you? Now, go on. Get out."

She gestures towards the door with the hairdryer.

"You go and skip around Leeds for the day with Lady Muck. Some of us have work to do."

She clicks the hairdryer on. Nothing. And again. Nothing. And again.

"Oi, what've you done to my hairdryer?" she shouts as I open the back door. "It's not working."

I stop in the doorway and turn around.

"Plugged in but *not* switched on," I say. "Just like you."

And with that I slide my sunglasses on top of my head and swish out the door, feeling like Dr Cathy Gale and whistling the theme tune to *The Avengers*.

CHAPTER
FOURTEEN

Friday 20 July 1962

Walking up Mrs Scott-Pym's drive always makes me happy. Today, though, I'm extra excited (despite the wedding and Maureen's salon and Christine). The blue summer sky seems extra blue and the crunchy gravel drive seems extra crunchy. It's like that bit in *The Wizard of Oz* when everything goes from black and white to colour.

As I get near to the house, I notice three things:

1. The music — opera (again). Today it's even louder than ever. A woman is shouting and somehow managing to sound both hysterical and very sad at the same time. Caroline must be an opera lover, just like Mrs Scott-Pym. Is that how it works? Can my love for Adam Faith be traced back to my *Vermicelli Souffle-cooking* mother?
2. The smell — something strange and alien. Not cooking or baking. More like a musky, malty, smoky, earthy kind of smell. Is this what London smells like?
3. The car — a Mini! In our village! It's bright

red with a white roof and a smiley face and it looks even smaller than they do on the telly.

When I go round the back of the house, I spot Caroline Scott-Pym through the open French windows. She's sitting in the kitchen, rocking precariously on the back two legs of a chair, her feet pushed up against a table leg. She has her eyes closed and is swaying her head in time to the music. One hand's on the table, tapping away next to a tiny cup and saucer, and the other, with a cigarette between two fingers, is flying around in mid-air, sending ash and smoke rhythmically around the room. Apart from the tiny cup, there are no other signs of breakfast.

I take a deep breath and knock.

"Evie, darling," she says, opening her eyes and waving the cigarette at me. "Come in! I'm almost ready, just finishing my fag."

She's wearing black capri pants, a black turtleneck top, and ballet shoes.

Amazing.

She picks up the tiny cup and knocks it back. It's the smallest cup I've ever seen. Not even big enough for a tea strainer.

"God, that's good," says Caroline, smacking her lips. "I'm hopeless in the morning before my coffee. Can't do a thing."

"I'm the same with tea," I say, trying not to stare at Caroline's doll-size crockery. "It takes a full pot to get me going."

205

"You're just like Mummy. She drinks gallons of the stuff. I'm more of a coffee girl myself."

She stands up and takes the tiny cup and saucer over to the sink. I notice a silver pot on the hob with splodges of dark brown liquid splattered all around it. I'm pretty certain the pot and the mess are responsible for the lovely smell. I've never tried coffee and suddenly feel more than a little overwhelmed by Caroline's sophisticated London ways.

"Speaking of Mummy," says Caroline, "I called her this morning. She sends her love."

"Aw, thanks. I really miss not having her around. It's funny without her."

"She'll be back soon enough, don't worry. Everyone says she's doing marvellously. She's as happy as Larry. Surrounded by books and magazines. And her room's like a florist's of course. I've even managed to sneak her in some sherry."

She winks a particularly naughty wink while taking another drag on her cigarette.

"She nearly choked when I told her I was taking you to Leeds. I think she thinks I'm going to corrupt you."

She walks round to the other side of the kitchen and stubs out her cigarette on a saucer lying next to the sink.

"I told her we're only going to get a little bit of pasta. Honestly. It's not as if we were going out for a bop or anything."

A bop! With Caroline! God, I'd love that.

206

"Now, where's Sadie? She went out in the garden for a pee just before you got here. You wouldn't mind getting her, would you, darling, while I grab a few things before we head off?"

And she slinks out through the door, heading for the sitting room and beyond.

(Being with Caroline is like being in the presence of a very glamorous cat.)

I go over to the open French windows and shout for Sadie.

Nothing.

I try again.

Nothing.

Where is she? I hope she hasn't run off. Mrs Scott-Pym's garden is massive and beyond it lies field after field of farmland. If Sadie has run off and we need to spend precious Leeds time looking for her, I won't be happy.

Just as I'm about to try again, Caroline re-appears. She's carrying a straw beach bag and wearing an enormous pair of sunglasses. She's like a creature from another world. She sticks two fingers in her mouth and blows a whistle so loud Mrs Scott-Pym can probably hear it in hospital.

A big rhododendron bush half-way down the garden rustles and shakes and then Sadie suddenly dashes out, covered in leaves and petals, looking more like a scarecrow than a Setter. As she bounds over to Caroline, her tongue flops around and long spools of drool come shooting out of her mouth like gelatinous bolts of lightning.

"Look at you, you messy old thing!" says Caroline, bending down and giving her a kiss.

Sadie stares up at Caroline, her eyes locked in hero worship. She's sitting down at Caroline's feet, bum wiggling, tail swishing, front paws dancing with excitement (I know the feeling).

"Come on now, you need to tidy yourself up," Caroline goes on. "Don't think I'm taking you to Leeds looking like that, young lady. Chop chop." And Caroline claps her hands twice.

Sadie gives herself a massive shake, sending leaves and twigs flying, then spins round and sits down again, mouth open, staring back up at Caroline.

"Is Sadie coming to Leeds with us?" I ask, not quite managing to hide the surprise in my voice. "Aren't we leaving her here?"

"Darling, of course Sadie's coming with us," says Caroline, tickling Sadie's back. "She'll love Leeds. Poor old thing. We can't leave her here whilst the two of us skip around town."

I'm not sure what Mrs Scott-Pym would say about Sadie going off to Leeds and skipping around town. Sadie's naughty enough in the confines of our village let alone the cosmopolitan hubbub of Leeds.

"Right, time to make a start I think," says Caroline. "Come on, ladies, your carriage awaits." And she marches off round to the Mini, swinging her big straw bag ebulliently (*adverb — full of life and high-spirits*).

When she gets to the car, she yanks opens the driver's door.

"In you go!" she says, looking at Sadie and gesturing with her head.

Sadie clambers up onto the back seat, a clumsy mess of limbs, fur and spittle.

I open the door to the passenger seat. This is my first time in a Mini. I feel like I'm crossing the threshold into another world.

Caroline gets in and immediately winds down her window.

"Oh, this is fun, isn't it!" she says, throwing her bag onto the back seat, narrowly missing Sadie.

I have come prepared and offer round fruit gums. Caroline takes two and Sadie manages to wolf down four before I wrestle back the pack.

"Thank you, darling," says Caroline, starting the engine and looking over at me. "Ready, then? Three, two, one. Off we go!"

And we speed off down the driveway, scattering gravel everywhere.

Sadie sticks her head out of Caroline's open window. It's hard to see whose hair is blowing most: Sadie's or Caroline's.

"Next stop, Leeds!" she shouts, her voice booming through the air (and hair).

An enormous feeling of adventure comes over me.

This is 1962. I'm in a Mini going to Leeds with someone who lives in London and does something in fashion, someone wearing black capri pants, a black turtleneck top and ballet shoes. And a dog.

This is surely how it's meant to be.

This is life.

Forty minutes later, we're in Leeds. Caroline's driving is like Christine's cooking: terrifying, in need of a health warning and almost certainly criminal. She clearly has no concept of road signage or the Highway Code and somehow manages to get the Mini going faster than Arthur's MG.

To park, Caroline ignores anything resembling a parking space and instead leaves the car semi-mounted on the pavement in front of the Corn Exchange.

"Here we are," she says, grabbing her bag from the back seat before flinging open the driver's door. As she gets out, Sadie shoots straight after her, dancing round Caroline's ballet shoes, barking and staring up in adulation.

"Good old Leeds," says Caroline as I get out of the car.

She looks around, taking in the city.

"Queen of the North. That's what they call her, isn't it?"

Is it? I have no idea. But, then, even after just one car trip with Caroline I've got the feeling there are lots of things I have no idea about.

"Hold on a mo." She rummages in her bag and pulls out a brush. The next thing I know, she's flipped her head down between her knees and is busy brushing her hair upside down. A few seconds later and she's back upright again, shaking her hair like the women do in shampoo adverts.

"That's better," she says, putting on her big round sunglasses. "Let's get the food shopping done first, shall

210

we? And then we can relax. Work before fun, at least that's what Mummy always used to say."

"Aren't we going to put Sadie on her lead?" I ask, suddenly feeling a bit like Margaret.

Caroline looks down at Sadie.

"What do you think?" she says. "Do you want your lead?"

Sadie barks, sending a shower of spittle all over the pavement.

Caroline reaches into her straw bag, pulls out the lead and fastens it to Sadie's collar.

"And the perfect finishing touch," she says, getting a fancy silk scarf out of the bag and tying it round Sadie's neck. "There, you look beautiful, darling. Now, come on. We've got work to do."

And she throws her bag over her shoulder and sets off. I dash after them, feeling like an unfortunate country yokel on account of being out-dressed not only by Caroline (of course) but now by Sadie too.

My previous outings to Leeds have stuck pretty firmly to the holy trinity of Schofields, Lewis's, and the clothes and record stores up on The Headrow. Caroline takes me off in a completely different direction, though, and I soon feel lost in a confusing jumble of back streets and funny little shops.

"Almost there, darling," says Caroline, looping her arm into mine. "Well, at least, I think we're almost there. Everywhere looks the same around here, doesn't it?"

She's been telling me about what she does in London. I think she works for a magazine or possibly someone who makes clothes. It's hard to tell as she doesn't really seem to do much other than go for coffee with people and attend parties. Whatever it is she does, it sometimes requires going to meetings in swanky offices in Mayfair (the really expensive square on a Monopoly board), which I think sounds very exciting and grown-up but Caroline considers "a big snooze".

As we get close to a small, chaotic-looking shop, she stops.

"A-ha," she says, pushing her sunglasses up onto her head. "Here we are."

The shop is half-market stall, half-greengrocer's. At first glance, it all looks a bit of a mess, but then you realise that everything — the baskets outside full of bright yellow lemons and the exotic-looking things piled in the window — is artfully arranged.

I look at the shop front. Across the top is a large sign saying *"di Pasquale"* in red letters painted on a green background. Dozens of red, green and white streamers and tiny flags are scattered around the displays, giving the window a feel of Christmas — a bit disconcerting on a boiling hot day in August.

"Come on," says Caroline, opening the door. "You're going to love this."

As we step in, the most amazing lemony, cheesy, salty smell hits me and I hear a machine gun of vowels coming from a group of small, moustachioed men deep in conversation, gesticulating like puppets.

This is what being abroad must feel like.

"Buongiorno, signorine!" shouts a stocky, bald man, flashing a warm smile. "How I help you?"

Caroline steps forward, tells Sadie to sit still, and then launches into the most lovely jangly foreign language I've ever heard. The moustachioed men are beaming manically, obviously amazed that anyone in Leeds can manage anything other than a badly garbled version of English. The arm waving goes up several gears. Everyone is shouting at once, including Caroline, and vowels swing around the room like thousands of tiny pendulums. Every now and then I hear a word I think I recognise: *bella, grazie, Roma, Napoli.* But these words are few and far between and on the whole I just stand there, hypnotised by the drama of it all.

While Caroline and the moustachioed men are busy shouting and waving, I have a good look round the shop. The place is stuffed full of strange, alien objects. Sausages as big as an arm hang down from the ceiling. Plastic buckets full of shiny little green and black balls sit on a table. Funny architectural-looking vegetables are piled up in wicker baskets. I'm staring at a washing line that stretches across part of the shop and carries four dry slabs of meat, each as big as a guitar, when I realise everyone has stopped talking and is looking straight at me.

"Evie," says Caroline, switching back to English. "They're asking if you'd like to try an olive."

An olive?

The stocky bald man is over at the buckets of green and black balls. He's put a small green ball on a huge spoon and is offering it up to me.

Ah, an olive.

Everyone looks at me looking at the olive.

"Is *buonissima* olive from Puglia, *signorina*," says the stocky bald man, smiling and moving the spoon closer to me.

All the other moustachioed men smile and lean forward.

"Darling," says Caroline. "Have you had an olive before?"

I don't know what to say. My natural instinct is to lie and say yes so that I don't appear even more unsophisticated. If I were with anybody else, this is exactly what I'd do, but something tells me that it's best not to try blagging with Caroline so I decide to tell the truth.

"Oh, your first olive!" she says, sounding as if I'd said it's my first Spam fritter or Bourbon Cream. She swings a few vowels over to the Italians, triggering lots of hand gestures and shocked faces, and then turns back to me and says, "You're in for a treat, darling. They're delicious."

Delicious. That's a good sign. Delicious means something like a fruit Spangle or Terry's Chocolate Orange.

I take the olive from the spoon and pop it into my mouth.

Two things happen at the same time:

1. The Italians all start clapping and shouting, as if I'd just scored a goal or passed my driving test.

2. A really horrible salty taste hits my tongue and then very quickly makes its way round my mouth.

It's disgusting, like a mouthful of seawater. In self-defence, I screw my face up, hoping I don't look too much like vinegar-faced Vera. I can feel my eyes watering and have a strong desire to spit the olive out but instead I soldier on, not wanting to disappoint Caroline. After what seems a lifetime, I swallow the olive and open my eyes.

The first thing I see is Caroline pointing a camera at me.

"Don't worry about me, darling," she says. "Just taking a few snaps. Nothing to worry about."

She turns round and takes a photo of the Italian men, the stocky bald one now holding the spoon up in the air like a trophy. Then she swishes her hair and says something in Italian that makes them all laugh.

"It's for a photo diary. So much more fun than writing. And I like to show Digby what I've been up to."

Digby?

Who's Digby? Caroline's boyfriend? Her boss? Her lover? Mrs Scott-Pym has never mentioned a Digby. Although, until very recently, she'd never mentioned a Caroline either.

I don't have time to ask (or think) about Digby, though, as the stocky bald man has reached up with a long stick for one of the guitar-sized slabs of meat, cut some off and is passing me a slice. It's the thinnest piece of meat I've ever seen, so thin I can see my fingers through it. Vera would not be impressed.

"Is *delizioso prosciutto* from Emilia-Romagna," the man says, smiling encouragingly and waving his hands.

I look to Caroline for guidance but she's in full swing talking to the men behind the counter and sending them after various packets, tins and bottles so I take a deep breath and stuff the slice in my mouth.

It's disgusting. Italian food is basically just salt.

"*Che bello*, eh?" says the stocky bald man, throwing his arms around me and kissing me on the cheek. "Is the best *prosciutto* in the all of York Shiiirrre."

"Darling," Caroline says, walking over to the stocky bald man. "I'm pretty sure it's the *only prosciutto* in the all of York Shiiirrre!" And she takes a slice of meat and pops it in her mouth.

"Mmm, delicious," she says, taking two more slices: one for her, one for Sadie.

The Italian men are shouting again. They all appear to be desperate for Caroline's attention. Arms are thrown up in the air, hands waggle around, fingers open and close. It's like watching human fireworks. One of them, a particularly short one with an Elvis quiff and big walrus moustache, has Caroline's bag full of shopping but the others all seem desperate to take it so that they can pass it to her. Vowels are being flung around all over the place, which sets Sadie off barking. The man with the bag pushes towards Caroline and thrusts it at her. He seems tiny next to her, like a bucket passing a bag up to a broom.

216

"*Grazie*, darlings," says Caroline, surrounded by the men. "*Grazie mille*."

She glides through the scrum, taking Sadie and the bag full of shopping with her.

"*Grazie. Grazie. Siete molto carini*," she sings, her vowels swinging so hard that they could probably knock down a wall. The men scurry around opening doors and stroking Sadie. There's lots of shouting, waving, hand holding and even some hand kissing too. You don't get all this with Mr Mullins, our village greengrocer. Shopping on the continent must be exhausting.

As we step outside the shop, there's a chorus of *ciao belle*, accompanied by lots of hanky waving.

"Come on," says Caroline, linking her arm through mine and striding off down the street. "Let's find a caff. I'm gagging for a coffee."

Five minutes later and I'm sat in another alien space. No swinging vowels or funny-shaped veg this time, but there are lots of beards and polo necks. Caroline has brought me to a milk bar. The men are nearly all wearing glasses and seasonally inappropriate knitwear. The women are all kohl eyes and neckerchiefs. There's not a sticky-out dress in site. Thank god I'm in my pedal pushers.

It's even noisier here than in the Italian grocer's. Everyone is speaking at the same time and, unlike when Arthur takes us anywhere to eat, nobody seems bothered about keeping their voices down. There's a jukebox in the corner (unfortunately full of jazz) and louder than everything else are the hissing pipes and squirty taps of the huge stainless steel coffee machine on the counter.

I ignore the coffee machine and stick to tea (the olive and ham experience have been enough food adventure for the day). Sadie gets a bowl of water (and some fruit gums) and Caroline (the coffee queen) is having something strong and dark in another tiny cup and saucer.

"Well," she says, sitting down and sighing. "Good to get all that shopping out of the way. Thanks for coming with me, darling. It's years since I was last in Leeds so it's nice to have someone to run around with."

She bends down and strokes Sadie.

"How's your tea by the way?" she asks, gesturing at my cup.

"Nice," I say, looking down at the familiar milky-brown. "I needed a tea after all that funny Italian food."

"Darling, don't be so hard on the poor old olive!" says Caroline. "We should have started you off with something sweet, like some *panforte* or maybe a nice *crostata*."

When she says *panforte* and *crostata*, her swinging vowels come back. It's lovely, like a quick burst of church bells.

"I love it when you speak Italian," I say. "It's like listening to music. How come your Italian's so good?"

"Well, there's school, of course. And then Mummy always had opera blaring out at home so I must have

218

picked up something there. But I suppose it's only when I ran away that I really learnt it."

Ran away? I can't keep up with Caroline. She makes Mata Hari look dull.

"You ran away?" I say. "What, to London you mean?"

"No, darling," she replies, laughing. "To Italy. I was almost seventeen. It was great fun. I lived there for quite a while."

"What happened?" I ask. "Why did you run away?"

Caroline stops for a moment and runs her tongue across her teeth, all the way from one side to the other and back again.

"Well," she says, slowly unfolding the word like a napkin. "Mummy and I had a disagreement, I suppose you could say." She stops again, tapping her finger on the side of her tiny coffee cup. "There was a bit of a flare-up one day. It all got quite nasty. You see, she tried to change me — well, change part of me, and I'm far too much of a stubborn old donkey to be changed. It was very hard at the time. Very hard for her too of course. Still is, I think. Poor old thing."

She takes another swig of coffee then sighs and smiles a little sad smile.

"Anyway," she says. "Enough of naughty old me. Tell me more about you. Mummy says you sometimes practise your French with her."

This is true. Mrs Scott-Pym helped me get ready for my O level oral exam. She was trying to improve my accent but I have a feeling my French is still very much of the Yorkshire-farmer variety.

"Yes, we sometimes switch into French for a bit; we seem to talk mainly about cakes to be honest," I say, thinking about Mrs Scott-Pym's almost infinite vocabulary of French patisserie. "But my French isn't a patch on hers. It's not even as good as Dad's."

"Your dad speaks French?" says Caroline, looking genuinely surprised.

"Yes, and my mother too apparently. Mrs Scott-Pym told me."

"It's in your genes, then, darling," says Caroline, reaching over and grabbing my hand. "Anyway, *revenons à nos mouton*, as the French say. Come on, tell me something else about you. Anything. Everything!" she adds, rolling her eyes mischievously.

My mind goes blank.

"Erm, well. I'm sixteen and half."

"Yes. And?"

Caroline's looking at me expectantly. Oh God. What else is there to say?

"I've just finished my O levels. I'm quite good at lacrosse. I like reading. Swimming. Driving."

She laughs. In a good way, I think.

"And I like dancing too. I'm the tallest girl at our school. I have two enormous Adam Faith posters on my bedroom wall, Sophisticated Adam and Brooding Adam, and a signed autograph of him on my bedside table."

"Oh, I think that's quite enough Adam in the bedroom!" says Caroline, laughing even more.

"I can play the piano, badly. My best friend's called Margaret. My favourite colour is blue. Navy blue. I'm

Sagittarian. I love *Juke Box Jury*. I once ate four of your mum's scones for breakfast."

"Four! Good God — I'm surprised you're not the size of a bull."

"My favourite place in York is Clifford's Tower, closely followed by Bettys. I'd like to fly a plane. And walk on a hot Mediterranean beach. And learn how to water ski. And normal ski. And skate. I'm really ticklish. I've got freckles on my shoulders. I'm going to do A level History, English and French."

"Clever clogs," says Caroline, pulling a funny face.

"I like Marmite. And raspberries. And custard tarts. And fish finger sandwiches. My favourite word is skulduggery. Or splendiferous. Or leatherette. I've got one wisdom tooth already. I wear my mum's wedding ring on my necklace as a lucky charm." (I give her a quick flash of the ring.) "I love dogs. And cakes. I know how to change a tyre and milk a cow. I've been to Manchester twice. I don't like bananas, except when they're a bit green. I can tie three types of Butcher's Knot. I'm allergic to penicillin. And tomorrow I'm starting work at Maureen's stinky salon."

Caroline raises her eyebrows.

"What? Maureen's? Why are you working there, darling?"

I tell her about Christine. Everything. From the new turquoise oven and all the missing things to the engagement announcement at the Royal Hotel, Beverly and the horrible prospect of Christine's and Arthur's wedding.

"Hmm," says Caroline, lighting up a cigarette. "This Christine sounds a nasty piece of work."

She sucks on the cigarette and blows out a ring of smoke. Amazing.

"Now, from what I understand, you don't *want* to work at Maureen's stinky salon, do you?"

I screw up my face.

"Then why are you doing it, darling? Why do something you don't want to do?"

"Because Christine says it'll make Arthur happy," I tell her.

Caroline looks straight at me with her enormous brown eyes, tapping her fingers on an ashtray.

"Hmmm. I see."

She takes a puff of her cigarette and blows another smoke ring.

"Look, when I was little, probably just a bit younger than you, I used to come to Leeds a lot," she says. "For the shops, of course, and for the life and the people. I felt that I belonged here much more than I did back home in the village or at school in dusty old York. But I also used to come here for the art gallery too. I used to love going round looking at all the paintings. It was like another world. Something magical. And there was one particular painting that I liked more than any of the others. *The Lady of Shallot*. Do you know it?"

I shake my head.

"She's beautiful, darling. A gorgeous, ravishing dark-haired vision with alabaster skin and rich red lips. You need to see her. Anyway, she's there, trapped in a castle, poor thing, destined to do nothing but weave a bloody tapestry for the rest of her life."

She jabs her cigarette in my direction.

"No wonder she looks so hacked off. Anyway, one day she sees Sir Lancelot, a handsome knight with coal-black curls, and she falls in love. She escapes the castle, gets in a boat and sets off down the river to Camelot."

"Fantastic!" I say.

"Well, not entirely, darling. You see, she's cursed."

She stubs out the cigarette and leans forward, so close I can smell the flowery, lemony, soapy scent of her perfume. And then she lowers her voice and says:

"She chanted loudly, chanted lowly,
Till her blood was frozen slowly,
And her eyes were darkened wholly,
Turned to towered Camelot.
For ere she reached upon the tide
The first house by the water-side,
Singing in her song she died,
The Lady of Shallot."

Caroline recites the poem with lots of rhythm and dramatic pauses and when she says "*she died*" she closes her eyes and flings her head down, so that her hair falls forward and covers most of the table. She should be on television.

After a few seconds, she throws her head back up and shakes her hair. Sadie is watching her and copies the shaking, sending wisps of fur into my tea.

"So she died, then," I say. "The Lady. She escaped from the castle and then died. What a shame. It's not much of a happy ending, is it?"

"But we don't *all* die before getting to Camelot, darling. Some of us escape from whichever castle we happen to be locked in and find happiness and love and all sorts of things."

Love?

"Look, the important thing is the escaping. Not being stuck weaving tapestry after tapestry all your life for other people. You should do whatever you think's right for you. No matter what. Come on," she says, getting up and putting on her sunglasses. "I want to show you the painting. You'll love her, darling. Just don't tell Mummy."

And Caroline throws her bag over her shoulder and strolls out the door, closely followed by Sadie.

Bugger. I thought she was going to tell me about Digby.

Interlude

18 August 1952
Rosamund Scott-Pym looked at the postcard on her coffee table. The picture on the front showed a glorious blue bay, gilded with brilliant sunlight.

Saluti da Napoli

It had all happened so suddenly, getting out of hand before she knew it. They'd both said terrible things. There'd been shouting and tears, broken crockery and Edward's poor car, and then suddenly, just like that, she was gone.

Rosamund leant back and took a large gulp of sherry.

What had she done wrong? How had all this happened? Would things have worked out differently if Edward had still been alive? She looked round the room, taking in the sage-green walls and the clock on the mantelpiece, her gaze finally coming to rest on the family photographs on the sideboard behind her. Caroline as a baby, at school, in her Brownies uniform, on a horse at the local gymkhana. Relics of another age. Then she picked up the postcard and read Caroline's message again.

225

> *I'm safe and happy. Don't worry.*
> *But I'm not coming back.*
> *I can't change.*
> *I'm sorry.*
> *Love, lots of love, always . . .*
>
> C_x

Rosamund wanted forgiveness, of course, but how could she ask for it? How could things ever go back to how they were before? Her eyes filled with tears, welling up from somewhere deep, and then she let it all out, emptying herself of everything.

CHAPTER
FIFTEEN

Friday 20 July 1962
Phew.

What a day.

I spent the whole day in Leeds, eating salty Italian food and looking at strange ladies in art galleries (painted ones, not real ones). I'm back at home now with Arthur and Christine having fish and chips, our tea of choice every Thursday. I'm busy polishing off a cod the size of a battered cricket bat whilst Christine tells us about her shopping trip to York. We're currently being shown the fruits of her labour.

"What do you think of this one?" she says, holding up a pink-and-blue striped blouse.

It looks awful.

"Lovely," I tell her.

"And then I got these," she continues, holding up a turquoise-and-green striped skirt and a pair of red-and-white striped gloves.

"Really lovely," I say, thinking that if she's not careful she's going to end up looking like a collection of deckchairs.

Arthur looks up from his fish and chips. I can tell from his face that he's as unimpressed with

Christine's purchases as I am. He shuffles on his chair, looking uncomfortable, and stares at the new skirt and gloves.

"Aren't they a bit, well, you know, loud?" he says to Christine.

"Loud?"

"Well, yes, maybe just a bit, love. I just thought it might be nice to get something a bit more . . ." He trails off, clearly searching for a word that is as non-incendiary as possible. "Subtle."

"Subtle?" repeats Christine. "Subtle?"

(It's like living with a colour-blind echo.)

"What are you going on about?" she says, waving the stripy gloves at Arthur. "They're lovely. The woman in the shop said they could have been made for me. She said I reminded her of Diana Dors. When I'm in need of your fashion advice, Mr Dior, I'll ask you for it. Ooh, I nearly forgot . . ." She goes on, rummaging around in various bags. ". . . while I was there I got something for you too."

She's pulling out various clothes and putting them on the kitchen table.

A pig-pink girdle.

A blue-and-white spotted swimsuit.

A pair of yellow knitted shorts.

"Here," she says, triumphantly lifting up something with a print so loud it hurts my eyes.

Arthur puts down his knife and fork and looks at what Christine's holding.

"What is it?" he asks, clearly in shock.

228

"It's a cabana set," says Christine, the foreign-sounding word rolling off her tongue with all the ease of setting concrete.

Arthur blinks.

"A what set?"

"A cabana set. They're all the rage. Like pyjamas for the beach. Elvis wears them. And Kenneth Williams."

She holds up the cabana set so that we can have a good look at it. It's a chaotic mess of palm trees, beach balls and exotic-looking cocktails. It looks truly awful, with all the sun-kissed sophistication of a pair of inflatable armbands.

"You'll look lovely in it. Very handsome, like President Kennedy."

Arthur wipes his forehead with the back of his hand.

"I'm not sure it's really me, though, love."

"Oh, stop being such an old fuddy-duddy," says Christine, prodding him in the belly. "You've got to move with the times, you know."

Arthur is staring at the cabana set. He has the blank look of a horse doing a pee.

"I thought it'd be perfect for the honeymoon," Christine goes on, doing her best come-hither smile and resting her hand on Arthur's shoulder. "You need something beachy. We can't be skipping around with the jet set on the Costa Brava with you in your corduroys and a V-neck sweater, can we?"

What?

"The Costa Brava?" I say, glancing over at Arthur. "I didn't know you were going to the Costa Brava."

Christine shoots me a look that could swat flies.

"Yes, the Costa Brava. Sorry, Evie, I didn't realise we had to ask your permission."

Arthur looks over at Christine. On his face, I'm sure I can see the beginnings of a frown.

"Christine, love, I thought we'd agreed to go to Torquay. You know we're having to be a bit careful with money at the moment."

"Torquay?" says Christine, back in echo mode. "You promised me a foreign holiday, Arthur Epworth. I'm not bloody going to Torquay. And what do you mean having to be a bit careful? We'll be rolling in it when we sell this place. I've told you, the sooner we sign, the better."

My mouth opens and I'm just about to say something when Arthur turns to me and, squeezing my hand, quietly says, "Not now, Evie."

"Well, it's not quite as simple as that," he goes on, turning back to Christine. "There are . . . complications. I want to make sure everything's done the right way."

He sighs and takes a chip.

"Don't worry, it'll all work out in the end," he adds, smiling unconvincingly.

"Well, it better had," says Christine, getting up from the table. "I'm not living in this old dump when we're married."

She's busy clattering bowls and opening and closing various appliance doors.

"Oh, by the way, I had a look at one of those automatic washing machines at the electricity board today," she goes on, mid-clatter. "It's 1962. It's not right me doing everything by hand."

(I think she must mean it's not right Vera doing everything by hand.)

Arthur pushes his plate to one side.

"Yes, of course, love," he says. "In a couple of months. I just want to make sure everything's all tied up first. We can't be spending money we haven't got yet, can we?"

"One's coming a week on Tuesday," Christine says, banging two pudding bowls down on the table. (She has the waitressing skills of Genghis Khan.) "I got it on the never ever."

Christine has never had it so good. She's like our very own Viv Nicholson (pools-win queen), except as well as *spend spend spend* she also *borrows borrows borrows*. Along with the freezer and now apparently the washing machine, she's bought a food processor, a porcelain shepherdess and a leather pouffe, all on the "never ever". Mr Macmillan must be very happy.

"Well," says Christine, sitting back down at the table and crossing her arms. "What am I meant to do? Just go around not buying things until you pull your finger out? Do you want to see me running around like a pauper? Ruining my lovely hands doing your bloody washing? Maybe I should just take to wearing a sack?"

Christine goes on and on and on. Poor Arthur. He must be desperate for a *Yorkshire Post*. We both look down at the bowls in front of us.

Strawberries and cream.

Arthur's favourite.

Christine is obviously trying to bring him round to the joys of automatic-washing-machine ownership.

Ignoring Christine (still going on and on), Arthur picks up a spoon and lifts a strawberry and a good measure of cream up to his mouth. He sighs again and a smile slowly inches across his face. I know that look. As soon as the strawberry and cream are in his mouth, he'll be purring like a cat.

In it goes . . .

"*Aarghh!*" he shouts, dropping the spoon and shooting both hands up to his mouth, clearly in pain. "My teeth!"

Christine, with possibly the least sympathetic face ever, starts jabbing her finger at him.

"Don't you go trying to show me up in front of Evie, Arthur Epworth. There's nothing wrong with them strawberries. They're fresh out the freezer."

"Fresh out the freezer?!" shouts Arthur. "Are you mad? They almost broke my bloody jaw."

He pushes back his chair and stands up. This is high drama indeed for a Yorkshireman.

"I've had just about enough today. I'm up to here, I really am. Sod the washing machine. And sod the strawberries too. Sorry, Evie." And he walks out of the room, muttering about frozen bloody strawberries.

"Well," says Christine, turning to me. "What a cheek. Here I am, grafting my fingers to the bone and what thanks do I get? None. And he says *he's* just about had enough — what about me?" She shoves back her chair, making a nasty scraping noise on the tiles. "I'm off to my room for some peace and quiet. *You* can get all this tidied up."

She flicks her hand round the kitchen.

"I'm not doing any more today," she goes on. "I deserve a good rest. I'm just give, give, give, me, that's my problem. It's all wasted on you lot, mind."

She gets up and is about to walk out the room when I strike.

"Just a minute."

She stops and turns.

"Where's my Adam Faith clock?"

The clock, featuring a smiling Adam and guitar clock hands, was a present from Arthur (after much hinting) and it normally hangs in the kitchen just next to the back door. When I got back from Leeds today I noticed that it had been replaced by a chicken-in-a-bonnet clock, with an egg where each hour should be. It's truly horrible and could only have been bought by a moron (*noun — a person notably stupid or lacking in good judgement*).

"Lovely, isn't it?" says Christine, pointing at the chicken. "Mum got it. We needed something nice and kitchen-y in here, didn't we?"

"So where's my Adam Faith clock, then?" I ask again.

"Here," she says, opening a drawer next to the sink. "With all the other tat we've got hanging around."

"It's not tat," I say. "It's official Adam Faith Fan Club merchandise. There's a sticker on the back."

"You can go and stick him upstairs on your wall, if you like," she says. "But I don't want him in my kitchen."

"*Your* kitchen?

"Yes, *my* kitchen," she repeats, banging the clock down on the kitchen table. She stomps towards the door. "And mind you're up early tomorrow for Maureen. Your dad's proper made up about you getting that job. You wouldn't want to disappoint him, would you? Not after all that . . . Ow. Bloody hell," she shouts, stubbing her toe again on the big ceramic bear (he's definitely growing on me). "For God's sake, this bloody bear."

And she slams the door and hobbles off upstairs.

When I hear her bedroom door bang shut, I take down the horrible chicken clock and replace it with lovely Adam and his time-telling guitars. Then I get a hammer and nail and spend the next few minutes putting up Christine's chicken and its twelve eggs in the downstairs loo.

If only it were as easy to shunt Christine out of our lives. Mrs Scott-Pym's magic doesn't appear to have done anything at all.

Everything's a big mess.

It's at times like this that I wish I had a Mum. A real Mum. One who makes you smile and tells you about life and helps you make sense of everything and puts her arm around you and says that everything will be all right. One who can speak French and make *Asparagus Ice* and *Vermicelli Souffle*. One with a monogrammed nutcracker and a polished black range oven. One who's beautiful and patient and kind.

Looking over at the bright patch of wallpaper around Christine's new cooker, I reach inside my top and clench the wedding ring looped onto my necklace, feeling its curve in the folds of my palm. What I'd love more than anything right now is to crawl into the paper, deep inside its happy colours, and let all its hidden memories wrap around me.

After a bit I realise it's getting dark so I go upstairs, passing the gruesome strains of Mantovani's "Greensleeves" outside Christine's room and then, just a little further along, the reassuring voice of John Arlott and *Test Match Special* coming from Arthur's room.

As soon as I get in my room, I switch on my Dansette and play "Who Am I", my favourite Adam Faith song. Sophisticated Adam and Brooding Adam look down from the wall, singing along with Dansette Adam. I join in with them, a quartet of angelic voices.

"I never meant to aim so high,
Who am I, who am I?
Well, now I ask you what am I to do?"

After the song, I switch off my Dansette (g'night, Adam) and go and sit by the window. The sky is even darker now, a hazy smudge of grey, but the warm buzz of summer still lingers in the air. I'm suddenly reminded of Caroline's Lady of Shallot, looking out from her castle window. Is that me? Trapped. Stalled. Hemmed in by a huge pile of tapestries, with horrible pink threads knotted around my legs?

Outside, the flat open landscape stretches out across the fields. What's out there? Waiting beyond the trees and the cows and the stream? Maybe it's just more of the same. Maybe it's nothing. But I hope somewhere, over the fields, over the horizon (over the rainbow), there's something different. Something magical. Something forming. Bit by bit. Unseen and unheard.

I reach over and take my mother's recipe book from the bedside table and then, clutching its dappled cover, stare up into the colossal sky.

CHAPTER
SIXTEEN

Saturday 21 July 1962

It's nine in the morning. I've been standing outside Maureen's salon for the past twenty minutes. There's been no sign of Maureen or Mrs Thwaite and her perm or even Mr Teasy-Weasy for that matter. In fact the only sign of life is the chemical stink that permanently hangs around the shopfront like a pair of foetid curtains.

I'm not very happy about starting work at Maureen's. I'd far rather be outside on the farm or doing something Exciting with Caroline or something Not Exciting with Margaret. I'm not in the least bit interested in hair and I'm sure I'm not safe to be let loose with all the peroxide, scissors and hot tongs waiting for me inside. Plus Christine is behind it, which means it can't be good. On the other hand, it'll make Arthur happy (he seems obsessed about me "getting a trade"), give me a little extra spending money, and keep me out of Christine's way. And they have hairdressers in London, don't they?

So here I am, waiting to give it a go.

"Coooo-eeeeee."

That's Maureen, the only person in the village who makes Christine look like a quiet dresser. Today she has come as a heavily accessorised coral reef.

"Evie, love," she shouts, marching towards me. "Sorry I'm late. I've had a terrible time."

She stops and leans against the brick wall, dabbing her nose with a lacy hanky.

"It's my piles. They've been playing up all night. You youngsters don't know you're born."

I smile, unsure of the correct way to respond. Being with Maureen is an etiquette minefield.

She puts her key in the door and opens up shop. "I'm meant to have Mrs Thwaite coming first thing. I don't know where she's got to. I hope she's not stuck in her bloody bath again. It took three of us to get her out last time."

It's really strange being inside the salon and not being a customer. I've been here loads of times to have my hair cut but, like all Maureen's customers, I usually stick to the permitted spaces of the small sofa at reception, the basins, and one of the big hair-dressing chairs. Today, though, I'm let loose, free to go wherever I want. Or, to be more accurate, wherever Maureen wants. As soon as we walk in, she starts giving me a list of things to do. Wipe the mirrors. Rinse the brushes. Sweep the floor. It's worse than Girl Guides.

"But first," she says, walking over to the coat rail, "you'll need to put on one of these."

She's holding up a bright pink apron. It has a kangaroo-style pocket (complete with hundreds of

238

attached hair grips) and a huge pair of cartoon scissors embroidered across the front. It's the type of thing that Christine would design. I hate it.

"Er, do I have to wear it, Maureen?"

"Of course you do. It's like a uniform. I've got one too. Hey, we'll look like twins."

Yes, Pinky and Perky.

I put the apron on and immediately feel thirty years older.

"You look lovely," says Maureen. "Now, before you do anything, could you put the kettle on, please, love? I'm dying for a brew. Get one for yourself too." And she starts checking her make-up in the huge mirror in front of her.

Now that I'm wearing the apron, I notice that it really stinks. Mainly of bleach and other chemicals, but there's also a faint undercurrent of cigarettes and Liquorice Allsorts. Why is it that everything in a hairdresser's is so smelly? I walk into the staff room and that stinks too. It's like being in the school chemistry lab, with bottles of nasty-looking liquids everywhere. I put the kettle on and have a look around. There's a couple of stacks of well-worn towels in one corner and, next to the loo, a shelf full of small boxes, all with strange names: Sunshine Blonde, Burnt Copper, Chestnut Flickers, Bolshoi Blue.

As I'm brewing, a bell pings. It's the salon door.

"Evie, love," shouts Maureen. "Mrs Thwaite's just arrived. Can you come and look after her, please?"

I pop my head round the door. Maureen is still on the chair in front of the mirror doing something to her fringe. I shout and tell her that I'm just brewing up but she smiles and shouts back that I can do that after I've taken Mrs Thwaite's coat. I bet Leonard of Mayfair doesn't have to do all this.

After I've de-coated Mrs Thwaite (eighty-two, tomato grower, moustache) and sat her down on the sofa next to reception, I go back to the staff room to finish the teas (three now, not two). I'm busy looking for the sugar when I hear Maureen shout my name again so I pop my head back round the door.

"Can you get Mrs Thwaite ready for her perm, please, love?"

"I'm just making the tea," I tell her. "I'm almost done."

"Yes, you can finish that after, Evie," replies Maureen, still sitting and fiddling with her hair. "I need my lady shampooing."

I spend the rest of the morning shampooing, sweeping, making drinks and wiping mirrors. I also spend a lot of time standing next to Maureen and passing her things. Rollers. Perm rods. Brushes. Cups of tea. There's a lot of standing up in hairdressing. You need legs like Roger Bannister's.

I've discovered four things working in Maureen's salon:

1. Quite a lot of the stuff that gets squirted on people's hair smells like cat pee.
2. When old ladies sit under a hood dryer, they fall asleep almost instantly.

3. Hair gets *everywhere*.
4. Hairdressing is definitely not for me.

My two highlights of the morning were when Miss Cherry (ex-nurse, spinster, croquet enthusiast) fell asleep under the hood dryer and produced a huge stalactite of dribble worthy of Sadie and when Mrs Gadsby (Quaker, menopausal, Welsh) came out of the loo with the back of her gown tucked into her knickers.

I'm in the staff room mixing up a hair colour (Bruised Brisket) for Maureen's 11.30 lady when I hear the bell go again and Maureen's now familiar voice shouts, "Evie, can you see to my lady, please?"

When I step out of the staff room I can't believe who's standing there.

Caroline Scott-Pym.

Maureen is talking to Caroline at the reception desk. She's looking up at Caroline in the same way Sadie does, clearly star-struck. Every head in the salon is craning over to reception and gawping at her.

She looks amazing.

She's wearing a beautiful navy blue tailored jacket and skirt, some silk stockings, a pair of very smart high-heel shoes, and a huge lampshade-style hat. Under the hat, her hair is a mass of red curls and wavy flicks. The combination of heels, hat and hair makes her seem about eight feet tall. She looks magnificent, like a *Vogue* model or a be-suited Good Queen Bess about to see off the Armada.

"Evie, can you take Dr Scott-Pym's coat, please?" says Maureen, using a voice that is much more mindful of her Ps and Qs than usual.

Dr Scott-Pym?

I just stand there. My brain is struggling to deal not only with this new piece of information about Caroline but also with the shame of her seeing me in a horrible stinky pink apron.

"Evie? Could you take Dr Scott-Pym's coat, please?" repeats Maureen, smiling at Caroline. I'm sure there's even a hint of a curtsey too.

Caroline passes me her hat and coat without saying a word, smiles, and then strides over to the basin.

"I didn't know you were a doctor," I say as I put a towel round Caroline's shoulders.

"Don't be silly, darling," she whispers, leaning forwards and sending a waft of her lovely perfume up my nose. "Of course I'm not a doctor."

"Oh, but what was all that Dr Scott-Pym business, then?"

"It's groundwork. All warfare is based on deception. Honestly, don't they teach you anything at school these days?"

What?

Our conversation is cut short by the arrival of Maureen.

"Here we are," she says, sotto-voce, holding up a fancy-looking glass bottle. "I've got some lovely shampoo for you, Dr Scott-Pym. Something for our special ladies," she adds, over-annunciating every syllable. "It's French."

"Ah, *merci*. *Très gentil*," replies Caroline, reaching out and touching Maureen's arm.

Maureen looks like she's just been given a guinea tip.

"Well, I have some very refined clientele, Dr Scott-Pym," says Maureen, almost purring. "And I like to keep a few products to one side for them. Special-like."

"That's very kind of you," says Caroline, smiling a smile last seen in Hollywood. "Do you know, this gorgeous salon of yours is just like the one I go to in London. I love it."

Maureen looks like she might explode.

"Now," continues Caroline, "let's give this lovely French shampoo a try, shall we?"

And she swings her chair round and puts her head forward into the basin.

Maureen leans over and whispers in my ear, "Mind you give her a good wash, Evie. Two shampoos and a cream rinse," and then walks off.

I switch on the water, give the pipes under the basin a good kick, and then start to wet Caroline's sumptuous red hair.

"What's happening?" I say, dolloping a good measure of French shampoo on her head.

"I've got a plan."

"A plan for what?"

"A plan to get you out of here," she says (although it's not easy to hear what she's saying because she's got

243

her head bent over the basin). "You do want to get out of here, don't you?"

Do I? Is a summer spent shampooing old ladies worth it if it makes Arthur happy? Can I put up with the horrible smells, the relentless standing and the underwear full of other people's hair if it brings a smile to Arthur's face?

Bugger that. This isn't for me. If I'm happy, Arthur's happy. That's how it works with fathers and daughters, isn't it?

"Yes, of course I want to get out of here," I tell Caroline. "But I'm stuck with it until school starts."

"Rubbish. Mummy would be furious with me if she knew I'd abandoned you here. And to be honest," she says, turning her head slightly and looking at me out of the corner of her eye, "you're really not cut out to be a hairdresser. You're shampooing me as if I were a bull in a field, darling. Now, don't worry. I'm going to rescue you."

Suddenly, I feel like Wendy Darling being rescued from Captain Hook. I have never been rescued from anything before and am expecting an elaborate plan involving lots of derring-do and clever intrigue.

"Here, take these," she says, passing me two small bottles.

I look at the bottles. A pink food dye and a blue food dye. It's hardly the stuff of *The Thirty-Nine Steps*.

"I found them in a cupboard in Mummy's kitchen," she says.

"Yes, we used them to make a cake for Arthur and Christine," I whisper. "What are we meant to do with them?"

"Well, you're going to pour them all over your arms and then you're going to sit back and let me do the rest," whispers Caroline. "Come on, hurry up whilst no one's looking."

I take the pink food dye first and splash it over both my arms in the basin. My arms immediately look like two long strips of angry Red Windsor cheese. Then I do the same with the blue food dye and my arms go from an angry pink to a grotesque blotchy purple. Horrible.

Caroline pulls out a black towel from her bag and starts dabbing at my arms. When she's finished, she stuffs the towel back in her bag and stands up dramatically, her hair still covered in shampoo so that she looks like a Mr Whippy ice cream.

"Good Lord," she shouts, immediately getting the attention of everyone in the salon. "Maureen, this girl is ill."

The whole salon stops and stares at me.

"It's clearly a bad reaction," says Caroline, leaning over and having a good look at my arms. "She needs to go home immediately."

Maureen (ever the drama queen) rushes over and puts her arm round me. "Oh, Evie, love, you poor thing. Whatever's wrong? Come and sit down." And she takes me over to the sofa at reception.

Mrs Burrows (bad breath, stubby neck) is clearly not happy about having her fringe trim interrupted. She

245

comes over and has a look at my arms, reaching out and trying to touch the purple marks.

"No touching, please," Caroline says, sounding terrifyingly imperious. "We can't risk any infection."

"Just looks like a funny bruise to me," says Mrs Burrows, screwing up her face into a frown. "She'll be fine."

Caroline stares at Mrs Burrows.

"Well, I'm sorry," she says, mustering up far more dignity than anyone with a head full of shampoo should by rights be able to, "but I'm a doctor and I can assure you that it is a reaction. It looks like a bad case of . . ."

She flicks her eyes around the room.

". . . *prosciutto cruditis.*"

Everyone looks blank.

"It's quite a rare reaction," she goes on. "Chemicals. Particularly chemicals found in hair salons. It can be *quite* disfiguring."

Maureen gasps and puts her hand up to her mouth. Mrs Burrows is still frowning, our very own hairclip-wearing bulldog.

Caroline reaches into her jacket pocket and pulls out what appears to be a wooden lollypop stick (without the lollypop).

"Could you put your tongue out, please?" she says.

I stick my tongue out and Caroline jabs the lollypop stick on it.

"And now say *ah.*"

"*Aaaahhhhhhhh,*" I say, trying not laugh.

"Definitely *prosciutto cruditis,*" she confirms, flicking her vowels authoritatively. "This girl needs to go home immediately and sit in a bath of warm water for at least an hour."

"Oh my god," says Maureen, definitely enjoying the drama of it all. "Evie, you get going, love. Do whatever Dr Scott-Pym says."

"Yes," says Caroline, twinkling her eyes. "You go straight home, young lady. Bath and then bed. And think yourself very lucky to have such a wonderful boss." She turns to Maureen and smiles. "Although with such a bad case of *prosciutto cruditis*, I'm afraid her days of working in a salon are over. We can't risk another reaction."

As she speaks, Caroline is ushering me out of the door.

"I'm really sorry, Maureen," I shout. "It's been lovely working here but it looks like I'm just not up to it."

"Don't worry, love," replies Maureen. "I understand. It's not for everyone, the hairdressing game. You need to have skin as tough as tractor tyres."

Outside, Caroline's wet hair has flopped down (no more Mr Whippy) and she's dripping water everywhere.

"Off you go, darling," she says. "It'll come off easy enough. Just give your arms a good rub with toothpaste — it gets rid of more or less anything. You'll be fine again in no time."

She winks and heads back inside the salon.

Brilliant. No more stinky salon to worry about.

Now I just have to do something about Christine.

CHAPTER
SEVENTEEN

Saturday 21 July 1962

As I approach the farmhouse, I can tell straight away that Vera's here because all the windows are wide open.

Vera is obsessed with airing. It drives me and Arthur mad. At various times she's said that fresh air kills germs, stops dust, reduces damp, controls rheumatism, slows wrinkles, improves the taste of food (helpful with Christine's cooking), and significantly increases your chances of winning at bingo.

With all its windows wide open, the farmhouse reminds me of an advent calendar just before Christmas day, each open window offering a festive object to surprise and delight. If you could peel back our little advent calendar windows, I wonder what you'd see? Christine's hairdryer? Arthur's *Yorkshire Post?* My mother's recipe book? And what would my advent-calendar object be? An old Lacrosse stick? An Adam Faith LP? A written-off MG? Maybe that's all we really are in the end. Just a collection of dusty objects lying behind a few glittery cardboard windows.

(I'd better watch out, having depressing thoughts like this. I'll be listening to opera next.)

Through the open windows, I hear another sure sign that Vera's around: the all-too-familiar drone of the hoover. The hoover is Vera's latest obsession (as well as bingo, airing and the hoover, she's also obsessed with *The Billy Cotton Band Show*, Mint Imperials and clinically clean doorsteps). Arthur bought Christine the electric upright hoover last January. Christine didn't appreciate the gesture quite as much as Arthur hoped, but Vera did and she's had the hoover out most days ever since.

Suddenly the hoovering stops, replaced by a high-pitched shriek.

It's Christine, not sounding happy.

"For God's sake, Mum, you've just hit me again. If you ladder my tights with that bloody thing, you can forget about coming to the wedding."

This is followed by a loud tut and then the hoover kicks in again.

It sounds like the hoovering is coming from Arthur's study. This is good as it means I can sneak in the back door and avoid both of them. I don't want Christine to know yet that her plan to condemn me to a life of shampooing servitude has failed. Knowledge is power, as I'm sure Elizabeth Bennet would say.

I tip-toe round the corner and enter the house through the back door, left wide open as part of Vera's airing regime. Now that I'm inside I can hear Christine and Vera much more clearly. They're definitely in Arthur's study — I can hear various sounds (Christine's tuts, Vera's clatters, drawers being opened and closed) ricocheting down the corridor. I think it's time to do some Miss Marple-ing so I position myself strategically at the door leading from the kitchen to the hallway and corridor beyond, a perfect spot to eavesdrop.

"I can't believe it," I hear Christine say, her voice jumping through a series of high-pitch hoops. "I can't bloody believe it."

"What is it, love?" says Vera. "What have you found?"

"Nothing. That's what I've found. Nothing. Well, practically nothing. Hardly enough for a new kitchen let alone an executive detached house and a trip to the Costa Brava."

Is Christine looking for money in Arthur's desk? She can't know him well if she thinks he keeps his money there. (He keeps his money in a shoebox in his wardrobe, next to his wedding photos and a navy cashmere scarf that belonged to my mother.)

"What do you mean, love?" says Vera. "He must have plenty of money. Are you sure you're looking at the right account?"

"Yes, of course I am. I'm not stupid, Mum. Look. A hundred and eighty one pounds sixpence in this account and just three bloody bob in this other one. Pass me a pen. I want to write all this down."

"Ay, don't forget about this other stuff, love. There's a Post Office savings book here, look. And some of those Premium Bonds."

"He's not said anything about them. The sneaky sod. I only asked him last week. How much is there?"

"Sixty quid in the Post Office and another fifteen in Premium Bonds. Ooh, look, there's three books of Green Shield stamps here too. Must be at least five quid's worth."

"Right, hold on, let me add it all up."

Christine's brain slowly clicks round, tooth by clockwork tooth. It's two hundred and forty one pounds, three shillings and sixpence, you moron.

"About two hundred and fifty quid I think," says Christine, eventually. "Is that all?"

"I thought he'd have much more than that," says Vera, sounding surprised.

"Me too. It's unbelievable."

"Unbelievable."

"I can't believe it."

"Me neither."

"I really can't."

"I know."

"Shifty bugger."

"Ay."

"What's the point of getting married to someone who's only got two hundred and fifty bloody quid to his name?"

"But he's got the farm, love, too, don't forget that."

Christine lets out a sigh so big I'm surprised it doesn't raise the ceiling a couple of inches.

"Yes. But something's not right, you know. He's being funny about selling the farm. I'm trying to get to the bottom of it but you know what it's like talking to Arthur. It's easier getting information out of that bloody wall."

This is true. We Epworths are an inscrutable bunch.

"He must have more stashed away somewhere, love," says Vera. "You know what farmers are like."

"He better have. He's got another thing coming if he thinks I'm going to put up with him and his bloody daughter for only two hundred and fifty quid."

Then there's a noise that sounds like something being kicked, probably the hoover, although, knowing Christine, it could just as easily be Vera.

"If he's got any money stashed away, I want to know about it," Christine goes on. "I'm not sharing anything with that crackpot bloody girl of his. Come on. I'll go through the bookshelf and you have a look round the rest of the room."

I can't believe it. I knew Christine was a cow, but not this much of a cow.

My thoughts are interrupted by some mooing coming from outside. Some of the non-Christine cows must have wandered into the courtyard again (a regular occurrence). There's more mooing (inside and out) and then I hear Christine telling Vera to put everything away, someone's coming.

Bugger. I don't want to get caught earwigging, so I dash into the only hiding place available: the pantry.

"Only me," shouts Mrs Swithenbank, coming in through the back door and putting down two bulging shopping bags.

I'm perched on an old crate, surrounded by tins of corned beef, condensed milk and mulligatawny soup, peeping through a crack in the rickety old pantry door.

"Oh, hello, Doris," says Christine, walking into the kitchen. "We're up to our necks cleaning. We've been at it all morning. I'm exhausted."

There's a clatter down the corridor and then Vera comes into the kitchen, carrying the hoover, a mop and a bucket full of cleaning things.

"Hello there, Doris," says Vera, manoeuvring the hoover and mop up against the table. "Lovely day for it."

"Ay," says Mrs Swithenbank. "Although I wish this hot spell'd hurry up and end. I'm getting through a tin of talc a week. Anyway, I won't stay for long," she goes on, sitting down. "I just wondered whether you'd heard about Clara Gilberdyke? I was in the butcher's just now and I bumped into Edna Mayhew and she said . . ."

And on and on they go. It's wall-to-wall village gossip. Mrs Gilberdyke's cystitis. Ada Johnson's new windows. Tom Wilson's affair with the lady in the mobile library.

A very long twenty minutes later, I hear Mrs Swithenbank getting up to leave. Hallelujah. There's a good deal of chair scraping and table knocking (Mrs Swithenbank and her bags need a large berth) followed by lots of *bye, love-ing* and, as she gets outside, more mooing.

"Right then," says Vera, walking over to the mop and hoover. "Back to the cleaning."

"You what?" says Christine. "Bugger that. I'm not going to work my fingers to the bone just for Arthur and bloody Evie. No, come on. Let's go to the Red Lion and get a ploughman's lunch."

"Oooh, good idea, love."

"And maybe a nice sweet, too," says Christine, taking off her leopard-print pinny. "I love Janice's treacle sponge."

Vera unbuttons her paisley pinny, all the while going on about the pros and cons of the Red Lion's various sponges (treacle, jam, chocolate). She folds the pinny neatly and pops it on top of the bucket. Christine, meanwhile, has tossed hers over a chair and is busy with her mirror and compact.

"Don't forget your purse, Mum," she says, heading for the door.

"Right, love," replies Vera, grabbing her handbag from the back of a chair.

"Don't worry," shouts Christine, now out in the courtyard. "As soon as I get that ring on my finger, I'll take you out for a slap-up dinner."

"Aww, you're a good girl," says Vera, going out the door and pulling it closed after her.

Their voices rattle around the courtyard, accompanied by more mooing, and then slowly disappear as they head off onto the High Street towards the pub.

Coming out of the pantry, I'm met by whatever the collective noun is for a group of cleaning products. A mop and hoover are balanced against the kitchen table. A bucket and accompanying array of bottles and cloths are up on the draining board. Two rubber gloves are flopped over the cold tap like barren udders. There's a

254

duster lying on the floor. I pick it up, put it next to Vera's neatly folded pinny, and pour myself a glass of dandelion and burdock. I sit at the table, take a long sip and start to think things through.

Christine is clearly bad news. I've known this for a while but I thought bad news as in being bossy, annoying and a terrible cook, not bad news as in planning to get her scarlet hands on all of Arthur's money.

I wish it could just be me and Arthur again.

Or, even better, me, Arthur and my mother. The three of us. The Three Bears. The Three Kings. The Three Musketeers. A glorious trio of which I have no memory at all, just a few faded photos, a ring on a necklace, and an old recipe book full of beautiful, looping writing.

I'm trying to have a profound moment but it isn't easy as Christine's horrible leopard-print pinny is draped over the chair next to me, loudly sucking all taste out of the room. Peeping out from one of the pockets, I can see the list she made of Arthur's money. Naturally, being an inquisitive Sagittarian, I pull it out and have a good look. The paper's covered in her bubbly cartoon handwriting. Bank accounts. Savings accounts. Premium Bonds. Everything. She's even noted down how much the Land Rover's worth (£480).

I turn the paper over in my hands. Should I hold on to it and show Arthur? What would he make of it? Would he be angry? Happy? Sad? It's hard to tell with him. The note's not that much on its own. It's a bit like one of those pictures where you can see two things at the same time, like two faces and a wine glass. Arthur would very much only see one thing. The good thing. He's too kind to see the bad thing.

Unless, of course, someone (me) helps him see the bad thing (Christine's evil plan).

I slip the piece of paper back into the pinny pocket. While I'm at it, I might as well check the other pocket too, mightn't I? That's what Miss Marple would do.

I push my hand inside. Right down at the bottom, amongst fluff balls and a safety pin, I find a crumpled piece of paper. I pull it out and put it on the table, flattening out the creases. It's a receipt from Bettys.

I knew it.

Interlude

28 November 1945

"Fat rascal?"

Diana looked at Arthur from across the table, her hands propped on top of her heavily pregnant stomach.

"I didn't say you looked like one!" said Arthur. "I was just asking if you wanted one." He smiled, arching his eyebrows mischievously. "They're delicious, you know."

They were in the grand tea rooms at Bettys in York finishing off lunch. They'd come into town to buy Diana a new scarf, an excuse really to get out of the farmhouse and enjoy a day out before it got too close to the baby's arrival.

"Well, I can only just about squeeze through the streets as it is," said Diana, patting her bump. "Oh, I do hope the poor little thing will be on time."

"'Course he'll be on time," said Arthur. "Like all good Yorkshiremen."

"Well *she* might be fashionably late, darling," replied Diana, leaning forward and running a hand through his hair. "Just like her mother."

Arthur beamed and then had a slurp of tea, happy with all that life had given him.

"Anyway," she went on, getting something out of the small Browns bag next to her chair. "What do you think?" She was wrapping a navy blue cashmere scarf round her neck. "Do I pass muster?"

"Beautiful," said Arthur.

"Beautiful?" repeated Diana.

"Yes, beautiful. Like a beautiful big snowman."

Diana smiled, lifted her foot and kicked Arthur under the table.

CHAPTER
EIGHTEEN

(Part I)

Saturday 21 July 1962

Here I am again, walking down Mrs Scott-Pym's drive. There's the familiar crunch of gravel under my feet and the sweet, comforting smell of the border flowers. But something's different.

No one is shouting. No one is dying. No one is screaming at the top of their voice while an orchestra swirls dramatically around them. Instead, a strange alien sound is tugging at every bit of my body.

Bum. Bum. Bum. Bu-bu-bum.

Bum. Bum. Bum. Bu-bu-bum.

Some men are singing but it's not opera. It's nothing like opera. It's more like an atomic Adam Faith with booster rockets and a harmonica.

It's the most wonderful sound I've ever heard.

I go round the back of the house and the music gets even louder, blasting out through the open French windows and hitting me like a great waft of something new. The harmonica comes in again, sounding sad but at the same time irresistible. And then the voices, running together like melting ice cream.

Love.

Love.

Me.

Do.

It's amazing.

There's no sign of Caroline in the kitchen so I follow the music through into the sitting room, which is where I find her, tapping a cigaretted hand to the beat, curled up on the sofa with Sadie.

"Darling!" she says as I walk into the room. "Isn't it marvellous? I've been playing it all afternoon."

She's wearing a black painter's smock and a pair of shorts that make her legs go on forever, all topped off with some kind of twisty turban thing. I've never seen anything like it. She is half Brigitte Bardot, half Dame Edith Sitwell.

"It arrived in the post today. A friend who works at a record company sent it. It's all very hush hush and hot off the press. I can't stop playing it."

The music thrusts round the room, occupying every single bit of space.

"It's great," I say. "I love it. Who is it?"

"It's the latest thing, darling. A group. Four boys from Liverpool."

She takes a puff of her cigarette, all the while moving her head from side to side and tapping Sadie's belly rhythmically.

"They're amazing," I say, sitting down on the sofa and pushing my feet under Sadie's bum.

"Yes, that's what everyone says apparently."

She stubs out her cigarette and jumps up, sending Sadie along the sofa.

"Hold on a sec," she goes on, walking over to the sideboard. On top of the sideboard is a strange machine with loads of buttons and dials and two big reels moving round and round in tandem. She pushes a button, stopping the reels and the music. "There, that's better," she says, coming and sitting back down on the sofa.

"I can hear you now."

"Oh, I was enjoying that," I say. "They're very good, these four boys from Liverpool."

"Don't worry, darling, we'll have them back again soon. I just want to hear how you got on today. Are you okay? Did you manage to get all that horrible food dye off?"

"Yes, back to normal now, thanks to ten minutes in the bathroom and half a tube of Colgate," I say, holding out my arms for inspection.

"Sorry about that, darling. But it did get you out of the salon, didn't it?"

"Yes, thank you. Maureen's lovely but, oh, I really don't want to work there."

"Well, hairdressing's definitely not for you. I'm not even sure whether it's for Maureen to be honest. I walked out of there looking like Harpo Marx. That's why I'm wearing this." And she points to the twisty turban thing.

We both laugh. It's great sitting on the sofa with Caroline and Sadie. I feel like I've suddenly found a shoe that fits.

"Hey, you were a very convincing doctor by the way," I say, pointing at Caroline. "I felt like I was in

261

Emergency — Ward 10. I'm sure Maureen won't forget about *prosciutto cruditis* for a while."

"It was the first thing that came into my head!" says Caroline, throwing her head back and laughing. "It must have been those lovely little Italians we met in Leeds. I've been thinking about that ham ever since. In fact, my brain's squashed full of food most of the time. No room for anything else, as Mummy always used to say."

Sadie plops her head back in Caroline's lap.

"She sends her love by the way. I spoke to her on the telephone half an hour ago and she was asking after you. She always does. She's got a very soft spot for you, you know."

"Oh, she's wonderful. You're so lucky to have her."

"Hmmm," says Caroline, looking out the window and staring at nothing in particular.

"How is she today?"

"Still making good progress. I've told her to get her skates on and come home. She's greatly missed by this one here," says Caroline, giving Sadie a big rub.

"We all miss her," I say. "I can't wait for her to get back."

"Darling, I think you just miss all those cakes! I know what Mummy's baking's like. I could easily hoover up an entire batch."

"Me too. And lick all the bowls. And the spatulas. Not like when Christine cooks."

"But I thought Christine was a good cook?" says Caroline, looking puzzled. "Didn't she win the fruitcake competition at the fete?"

Oh. The cake.

"She bought it," I tell her. "I found the receipt this morning, scrunched up and shoved in her pinny. The day before the fete she got a deluxe vintage port and ale fruitcake from Bettys. No wonder she won."

Caroline's eyes go from shocked tennis balls to small angry slits.

"I can't believe it," she says, shaking her head. "The devious little madam. Cheating at the village fete."

"I know. She's horrible."

"Well, yes, I really think she is," says Caroline, sitting bolt upright. "We have to do something."

"Mrs Scott-Pym was trying to use some Yorkshire magic on her. A spell from an old book. *Songs to Unshroud a Scarlet Woman.*"

"Yes, I heard about that. I thought Mummy was going do-lally when she told me. But then I saw the clever old thing polish off the *Times* crossword in less than twenty minutes and decided she still had a few marbles left."

She beams a huge, mischievous smile.

"Anyway, come on, aren't you going to tell me more about Mummy's Yorkshire magic?"

"It didn't work," I say, leaning over and stroking Sadie. "I don't suppose it ever really stood any chance of working. I wanted to believe in it, though, mainly just because Mrs Scott-Pym did. But nothing happened, of course." I sigh a big, un-magical sigh. "I don't believe in magic any more."

"Nonsense, darling. We all need some magic in our life," says Caroline, taking my hand.

"No, I think magic is just silly, something for children, like fairy tales."

"Look, fairy tales annoy me too. All those helpless princesses waiting to be rescued by a handsome prince and then whisked off for a life of drudgery in some boring old castle. No, thank you."

She's rubbing my hand and I can't help but smile.

"And it's always irritated me that in most fairy tales there are three children and it's the youngest one that's the special one. That's rubbish. It's the only child who's the special one, darling. That's you." She jabs her finger on my arm. "And me. It's the only child who has to be clever and brave and crafty and sneaky. That's our magic, darling. And who knows?" she says getting up. "Mummy's spell may well be working; it's just a slow burner, magicking away in the background. That's how modern magic works perhaps. Now, I think it's time for a drink, don't you?" And she walks off into the kitchen, closely followed by Sadie.

I lie back on the sofa, stretching out my legs and hugging a nice flowery cushion. Am I too old for magic? Caroline clearly thinks not. It's so confusing. I close my eyes and try to think marvellous, mysterious, magical thoughts.

"Darling, don't move!"

It's Caroline, standing over me with a tray.

"Aargh, what is it?" I shout. "Is there a wasp?!?!"

"No, darling, don't be silly. It's the late afternoon sun on your face. You look wonderful. Angelic. Like a Vermeer milkmaid."

264

What?

"I want to take a photo. Stay there. Don't move."

I hold my pose while Caroline puts down the tray and fetches her camera from the sideboard.

"There," says Caroline, after clicking the camera a couple of times. "All done. You look marvellous, darling."

"Can I move now?"

"Yes, of course," she says, putting the camera down and bringing over the tray. "Have a good wriggle around. Now, I want to ask you a favour."

"A favour? Me? Yes, of course. Anything."

"Thank you. Okay, you know the reason I'm always taking photos is for the scrapbooks I make, the ones I like to show Digby."

Digby! I'm dying to know who he is but Caroline's in mid-flow so I just nod my head.

"Well, I've also started recording a kind of audio diary. It's all very modern. A friend at the BBC does it and so I thought I'd give it a go too. That's why I got the reel-to-reel." She points over to the machine on top of the sideboard. "Now, I thought it'd be fun for you to record a little something for Digby too. Just a quick hullo and then whatever takes your fancy."

"Make a recording? What, like a news announcer or politician, you mean?"

"Well, hopefully not *that* much like a news announcer or politician. I thought something a bit livelier and more fun. Just be yourself."

Right. Now's my chance to find out about Digby. *Carpe diem*, as Miss Weston, my old Latin teacher, would say.

"But who *is* Digby?" I ask, trying to sound as nonchalant as possible. "I don't know him."

Caroline smiles and sits down next to me on the sofa. Sadie comes and joins us too.

"Darling, look, there's something I need to tell you. You're going to be shocked I think but the world's full of shocks so it'll be good for you."

Oh. I brace myself.

"I'm a lesbian."

Caroline stares at me, waiting for a response.

I have no idea what she's talking about, just like when she said I was a Vermeer milkmaid, so I just look back at her and smile.

She cocks her head slightly to one side and looks a bit puzzled. "You don't understand, do you?" she asks. "A lesbian, darling. Sapphist. Dyke. A homosexual. Digby's not a man; she's a woman."

A woman? And Caroline's a woman. That's two women. Not a man and a woman. A woman and a woman. Together. As in *together* together. As in a couple. As in man and wife. Or wife and wife.

Amazing.

"I've never met a lebesian before," I say.

"Well now you have. And it's *lesbian* darling, not lebesian. Lebesian sounds like a breed of cow."

I'm gawping, I know. Not very polite, but I'm in shock.

"Look, here's a photo of Digby," says Caroline, pulling a wallet out of her painter's smock. "Isn't she adorable?"

266

I look at the photo. Caroline's on a beach in a spotty bikini and next to her is a lady in culottes and a stripy fisherman's top. The lady is older than Caroline, a good ten years older I'd say. She's smaller, too, and wider. Caroline and Digby are holding hands and they look happier than virtually anyone I've ever seen in any photograph.

"So, she's like your husband?" I say, hesitating over every word.

"Well, I suppose you could say that. But we're more like a partnership. A perfect little team. She's divine. The nicest, funniest, kindest, filthiest person I know. We met in Italy, after I ran away there. I was in Naples, doing some teaching and just enjoying life, and we bumped into each other in a gorgeous little bar in the *centro storico*. She stayed with me for a year or so and then went back to London. I followed her and we've been together ever since."

"Oh," I say, mainly because I don't know what else to say. It's such a turn up for the books. A perfect little team of lesbians. It really is 1962. It's like we're living in the future. We'll have robots and flying cars next.

"But what about Mrs Scott-Pym?" I ask. "Has she met Digby?"

Now it's Caroline's turn to hesitate.

"Ah. Well. No."

She reaches up and adjusts her twisty turban thing with both hands.

"It's all very difficult. Mummy doesn't approve. Well, actually it's more like she doesn't understand. To be honest, she took the whole thing very badly. It was an awful shock for her. We had a terrible row and that's when I ran away."

"So you ran away because Mrs Scott-Pym found out about Digby?"

"No, darling. Digby was later. The row came about because of somebody else. A very beautiful Yorkshire girl."

Caroline sighs and rubs her hands through Sadie's soft curls.

"It was all very dramatic. Mummy was yelling like a fish wife. Me too."

She smiles, a sad, nostalgic, thoughtful smile.

"We both said some really terrible things. And that's why I ran away."

"Oh, so you ran away because you were offended by what Mrs Scott-Pym said?" I ask, pretty confused at this point to be honest.

"Offended by Mummy? No, darling. She said some pretty nasty things but then again, we both did. I wasn't offended at all. More embarrassed really." She turns and looks me straight in the eye. "No, Mummy didn't offend me. She threw me out."

"She threw you out?" I repeat, shocked. This isn't like Mrs Scott-Pym at all; in fact, instead of *throwing out*, she seems to spend most of her time *taking in*. Dogs. Hedgehogs. Birds. Me.

"Well, it was six of one and half a dozen of the other really," Caroline goes on. "She told me to leave so I left. But I was so angry with her that I just never came back. And that's how I ended up in Italy. Running away."

I have a slurp of my tea. It's barely even lukewarm at this point but cold tea is better than no tea. Especially after such a shock.

"I was angry about it for years. I was so young. It's been really hard to forgive her to be honest. I had to think long and hard about coming back when I heard she was in hospital. We've had very little contact over the past ten years. Just cards and a small note for birthdays and Christmas and the odd strained phone call."

She rubs her long legs with her hands.

"But I have to remember that in a strange way it's because of Mummy and what happened that day that I met Digby. I should really, I suppose, be grateful to her in some way," she goes on, laughing gently. "It would all be so much easier if she weren't so terribly embarrassed by the whole thing. Well, more than embarrassed. Ashamed really. She had no idea how to deal with it. Still doesn't, in fact. And she wouldn't talk to anyone about it either. She was just mortified by it all." Caroline stares out of the large sash windows and shakes her head. "Even when we'd re-established a very loose contact, she still wanted to keep a distance. She wouldn't let me come and see her just in case I bumped into one of her friends and they somehow noticed I was different. She can be such an old prude sometimes. And, of course, she's so worried about social standing and all that. But then I suppose she's from a very different world. A different time."

By now I've finished my (cold) tea and just sit holding my empty cup and saucer, transfixed. This is even better than *Armchair Theatre*.

"And it must have come across as such a huge shock to her too," says Caroline. "It was different for me as I'd known about it for years, of course. Practically all through school. It had just become part of me. But for Mummy, to find out like that — bang! — well, it must have been awful, I suppose."

It's all beginning to make more sense now. So that's why Mrs Scott-Pym didn't speak about Caroline or have any photos of her downstairs in the house. How strange. I'm shocked all over again.

"But you're speaking again now, aren't you?" I ask. "On the phone, I mean, before I got here and then when you go and visit her in hospital."

"Well, of a sort, darling. It's all very practical and business-like. Pay the butcher's boy on Wednesday, have the laundry ready to collect on Thursday, that kind of thing. And we talk about Sadie of course. Mummy's always checking I've remembered to feed her. And we talk about you too — she loves talking about you. She's got a real soft spot for you, you know."

"Oh, I've got a real spot for her too," I say, beaming. "She's amazing. I don't know what I'd do without her. You're really lucky to have each other."

"Hey, *you've* got us too," says Caroline, leaning over Sadie and prodding me in the arm. "You're not going to be able to get rid of us, you know. We're neighbours, remember. And the way Mummy thinks about you, you're practically my little sister."

I suddenly feel cocooned, swaddled in neighbourly, sisterly love.

"You'd be an amazing big sister," I say.

270

"And you, darling, absolutely are an amazing little sister. Digby's going to love you."

My eyes suddenly feel warm and full and I realise I'm fighting very hard not to do a sad-happy cry. If I had a *Yorkshire Post*, I'd be barricading myself safely behind it. Instead, I push myself back into the sofa as far as possible, beaming, and cross my legs.

Quick as a flash, Sadie barks and jumps onto the floor. Before I know it, she's mounted my crossed leg and is enthusiastically humping away at my shin, wagging her tail excitedly and sending long spools of drool over my pedal pushers.

"Sadie!" shouts Caroline, reaching over and pushing her off. Sadie gives a yelp of surprise. "What have I told you about that, young lady?" Poor old Sadie hangs her head before slinking back onto the sofa, rebuked. "Sorry, darling," Caroline goes on, turning back to me. "She's such an old strumpet. I really don't know where she gets it from. Marvellous way to polish boots, though."

And she belly laughs, setting me off too.

"Anyway, look, are we going to get this recording done or not? It'll be such a wonderful surprise for Digby. I've told her all about you. Come on!"

And she grabs my hand, pulls me off the sofa and leads me over to the sideboard.

Interlude

16 July 1952

Rosamund Scott-Pym felt a strange wet sensation on her hand. Was she dreaming? Her brain steadied, the real world slowly becoming more solid. The wet sensation became rhythmic. A lick. Then another. And another.

She thought about opening an eye. Gingerly. Barely. Through a fuzzy slit she saw Gladstone, her English Setter. Her arm had fallen off the sofa and was dangling, ripe for licking.

She must have nodded off.

She was lying on the sofa with the *Listener* magazine across her chest. How long had she been asleep? She swung her legs onto the floor and sat up. One thing was certain. She needed a tea.

In the kitchen she looked out through the French windows expecting to see Caroline and Flora reclining on their deckchairs, taking the afternoon sun. The terrace, though, was empty, and even the annoying tinny hammering of the wireless had ended. They must be cleaning Edward's car in the garage, she remembered. That was good of them. Maybe there was hope for her recalcitrant daughter after all.

As she waited for the kettle to boil, she readied two pots — one for her, one for the girls — and laid out a tray with cups, saucers and plenty of cake. She poured the boiling water into both pots then stood for a moment, stretching her arms up into the air, trying to wake herself up.

The sun outside was still hot and, as she carried the heavy tray across the lawn to the garage, Rosamund felt tiny beads of sweat appear on her skin. The main garage doors were closed, but, anyway, the small side door was much easier to manoeuvre through with the tray. She balanced the tray in one hand, turned the door handle with the other and nudged the door open with her hip.

Edward's car was just inside. Pushed up inside the car's backseat window was a large expanse of flesh. The flesh, a blotchy map of white and pink, was magnified slightly by the glass, its features strange but somehow still familiar.

A young girl's back.

She dropped the tray.

An enormous clatter and smash splintered round the garage.

In the car, the squashed back shot to one side, revealing her daughter's impassioned face behind it. Mother and daughter stared, frozen, each appalled in her own way. There was silence for a second, then Flora screamed and Caroline, pushing both hands back through her sticky, moist hair, cocked her head back and mouthed a single word.

"Fuck."

CHAPTER
EIGHTEEN

(Part 2)

Saturday 21 July 1962

"It looks very complicated," I say, standing in front of the reel-to-reel.

"No, it's simple, darling," says Caroline. "Very easy. I ignore most of the buttons except for this one here, which is to play, and this one here, which records. I just have to remember to change the reel when I record so I don't talk over the four nice boys from Liverpool," she adds, removing the reel from the machine. "I lost a lovely version of 'Dido's Lament' like that, recorded over by me banging on about a picnic in Greenwich. Very annoying."

"Absolutely," I say, even though I suspect this might be opera and so actually replacing it with Caroline's lovely gravelly voice seems like a Very Good Thing.

"Ready for Digby, then?" she asks, winding a new reel onto the machine.

"Oh, yes, okay. Digby. I don't know what to say."

"Just say anything, darling. She'll love it. Okay?" She sticks her thumb up and pulls an encouraging face. "Three, two, one. Recording."

Caroline flicks a big switch and the two reels start moving slowly round in unison, like someone rolling their eyes.

"Erm. Hello. This is Evie. Evie Epworth. Hello. Oh, I've said that already, haven't I? Sorry. Erm. I'm Caroline's neighbour. Well, Mrs Scott-Pym's neighbour. I'm here with Caroline and Sadie. Do you know Sadie? Yes, of course you do. Anyway I'm here with both of them, in Mrs Scott-Pym's sitting room, and Caroline's asked me to record a message for you, a bit like the Queen at Christmas."

Caroline smiles and nods encouragingly.

"I'm having such a good time with Caroline. We've done loads of things. We've been to Leeds, where I had an olive. And some Italian ham, which tasted like salty blotting paper. She's lovely, by the way, Caroline I mean, but I suppose you know that already. Anyway, it's very exciting to speak to you because you're in London and it's exciting to speak to someone in London. Oh and it's exciting too because it's the first time I've spoken to a lesbian. Well, the second time actually. Caroline, just now, was the first time. Well, I think the first time. Miss McMinn, our games tutor, quite often wore a tie."

Caroline turns away and coughs.

"I hope all's well in London and that you're not missing Caroline too much. I'm sure there must be plenty to do down there, what with all the parties and celebrities and spies and political things. It's lovely having Caroline up here — it's like having a bit of London in the village. And she's even brought four nice boys from Liverpool with her — we were listening to them just now. You'll love them. Well, at least I think you will. I don't really know what kind of music you like, do I? Although I suspect it might be opera."

Caroline, with one hand over her mouth, sticks the other hand's thumb up.

"Right. Well. I think it's time to say goodbye. So, er, very nice to meet you. Well, to speak to you. Or rather speak *at* you. It'd be really lovely to meet you sometime. You look lovely on the photo Caroline showed me. And that's it. Bye-bye. Cheerio. Over and out."

Caroline clicks the switch on the machine and the reels stop turning.

"You were wonderful, darling," says Caroline, smiling like a Cheshire cat. "She'll love it."

"Really? I thought I was terrible."

"No, you were brilliant. The essence of Evie-ness."

"Oh. Is that a good thing?"

"Of course, darling. It's an extraordinarily good thing. It'll get you far."

She's busy taking the reel off the machine, carefully spooling the tape to the end.

And then a thought pops into my mind.

"Caroline?" I ask, trying to sound as casual as possible.

"Yes, darling?"

"Do you think I could I make another recording?"

"Another one? Yes, of course. But there's no need to; that one was great. Digby will absolutely love it."

276

"No, the new recording wouldn't be for Digby," I say. "It'd be for Mrs Scott-Pym."

"For Mummy? Whatever do you want to make one for Mummy for?"

"I've got an idea," I say, smiling and moving the idea around in my head.

Caroline smiles back. "Curiouser and curiouser. They should have called you Alice."

(Actually I often wander off into a literary daydream inserting myself into various book titles and imagining what the consequences would be. *Evie Flanders*. *Evie of Green Gables*. *Evie Poppins*. *Evie Eyre*. *Evielina*. *Evie of the D'Urbervilles* (hopefully with a much happier ending). My definite favourite, though, is *Evie in Wonderland*. I can easily see myself falling down a rabbit hole and having tea with a mad hatter and getting on the wrong side of a bad-tempered old queen. Where exactly is my Wonderland, though? Is it in my sworl-of-cashmere, fully parented past? Or is it out there somewhere, unseen, lost in the messy blur of my future?)

Caroline rests her hand on my shoulder.

"You can make as many recordings as you like, darling. I'm sure Mummy will be delighted."

And she starts getting a new tape ready while I try to think what to say.

"Okay," says Caroline, finishing off whatever she was doing with the machine. "Right, just do exactly the same thing again. You're a natural. Mummy's going to

277

love this. Three, two, one. Go!" And she flicks the big switch.

"Hello, Mrs Scott-Pym!" I say, feeling a bit more relaxed now that I'm speaking to someone I know. "It's Evie! I'm here with Caroline and Sadie in your sitting room. We're recording on Caroline's tape machine thing. It's all a bit strange but good fun too. Caroline's amazing, Mrs Scott-Pym. She saved me from working at Maureen's stinky salon. And she took me to Leeds and we bought lots of Italian food and went to the art gallery. You'd have loved it. It was really good. I think we should all go together when you get out of hospital. Sadie too!"

Caroline smiles and looks down at her feet.

"And she's told me all about London. And about working in fashion. She's so clever. You must be really proud of her. I wish I had a sister like Caroline. Funny and sophisticated with lots of friends and doing lots of brilliant things."

Caroline keeps her head down but I can see that she's still smiling.

"And she's told me about Naples. And all about being a lesbian. It's all very exciting. It's the modern world, Mrs Scott-Pym, just like you always say. Like spaceships and non-stick pans and women reading the news on the BBC. I know it must all seem strange to you but it's not strange really, is it? You told me once that before the war people did a lot of incredible things. Well, we still do a lot of incredible things. Incredible lovely things. And Caroline is incredible and lovely. I just wanted you to know that, Mrs Scott-Pym. You're

278

both incredible and lovely. And Digby is incredible and lovely too — Caroline showed me a photograph of her and said she's funny and warm and kind. She's like a wonderful new daughter for you, Mrs Scott-Pym. Or maybe a wonderful new son? I'm not really sure. Anyway, it's like that poem you showed me last year — the one about the war. *We must love one another or die*. That's what it said. And it's true. That's what we need to do."

Caroline's hand moves up to her face.

"But not Christine, though. Obviously. We don't have to love her. Oh, speaking of which, I almost forgot! Some top-secret news. Christine cheated at the village fete — her cake was from Bettys. Can you believe it? You were right, Mrs Scott-Pym. She's a scarlet woman. Horrible. Anyway, I think it's time to go now. Please hurry up and get well so that you can come home. We'll all have a big party when you get back, with lots of cake and tea. Oh, and sherry. Bye, then, Mrs Scott-Pym. Lots of love. Bye." And I wave goodbye to Mrs Scott-Pym (even though she can't see me).

The tape loops round for a few seconds. Caroline reaches over, her hand hovering above the stop button. She stands as still as a statue, hesitating, her eyes locked on the turning tapes, and then starts speaking into the microphone.

"Hullo, Mummy. I've missed you, you know. Really missed you. It's good to be home."

And she clicks stop.

She wipes her eyes with her black smock.

"You were brilliant, darling. Really brilliant," she says.

"Do you think she'll like it?" I ask.

"Like it? I think she'll love it," replies Caroline, giving me a big hug. And we stand there, hugger and huggee, both lost in beautiful thoughts of Mrs Scott-Pym.

"Here we are," says Caroline.

It's almost half past eight at night. We've just spent the past forty minutes rocketing along various country lanes to get to Mrs Scott-Pym's hospital. Mrs Scott-Pym's hospital looks very different to the hospital I was in. My hospital was the size of a factory and was all concrete and glass and wall-to-wall bossy signs. Mrs Scott-Pym's hospital is basically a big old posh house on the outskirts of York. There's gravel on the drive and nice old trees everywhere. It's lovely.

Caroline squeezes the Mini in between a Jaguar and a huge old Bentley (I'm very careful getting out) and we set off inside. Caroline's carrying a huge bunch of flowers, some chocolates, some periodicals (magazines) and a clandestine bottle of sherry, and I've got the bulky reel-to-reel machine.

Visiting hours must be long gone but Caroline has said, repeatedly, that this won't be a problem. We'll see. If it's anything like the hospital I was at, getting past the nursing staff outside of visiting hours will be harder than getting past a gang of marauding Vikings.

"Hullo there," says Caroline to the nurse on reception. The nurse looks up from her paperwork (*Woman's*

Weekly), clearly not happy about visitors arriving at this late hour. "I was wondering if you could help us. It's my mother's birthday tomorrow and we've brought a few things over to arrange a little surprise."

"Oh, really," says the nurse, not sounding very impressed.

"What's your mum's name?"

"Rosamund Scott-Pym."

The nurse flicks through a ring binder with lots of little stickers on it.

"Says here that your mum's date of birth is in March." She props her elbows on the desk then puts her hands together and leans forward. "That gives you nigh on eight months to get the surprise ready, doesn't it."

She stares at Caroline.

Caroline stares back. This isn't going well.

(Caroline is clearly not used to such a wall of indifference. If I'm honest I don't think her outfit is helping much. She's still wearing the black painter's smock, shorts and twisty turban thing. She looks like she might just have escaped from the local madhouse.)

Caroline smiles at the nurse. The nurse doesn't smile back.

"Look, darling, you're absolutely right. It's not my mother's birthday. I'm very sorry. But we *are* going to surprise her. See this tape machine." She points at the reel-to-reel I'm holding. "Well, Evie here has recorded a wonderful surprise message for Mummy and it's really important that she hears it. It will make an old lady very happy."

She smiles at the nurse.

Nothing.

"Really happy," she adds, placing the box of chocolates on the desk and slowly pushing it forward.

"Really happy?" asks the nurse. "Or just a bit happy?" she adds, looking at the box of chocolates as if it were a small pile of cow dung.

"Really, really happy," says Caroline, putting the huge bunch of flowers on top of the chocolates.

The nurse doesn't move. I would hate to play her at poker.

Caroline starts to put the magazines on the desk next to the chocolates but the nurse tuts and shakes her head.

"Got any fags?" she asks.

Caroline gives her the kind of Look that could have come from Christine.

"Look, darling, no fags, but I do have this," she says, pulling Mrs Scott-Pym's contraband bottle of sherry out of her bag. "And that's it I'm afraid. You've sucked us dry now."

The nurse takes the chocolates, flowers and sherry and puts them on the floor under her desk.

"Right," she says, finally loosening up (there's even the faint glimmer of a smile). "Do you want to follow me, then?"

As she comes out from behind the desk, Caroline stops her and whispers something in her ear. The nurse listens, impassive, and then, when Caroline's finished, asks her if she's sure. Caroline nods and then the nurse points towards a door down the corridor, tells us to wait in there for twenty minutes, and then walks off.

"Come on, then," says Caroline, striding down the corridor. "You heard Nurse Ratched. Let's wait in here for a bit then we can go and see Mummy. Honestly, private healthcare just isn't what it was," she adds, entering a room with a big *Patients' Lounge* sign on the door.

Twenty minutes later, we're up in Mrs Scott-Pym's room. Mrs Scott-Pym is fast asleep and I'm tip-toeing around trying to be very quiet. Caroline, noisily setting up the reel-to-reel on Mrs Scott-Pym's bedside table, has no such qualms.

"Shouldn't we try to be quiet?" I whisper, pointing at Mrs Scott-Pym asleep in bed.

"No, don't worry, darling," she says. "I asked Florence Nightingale to give Mummy a sedative. She'll be out for hours. If a jet engine went off under her bed, it wouldn't wake her up. Now, could you pass me the card you made, please?"

I get the card out of the bag and pass it to Caroline. On it is a big arrow with the words *PRESS HERE* written above it in thick red writing. Caroline puts the card on the reel-to-reel, making sure the arrow's pointing right at the play button, then stands back and admires her handiwork.

"Excellent," she says. "Right, come on, let's get off before that nurse comes back and starts demanding the clothes off our backs. Not that she'd suit hot pants and a turban."

I grab the bag and walk out the room. When I look behind me, I see Caroline through the open door rubbing Mrs Scott-Pym's hand and kissing her gently on the forehead.

On the way home in the Mini, I have another brilliant idea.

CHAPTER
NINETEEN

Sunday 22 July 1962

It's eleven o'clock in the morning the next day and I'm standing in a field surrounded by a herd of cows.

Last night, when Christine found out that I couldn't work at Maureen's salon because of medical reasons (*"Prosciutto cruditis! What the bleeding hell's that?"*), she showed all the sympathy and understanding of Caligula. Arthur, ever the diplomat, asked me to go up to my room, so I went and put on my favourite Adam Faith LP, but, even without all the acoustic interference of Christine's yelling, it somehow didn't feel the same now that I'd heard Caroline's tape of the four boys from Liverpool. Later on, Arthur came up and told me to keep today free as he wanted to show me something — and he said not to tell Christine. It was all very mysterious, which isn't like Arthur at all.

So here I am. In a field of cows. With Arthur. And with Mr Baxter, the horrible builder who wants to knock down our farm and build a shiny new housing estate.

Mr Baxter looks like a Toby jug. He's wearing a pie-brown suit that must be at least two sizes too small for him and a great bulge of white shirt is poking out over his trousers, making a bid for freedom. Summer is obviously an unfortunate time of the year for Mr Baxter, as a growing damp patch lurks under each of his armpits, and his round face, which reminds me of a well-inflated football with a comb-over, is covered in a sheen of sweat.

"And the new garden would end there," says Arthur, smiling and pointing to a spot near the stream. "So, you can see, you'd still have plenty of space outside. Enough even for a dog, maybe."

Arthur has been on a charm offensive for the past half-hour. I've heard all about how lovely the new estate will be. How pretty it will be. What good neighbours we'll all be and how happy everyone'll be. And I've heard about our wonderful new house and its wonderful porch and wonderful drive and wonderful double garage. Now Arthur seems to be playing his joker: I can have a dog.

I've never seen him be this effusive about anything before. Not even the cricket. Something strange is happening.

"So will the stream be in our garden, then?" I ask.

"Er, yes," says Arthur, glancing over at Mr Baxter.

"Well, yes *and* no," says Mr Baxter (rooting hog, saucy lackey, cream-faced loon). "You see, we'd need to fill in the stream and concrete it over. So the stream would technically still be there, it's just that you wouldn't actually be able to see it any more. And there'd be no water, of course. But you *would* have a lovely fishpond, remember, with a fountain in it too if

286

you like. Better than a dirty old stream, love," he continues, speaking to me as if I were ten. He walks up to Arthur, puts his sweaty arm around him (poor Arthur) and exudes a clammy smile.

"But what about the newts?" I ask. "Loads live in the stream. Where will they all go?"

Mr Baxter's smile flickers.

"Well, they'll go and find a new stream, won't they, love? Yorkshire's hardly short of streams, is it? It's a good fast bowler we're lacking, eh, Arthur?" he adds, slapping Arthur on the back.

"And what about the copse?" I say, pointing to a small wood which has a carpet of bluebells every spring. "Is that going too?"

"Well, I'm sure Mr Baxter will be keeping as many trees as possible, love," says Arthur. "Won't you, Bill?" he adds, looking at Mr Baxter.

"Aye, we'll keep a few. Of course. People like a bit of greenery around. We can't go crazy, mind. Land is money, eh, Arthur?" And Mr Baxter, half winking, half gurning, bursts out laughing even though he hasn't said anything remotely funny.

"I'm not sure," I say, unconvinced by Mr Baxter's bonhomie and roast-ham smile. "It all sounds such a shame. Knocking the farmhouse down and building over the land, I mean."

Mr Baxter looks at me as if I'm a problem (I recognise the look — it's the same one I get from Christine).

"Arthur," says Mr Baxter, turning around and gesturing to Arthur. "Can I have a quiet word?"

They walk a few yards and stand with their backs to me, with Mr Baxter's arm looped over Arthur's shoulder. They're talking but I can't hear a thing. At times like this, I'm jealous of Christine and her radar hearing.

After a bit Arthur turns round and glances back at me. I pretend to be busy with a stick and clod of grass and he turns back round and carries on talking to Mr Baxter. There's a flurry of head shaking (Arthur) and back slapping (Mr Baxter) and then they both finally turn and face me.

"Riiiiiiiiiiiiiight," says Mr Baxter, unnecessarily spreading the word out. "Look, I don't want to keep you both, so do you have any more questions, young lady, before I get going?"

"Yes, what about the cows?" I ask. "What'll happen to them when you build all the houses everywhere? Will they still have a home?"

"The cows?" repeats Mr Baxter, shooting his voice high into the air (just like Christine). He turns and raises his eyebrows at Arthur. "The cows? Eh, she wants to know about the bleedin' cows?" He turns back to me, staring at me with his beady, gammony eyes. "Look, love, let's just say it'll be steak and ale pie all round!"

I stare at him, fighting the urge to push him into the stream and then concrete it over.

Arthur looks across at me. The sun's beaming down onto his lovely blond hair and his butterfly-blue eyes flash. He suddenly seems taller. And broader. A tweedified Yorkshire Viking.

288

"I think it's best if you go now, Bill," he says, cocking his head back slightly. "We'll talk business later. I want to spend some time with Evie first."

"Right you are, Arthur," says Mr Baxter, shaking his head and putting his fat stubby hands into his pockets. "Let's talk later. Just you and me, eh?" He starts walking off. "I'll bring the contract. And, ey, just think of all that money and the new house for you and your dolly bird."

Arthur winces.

"You'd be a fool to miss an opportunity like this," shouts Mr Baxter, heading back towards the farm.

Horrible sausage roll of a man.

Arthur and I go and sit on a big tree that blew down last winter and watch Mr Baxter walk off. Our telepathic antennae are twitching and I can tell he wants to speak to me about Something Important.

"Well, I've known nicer," he says, in a textbook example of Yorkshire understatement. "But his money's good. What he's offering could really help us out, love. You know the farm's barely keeping afloat, don't you?"

I want to mention all the money Arthur spends on Christine but I don't.

"It'd set you up too, love," he adds. "I know the hairdressing didn't work out but if we sold the farm, you'd have enough to get yourself a nice little florists or a dress shop. Or you could train up for something. Typing. Shorthand."

He does his best encouraging smile. I try to respond but I just can't.

"And the farmhouse is old, love," he goes on, pushing his fingers through his hair. "Having one of Bill's new houses makes sense. There'd be no leaks or drafts, no low ceilings or broken floorboards. You'd have a nice big bedroom, really light, with a desk and walk-in wardrobe. You'd have your own bathroom too. Everything'd be new."

"But I don't want everything new," I say, calmly and clearly. I'm looking down at my feet, tracing shapes in the dirt with the tips of my shoes. What I really want is for everything to go back to How It Was Before. Pre-Christine and her man-made fabrics and Tupperware vases. Pre-bingo, burnt teas and wall-to-wall commercial television. Pre-endless talk of weddings and Olympic-scale nagging.

Just pre.

I sigh. A big, fat, shoulder-shaking, belly-emptying sigh.

"But if you think we need to sell the farm," I go on, "that's what we'll have to do. We don't really have any choice, do we? I just want you to be happy, Dad."

Up until now, Arthur had been staring down at his feet too, but when I say this he closes his eyes tight shut and looks like he's in pain.

After what seems like ages Arthur opens his eyes, looks at me and smiles. His eyes are pink and a bit puffy and I suspect he might be coming down with a summer cold.

"There's something I want to talk to you about, Evie, love," he says, reaching out and holding my hand. "Something important. It's about your mother."

This is really strange as:

290

1. Arthur never holds my hand.
2. Arthur never talks about my mother.

He fidgets around a bit, looking even more awkward than usual, and squeezes my hand.

"Is this about the recipe book?" I ask, trying to help out.

"What recipe book?" says Arthur, clearly caught off guard.

"Mum's recipe book, the one with all the amazing recipes in it. Mrs Scott-Pym gave it to me."

Arthur stops staring at his feet and turns to look directly at me.

"Diana's recipe book?"

For a second, the air shimmers and glows.

"Where did that come from?" he goes on. "How did Mrs Scott-Pym get hold of it?"

"Mum lent it to her apparently and it's been sitting on one of Mrs Scott-Pym's bookcases ever since. It's incredible, full of recipes for things like *Lemon Syllabub* and *Asparagus Ice*."

"Diana's recipe book," repeats Arthur, staring at the sky and clearly not really listening to me.

"It's lovely," I explain. "Full of beautiful writing, looping and curling. I wish I could write like that."

Arthur doesn't say anything. I think he's back somewhere in the Olden Times.

"And she stuck in some recipes from old newspapers too," I go on. "But they've all gone a bit yellow and brittle. There's even one from a French paper."

Arthur closes his eyes and laughs. When he opens them, I see that they've progressed from pink to red.

"Yes, that'd be your mother," he says, his eyes fixed on a patch of inconsequential sky. "She could speak French better than a Frenchman, you know. Cook better than one too. She was a wonderful cook, your mother. In fact, she was wonderful at most things."

"That's what Mrs Scott-Pym said when she gave me the recipe book. She said Mum was a real gem," I tell him, even though I still don't think he's really listening to me. "I was going to tell you about the recipe book before but I just wanted to keep it to myself for a bit because I was worried Christine might take it away."

"What's that, love?" he says, time-travelling back to 1962.

"I said I was going to tell you about the recipe book, but I haven't got round to it yet. I was worried Christine would take it away, like she did with all the other things."

Arthur lets go of my hand, puts his head down, closes his eyes (again) and lifts both hands to cover his face. His shoulders bob up and down slightly and he makes heavy breathing noises through his palms.

I'm not really sure what to do.

"Sorry for mentioning the recipe book, Dad," I say. "Was that what you wanted to talk to me about? Or was it something else?"

Arthur doesn't reply. His face is still covered, his shoulders still bobbing, and his breathing still heavy.

"No," he says eventually. "But it doesn't matter, love. Not now. Let's talk later. You stay here and keep the cows company."

And he gets up and walks off, looking over at the house not at me.

Interlude

14 May 1946

Diana carefully placed the wicker basket down on the grass and sat down next to it, folding her long legs by her side. She leant over the basket and peered in. A tiny beaming face, swaddled in a great whorl of cashmere, peered back at her.

She was meant to be in mourning.

The news of her father's death had come out of the blue. A noisy crack breaking years of silence. Mourning wasn't easy, though. Not after being shut out of his life for all these years. And how could anyone mourn when there was Evie? Diana looked down at her baby daughter and smiled. What was it Keats said? Something about a shape of beauty moving away the pall from our dark spirits. Evie was her shape of beauty. Her balm.

"Oi! Are you day-dreaming again?"

It was Arthur, bringing supplies.

"Oh, I think I must have been. Sorry!" said Diana, looking up to see her husband walking towards her.

"You were staring at Evie," said Arthur. "She must have hypnotised you."

"Yes, I think we might have an enchantress for a daughter," said Diana.

"Well, she gets it all from her mother," replied Arthur, sitting down next to Diana and kissing her. He leaned over the basket, looking at Evie. "And how is my lovely little fairy?" he said, bending in and kissing her on the forehead.

"She'll be turning frogs into princes before we know it," said Diana.

"Really? Well, she's not the only one around here who can do magic. Close your eyes."

Diana smiled and did as she was told.

"No peeping," said Arthur, starting to unpack the bag.

She drummed her fingers on her summer-honeyed arms, listening to assorted rustles and chinks, happy to play along.

"Can I open them yet?" she said after a while.

"No! Hold on, nearly there," he replied, taking out the last few items. "Okay, you can open them now."

Diana opened her eyes to see two Scotch eggs, two ham sandwiches, two packets of crisps and two bottles of beer all laid out on one of her best gingham tea towels.

"A feast! Wonderful!"

Arthur smiled broadly.

"It's nothing fancy," he said.

"Nonsense," said Diana. "It's perfect. Just what I wanted."

"Really? You sure you wouldn't rather have some of your fancy French food?"

"Absolutely not," said Diana. She reached for a Scotch egg and took a big bite. "Mmmm, this is good," she said, smacking her lips noisily.

"Hey, did nobody ever tell you it's not polite to speak with your mouth full?" said Arthur. "I thought you were meant to have been brought up a lady?"

"I was, darling," she replied, taking another bite. "And now look at me," she went on, chewing and speaking. "Lady and the tramp."

"Cheeky bugger!" laughed Arthur.

Diana swallowed, took another bite, and then threw the rest of her Scotch egg at Arthur.

"Oi!" he said, ducking out of the way. "I'll tell Mr Jackson what you're doing with his Scotch eggs! Wasting them like that. Just because you've got money to throw around now. It's all right for some."

Diana craned her neck back and looked up at the sun.

"Oh, you're not going to nag me again, are you?"

"Yes," said Arthur. "That's my job."

When Diana's father died, she found that she'd been left a considerable bequest. He hadn't left her everything (his old school and college had got the lion's share plus he'd left other odd bits to various staff and local charities), but she'd still ended up with a large pot of money and countless shares. It had all come as a big surprise to Diana. There'd been no contact with her father for years and so she hadn't expected anything else at all. But then, suddenly, there she was. Rich.

"You can't just leave it all sitting in the bank, love," said Arthur. "Money's like a man. It needs to work."

"I know," said Diana, drawing out the word and rolling her eyes.

"It needs looking after."

"Like the cows, you mean?"

"Very funny. But it's not really something we should joke about, love," said Arthur, reaching over and holding her hand.

"Yes. I know. You're right, of course." She sighed. She really didn't feel like another conversation about the money. "I'll go and see old Mr Anderson about it next week."

Mr Anderson was Diana's father's accountant. He'd been with the family for years, overseeing her father's investments and advising on all matters financial.

"Mr Anderson?" said Arthur. "But he's older than the Dales, love. Things have changed since before the war. It's a different country now. There are new ways to make money. I've told you, you should talk to Bob."

Diana winced. Bob was from Arthur's football days. The club accountant, officially, but he had his fingers deep in many pies, helping the players at the club build up tidy little nest eggs. He seemed to have a knack with money and the whole team trusted him. But Diana wasn't so sure.

"But Mr Anderson is so nice, darling. And reliable. He's practically Victorian. It's like having Disraeli look after the money."

"But that's the problem, isn't it? We're not Victorians any more. It's a new world out there."

"O brave new world that has such people in it," said Diana, having a swig of beer.

"What?" said Arthur.

"Shakespeare," said Diana, suddenly feeling tired. She sighed. "I'm using my expensive education. Just like Mr Anderson does."

Arthur looked at Diana. It was different for her. She was used to money. It came and went but then always came back again. She'd never really wanted for anything. How could she understand?

"I really think you should speak to Bob, you know. He's the right man for this."

"But I just don't like him," said Diana sharply.

"You should give him a chance. All the boys at the club use him," said Arthur. "Mr Barrett and the chairman too. And they both know what they're doing. Bob's got his head screwed on good and proper, you'll see."

"Are you asking me or telling me?"

"Don't be like that," said Arthur. "I'd feel terrible if we didn't get in touch with him. It's not how things are done. You know what it's like at the club. He looks after everyone and he'll look after us too. Bob's our man."

"Can't you just let me get on with it in my own way?" snapped Diana. "I managed perfectly well doing everything by myself all the way through the bloody war."

"I'm just trying to help," he said, shaking his head. "That's all. For God's sake, Diana."

"What?" Diana felt her head throb. "Look, I don't trust Bob. Not with all that money."

298

"You're wrong about him. He might be a bit of a rough diamond but he's a bloody good man and sharp as knife when it comes to money."

"Oh really?" said Diana, raising her voice.

"Yes, he'd be a damn sight better with the money than old Mr Anderson," shouted Arthur. "Remember, it's not just your money," he went on, pointing at the sleeping baby. "It's hers too."

"Do you think I don't know that?" Diana shouted back. "I've told you, I don't trust Bob. And I don't like him either. There's something of the spiv about him."

"Don't be such a snob, Diana."

"You of all people should know I'm no snob," she snapped back.

Silence crackled around them.

"Look," said Arthur, "if you don't call Bob, I will." And he threw his sandwich on the floor and walked off across the field.

Diana watched him go, her cheeks flushed and her eyes red.

CHAPTER
TWENTY

Monday 23 July 1962

"Darling, thank you."

That's Caroline, lounging across the sofa, cigarette in one hand, tiny cup of coffee in the other.

"You're such a clever old thing. I don't know how you thought of it."

It's 9.30 in the morning and I've come next door to see Caroline and pick up her reel-to-reel. She collected it from Mrs Scott-Pym's hospital yesterday and has it primed ready for today's action (Brilliant Plan Number 2). But first I'm being told all about the recording we made for Mrs Scott-Pym (Brilliant Plan Number 1).

"It was wonderful, darling. Mummy listened to the tape as soon as she woke up, over and over again apparently, and there were lots of tears, lots of happy tears."

"Aww," I say, feeling that there may well be some happy tears here soon too.

"Anyway, she called me straight away. We spoke for hours. Oh," she says, wiping her eyes with the little finger of her cigarette hand, "we went over everything, absolutely everything. We must have said sorry a hundred times. A thousand maybe! It really was marvellous. And it's all because of you, darling."

She reaches over and gives me a big kiss on the forehead, putting her tiny cup down on the coffee table while she's at it.

"Well, of course," she goes on, "after all that we just had to see each other so I jumped straight in the car and drove over to the hospital. Mummy was waiting for me in her room and I just threw myself into her arms. And there we were, holding each other, hugging and blubbing."

She wipes her eyes again (with her non-cigarette hand this time). I take the opportunity to have a good eye-wipe too, using the sleeve of my top.

"There was lots of talking, kissing, crying — it was like being back in Italy, darling! Everything came out. All these years of silliness. All the hurt. All the anger. It's all behind us now."

She gestures vaguely in the air, sending little puffy clumps of ash over Mrs Scott-Pym's sofa.

"We're back on an even keel — at last — after all these years. And it's all thanks to you. You really are the cleverest girl in Yorkshire, you know."

And she comes over and gives me a big, grateful, joyful, finally-at-peace hug.

It's lovely.

"Anyway, darling," Caroline says, getting back on the sofa, "enough of all this. We've both got work to do. You've got to take that thing next door," — she points at the reel-to-reel sitting on Mrs Scott-Pym's sideboard — "and I've got to get ready for a guest arriving."

301

"Oh," I say, quite excited by the possible arrival of another Caroline (if such a thing exists). "Is Digby coming up?"

"Digby? No, not Digby, darling. Someone else. You'll meet her soon enough, don't worry. Now, come on, chop chop." She stands up and goes over to the reel-to-reel. "You've got your wicked plan to set up. We need everything ready before the two evil old hags get back!"

"Absolutely," I say, taking the reel-to-reel from her.

"Now, *bonne chance*, darling," she says, kissing me on the cheek. "I'm sure you'll be brilliant. As always."

And off I go. Heading for the farmhouse with the reel-to-reel in my hands and my spirits high in the sky.

Magically high.

I know that Christine and Vera won't be around for a while because today is Monday and Monday morning is shopping morning. They'll both be busy in the village trudging round shop after shop, buying tins of spam and haggling over the price of onions. I want to put the reel-to-reel somewhere in the kitchen because Christine and Vera always come back from shopping and have a brew here, moaning, nattering and gossiping. I'm going to record all their moaning, nattering and gossiping in the hope of finding some incriminating evidence (Brilliant Plan Number 2). So I'm trying to find somewhere to put the reel-to-reel where it can't be seen but can still easily pick up what they're saying.

It isn't easy. At first I thought I'd be able to hide the reel-to-reel in the pantry, but if I just put it there, they'll see it when they put the shopping away. And if I hide it in a box, it won't be able to pick up what they're saying through the box *and* the pantry door. Other places are unsuitable too:

Under the sink (too exposed).

In the bin (too small).

Under the table (too obvious).

It's very frustrating. They never have problems like this on *Z Cars*.

So now I'm tip-toeing on a rickety old chair trying to put the reel-to-reel on top of the kitchen cupboards. Even with my great height, it isn't easy. The machine weighs a ton (it feels as heavy and cumbersome as a new-born calf) and lifting it up to the small gap of space between the cupboards and the ceiling requires the strength of a forklift truck. I struggle for a bit but then give up.

And then I see it. Down below. Christine's horrible new cooker. The turquoise terror. The reel-to-reel looks like it might fit in the oven. Excellent. Christine could be hoist with her own pastel petard.

I open the oven door, take out all the shelves, and, gently, carefully, slide the reel-to-reel in.

It fits.

Bingo.

There's absolutely no chance of Christine and Vera using the oven when they get back because every Monday they pick up a couple of beef dripping baps from Mr Jackson, the butcher, plus a bag of crisps each and a custard tart for afters and have it all (with gallons of tea) as soon as they sit down.

It's a fail-safe plan.

But then I realise that when the oven door is closed, the reel-to-reel won't be able to pick up Christine and Vera's voices clearly. They'll just be echoey muffles (possibly an improvement). I need to find a way to keep the door open enough to let the sound pass through but not open too much so that Christine and Vera notice it.

Hmmm . . .

I push my hands in my pockets (always conducive to a good think).

And there, deep down, like a miraculous holy relic, is where I find it. My Bazooka bubble-gum. The stickiest, claggiest thing known to man.

I've soon got the entire pack in my mouth (the equivalent of chewing a tennis ball) and within a very short space of time three big blobs of well-chewed bubble-gum sit on the inside of the oven door, allowing enough of a gap to record Christine and Vera's voices without risking the door falling wide open.

I am a genius.

Now all I need to do is wait for Christine and Vera to get back.

It's not long at all before I hear the familiar clatter of Christine's kitten heels on the cobbles outside. I've been sat by the oven, ready to strike, ever since I put the reel-to-reel in. I press "record" and gently close the oven door onto the bubble gum then dash round to the other side of the kitchen table, sitting on the chair furthest away from the oven so that Christine and Vera will have to sit as close to the reel-to-reel as possible.

"Oh," says Christine, bag-less, walking in through the open door. "You're here. What are you doing?"

"Hello," I say, mustering up the best smile I can. I'm just about to say more when Vera walks in, carrying two huge bags stuffed full of assorted village fare. She's panting quite heavily and looking very much in need of a chair.

"Oh, Evie," says Vera, managing to sound both surprised and disappointed at the same time. "What are you doing here?"

"Oh, nothing," I say. "I'm just resting."

"Just resting, are you?" says Christine, sitting down and slipping off her shoes. "It's all right for some."

Vera heaves the two shopping bags up on the worktop and then comes and sits down with us. They're both within easy range of the reel-to-reel. Brilliant.

"I said it's all right for some, Mum," Christine goes on, turning round to Vera and gesticulating a thumb in my direction. "Evie, here, lounging around while we traipse round the shops all morning carrying big heavy bags. She's got a life of Riley, hasn't she?"

"Yes, love," says Vera, but I don't think she's really listening as she's busy wiping her forehead with a hanky.

"Oh, it's nice to sit down after being on my feet all morning," Christine goes on, leaning back in her chair and adjusting her bra-strap. "Are you putting the kettle on, Mum? I'm parched."

"Right, love," says Vera. She pushes back her chair and stands up with all the enthusiasm of Eeyore. "I suppose you want one too, Evie?"

"No, thanks, Vera, I'm going out," I say, getting up and heading for the door. "I've got a few things to do."

"Oh, listen to her," says Christine. "She's got a few things to do. What, do you mean things like sitting around on your backside all day reading?"

"Yes," I say, turning round in the doorway. "Very important things like that." And I stride off across the courtyard, wishing I was carrying a book.

I don't go far.

Earlier on, I'd stashed a bottle of dandelion and burdock, some Cadbury's Fruit & Nut, and this week's *Melody Maker* in our barn. Caroline's put a four-hour tape onto the reel-to-reel, which means I've got about three hours forty-five minutes before I need to go back to the kitchen, get rid of Christine and Vera, and retrieve the tape from the oven. This means I can put my feet up, snuggle down on the haystacks and enjoy some much-deserved quiescence (*noun — a state of tranquil rest*).

Three and half hours later (mainly spent doing *Melody Maker*'s "Pop-o-rama" word puzzle) and I'm readying myself for the next part of the plan: getting Christine and Vera out of the kitchen. I have put much thought into this and have come up with a brilliant ploy (otherwise known as a lie). It's going to require some acting skills so I'm trying to remember what I learnt when I played Edith the maid in our school's production of *Blithe Spirits*. I can't remember much to be honest other than it seemed to require a lot of tray carrying.

306

"You'll never believe it," I say, bursting into the kitchen and finding Christine and Vera still sitting at the table (moaning, nattering and gossiping).

They look at me with the welcoming warmth of the Kray twins. "What?" says Christine, curling her lip (but not in an Elvis kind of way).

"It's the rugby team. They're all running around starkers," I say (lie).

"What?" says Vera. "Starkers? What do they want to be doing that for? Silly buggers."

"Are you sure?" asks Christine.

"Yes," I say (lie). "They're over on the rugby pitch now. It's something to do with a bet apparently."

"Come on, Mum," says Christine, standing up and marshalling her chest. "We've got to see this." She's already by the door, tapping her foot. "Are you coming, then?" she goes on, looking impatiently at Vera. "Get a move on. We don't want to miss them, do we?"

Vera grabs her hairnet and scrambles out the door.

"You stay away, Evie," Christine shouts as she canters across the courtyard. "It's not a sight for young eyes. Stick to hockey."

And I hear her and Vera burst out laughing.

I bolt over to the oven and take out the reel-to-reel. It's still turning, one big spool of tape being fed by a tiny little one. Brilliant. I press the stop button and both spools jolt still.

For the next part of the plan, I need to get the reel-to-reel out of the farmhouse and back round to Caroline, so I lug the heavy thing all the way round to

Mrs Scott-Pym's as quickly and surreptitiously as possible (not easy).

When I get there, the kitchen is empty and there's no sign of life other than an ashtray full of cigarette ends, so, still carrying the reel-to-reel, I push open the door to the sitting room with my bum and go in backwards.

When I turn round I'm confronted with the sight of two impossibly glamorous women sitting across the coffee table from each other. One is Caroline (a vision in a sky-blue pinafore dress) and the other must be the friend she mentioned earlier. I stare at them both for a second. Dumbstruck. How can two so incredibly chic people exist in the same space and time?

"Evie, darling," says Caroline, standing up and walking over to me. "There you are! I've just been telling Élise all about you."

Élise. Oh, what a lovely name. It sounds foreign. Or maybe lesbian.

"Here, let me take that for you," Caroline goes on, taking the reel-to-reel from me and putting it on the sideboard. "Now, Élise, I'd like you to meet Evie, Mummy's wonderful neighbour and my marvellous new friend. And Evie, I'd like you to meet Élise, the sweetest, kindest, most magnificent Frenchwoman I know. And I know quite a few, darling."

Élise comes over, says *enchanté* and then kisses me on each cheek. I feel like I'm in a Brigitte Bardot film. This air of sophistication doesn't last long, though, as Sadie, clearly not happy about missing out on the introductions, lollops over and starts rubbing her pink bits on Élise's leg.

308

"Sadie, darling!" says Caroline, pulling Sadie away. "Good grief, whatever will Élise think."

Élise smiles and gestures Gallic-ly with her hands.

Caroline's already back on the sofa, with Sadie close behind her. Soon we're all sat down, Élise on an armchair and me sharing the sofa with Caroline and Sadie.

I can't stop staring at Élise. She's stunning. Her skirt and blouse are the colour of caramel and she's wearing a thin golden belt on her tiny waist with a red-and-blue silk scarf neatly tied round her neck. Her short, wavy hair is like polished mahogany and her skin is tanned and looks like summer. She is glorious, as out of place in our village as an Eskimo.

"Evie's been doing some recording," Caroline says to Élise, pointing at the reel-to-reel.

"Really!" says Élise, with an accent that could melt stone. "And what have you been recording?"

"Cows," I answer.

"Cows?" repeats Élise, looking a bit bamboozled. "Ah, well, you have such nice cows here. I'm sure they moo very nicely."

"Well, not all of them," I say.

Caroline has been busy lighting a cigarette. She passes the lighter to Élise, who takes it with a *merci* and then picks up Caroline's Gauloises from the coffee table.

"Élise is up from London, darling," Caroline says to me. "The cows are all madly exotic for her. She's very kindly come up for a few days to help me get the house ready for Mummy."

"Mrs Scott-Pym! Is she coming home?" I ask. This is Very Good News.

"Yes, darling. On Friday. So it's all hands on deck to get the place ship shape. I dragged poor old Élise up here from her job at the Lycée to help out."

"Oh, what's the Lycée?" I ask, turning to Élise.

"It's the French school," she says. "We teach children how to be good little French boys and girls. We have lessons in grammar, smoking and beret wearing."

"Sounds marvellous," says Caroline.

"And there was definitely no dragging," Élise goes on. "I am a country girl. I do not need much of an excuse to escape from London with all its noise and rush and smoking chim-i-knees."

I look at Élise and Caroline with their Gauloises. Two very stylish smoking chim-i-knees indeed.

"Well, I'm very glad you came, darling," says Caroline. "The only noise you need to worry about up here is Evie playing Adam Faith at full blast with her window open." And she turns and winks at me.

"Oh no, sorry, I had no idea you could hear that," I say, deeply embarrassed. (I'm actually going off Adam Faith to be honest. It's very strange. All I can think about now are the four nice young men from Liverpool.)

"Just pulling your leg. You play your music as loudly as you want, Evie. I can always drown it out with some Strauss." She grins and arches her eyes. "Now, look, we've been gassing all this time and I've forgotten to offer you a drink. How extremely rude of me. Mummy would be furious. Another coffee for you, Élise? And

310

what about you, darling?" she says, turning to me. "Tea?"

Obviously I'd normally have a tea. The drink of the gods. Nectar of the Dales. Liquid gold. But I'm wavering. Something strange is happening. I feel like I've suddenly reached a crossroad, something that will shape me for years to come. Something important and elemental.

I feel like I'm about to choose what kind of a woman I want to be.

I take a deep breath.

"Coffee, please."

"Darling, are you sure?" says Caroline. "I can easily make a pot of tea."

"No, coffee would be lovely, thank you."

"Coffee it is, then!" And she marches off into the kitchen, closely followed by Sadie.

Élise smiles, a beautiful warm smile that fills the room.

I'm momentarily rendered incapable of speech. Apart from Caroline (and Mrs Scott-Pym I suppose, but she's different), I don't know any sophisticated ladies. Or sophisticated men either for that matter. I glance down at the magazines on the coffee table. Mrs Scott-Pym's *The Listener* and *Radio Times* have been replaced by a French *Vogue* and something called *Elle*. This just makes me even more nervous. What on earth are you meant to say to a sophisticated Frenchwoman on a Friday afternoon?

"Are you a lesbian too?" I try.

Élise coughs.

"No, Evie," she says, the cough turning into a laugh. "I was married to a wonderful man but he died ten years ago."

"Oh, I'm sorry," I say. "I hope I haven't offended you, I just didn't know what to say. I always put my foot in it when I'm nervous."

"No, you haven't offended me at all," she says, smiling and shaking her head. "You just surprised me. I always thought that the English were very discreet. You, my dear, could be French."

"Oh, thank you," I say, very happy with the compliment (Caroline's continental ways must be rubbing off on me). "I'd love to be French. All those nice clothes and crusty baguettes. I think I'm probably too tall though."

Élise laughs even more. I'm not sure why. Maybe it's a French thing.

"*Alors*," she says, dabbing at her eyes with a very small hanky. "Caroline always says the Yorkshire people are a different breed from the other English. Now I see that. They are very direct, no?"

"Oh, I don't know. Are we? Dad always says we should call a spade a spade, which, to be honest, I think is a really funny thing to say because what else would you call a spade?"

"*Un bêche*," says Élise, shrugging her shoulders and doing something foreign with her hands.

"*Un bêche*," I repeat, rolling the vowels in my mouth. "It sounds so much nicer in French, doesn't it? Just like food. You probably have much fancier spades in France than the ones over here."

312

"Oh, I don't know. I'm sure your spades are lovely. Like your cows."

We both have a little laugh. I'm feeling much less intimidated now by Élise's sophisticated French ways.

"Have you been to Yorkshire before?" I ask.

"No, this is my first time. I am very much looking forward to seeing it all. The Minster. The Dales. The fish and chips. The Moors. The Heathcliffs."

"Hmmm," I say, trying to think how I can let her down gently. "The Minster, Dales, fish and chips, and Moors are all okay but I'm afraid you might be in for a bit of a disappointment with the Heathcliffs. We don't really have many Heathcliffs up here these days."

"What's all this about Heathcliff?" says Caroline, coming back into the room carrying a tray. "Are the two of you having an intellectual conversion?"

"We're talking about Yorkshiremen," says Élise. "Evie says the Brontes were lying. Yorkshire is not full of Heathcliffs."

"Evie, darling, don't say that," says Caroline, putting the tray down on the coffee table. "You're meant to be flying the flag. You can't say what wonderful cows we have up here but then go on to demean all our lovely menfolk."

"I will go back to London immediately," laughs Élise.

"No, darling, you're staying. Evie doesn't know what she's talking about. She's only got eyes for Adam." Caroline winks at me again and then passes Élise a tiny cup of black coffee. "Milk and sugar?" she asks, turning back to me.

"Er, I'm not sure. How do you take yours?" I say, turning to Élise.

"The French way. Black, two sugars."

"I'll have mine like that then," I say. "Black, two sugars."

"*Bien sûr*," replies Caroline, taking the spoon from the sugar bowl and adding two heaped teaspoons of sugar to the dark brown liquid. Then she takes another teaspoon and stirs it all up before passing me the tiny cup and saucer.

It smells delicious.

Caroline and Élise are busy talking about Yorkshire but I focus on the coffee. There's hardly anything there, just a thimble-full. I give it another stir and then lift the cup up to my lips and have a little sip. The coffee is somehow smoky, bitter and sweet at the same time. Very nice. I have a bigger slurp. Then another. And another. Then it's gone.

"Darling," says Caroline, watching me put the empty cup and saucer back on the tray. "That was practically down in one. And here's me thinking you were a tea-totaller."

Élise laughs. "You see, Caroline, I think Evie is actually French. She could be *une Parisienne*. She is very *direct*. And is *très chic* with her beautiful dark hair and French *pantalon*."

I glance down at my pedal pushers.

"And now we know she likes the French *café* also. Evie is clearly a *femme française*. A *fleur-de-lis* planted in the heart of Yorkshire."

I like Élise a lot.

The conversation swirls round. We talk about loads of things. Bettys cakes. English summers. The Brontë Parsonage. Lipstick. Someone called Bob Dylan. Scottish castles. Spanish painters. The Al. Marilyn Monroe. *Billy Liar*. Hyde Park (London). Central Park (New York). Dry hair.

I keep managing to chip in even though most of the time I've no idea what to say. It's very exciting. When it comes to adult conversations, I'm usually happy to take the Wimbledon approach: quietly watching from the side lines and turning my head from side to side to keep up with all the action. But today I'm down on court, chasing after the ball and even managing a few good rallies. Amazing. I feel like a left-bank intellectual (or is it right-bank?).

After a while, Sadie lets out a big yawn. She's lying down, legs akimbo, on the sofa, her head slouched across Caroline's thighs.

"Darling," says Caroline, looking down at Sadie. "Are you bored?"

Sadie yelps.

"Well, that told us, didn't it!"

Sadie yelps again.

"Actually, I think she's telling us it's time for you to start your homework, darling," says Caroline to me, doing her best schoolmarm-ish look (which isn't very good).

"Homework?" I ask. "What homework?"

"Well, you've got four hours of tape to work some magic with. Sounds like homework to me."

Oh, the tape! Why am I so easily distracted?

"Come on," Caroline goes on, standing up and sending Sadie's head flopping back onto the sofa. "Let's get you started. This is going to take a long time."

She's over by the sideboard, getting the reel-to-reel. As I go and join her, I turn to Élise and say how much I've enjoyed meeting her.

"*Moi aussi*," she replies. "*Un plaisir*. Now, enjoy your cows!"

Caroline takes me to Mrs Scott-Pym's study, a wonderful room stuffed full of books. It's one of my favourite rooms in Mrs Scott-Pym's house but I don't really come very often as we mainly stick to the kitchen or sitting room. The room has a particular smell, old books mixed with good breeding and house plants.

Caroline puts the reel-to-reel down on the desk in front of the large sash window.

"You sit yourself down and get comfortable. I'll be right back." And she leaves the room.

I sit down at the desk and look at the reel-to-reel. What secrets are waiting inside? Am I wasting my time? Would I be better off just listening to the four young men from Liverpool for four hours?

"Here, put these on," says Caroline, coming back in. She's carrying a big pair of headphones. "You'll be able to hear everything so much better, darling. The recording probably won't be great — it's not easy to record from inside an oven. We need to use every resource we have. And these are a very good resource. The best EMI has."

316

She puts them on over my ears. Everything suddenly sounds like I'm underwater.

"There. How do they feel?" shouts Caroline, pointing at her ears.

My ears are squashed and I'm sure I look ridiculous.

"Great," I lie.

"Wonderful, darling. You look fabulous," she lies back.

I sit and roll my neck, weighing up the headphones; all the weight has shifted to the outside of my head, making it feel like my head is hollow (this must be how Christine feels).

"Now, can you remember everything I showed you?" she says.

I nod.

"Good. You know where I am if you need me." And she bends down and kisses me on the cheek and then leaves the room, shouting *bonne chance* and waving two sets of crossed fingers.

I listen to the fuzzy echoey silence for a few seconds and then pick up a pen, take a deep breath and press play.

CHAPTER
TWENTY-ONE

Wednesday 25 July 1962
It's all go here today.

As well as Christine, the wedding, my future, Mr Baxter and the new housing estate, my O level results, Mrs Scott-Pym's herniated disc, global thermonuclear war and my Brilliant Plan Number 2 to worry about, I'm having to deal with an Aesculapian emergency (*adjective — medical; from Aesculapius, the Roman god of medicine*).

I've had to temporarily interrupt my reel-to-reel editing for a humanitarian trip to see Mrs Swithenbank. Last night, I found out from Margaret (who found out from Julie Turner's mum, who found out from Mrs Nyburg, font of all village gossip) that Mrs Swithenbank has been in bed for three days with a bad flu. I want to go and see how she is and try and cheer her up. And with Mrs Swithenbank the best way to do this is with food.

So I spent a very enjoyable couple of hours going through my mother's recipe book trying to find:

1. Something that Mrs Swithenbank will like (I'm

not sure she's quite ready for *Matelote d'Anguille*).

2. Something that I can cook.

This wasn't easy. Most of the recipes in the book seem very complicated and require culinary skills way beyond my usual range of cheese on toast or a poached egg. I also need the recipe to be relatively quick and mess-free as I don't want Christine to know about it (we only children are instinctively secretive and, as far as sharing knowledge of anything with Christine is concerned, less is definitely more). I know that Christine is out this morning (in Scunthorpe seeing a chiropodist on account of her hammer toe), so that gives me a couple of hours to make something for Mrs Swithenbank and clean up afterwards.

After rejecting a lot of unsuitable recipes (*Lièvre à la royale* — too complicated; stuffed quail — too anatomical; Chorley cakes — too Lancastrian), I eventually found the perfect thing: *gougères*. They sound delicious. Substantial and comforting (just like Mrs Swithenbank). The ingredients list, for once, is remarkably short (most of the recipes in the book have an ingredients list that stretches on and on forever, like a Robert Browning poem):

Half a pint of milk
Quarter of a pound of plain flour
2 oz unsalted butter
A pinch of salt
4 eggs

3 oz Gruyere cheese

(I've no idea what Gruyere cheese is so I'm using a bit of everything I can find in the fridge: Cheddar, Wensleydale, Red Leicester, and a small block of Caerphilly that had fallen into the veg drawer.)

It sounds really easy to do, but then again so did nipping out to deliver a few bottles of milk in Arthur's MG, and look what a mess that got me into. Anyway, here goes.

First, the recipe says to heat the milk in a pan (where else?). I'm a dab hand at this as I often make Arthur and me an Ovaltine at bedtime. While the milk's heating, I cut the butter into smallish cubes and then drop them in, giving it all a good stir. Very soon the butter starts to melt, creating a lovely oily yellowy layer on the top of the milk (more mixing at this point). The recipe then tells me to sift the flour into the milk while stirring, not an easy thing to do (people were obviously much more agile kitchen-wise back in my mother's day). Apparently I have to stir until everything sticks together to make one big doughy blob. So I stir
and stir
and stir,
all the time wondering if it wouldn't just be easier to buy Mrs Swithenbank a piece of Parkin and a small pot plant.

My mother's recipe is quite firm with the next instruction — it's time for the eggs, but they must be added one at a time (underlined) and only when the previous egg has been blended in (who knew recipes could be so bossy?). I take the pan off the heat, crack an egg in the mixture and stir. It immediately all goes a bit claggy but the recipe (now reassuring) tells me not to worry if it appears to have curdled — I just need to keep on stirring. So I stir.

And stir

A n d s t i r.

A n d s t i r.

A n d s t i r.

A n d s t i r.

A n d s t i r.

The egg *finally* blends into the mixture. It feels such a shame to have to mess it all up again by adding another one, let alone another three. I'm not sure I've got the energy for it to be honest. By the time I'm done, I'll have arms like Popeye.

But there's no turning back now so I put in the second egg.

(stirstirstirstirstirstirstirstirstirstirstirstirstirstirstirstirstirstirstirstir)

And the third egg.

(stirstirstirstirstirstirstirstirstirstirstirstirstirstirstirstirstirstirstirstir)

And the fourth.

(stirstirstirstirstirstirstirstirstirstirstirstirstirstirstirstirstirstirstirstir)

After the fourth egg has unclagged and disappeared into the gooey mixture (phew), I give my forehead a quick wipe and then add a pinch of salt (so much easier than adding the eggs). Now it's time for the cheese, so I grate some of each type onto the kitchen scales (almost losing a bit of nail on the big metal grater when I do the Caerphilly) and add it to the mixture.

More stirring.

(I honestly can't believe that such a short recipe can require so much hard work.)

Then, using a teaspoon, I deposit little blobs of the mixture onto greaseproof paper, grate a bit more cheese on top (improvising — you can never have too much cheese), and put the baking tray in Christine's oven. The recipe now gets very bossy again. The *gougeres* need to cook for twenty minutes AND THE OVEN DOOR SHOULD NOT BE OPENED IN THE MEANTIME.

Not even for a quick peek.

Twenty minutes is easily long enough to tidy everything up, so I check the time on my Adam Faith wall clock and set to with a dishcloth and some Ajax.

After about ten minutes the most amazing cheesy smell starts to fill the kitchen. This is good because it means that the *gougeres* will hopefully taste nice but also bad because the smell is a dead giveaway that I've been cooking, so I take a page out of Vera's book (a very thin book, probably with pictures) and throw open the door and all the windows to let the room air.

Ten minutes later and I'm hovering by the oven watching Adam's guitar-clock hands tick round. I can't wait. The smell is incredible — I wish Mrs Scott-Pym were here to see it (or rather smell it).

And then it's time.

I open the oven door and, very gingerly, pull out the baking tray.

322

It is baking perfection.

I stare, goggle-eyed, at the thing of beauty in my hands.

Thirty golden balls of sweet dreams and health. I can't believe it. I put the tray down and take one (just to try — cook's prerogative). It's really hot and burns my fingers a bit but it's worth it just for the smell (a heady waft of cheesy balm). I stand smelling the *gougere* for a while longer, then I put it in my mouth, biting into the hot, squishy pastry.

It's *Fromage* Heaven.

I have another bite. Bliss. They are little parcels of pure joy. I could easily wolf them all down right now. But I won't. They are for Mrs Swithenbank in her hour of need. So I load them up into an old biscuit tin and head off.

From the street, Mrs Swithenbank's cottage has a short path, flanked by foxgloves and lupins, leading to her front door (an explosion of climbing roses). I hesitate slightly outside the door and then knock loudly three times.

"Come in, whoever it is," I hear Mrs Swithenbank shout.

I push open the door and walk inside.

The door leads directly into Mrs Swithenbank's sitting room and it's there that I find her, perched on a high-back armchair, in a full-length purple nightie, a frilly lilac hairnet, and a pair of thick woolly socks.

"Evie, love," she says, beaming from ear to ear. "It's grand to see you. Come in. Take a seat." And she gestures over at the empty sofa.

"How are you feeling, Mrs Swithenbank?" I ask, sitting down and making myself comfy.

"Hold on, love. Let me turn the wireless off," she replies, leaning over and turning off the big, old Bakelite set.

"Don't turn it off for me, Mrs Swithenbank."

"Oh, don't worry, love. I'd had enough of it anyway. It was only Val Doonican and his bloody guitar. I wasn't really listening. I only had it on ready for Jimmy Young. Now, what were you saying?"

"I heard you'd been ill," I say, "so I wanted to come round and see how you were."

"Oh, that's right nice of you, Evie, love. Well," she goes on, untucking a lacy hanky out from her sleeve and dabbing at her forehead. "Fair t'middlin' now, thanks. But I've been proper jiggered. I was burning up like a chip-pan a few days ago. I had a dizzy turn and nearly went all my length on t'kitchen floor." She shakes her head. "I'm on the mend now, though. I'll be back in fine fettle soon enough, don't worry."

(I suspect if Mrs Swithenbank were ever to go to London, she'd need to take an interpreter.)

"I've brought you these," I say, passing the biscuit tin to her. "I made them for you just now."

Mrs Swithenbank takes the tin and prises off the lid.

"Oh, they smell lovely," she says, having a big sniff. "What are they?"

"*Gougeres.*"

324

"What?"

"*Gougeres*. They're French."

"Oh, look at you, cooking French food. By, you're a clever lass."

"I found the recipe in Mum's book," I say, blushing a bit. "It was easy, really. I thought they might make you feel better."

"Well, I'm sure they will, love. Ey, I tell you what, how about having a couple now with a nice brew. I'm parched."

"I'll make it, Mrs Swithenbank," I say, getting up. "Milk, three sugars?"

"Oh, you're a good girl, Evie. Aye, milk, three sugars. It's all in the cupboard over the kettle," she goes on, pointing towards the kitchen. "And help yourself to biscuits while you're in there."

"Thanks!" I shout, walking through into the small kitchen at the back of the cottage.

"Sorry it's a bit of mess in there, love," shouts Mrs Swithenbank as I'm filling the kettle. "I've not been able to do any cleaning for days, what with being so off colour."

The kitchen is spotless, like it's just been cleaned and polished by a troop of squaddies.

"It's lovely, Mrs Swithenbank," I reply. "You've got a great view from your kitchen." The kitchen window looks onto Mrs Swithenbank's joyfully blooming back garden and then out across the ancient graveyard to the church.

"Thanks, love," she shouts back. "Aye, it's not bad. How are you getting on in there? Cups and saucers are in the cupboard next to the fridge. Can you find everything?"

"Yes," I shout, getting the tea and sugar out of the cupboard.

"Got them."

"Ey, love, these things you've brought me really do smell lovely, you know. What did you say they were called again?

"*Gougeres.*"

"Oh, yes, that's it. And how do you make them, then?"

"Well, it's flour, eggs, milk and butter," I shout, getting all the tea things ready on a tray. "And lots of cheese. Then you just dollop it all up on a baking tray and pop it in the oven. It's really easy."

"Oh," Mrs Swithenbank says as I walk back into her sitting room with the tray. "Like cheese puffs you mean?"

"Cheese puffs?"

"Aye, the recipe sounds exactly like the one I use to make cheese puffs."

I slump down on the sofa, feeling slightly defeated by the cheese puffs. (Surely all that endless stirring deserves a fancy French name?)

"Anyway, thanks for making the tea, love. You're an angel. It's really good of you to come round, you know."

"It's no trouble at all," I say. "I know how boring being ill is, so I thought a bit of company might be just what you need."

"You're absolutely right there, love," she says, leaning over and pouring the tea. "I had Sheila here from next door earlier, and Mrs Wellburn from number 19 popped round yesterday."

"What about Christine and Vera?" I ask. "Have they not been round?"

"No, they haven't, love," she replies, having a slurp of tea. "Happen they've been too busy with the wedding plans. It's all they blether on about these days."

We look at each other and exchange eye-rolls.

"Speaking of which, how's your dad? Full t'brim with wedding joy?"

I take in the assorted plates, pictures and ceramic ducks ranged across the sitting room wall and wonder how diplomatic I need to be.

"He doesn't really talk about it much, to be honest."

(Unlike Christine and Vera.)

"Aye, well, he's busy with the farm, isn't he. He's got a lot to keep him occupied. Although I bet a herd of cows and a hundred acres are far less trouble than young Christine!"

I smile and pick up my tea, giving it a good stir, while Mrs Swithenbank taps her knee gently with her hand.

"And what about you, love? she asks. "How do you feel about the wedding?"

I stop stirring and put the teaspoon down. It tinkles slightly as it comes to rest on the china saucer.

"I wish it weren't happening, to be honest," I say. "I wish she'd just go away. We don't really get on,

Christine and me. And the funny thing is I'm not even sure Christine and Dad get on that much either."

"I see," says Mrs Swithenbank, still tapping her knee.

"I think Dad would be quite happy to forget about the whole thing," I go on. "But, knowing him, he just doesn't want to cause a fuss or feel like he's letting her down."

"I thought as much," says Mrs Swithenbank. She puts her cup and saucer on the table and reaches out. "Now look. There are some things that can't be changed and we just have to accept them," she goes on, holding my hand and looking me straight in the eye. "Things like gout and tax and your monthly visitation. But then there are other things that can be changed. They might not be easy to change, mind, and we might have to fight like billy-o to change 'em, and it might even bring a few tears along the way, love, but it's not a reason just to leave 'em be and do nothing." She gives my hand a big squeeze. "You're not daft, love. You've got a good head on your shoulders. You know what you need to do."

"Yes," I say, suddenly feeling brim-full of Yorkshire magic. "I know exactly what I need to do."

And we both nod conspiratorially then have a good slurp of tea.

CHAPTER
TWENTY-TWO

Friday 27 July 1962

It's a very special day.

The day Mrs Scott-Pym comes home.

Caroline has gone to pick Mrs Scott-Pym up from hospital and I'm here with Élise helping to get things ready for their return.

We're going to have a garden party, like the Queen. We've moved the kitchen table out onto the terrace and covered it with a beautiful red gingham cloth (perfect for a dress) and I've put out some stripy deckchairs.

The table is weighed down with food from another world. Lots of brightly coloured vegetables, roasted and slathered with a rich, greeny oil. Golden things called *quiche*, which are hot and fill the air with a wonderful cheesy smell. A big bowl of salad made with lentils (lentils! cold! in a salad!). Tomatoes as big as a cricket ball. Great slabs of herby, buttery chicken breasts. Warm, flaky, crispy, crunchy towers of cheese pastry. And lots, lots more. Élise has done most of the work, kitchen-wise, but I've helped out here and there, cheese grating, bowl filling and vegetable washing.

It's been great.

The only downside has been the reel-to-reel, perched on a small table on the terrace. Élise has been using it to play opera, which is very annoying as I've been desperate to put the four young men from Liverpool on all morning.

(I've actually been trying to force myself to like opera ever since I found out Caroline listens to it, but it isn't easy. I just can't get on with it at all. It must be something that comes with age, like gardening or drinking sherry.)

Élise is wonderful (despite the opera). She's charming, funny, and very kind. She's extremely glamorous too, but it's a different kind of glamour to Caroline's. Older. More sophisticated. She's basically Katherine Hepburn to Caroline's Audrey. I found out this morning that she's forty, which was a big surprise. Every forty-year-old woman I know wears a flowery apron and hairnet (not to mention rollers) when cooking; Élise has been wearing a stylish bottle-green skirt and top, diamond earrings and a colourful silk scarf tied elegantly round her head. Amazing.

As I'm putting out a large bowl of grapes, I hear the familiar clod-hop of Christine and her kitten heels.

"What's all that nonsense round the front?" she says, crunching her way across the gravelled terrace, Vera in tow. "Buy-en-ve-noo. Ay, I knew your spelling was bad but not that bad."

"It's French," I say, referring to the banner that we'd hung across the front of the house this morning. "*Bienvenue a la maison*. It means welcome home."

"French?" asks Vera. "French! What on earth have you written it in French for? What's wrong with English?"

"I know," says Christine, shaking her head and tutting.

"It was good enough for Shakespeare and Robin Hood. And anyway, what a waste of time doing anything in bloody French. The French'd all be writing in German if it weren't for us."

"*Bonjour*," says Élise, coming out onto the terrace and carrying a large dish of food. She's doing her room-filling smile but I'm sure she must just want to crack Christine with the dish.

I introduce Christine and Vera to Élise (*enchanté*) and then Élise to Christine and Vera (*ow do*). The atmosphere has all the Anglo-Gallic cordiality of Agincourt.

Each side is holding its weapon of choice. For the French, Élise has a dish filled with beautifully arranged cold meats and cheeses, garnished with some elaborately cut tomatoes and a few sprigs of parsley. For the English, Vera is holding two potatoes wrapped in foil, each with a salvo of cocktail sticks holding an assortment of cheese squares and burnt mini sausages.

Christine takes the foil-wrapped potatoes from Vera, weighs them in her hands like grenades, and offers them to Élise, who, after looking at them quizzically for a second, takes them.

"Ah, thank you," she says, putting the potatoes down on the table with a slight thud. "That is very kind of you. You really didn't have to bring anything."

331

"Well, we wanted to help out," says Christine. "Can't be easy for a foreigner to make proper garden-party food."

"You are too kind," replies Élise (still smiling). "But, as I said, you really shouldn't have."

Christine and Vera survey the table.

"Well, it all looks very . . . interesting," says Christine. "Shame you've got no sausage rolls."

"Hmmmm," says Vera, looking like she's got a mouthful of sour milk. "I could have got some out of the freezer. Never mind."

"And I can't see any pickled onions either," Christine goes on, scowling at the bacchanalian feast laid out on the table.

"That's because they're not there," I say.

"Hmm. Like your naked rugby players," counters Christine, giving me yet another Nasty Look (she has the memory of an elephant). "Is it French?" she asks, turning back to Élise and making being French sound like an embarrassing ailment.

"*Oui*, all French. You English are not the only ones who have *le pique-nique*, you know."

Christine bristles.

"Hmmmm. Well, we know all about French food, don't we, Mum? We went to the Royal Hotel Beverley a few weeks ago. The food was all French. Very oily, mind."

"Aye, and everything swimming in sauce," adds Vera. "Garlic everywhere too. Stank like a sewer."

This is not going well (Christine and Vera have the diplomacy skills of Attila the Hun).

"Where's Dad?" I say, hoping to distract Christine and Vera from their general intolerance of all things French.

Christine rolls her eyes.

"With the bloody cows. Like he always is."

"He won't be long," adds Vera, scowling. "We just thought we'd come round early. Show a friendly face, like."

"That's very kind of you. Although actually," says Élise, putting her hand on my shoulder, "I've had a wonderful friendly face here with me all morning."

"Oh yeah? Who was that, then?" asks Christine.

"Me," I say. Honestly, some people.

"You? A friendly face?" Christine turns to Élise. "What, did you give her a family-size pack of Custard Creams or something?"

"Evie's been helping me get everything ready," says Élise.

"Oh, lucky you," says Christine. "I can't get her to do a thing at home. She's always got her head in a bloody book."

"Well. She is a girl of great intelligence."

"More like great laziness," replies Christine. "Now, would you mind changing this music, please? It sounds like someone's died."

"You don't like *Norma*?" says Élise.

"Who? What about a nice bit of Mantovani? Something bright and jaunty instead of all this doom and gloom. It's like being at church."

"Monteverdi?" asks Élise, cocking her head.

"Yes, have you got any?"

"Er, no, I don't think so. Something Baroque perhaps?"

"What? Look, how about a musical? Anything with a tune."

"Ah, a musical," says Élise. "Yes, Caroline has the *West Side Story*. Hold on a moment." And she heads back into the house to get it.

"Oooh good," says Christine, turning to me and Vera. "I like *West Side Story*. Do you know, loads of people say I remind them of Natalie Wood."

"Oh, yes, love," says Vera. "I can see what they mean."

"Does she have big feet too, then?" I ask.

Christine gives me a Look and then grabs the hem of her skirt and, waving it around like a can-can dancer, starts jumping around and singing.

"*La la la la la America,*
La la la la la America,
La la la la la America,
La la la la la America."

(Possibly the worst advert for musical theatre ever.)

"What's all this?" says Mrs Swithenbank, all in black and waddling round the corner of the house like a giant monochrome penguin. "Was that meant to be the Lambeth Walk?"

"Doris?" says Vera. "What are you doing here?"

"Young Evie invited me," says Mrs Swithenbank, berthing herself onto a deckchair. "I've been as rough as a badger's backside. Not that either of you'd know, mind."

"We've been busy, Doris," says Christine. "We've been sorting out my wedding, remember. There's a lot of work involved with matrimonials, you know."

"Hmmm," says Mrs Swithenbank, clearly unimpressed by Christine's matrimonials. "Well, thank God for young Evie popping round, that's all I can say. You've been brilliant, love," she continues, turning to me. "Very good company. You and the BBC. I haven't heard a dickybird's chuff out of some people," she adds, crossing her arms and staring pointedly at Christine and Vera.

There's an awkward silence. I wonder if the Queen has this problem at her garden parties?

"*Voila*," says Élise, thankfully stepping back outside and waving a reel in the air. "We have the *West Side Story*."

"Élise," I say. "This is Mrs Swithenbank."

"Call me Doris, love," says Mrs Swithenbank, getting up from her deckchair. "Everyone else does — except Evie, that is."

"Ah, Doris. I am so glad you could come," says Élise, holding Mrs Swithenbank's hands in hers. "Evie has told me all about you. You have the Paris style, no?" she goes on. "The sophisticated lady in black."

"Oh, do you think so, love?" She beams a large smile. "Well, I like to look my best."

Christine looks livid. Élise, understandably, has not commented on either her gaudy pink bouffant dress or Vera's nondescript cloud of brown.

"Sophisticated? She's been wearing the same black dress since 1916," says Christine. "It was war-issue, wasn't it, Doris?"

"Better than whore-issue," says Mrs Swithenbank, under her breath but still loud enough for us all to hear.

"Ladies, can I get you all a drink?" asks Élise, proving to be a far better diplomat than either Christine or Vera.

The Byzantine complexity of getting a group of Yorkshire women a brew defuses the tension; the never-ending permutations of which tea, how much milk, how many sugars, and how long to leave the tea brewing seem to go on forever. In the middle of it all, Arthur finally arrives.

"Sorry I'm late," he says, skimming along the gravel.

He's wearing an open-neck shirt under his best tweed sports jacket and his blonde hair glistens with Brylcreem. I feel a thump of pride.

He nods at Christine and Vera, says hello to Mrs Swithenbank, and then turns to Élise.

"This is Élise, Dad, Caroline's friend from London. And this is my dad, Arthur," I say to Élise. They smile at each other and shake hands.

"What's that?" says Christine, pointing at a bottle in Arthur's other hand.

"Some champagne. I thought it'd be nice for Rosamund, you know, to welcome her home properly."

He passes the bottle to Élise.

"Champagne! Oh, look at Mr Rockefeller." Christine rolls her eyes. "Last of the big spenders."

Élise has been looking at the label.

"*Mais non!*" she exclaims. "This is from my home town!"

"Really?" says Arthur. "You're from Beaumont-sur-Vesle? I was there in the war for a few months. That's why I picked it!"

"*Oui*, Beaumont-sur-Vesle!" says Élise, throwing her arms up in the air.

"*C'est un très beau village*," says Arthur.

"*Merci, vous êtes trop gentil.*"

"*Mon plaisir*," replies Arthur, now blushing slightly.

"*C'est merveilleux.* Very kind. *Si jolie.*"

Christine doesn't look happy. She swings past Vera and barges in between Arthur and Élise.

"All right, all right. Stop showing off," she says, glaring at Arthur and grabbing his arm.

Arthur winces.

"I think you'd better learn how to speak English proper, Arthur, before you start beggaring around in French. Honestly," she goes on, turning to Élise and shaking her head, "you can't get a word out of him most of the time but look at him now. Rabbiting away."

"I was just saying what a lovely place Beaumont-sur-Vesle is," says Arthur, not really looking at Christine. "Very beautiful. And very nice food too if I remember rightly."

Élise smiles at Arthur and does something French with her eyes.

Christine (our very own Jodrell Bank) spots this and weaponises her chest.

Arthur, meanwhile, looks like he's subtly trying to pull his arm away from Christine but she's got a grip like a bench clamp. I think it's time I helped out.

"Dad," I say. "Would you mind helping me move the garden bench? Caroline said we should bring it over near the table."

"Of course, love." He tugs his arm away from Christine. "Happy to help. *Excusez-moi*," he adds as he passes Élise.

As we walk off down the garden to get the bench, he puts his arm round my shoulders and whispers, "Thanks for that, love. Do you know what, sometimes you're almost as useful as a *Yorkshire Post*."

Five minutes later and we hear the sound of a very fast car coming tearing down the drive followed by a manic burst of car horn.

They're back!

We dash round to the front of the house and find the Mini parked haphazardly near the front door.

"Hullo," shouts Caroline, getting out of the car. She's wearing a really (*really*) short black dress and has her hair piled up on top of her head. All this finished off with some ballet pumps and a huge pair of sunglasses.

"Here she is," she goes on, running round and opening the passenger door. "The star of the day!"

And Mrs Scott-Pym, helped by Caroline, steps out of the car.

"Oh, what a fuss!" says Mrs Scott-Pym, steadying her feet on the gravel. "You really shouldn't have."

"Welcome home," we all shout.

"Thank you, everyone," says Mrs Scott-Pym. "It's lovely to be home again. And thank you all for keeping an eye on my disorderly daughter."

338

"Mummy, charming!" says Caroline, giving Mrs Scott-Pym another kiss.

Mrs Scott-Pym turns to me and holds out her arms. "Evie, my dear. Come here!"

I go and put my arms around her and she hugs me tight and I hug her tight. She's lovely and warm and I can feel her heart beating through her jacket.

"I have to say an enormous thank you for your wonderful recording," she whispers, her arms wrapped around me. "You are a marvellous, clever child. As wise as time." She kisses me on the forehead.

I squeeze her. And then squeeze her even more.

"It's so good to have you back, Mrs Scott-Pym," I say.

She puts her hand on my head and gently strokes my hair.

"Well, I'm home now, dear. And we've got a lot of cake-eating and book-reading to catch up on. Oh!" she says, looking up at the banner and laughing. "However did you manage to get that up there? *Bienvenue à la maison* indeed!"

Back round on the terrace, Mrs Scott-Pym has two things waiting for her.

The first is all the food laid out on the table ("Oh, look at this! It's marvellous! You really shouldn't have!").

And the second is Sadie. Up until now Sadie has remained firmly within dribbling distance of the food, staring at it as if it had magical hypnotic powers. But as soon as she hears Mrs Scott-Pym's voice, Sadie goes berserk. She yelps and then darts over to Mrs Scott-Pym, running round and round and jumping up in a big messy ungainly display of acrobatics, showering spittle and gravel everywhere. The yelping turns into howling and she suddenly bolts off down the garden and races back again before shooting into the borders and peeing on Mrs Scott-Pym's hollyhocks.

"Sadie!" shouts Mrs Scott-Pym, giving Sadie a big kiss and a very vigorous rub.

"Darling, calm down," says Caroline (I think to Sadie but with Caroline you can never be sure).

"She's missed you," I say to Mrs Scott-Pym.

"Oh, she's had you and Caroline, dear, running around after her. She doesn't need me." Mrs Scott-Pym bends down and takes Sadie's head in her hands. "She's only interested in me because she wants to know when the baking's going to start again, aren't you, dear?"

"Mummy!" says Caroline, clicking her fingers. "You've just reminded me about something. Hold on a sec. Back in two tics." And she disappears off round the front of the house.

Mrs Scott-Pym watches her go.

"Oh, it's good to be back," she says, looking around at everyone and smiling. By now, we're all sat round the table. Mrs Scott-Pym's at the head, with me next to her. The others are split into two groups: Mrs Swithenbank and Élise on one side of the table and Christine and Vera on the other. Arthur, I think, has spotted the obvious danger of the seating arrangement and is busy inspecting the flowerbeds.

340

Mrs Scott-Pym leans over to me.

"You've made a big impression on Caroline, dear," she says.

"She's wonderful." I reply. "I love having her here. It's like having a little piece of London in the village. Everything seems more exciting. Do you think she'll be coming up more often now?"

Mrs Scott-Pym pauses and looks down the garden.

"Do you know what, dear, I think she probably will."

And we both sit back for a moment, smiling and taking in the warm summer scene.

"Here we are," says Caroline, coming back from wherever she disappeared to.

She's carrying a big box with Bettys written on the side (the very best kind of big box).

"I left it in the car," she says, putting the box down on the table. "How could I forget!"

"Oooh, Bettys, love," says Mrs Swithenbank. "Very nice."

Élise leans over and looks at the box.

"Ah," she says. "It is the famous Yorkshire baker, non?"

"Yes, darling," replies Caroline. "Home of the deluxe vintage port and ale fruit cake." She looks at Christine. "Prize-winning, I gather."

Christine stares back at Caroline. Neither blinks.

"Caroline, dear. You're spoiling me," says Mrs Scott-Pym, reaching out and holding Caroline's hand.

"Well, you haven't seen what's inside yet. It might only be a scone."

341

"It'd be a bloody big scone, love," says Mrs Swithenbank.

"Aye," says Arthur. "Looks like we'll be needing more jam and clotted cream, Rosamund."

Everyone laughs (except Christine).

"Evie, I think you should open it," says Caroline, pushing the box across the table towards me.

"Oh yes, dear," says Mrs Scott-Pym. "Go on."

I unfold the tabs and then gently slide the lid upwards.

"Ta-dah!" I say, pushing back the lid and revealing a huge cake with the words *Welcome Home* iced across the top.

"Oooof," says Christine, our very own deflating balloon. "What a funny colour for a cake. What would you call it? Ruby?"

Caroline looks at Christine and smiles.

"No, scarlet."

The next hour is a delicious blur of food and bonhomie. Highlights include Vera going at a plate of French ham with the speed and destructive efficiency of lightning. Sadie jumping up and running off with all the cheese straws. Arthur expertly popping the champagne cork. Caroline toasting Mrs Scott-Pym and Mrs Scott-Pym almost crying. Mrs Swithenbank laying waste to three slices of the scarlet cake plus some extra icing.

And, throughout it all, Christine sits glowering like a monkfish.

342

"Right, everyone," I say, standing up. "I think it's time for some different music, don't you?"

A wave of nods surges round the table. (There's only so much *West Side Story* you can take on a sunny afternoon in the East Ridings.)

"I hope you're putting on something cheerful," shouts Christine, frowning.

"Yes," I say, walking over to the reel-to-reel machine. "Very cheerful."

I get a tape-reel out of my pocket, loop it onto the machine and press play.

There's a few seconds of silence, then a bit of crackle and fuzz, then the harmonica comes in and then the drum and then the four young men from Liverpool start singing. It's glorious. Caroline is swaying her head and Élise taps her hand on the table in time to the beat. Everyone (even Christine) looks happy.

"Oh, what's this, love?" shouts Mrs Swithenbank. "It's smashing."

"They're new," says Caroline. "From Liverpool."

"Liverpool?" replies Mrs Swithenbank. "Well, they're not bad for a bunch of scousers."

We all sit listening to the song. Even after hearing it hundreds of times, it still sounds bright and exciting, like the start of something new.

Then, all of a sudden, the harmonies of the four young men from Liverpool are replaced by the appalling wails of Christine singing "Kiss me, Honey, Honey, Kiss me". It's the aural equivalent of going from a slice of Élise's golden quiche to one of Vera's burnt cocktail sausages.

"Ey, that's me," shouts Christine. "Don't I sound good? Like Shirley Bassey."

(Perhaps the noise Shirley Bassey might make if someone were gouging her eyes out.)

Thankfully we only get the first verse before a new voice steps in.

It's Vera.

"*Ere, love. Do you know you're nearly out of loo rolls?*"

"It's you, Mum! Listen to you," says Christine, pointing at Vera. "Hey, you sound really funny."

"What's going on?" shouts Vera. "How the bleeding hell did that get on there?"

I know exactly how that got on there. I spent much of the weekend editing the four hours of Christine and Vera talking in the kitchen into a five-minute bouncing bomb. This is going to be fun.

The tape goes on.

"'*Course I know who's prime minister, Mum*," says Christine. "*Do you think I'm stupid? What do you think I've got between my ears?*"

"*Loo rolls*," answers Vera. "*Loo rolls, loo rolls, loo rolls.*"

"Wait, I didn't say that," says Vera.

"What's going on?" asks Christine, turning to me. "What's happening?"

I give her my best Cinderella smile.

"It's called splicing."

"You what?"

"To splice," I explain. "Verb. To unite two lengths of magnetic tape by overlapping and securing together."

She scrunches up her face and looks, not for the first time, completely clueless.

On the tape, Vera and Christine are talking.

"*I'm a . . . loo roll,*" says Christine.

"*You're a big . . . loo roll,*" says Vera.

Then the tape crackles a bit and we hear Christine interspersed with Vera:

"*She's got a life of Riley . . .*

Our Christine

Sitting around on her backside all day . . .

Our Christine

It's all right for some . . .

Our Christine

Are you putting the kettle on, Mum?"

Around the table, everyone's beginning to chuckle. Well, everyone except Christine and Vera.

"What the bloody hell's going on?" snaps Christine, growing more scarlet by the second. "That was a private conversation I'll have you all know."

"*Hey love, I wonder what Doris is up to? We haven't seen her for a while.*"

"Oi, stop the bloody tape," shouts Vera.

"Leave it be, Vera," says Mrs Swithenbank. "I want to hear this."

"*Doris!*" exclaims Christine on the tape. "*Don't talk to me about Doris. She can be a right nightmare.*"

"*Oh, I know, love. She's always been a bit of a handful.*"

"*I don't want her coming to the wedding, Mum. Her and her bloody bowel. She's embarrassing. Size of an* ostrich and the brains of one too. And she's dead common."

"Turn. It. Off," says Christine, getting up. She looks like she's wants to throttle me.

"You sit right back down, young lady," says Mrs Swithenbank, standing in front of Christine and pushing her back onto her chair. "Dead common, am I? Happen we might all learn something here."

The tape goes on. We're all listening to every word. It's like the Queen's Christmas speech.

"*Where do you want your Custard Creams, love?*" says Vera.

"*Same place as usual, Mum, where do you think? I've told you, if you stick 'em in the biscuit cupboard, Evie'll have the lot.*"

"*Right, they're in the bottom drawer, love.*"

"*Good. I don't want that annoying little madam getting her hands on them.*"

Around the table, there's a sharp communal intake of breath.

"Well it's true," Christine says, pulling a face that reminds me of the gargoyles at York Minster. "She's like a bloody gannet."

Arthur turns and looks at Christine but says nothing.

Back on the tape, Christine's voice is looping around.

"*Annoying little madam. Annoying little madam. Annoying little madam . . . Do you know what, Evie's really getting on my nerves.*"

"*Oh, yes,*" says Vera. "*You need to show her who's boss, love.*"

"Just wait till after the wedding. Things'll be very different. I'm not having her moping around my lovely new house. I want her and all her bloody stupid books gone, out from under my feet. She can sling her bloody hook."

Christine looks like she'd like to slip off but Mrs Swithenbank is standing guard behind her, a one-woman mountain range.

The tape continues. There's a couple of seconds of static buzz and then we're back to Christine.

"No, of course I don't love him. Don't be daft."

"Not even a bit, love?" asks Vera.

"Well he's harmless enough I suppose. I'll tell you what I do love, though. The chocolates, and the new dresses, and all the trips out to the races. And I love my new cooker. And new freezer. And I'll tell you what I'll REALLY love. My lovely new house and its lovely big garden."

"And don't forget about the lovely big bank account, love!" adds Vera, cackling.

"Oh yes, don't worry. I'll find out where he's stashed all his cash if it kills me."

"You've a right to know, love. It's your money too."

"I know. Exactly. It's my money. I bloody deserve it with all him and his idiot daughter put me through. Once I've got that ring on my finger, things'll change. Now, are you going to make me another brew?"

There's another crackle and then we hear Christine singing one last time.

"Ta-ra-ra-boom-dee-a
Arthur's money's coming my way.

Ta-ra-ra-boom-dee-a

Arthur's money's coming my way.

Ta-ra-ra-boom-dee-a

Arthur's money's coming my way."

The tape comes to an end and the empty spool flicks round and round, again and again. *Flick, flick, flick, flick, flick.*

Everyone is looking at Christine.

There's a stunned silence, like when snow sucks away all the sound.

Arthur's face is a collage of emotions (all of them bad).

"I think you should see these too," I say, passing two pieces of tatty paper to him.

"What are they?" says Christine, her face so red that her forehead looks like an angry slice of corned beef.

"Well, one of them looks like a list of my bank accounts," says Arthur. "And my Post Office savings. Pension. Premium Bonds. Green Shield stamps. Everything." He shakes his head. "Everything. All in the same handwriting."

He holds the paper in his hand and looks over at Christine (who's busy looking down at the floor).

"And then the other one," he goes on, scrutinising the second piece of paper, "is a receipt for a deluxe vintage port and ale fruitcake from Bettys." He flicks the paper with his fingers. "The day before the village fete."

There's another sharp intake of communal breath.

Arthur stares at Christine.

348

Christine looks up from the floor and stares back at Arthur. The only sound is Sadie's tail wagging against Mrs Scott-Pym's leg.

Clomp. Clomp. Clomp.

"I think you'd better leave," says Arthur, crossing his arms.

"Leave?" says Christine, bristling herself up to her full height (5ft 7). "Of course I'm leaving. Who'd want to stay all afternoon with you old fuddy-duddies? The food's bloody awful anyway."

"No, I don't just mean leave here," replies Arthur. "I want you to leave the farmhouse."

"What?" says Christine.

"I want you to leave the farmhouse. As soon as possible. I don't want you under the same roof as Evie."

Christine glares at Arthur.

"Ey, you can't do that, Arthur," says Vera. "It's Christine's home."

"Actually, Vera," says Arthur, "it's Evie's home. She owns the farm. It was Diana's and now it's Evie's. It was all left to her."

What?

"Evie's?" says Christine. "It was all left to Evie? It's *Evie's* farm? Not yours?"

She looks even more confused than normal.

(Although to be fair, I'm pretty confused too.)

"But what about the wedding?" she goes on, turning back to Arthur.

"It's off," he says, shaking his head again. "There won't be any wedding. I've been a bloody fool."

"Off!" shouts Christine. "You can't do that."

"He just has, darling," says Caroline, flatly.

Christine stands up, grating her chair across the gravel.

"Come on, Mum, we're off. We're not hanging around here with this lot. And you needn't worry about calling off the wedding, Arthur," she says, jabbing a scarlet finger at him. "No farm. No wedding."

Vera stands up. She's obviously trying to muster as much dignity as possible but it's difficult when you're the mother of someone who's just been exposed as a horrible, gold-digging old cow.

"Are you coming, Doris?" she asks.

"I'm bloody not," replies Mrs Swithenbank, picking up a tea towel and mopping her forehead. "I'm staying right here. And you can stuff your bingo nights. Rosamund's going to teach me bridge."

Mrs Scott-Pym looks at Christine and Vera and smiles a devilishly sweet old-lady smile.

"Well, you stay here with Mrs Fancy-Pants and her bloody foreign friends, then," shouts Christine. And she storms off across the terrace, with Vera close behind her.

After three steps, she turns round and yells,

"You can send my cooker round to Mum's."

Then another step.

"And the freezer."

Then another step.

"And the leather pouffe and cut-crystal Perry wine glasses."

Then they disappear round the corner of the house.

Gone.

"And all the bloody Tupperware too," we hear a faint, dismembered voice shout.

And then — finally — there's silence.

Arthur reaches over and puts his arms round me.

"I'm really sorry, love," he says, giving me an enormous, gigantic hug. "For everything."

"Don't worry, Dad," I say, folding myself into his arms. "It's okay."

As he hugs me, he rests his head against my cheek and I can smell his woody, leathery aftershave and feel his body gently shaking.

We all sit and look at one another. What a day.

"*Alors*," says Élise, doing a Gallic shrug. "And to think you English say the French are dramatic."

It's later on that evening and I'm sat in Mrs Scott-Pym's garden with Caroline. It's just the two of us; everyone else is in Mrs Scott-Pym's sitting room drinking sherry and talking. Outside, the bright daytime blue is slowly blurring to a velvety evening navy. The lights are on in the house and, high above us, the stars are beginning to prick the sky.

It's been a very strange afternoon.

Arthur has been a torrent of apologies. Apologies to Mrs Scott-Pym for the scene, the shouting, and the bad language. Apologies to Caroline for spoiling the lovely welcome home that she'd prepared. Apologies to Mrs Swithenbank for Christine's and Vera's nastiness. Apologies to Élise for spoiling her *pique-nique* and for his "appalling" French. And apologies to me for everything. For letting Christine barge into our lives. For letting her take over our home. For letting her boss me about. For being "no fool like an old fool". For not listening to me more. For not talking to me more. For not being with me more. For being "a terrible dad".

I told him not to talk rubbish, of course.

He's the perfect dad for me. We're a team, I reminded him. Maybe more Bridlington Town than Manchester United, but a team nevertheless. That made his eyes go red. Mrs Scott-Pym helped cheer him up, telling him again and again that he'd done the right thing now and that was all that mattered. But what really cheered Arthur up was Élise fussing round him all afternoon. By the time everyone went inside, he seemed like a new man, handsome and proud. A blond Yorkshire Viking.

Out in the garden, the moon is hanging low and big, so low and big that you can see all its shaded contours, like an Ordinance Survey map.

Caroline and I are lying on the daisy-spotted grass staring up at the evening sky. Our heads are almost touching, crown-to-crown, and our long legs stretch out like the hands of a clock (twenty to three).

"Darling?" asks Caroline.

"Yes?"

"How much do you know about your mother?"

A smile breaks out across my face.

"Well, I know she was tall and beautiful and elegant and spoke French and was kind and funny and liked

352

navy blue but didn't like celery. And now I know that she left me the farm."

"Mmm," says Caroline. "Nothing more?"

"Well, no, not really. Why?"

Caroline shifts her legs.

"Oh, nothing really. It's just that I found something at the bottom of one of Mummy's drawers when I was getting the house ready for her to come back."

"What? Something of Mum's?"

"Sort of."

I want to ask more but with (im)perfect timing, Sadie comes bounding out of the house and makes straight for Caroline, mounting her legs and giving her face an enormous lick.

Caroline yells and pushes Sadie away but Sadie, obviously in the mood for fun, jumps up again. She pushes her face into Caroline's and gives her another enormous lick. Caroline yells again (half scream, half laugh) and grabs Sadie, tickling her pink bits, before hoisting her up on her chest and rolling around on the grass together, yelping, howling, tickling and licking.

"Oh, I'm exhausted," says Caroline, when they've both calmed down a bit. "And I think Sadie's hungry. I'd better nip inside and get her some of that delicious quiche. I'll be right back, darling. Hold on."

And she runs into the kitchen, closely trailed by Sadie and her slobber.

I lie back down on the grass and look up at the stars, tiny little beads of light on a vast cloth of inky blue sky. In the next field I can hear the cows and their bedtime chorus and from somewhere inside the house come the sounds of people talking and glasses chinking.

The perfect end to a perfect day.

I stretch out my arms and legs and make angel wings on the grass for a moment or two. Then I roll over onto my side and look down Mrs Scott-Pym's garden, taking in the lupins and the delphiniums and the lavender.

And then I notice that, nearby, on the grass where Caroline and Sadie were playing, there's a folded-up piece of brown newspaper.

Obviously I should just leave it there. Caroline can get it when she gets back. It's not doing any harm lying on the grass . . .

I try not to look at it.

The paper sits there, shouting.

I reach over and pick it up. It feels old. Brittle and crisp. I try to see the date but the paper's folded up and the only things I can make out are a photo of some soldiers and an advert for Pears soap. I'll just have a quick look in. I'm sure Caroline wouldn't mind. It can't do any harm.

I unfold the paper carefully, crease by crease, flattening it out as I go.

Released, the headline roars its terrible news.

And at that moment the stars stop shining and the sky becomes burnt black.

Interlude

17 May 1946

Diana looked at the door.

It certainly wasn't what she'd expected.

She'd last met Bob Greenwood before the war. A rough diamond, Arthur called him; more like a wide boy, thought Diana. Either way, he was definitely not the type to have an office on "The Mount". She knew the area well, of course. It was York's 8th Arrondissement, its Kensington, a Georgian boulevard of old money and good taste. So how on earth had he ended up here? He'd clearly had a good war.

"Can I help you?" asked a small, middle-aged lady sitting behind a mahogany desk.

"Yes, I'm Mrs Epworth," Diana replied, smiling. "I'm here to see Mr Greenwood."

The lady, rather mousey with a tight-set head of curls, looked down at a large diary on her desk then back up at Diana and asked her to take a seat.

"Diana!" said Bob, coming into the waiting room and holding his hands out like Christ the Redeemer. "How lovely to see you again after all this time.

"Well, it's lovely to see you, too, Bob," replied Diana.

"You're looking wonderful," said Bob, giving her an exaggerated wink. "But then you always did."

Diana smiled politely. He hadn't changed at all, she thought. The oiliness was still there. The casual, easy glibness.

"You look even younger than when we last met," he went on. "Now, then, when would that have been?"

"Oh, I don't know," said Diana. "Sometime before the war."

"June 1939," said Bob, pointing his finger at Diana. "The York City chairman's wedding. Seven years ago!"

"And what a seven years," replied Diana, dealing with the broad sweep of the war's destruction and human misery in one understated phrase. "You seem to have done very well since then," she added, looking around the room.

Bob grinned.

"Well, I haven't done bad for myself, have I? And what about you and Arthur? A life on the farm, eh? Who'd have thought it!"

"We both love it. Arthur's become a real country gent. And now we've got Evie too, of course."

"Of course," said Bob. "Arthur told me about your little girl when he telephoned. He's very been on having all this money of your father's looked after for her."

Diana smiled again, not really feeling that Bob was striking the appropriate tone.

"Well, you've come to the right place. They don't call me Mr Money for nothing, you know. Now, shall we go into my office and talk about this a little more privately?" he said, gesturing with an open hand towards his office door.

It was too late to back out now, thought Diana. But she didn't have to sign anything today. She could go and see nice old Mr Anderson next week and instruct him to act on her behalf. Arthur would understand. Club connection or no club connection. She'd just get the next hour out of the way and then that would be that.

"Yes," she said. "Let's do that."

Bob walked Diana over to his office door, his hand on her back, guiding her like an animal at an agricultural show.

"You go in and make yourself nice and comfortable. I just want to have a quick word with Miss Gorse."

Diana walked into Bob's office, pleased to free herself of his hand.

Bob sidled up to his secretary's desk.

"Thanks, Mabel, love," he said, playing with his tie. "That'll be all for today, then. As I said, you get yourself off and have half a day on me. Go and have a look round the shops. I won't be needing you this afternoon. It'll just be me and Mrs Epworth."

And he strode into his office, rubbing his hands.

Miss Gorse sat for a moment then picked up her handbag and stood up. She was getting used to these little afternoons off. Another shopping trip. Perhaps she'd go to Browns. She could have look at the knitting patterns and maybe go for a scone in the cafeteria and then try and pick something up for tea.

Diana hovered by a chair in front of the large desk, waiting for Bob. His office was just how she expected it. Grandiose and flash. The office chairs were voluptuous and full-figured, their deep leather seats built for show not comfort. In the middle of the room hung an elaborate chandelier, more suitable for a room twice the size. And near the large sash windows was a chesterfield sofa, kept company by an ugly green onyx coffee table and a couple of leather armchairs.

"Oh, I thought we'd sit by the window," said Bob, walking in behind Diana. "It's cosier than being at the desk," he went on, taking Diana's hand and guiding her towards the sofa. "I hope you don't mind but I asked Miss Gorse to put out some gin and tonic. I thought we could have a friendly chat before we got down to business. No rush, is there?"

"Thank you," said Diana, already wondering when she could make a polite exit. "But tonic water will be fine. I need to keep a level head when it comes to talking about money!"

"Oh, a drop won't do any harm," said Bob, pouring some gin into each glass. "Just a sniff. It'll help oil the cogs. It's been seven years since we last met. I think we both deserve a drink, don't you?"

"Well, if you insist," said Diana, removing her gloves and taking a glass from Bob.

"Cheers, then." He held his glass in the air. "Here's to making lots of money for you all."

"Cheers," said Diana, forcing herself to smile.

358

"Well, it's nice to relax, isn't it?" said Bob, leaning back and making himself comfortable. "It's been non-stop ever since VE Day."

"Yes, it must be good to be busy. I suppose now that the war's over, people are wanting to get their finances in order. We're all thinking about the future again."

"Well, nice Mr Attlee's given us all a new future, hasn't he? A new Eden apparently. And that means lots of new opportunities, Diana." He leant over towards Diana, fondling his glass. "New ways to make money. We'll make sure your little girl's going to do all right out of Mr Attlee's new Eden, don't you worry."

Diana smiled politely again, sitting bolt upright and holding her glass in both hands.

"But we said we'd have a little chat, didn't we, before we got down to all the serious work?" continued Bob, still leaning over towards Diana. He slid his hand back and forth over the slippery leather sofa as if cleaning it. "Good to hear all's well out on the farm."

"We love it," said Diana. "It's hard work, of course, but we've settled into a routine."

"Yes, I've heard life out on a farm can be hard. It's proper graft for Arthur. I bet you don't get to see that much of him."

"Well, we manage. I ran the farm during the war so we tend to work things out together most of the time."

"Right, I see," said Bob, inching forwards. "But I bet it can be isolating, can't it? Living out in the middle of nowhere. Far away from the bright lights of York."

"No, not really," she replied, quickly. "We're lucky. We're in a little village with lovely neighbours. It's not isolating at all."

"Oh, village life! I've heard all about that. Three dozen cows and a village idiot — must be hard for a sophisticated young lady like yourself?"

Diana looked at the small beads of sweat on Bob's forehead and remembered how much she had disliked him.

"Well, one can find a village idiot almost anywhere these days," she said, trimming her smile.

Bob stopped sliding his hand on the sofa.

"But don't you find you miss company?" he said.

"Company?" asked Diana, taking a sip of her G&T.

"Aye, company," replied Bob. "All those parties and balls before the war. All the champagne. All the attention," he went on, reaching out and putting his arm across the back of the sofa.

Diana looked at Bob; he held her stare.

"All that male attention. Fussing around you. I'm sure you must miss it."

He leant forward and tried to pour some more gin into Diana's glass.

"No, really, Bob. Thank you," said Diana, pulling her glass away. "There's quite enough here already."

"Don't be such a spoilsport," said Bob, moving the bottle to follow the glass in Diana's hands. "Here, just have a little bit more."

He tried to tip some gin into Diana's glass but missed and a splash of gin fell onto her dress.

"Oh, blast, I'm sorry," said Bob, moving closer.

360

"It's quite all right," replied Diana, dabbing at her dress with her hand.

Bob took a handkerchief out of his pocket and placed it on the damp patch of gin, pressing his hand down firmly on her thigh.

"It's really not a problem," said Diana, putting her glass back down on the ugly onyx table. "It's just an old dress."

She glanced at her watch.

"Oh you needn't worry about time," said Bob. "We've got all afternoon. Plenty of time to get down to business."

Bob's hand was still pressing down on Diana's thigh.

"Actually," said Diana, wriggling away, "I think perhaps I'm having second thoughts. I'm really quite a cautious investor; it's something I get from Daddy. I don't think I'm ready to help build the new Eden."

Bob moved closer, taking both her hands in his.

"Well, I don't think you need to go just yet, do you? Come on, relax. Miss Gorse is away all afternoon. We've got the office to ourselves."

Diana tried to pull her hands away from his but he held his grip.

"Bob, please. Stop it. I think I should go."

"Come on, Diana, a little fun won't hurt anyone. You upper crust are all at it. I know what you're like."

"Bob, really. No," she said, hoping that she sounded firm. "Let me go."

"Just a little kiss," he said, moving in. "It's harmless enough. No one has to know. Come on, I'll scratch your back and you scratch mine," he said, winking. "That's what they say, isn't it?"

And he let go of one of Diana's hands so that he could run his fingers down her spine. Diana pulled her hand away with a jolt, sending it upwards and slapping Bob accidentally under the chin.

"Oh, I'm sorry," she said, instinctively.

Bob winced but carried on.

"I've always thought you were the most beautiful woman I knew, Diana. I've been waiting years for one little kiss."

And he moved his face close to hers.

"It can be our secret. Just a kiss."

She strained to pull her head away.

"Bob. No."

She tried to push him away but, as she pushed, her body slipped down across the smooth, well-plumped leather seat, knocking her off balance. Her head jolted sideward, sending it veering off the sofa, where it slammed into the corner of the green onyx coffee table with a loud, empty crack.

"I bloody hate doing this," said the driver, a young policeman who had just got engaged.

"Aye, son, me too," said the passenger, a married officer in his forties. "Come on, let's get it over with."

The two men got out of their car and walked up to the house.

As they passed a window, they both saw a blond-haired man on the floor playing with a little baby. The man glanced up, surprised, but the two men carried on walking, not stopping until they were outside the front door. The older one looked at his colleague.

"Ready?"

The young man nodded, his face hollow and grey.

And the older man lifted his hand up to the door and knocked three times.

CHAPTER
TWENTY-THREE

Sunday 20 January 1963

It's been a very strange six months.

In Mrs Swithenbank's words, there's been a lot of coming and going.

The best *going* has been the removal from our lives of Christine, now shrivelled into an ancient amourette (*noun — a trifling, insignificant brief affair*). She has only been seen once since the welcome-home party and that was to collect her horrible turquoise cooker (replaced by a lovely *coming*, a new range oven). After falling victim to Mrs Scott-Pym's Yorkshire magic, Christine decided to work some magic of her own with Mr Baxter, the gammony property developer. Apparently she walked into his office, a lean-to next to a chippy in Brigg, and announced her presence with a low-cut playsuit and a dual-control girdle. They started stepping out soon after that and now live together in a brand new Tudor-Georgian dormer bungalow just outside Pontefract. Vera is living with them too, keeping herself busy with trips to the local bingo parlour, the Pontefract Palace. *Tibi seris, tibi metis*, as my old Latin teacher, Miss Weston, would say.

A sad *going* was the return of Caroline to London, but she's been coming up and visiting every few weeks, so even though it's officially a *going* it should also be counted as a *coming*. And another *coming* (four times now) is Digby, Caroline's friend/girlfriend/wife/husband. We all think she's great, including Mrs Scott-Pym, who says she's not so much lost a daughter as gained a jolly good bridge partner.

Another nice *coming* were my nine O level passes. Nine! That's only one less than Margaret. I passed everything except "home economics". Amazing.

Adam Faith, I'm afraid to say, has been a *going*. I just grew out of him, like *Bunty* comics and pop socks. Sorry, Adam. A very exciting *coming*, on the other hand, has been the *coming* of the four young men from Liverpool (called The Beatles), coming not to our village, of course, but to our lives, radios and to my chest (I have three *Beatles* badges and one sweater).

But the most important *coming* has been my mother, Diana. She's come into my life in a way quite different from before, quietly present in almost every little thing I do, like sunlight. Arthur's told me everything about her. What made her smile. What made her cry. What she liked to do and read. Where she liked to go. How she spoke. How she danced. How she lived. How she died.

It was an extremely sad death, of course. Tragic. At least that's the word all the newspapers used. Thankfully it was quick, a blow to the temple followed by an immediate and catastrophic haemorrhage (*noun — a sudden and serious internal loss of blood*). She wouldn't have known anything about it. Arthur did his best to cope (he had to — he had me to look after) but it was hard. Every day was a new death. New time to fill. New guilt. Once the court case was over, he just retreated into himself and could never really find his way back. I was his everything, he said. The beating heart that kept the man alive.

Finding all this out about my mother and Arthur has been hard. The good thing, though, the really good thing, is that, after talking about it, finally, after all these years, Arthur seems like a different person. It's like he had his life hung away on a hanger in the wardrobe for years but has taken it out again, tried it on again for size, and decided to put it back on.

This might have something to do with another *coming*. Élise. She's come up to the village. To live. She's staying with Mrs Scott-Pym, helping out around the house and making delicious French food (which she often shares with Arthur and me). In fact she comes round to the farmhouse quite a lot and seems to have rekindled her Gallic interest in cows and fields and row-crop tractors. And when she's not here, she's often out on a day trip, to York or the Bronte Parsonage or Whitby or Brimham Rocks, driven by Arthur, who seems as happy as Larry about it all.

And as for me, am I *coming* or *going*? Well, you'll have to see . . .

"Evie, darling, do you need any help up there?"

That's Élise, calling from downstairs. She's in the kitchen, no doubt making something delicious, and I'm up in my bedroom, tidying and sorting.

366

"No, I'm fine, thanks," I shout back. "I'll be down soon."

Through the window, I can see field after field of snow, with sprinklings of cows standing out like currants in a currant bun. The two Adam Faith posters on my walls (Sophisticated Adam and Brooding Adam) have been replaced by ones of John, Paul, Ringo and George plus a reproduction of *The Lady of Shallot* from Leeds Art Gallery. And on my bedside table a photo of me and Caroline outside Castle Howard sits alongside the one of me, Mum and Dad taken in winter 1946, when I was four months old, an ample mass of wool and lace with a tiny beaming face. I look at the two photos, taken a life apart. My life.

Speaking of life, now I know what kind of Woman I'm going to be. No more kaleidoscopes of twisting futures going in and out of focus, blurring and disappearing. Now the future me is clear, with a sharp outline and bright colours.

I'm going to be an apprentice radio producer at the BBC.

Amazing.

Caroline, apparently, was very impressed with my tape splicing skills. Between the two of them, Caroline and Digby seem to know half the BBC and it really wasn't very long at all before I received a letter from The Hon. Lucy Grenville-Smith (Head of Radio Production) inviting me for a "chat" and a look around, which magically turned into lunch and the offer of an apprenticeship. And so I'm packing, leaving for

London, and going to live with Caroline and Digby in a place called Holland Park. I've never been so excited.

I put the two photos from my bedside table carefully in my duffle bag, next to my mother's recipe book and a framed photo of Arthur with a prize cow. In the bag, I've also got a Beatles photo album, full of photos of Arthur, my mother, Mrs Scott-Pym, Sadie, Caroline, Margaret, Mrs Swithenbank and Élise, plus a copy of the latest *Country Life* (from Mrs Scott-Pym), a York Minster tea towel (from Mrs Swithenbank), a tin of travel sweets (also Mrs Swithenbank), and a London *A-Z* (from Margaret, practical as ever).

I'm just sat wondering how much more I can fit in the duffle bag when there's a knock on my bedroom door, swiftly followed by the appearance of Arthur's head.

"Mind if I come in, love?" he says, smiling like Gene Kelly.

"No, 'course not," I answer, although I hope we're not going to have another Talk. Over the past few weeks, we've had lots of Talks.

We've had Talks about boys.

We've had Talks about men.

We've had Talks about women.

We've had Talks about money.

We've had Talks about eating.

We've had Talks about smoking.

We've had Talks about drinking.

We've had Talks about the Tube.

We've had Talks about the buses.

We've had Talks about foreigners.

We've had Talks about Southerners.

We've had Talks about Londoners.

And we've had Talks and Talks and Talks about London.

In some ways life was so much easier when Arthur and I didn't have Talks and just communicated everything telepathically.

Arthur comes in and sits on the bed next to me. He's carrying something wrapped in tissue paper with a navy-blue ribbon round it.

"Here," he says, putting the tissue-paper parcel on my lap. "Now that you're a sophisticated young lady like your mum, I think it's about time you had this."

"What is it?" I ask, looking at him and then at the parcel and then back at him.

"Well, there's only one way to find out, isn't there?" he answers.

I look down at the parcel, feeling its delicate crispness. It's light, hardly with any weight at all, and whatever's inside is soft and limp. I carefully untie the navy ribbon and then fold back the tissue paper, each unfolding bringing a little burst of colour into the room.

"It was your mum's," says Arthur, putting his hand on my knee. "Her favourite silk scarf. She got it in Paris before the war."

I lift the scarf from the tissue paper. It's beautiful. Swirls of cavalry officers on different shades of blue and red all bordered by a looping golden chain.

"I reckon it'll stand you in good stead in London," Arthur goes on. "It won't have been cheap, knowing your mum."

"It's wonderful, Dad," I say, squeezing his hand. "I love it."

I put it on, tying it around my neck like I've seen Caroline and Élise do.

"There, what do you think?" I ask.

For a moment Arthur doesn't say anything. He just stares.

"You look beautiful, love," he says, his eyes glistening. "Very grand. Just like your mum."

"Thanks, Dad."

And we both sit for a moment, lost in thought, giving ourselves up to the magic of the scarf.

Baaaaaaaaaaaaaaaaaaaaaaaaaaaaaaaaaaaaaaaaaaaaah.

Someone sounds a car horn out in the courtyard.

It must be Caroline.

"That'll be your coach and horses," says Arthur. "We'd better get downstairs."

"Surprise!!!"

The kitchen is crammed full of women. Old ones. Young ones. Big ones. Small ones. Dog ones. It's not at all what I expected when I opened the door.

Caroline is at the back of the pack, towering over everyone, wearing a bright mustard turtle-neck and, for some inexplicable reason, a tiara. Élise, plus beret, is standing next to her, a little French flag in each hand and some onions roped round her neck. In front of them is Mrs Swithenbank and Mrs Scott-Pym, both sitting down. Mrs Scott-Pym is perching gracefully on her chair in full twinset and pearls (plus another tiara), looking like she's about to have tea at the Ritz, whereas Mrs Swithenbank is, as usual, head-to-toe in black but with the addition of a burgundy feather boa and a World War I German helmet with a big spike on top. Margaret, sporting a Union Jack jumper, is standing next to Mrs Swithenbank and Mrs Scott-Pym; she's somehow managed to get hold of Mrs Thorneycroft's WC hat from the village fete and looks truly mad. Sadie, meanwhile, is running round all over the place, slavering and yelping, with a gold sparkly pom-pom tied to the top of her head.

It's like walking into a scene from *Cold Comfort Farm*.

(In contrast, I am at my most stylish. I'm wearing something that Caroline and Digby got me for Christmas: a sleeveless, tweed, pillar-box-red mini dress with a long, tailored pleat stretching architecturally all the way down the front. I love it. I love the feel of it. I love the smell of it. And, most of all, I love the look of it. It's Perfect. A dress I will love forever. Under it, I've got on a navy turtleneck pullover, now with my mother's silk scarf tied round the neck, and navy tights and I feel like royalty. Like very stylish, very chic royalty.)

"What's going on?" I ask, wondering if all the packing has had a hallucinogenic effect.

"We've come to say goodbye, dear," says Mrs Scott-Pym. "We wanted to surprise you."

"Aye, we thought we'd give you a right good send off, love," says Mrs Swithenbank. "Put on something special. Something you wouldn't forget."

"Well, you've definitely done that," I say, grinning from ear to ear.

"Darling, your scarf," says Caroline. "It's lovely. You look wonderful."

"Dad gave it to me," I say, putting my hand up to the scarf and stretching out my neck like a swan (I hope). "It was Mum's."

"Oh, you look lovely, dear," says Mrs Scott-Pym. "So grown up."

She gets up and, cupping her hands softly on my cheeks, adds, "Your mother would be so proud."

"She would, that," says Arthur, walking over to Élise and putting his arm around her. "Proud as a peacock."

Sadie barks, clearly in agreement.

By now everyone has moved out of their *surprise!* greeting position, leaving me with a clear view of the kitchen table. It's covered in cakes.

"What are all these?" I ask.

"Darling, they're your leaving presents," says Caroline, deftly side-stepping Sadie. "Everyone had the same idea. We obviously all know you very well."

There's a Battenberg cake (my favourite) from Mrs Scott-Pym, a huge Victoria Sponge from Mrs Swithenbank, a Bakewell Tart with a mini Big Ben on the top from Margaret, a chocolate cake with *Good Luck Evie* written in icing from Arthur (bought from Bettys), and Élise has made something called a *Paris-Brest*, a big wheel of a cake oozing cream.

"And I've made you these too," she says. "For the journey."

She points to two long baguette sandwiches and a quiche (cheese tart) on the kitchen worktop.

"Well, you're certainly not going to starve, love," says Mrs Swithenbank.

"No, we'll be like *Meals on Wheels*," says Caroline. "I hope we can fit it all in!"

"Speaking of which," says Arthur, looking at me, "I think it's time to start loading the car, don't you?"

When we all step outside, I get another surprise.

Parked across the courtyard is a bright red MG sports car.

I glance over at Arthur, suddenly feeling very guilty. He winks.

"What do you think, darling?" says Caroline.

"I love it," I say, going up to the car and sweeping my hand along its sculptured bonnet.

"I borrowed it from a friend," says Caroline. "Thought it'd be a fun way to arrive in London."

"Ee, you'll be arriving in style all right," says Mrs Swithenbank.

"Yes," says Arthur, grinning. "But just watch out for the cows."

With everyone helping, the car's packed in no time at all. The cakes are in the boot (neatly stacked in boxes and tins), as are my duffle bag and lacrosse stick (just in case). One suitcase is strapped on top of the boot and the other one slips in neatly behind the seats. It is a masterclass in packing.

"Right, then," says Caroline. "Time for off, I suppose."

I look around at everyone. It doesn't feel real.

I can't believe I'm leaving.

Margaret rushes up to me and gives me a big hug.

"You will write, won't you? Tell me everything about London. What it's like. Where you go. What you do. Who you see. And you promise to let me know if you bump into Cliff Richard at a party, won't you?"

"'Course I will," I say. "And if I do see Cliff, I'll give him your number."

"I'll miss you, Evie."

"And I'll miss you too," I say. And I really will miss her, even if she does ask more questions than the Spanish Inquisition.

"Come here, love," says Mrs Swithenbank, grabbing me and pulling me into the huge folds of her chest. "Let me give you a kiss." And she does. A big one. "You're a proper little lady now. You show those Londoners how it's done, love," she goes on, squeezing me tight. "Give 'em a bit of Yorkshire sophistication."

"I will," I say, squeezing her back. "Thanks for everything, Mrs Swithenbank."

"Oh, I do wish you'd call me Doris, love!"

I uncouple from her squeeze, take hold of both her hands, and, beaming a huge smile directly at her, say, "Thanks for everything, Doris."

"About bloody time," she laughs. "You look after yourself, love," she adds, wiping her eye with a woolly-gloved hand.

374

All this time, Sadie has been running around in the snow, chasing imaginary rabbits, but now she comes bounding up to me and nearly knocks me flying. She barks and jumps up, sending a sparkly rope of dribble across my duffle coat.

"Sadie!" I shout. "I'll miss you!" She barks again and dashes round my legs. I bend over, hold her noble face, look into her earl-grey eyes and give her a kiss, whispering to her to look after Mrs Scott-Pym. Our moment of affection doesn't last long though, as she is distracted by Élise holding a bag of food.

"*Voila!* Your lunch," says Élise, passing me the bag. "Enjoy London, Evie. It is a wonderful city. You will love it." She straightens my new scarf. "And it will love you too."

"Thanks, Élise," I say, smiling my best French smile. "And thanks for looking after Dad."

"Oh, it is my pleasure. He is *un Viking merveilleux*. I think I may have found my Heathcliff," she adds, whispering in my ear.

And she gives me two kisses, one on each cheek.

I look over at Arthur. This time it's my turn to wink.

"Evie, dear," says Mrs Scott-Pym, inching over to me. "You *will* try to look after that daughter of mine whilst you're down there, won't you?"

"I'll try, Mrs Scott-Pym, but I can't promise anything."

Mrs Scott-Pym and I have already said our goodbyes. There's been a lot of crying and laughing and tea and sherry-drinking over the past few days. It's going to be awful without her, although we'll be speaking on the telephone all the time plus she's promised to come and visit.

"Well, just do your best with her, dear. I'm sure you'll do a better job than me." She smiles and cups my face in her hands again. "Now, I've got another little present for you. Something I'd like you to have."

"But you've already given me loads of presents," I say. It's true. Over the past week she's given me: a subscription to *Country Life*; a complete set of Jane Austen; an art deco book-end; a small ceramic English Setter; a book of poems by Dorothy Parker; and (just now) a Battenberg cake.

"They were just trinkets, dear. Now I want to give you something for your new London life. Something special."

And she reaches up to her tiara, takes it off and puts it on my head.

"There you are," she says, adjusting the tiara. "You look wonderful, dear. I knew it would suit you."

I feel like Princess Margaret.

"But you can't give me this, Mrs Scott-Pym," I say. "It's too much."

"Nonsense, dear. I want you to have it. It's just a little *thank you*. You can't imagine what it's meant to me having you next door all these years."

She smiles and takes my hands in hers.

"Take the tiara — you'll be needing it in London. All those grand balls and society affairs. You look stunning. Just like your mother."

She squeezes my hands, gently.

I can feel my eyes welling up, which is really rubbish as I'd promised myself not to cry.

"Thanks, Mrs Scott-Pym," I say.

I don't know what else to say. My head feels like it's going to explode but I just can't put anything into words.

"Now, off you go, dear," she goes on. "No more blubbing. This is exciting, remember. You should be smiling." And she backs away, leaving me standing there with the tiara, trying to smile.

"Oh, very posh," says Arthur, coming over and nodding at the tiara. "You'll be having us all bowing and curtseying next. And you've not even got to London yet."

I look at Arthur, unsure whether to laugh or cry.

"Will it all be okay, Dad?"

"Okay? Of course it'll be okay. It'll be more than okay. It'll be brilliant."

He puts his arms around me and kisses me on the forehead.

"And if it's not brilliant, just come back — me and the cows will always be here for you."

I hug him tightly, burying my head into his thick sheepskin coat.

"You're my little fairy queen, remember. And always will be."

We hug, a great merging of sheepskin and duffle coat.

"Now, you'd better jump to it. Looks like Caroline's ready for off."

I look round and see Caroline sitting in the car. She's folded back the MG's roof and is in the driver's seat wearing her big sunglasses (plus tiara) with a blanket across her knees.

I give Arthur another big squeeze and a kiss and then walk over to the car.

"I'm going to blow the cobwebs off you," shouts Caroline, pointing to the folded roof. "I want you to arrive in London fizzing with life," she goes on, pulling on her driving gloves.

As I'm getting in the car, Margaret and Mrs Swithenbank unfurl a huge homemade banner with the words *"Good luck Evie!"* painted on. I feel like a football club setting off to the FA Cup final at Wembley.

Caroline throws a blanket over my legs and gestures at the glovebox.

"Have a look in there, darling," she says. "There's a little surprise for you."

I tuck the blanket under my bum and open the glovebox. Inside is a pair of sunglasses, huge and black, just like the ones Caroline always has on.

"Wow," I say. "They're lovely."

"I thought you'd like them," says Caroline. "I ordered the weather too, you know," she adds, pointing up at the sky.

It's a glorious winter day; there's snow on the ground but the sky above is the brightest blue.

"Put them on, then, darling. Let's have a look."

I slide the sunglasses on, making sure not to disturb Mrs Scott-Pym's tiara.

Caroline starts the MG and revs up, sending a gust of toasty heat down to my toes.

"Call us when you get to London," shouts Arthur, standing with Élise, their arms curled around each other.

"I will," I answer.

Caroline revs the car some more.

By now everyone's waving and shouting, even Sadie, who's howling for Yorkshire. I'm waving and shouting too and so is Caroline, which is rather worrying as she's driving, manoeuvring the MG out of the courtyard.

"Bye!!!" shouts everyone, waving madly.

Caroline turns the MG's horn into a great wall of sound.

"Bye!!!" I shout, watching all the people I love glide past me, then behind me, then come running after me as we swing onto the drive.

Caroline gives a final blast of the car horn, waves both arms in the air, shouts something in Italian, and puts her foot down and then that's that. We've left. Gone. Next stop, London.

I turn and give a last wave to the small gesticulating group outside the farmhouse and then turn back and look ahead, fixing my eyes on the open road.

I am the wind, skeeting across tarmac and whooshing over dale.

I fly. I loop. I race.

Here, now, in the car, sunglasses on and wearing my mother's silk scarf and Mrs Scott-Pym's tiara, I feel different. Excited. Vigorous. Alive.

I feel like a film star driving off into the sunset at the end of a film.

Driving off into a new life.

My new life.

The one that I've been looking for all this time.

Amazing.

Acknowledgements

I would like to thank Chris White, my extremely patient editor at Scribner, for being so great to work with and knowing exactly when to say yes and when to say no. And thank you to all the team at Simon & Schuster, especially Jess, Richard and Kaiya (font-detective extraordinaire): Evie is very lucky to have found such a wonderful home. I'd also like to thank my lovely agent Alice Lutyens at Curtis Brown — the most stylish agent in London and also provider of the best breakfasts. Speaking of food, many thanks to Dr Emily Mayhew, recipe auditor, scotch-egg obtainer and Cointreau pourer. Special thanks to my *chuffin' brillyunt* friend Chris for his cheeky Yorkshire banter and his in-depth knowledge of 1960s hairdressing techniques (which he practises every day). And thanks, too, to Claire Sheills, writing buddy and amazing company over the long slog. I met Claire at the Faber Academy and I would like to thank our tutor there, Shelley Weiner, for being so encouraging and wise, and also all my fellow classmates, especially Nina and Kara, who gave very useful feedback on early drafts. Many thanks to Carly and Anna, for keeping me well fed, housed and cultured. Thank you to colleagues at various workplaces over London for putting up with me over the four years it took to write the book, in particular the terrific team at CfAE Imperial College, who taught me about dangling participles. And to all my friends and family: thank you! Finally, lots of virtual belly rubs to two fantastic dogs, Lola and Sadie, who made me very happy indeed.

Other titles published by Ulverscroft:

THE SALT PATH

Raynor Winn

Just days after Raynor learns that Moth, her husband of 32 years, is terminally ill, their home is taken away and they lose their livelihood. With nothing left and little time, they make the brave and impulsive decision to walk the 630 miles of the sea-swept South West Coast Path. Carrying only the essentials for survival on their backs, they live wild in the ancient, weathered landscape of cliffs, sea and sky. Yet through every step, every encounter and every test along the way, their walk becomes a remarkable journey. *The Salt Path* is an honest and life-affirming true story of coming to terms with grief and the healing power of the natural world. Ultimately, it is a portrayal of home, and how it can be lost, rebuilt and rediscovered in the most unexpected ways.

SHORT RANGE

Stephen Leather

Dan "Spider" Shepherd's career path — soldier, cop, MI5 officer — has always put a strain on his family. So he is far from happy to learn that MI5 is using teenagers as informants. Parents are being kept in the dark, and Shepherd fears that the children are being exploited. As an undercover specialist, Shepherd is tasked with protecting a fifteen-year-old schoolboy who is being used to gather evidence against violent drug dealers and a right-wing terrorist group. But when the boy's life is threatened, Shepherd has no choice but to step in and take the heat. And while Shepherd's problems mount up on the job front, he has even greater problems closer to home. His son Liam has fallen foul of the Serbian Mafia, and if Shepherd doesn'tintervene, Liam will die . . .